PRAISE FOR THE NOVELS OF
P. T. DEUTERMANN

THE FIREFLY

"Complex...fascinating."

—*The Washington Post*

"A first-class page-turner."

—*Atlanta Journal-Constitution*

"A deft thriller...impeccably authentic!"

—*Library Journal*

"A top-notch thriller from a top-notch writer. *The Firefly* may be Deutermann's best novel to date—reminiscent of *The Day of the Jackal*."

—Nelson DeMille

"Addictively enthralling...wait till you get to the jaw-dropping ending!"

—*Entertainment Weekly*

HUNTING SEASON

"Explosive tour de force....The author exceeds his near-perfect *Train Man* with this ripped-from-the-headlines plot pitting a middle-aged Rambo with a small but deadly arsenal of spy gadgets against spine-chilling villains, corrupt agency brass and powerful political forces. Deutermann never sounds a wrong note in this nonstop page-turner."

—*Publishers Weekly* (starred review)

MORE...

"You think you have read this before. Trust me. You haven't. And you should…a great read."

—*Tribune* (Greensburg, PA)

"One of the lasting conventions in thriller-writing involves putting the hero in a situation where the reader is forced to ask, 'How can he possibly get out of that?'…Deutermann… exploits that convention to the hilt in *Hunting Season.*"

—*Houston Chronicle*

"Enough techno and black ops to satisfy Clancy fans, enough double-dealing, back-pedaling internecine treachery to keep Carré fans reading and enough plot turns and suspense to keep Crichton and Higgins Clark devotees guessing."

—*The Florida Times-Union*

"Deutermann's previous novel, *Train Man,* was a marvelous, bang-up action novel…in *Hunting Season* he equals the thrills…Deutermann writes with authority and inventiveness. Add in top-secret gizmos, heroes meaner than villains…and you've got one of the best by one of the best at what he does."

—*Telegraph* [Macon, GA]

"The tale is loaded with political and bureaucratic skullduggery, and there are plenty of well-banked curves and clever twists. A solid read from an author whose own tradecraft is every bit as good as that of his characters."

—*Booklist*

"Deutermann has sold three novels to Hollywood already. They're blind if they pass on this one."

—*Kirkus Reviews*

DARKSIDE

"Gripping…thoroughly absorbing."   —*Publishers Weekly*

"Deutermann…writes page-turners. And this one has a surprise ending—one that comes as a bombshell."

—*Houston Chronicle*

"Deutermann's inside knowledge of the Navy and Pentagon politics, coupled with his likeable protagonists, make this a gripping new addition to his line of naval mysteries."

—*Publishers Weekly*

"A fine page-turner."

—*Library Journal*

OFFICIAL PRIVILEGE

"A tight story line...An attractive combination of murder mystery and naval politics."

—*The New York Times Book Review*

"P. T. Deutermann has become one of our best thriller writers....A keenly entertaining, fascinating mystery."

—*Observer* (Florida)

"Superb plotting and characterization are here, as is suspense and a clear awareness of the dangers and dalliances that can thrive in official Washington...*Official Privilege* is more than just a whodunit and a Navy story; it is a suspenseful indictment of power politics."

—*Florida Times-Union*

THE EDGE OF HONOR

"One heck of an exciting voyage...P. T. Deutermann ships a reader onto the bridge in that special place—where men go down to the sea in ships. He adds a first-rate suspense novel as a bargain."

—*Tampa Tribune and Times*

"*The Edge of Honor* is the rare book that addresses the complexities of war at the front and also at home. The author captures the Vietnam period and its confusion perfectly. Particularly interesting—and horrifying—is the culture depicted on the *Hood*, a real-life ship around which the novel is set."

—*The Baltimore Sun*

"*The Edge of Honor*…is headed up the bestseller list."
—*The Atlanta Journal-Constitution*

"A powerful human wartime thriller with a steady flow of action, both military and human. One of the best plots to come our way in years."

—*Neshoba Democrat*

"Utterly convincing…Unlike many techno-thriller writers, he has as good a grasp of what makes people tick as of what makes a modern warship function. Deutermann's clear mission is to picture Navy life in a depth we have not seen before, and he succeeds brilliantly. His craftsmanship is amazing."
—*The San Diego Union-Tribune*

SCORPION IN THE SEA

"Realistic with fast-paced action that carries the story to a crashing, pounding climax."

—*Florida Times-Union*

"Fast-paced...A page-turner...Exciting."
—Rear Admiral M.A. McDevitt, *Proceedings*, a U.S. Navy Publication

"High-octane compound of techno-thriller and military procedural that satisfies on several levels."

—*Publishers Weekly*

ST. MARTIN'S PAPERBACKS TITLES
BY P. T. DEUTERMANN

The Firefly
Darkside
Hunting Season
Train Man
Zero Option
Sweepers
Official Privilege
The Edge of Honor
Scorpion in the Sea

THE CAT DANCERS

P. T. DEUTERMANN

ST. MARTIN'S PAPERBACKS

This is a work of fiction. All of the characters, organizations and events portrayed in this novel are either products of the author's imagination or are used fictitiously.

THE CAT DANCERS

Copyright © 2005 by P. T. Deutermann.
Excerpt from *Spider Mountain* copyright © 2006 by P. T. Deutermann.

Library of Congress Catalog Card Number: 2005046583

ISBN: 0-312-93342-8
EAN: 978-0312-93342-5

Printed in the United States of America

St. Martin's Press hardcover edition / December 2005
St. Martin's Paperbacks edition / November 2006

St. Martin's Paperbacks are published by St. Martin's Press, 175 Fifth Avenue, New York, NY 10010.

10 9 8 7 6 5 4 3 2 1

1

INCH BY METICULOUS INCH, he slides down the 10.5-mm rope, twisting and releasing the figure-eight descender in tiny, silent increments. He is sitting on a trapeze bar, which, in turn, is suspended from the rappelling device. Every time he twists the ring, the bar descends a few inches. He wears a webbed climbing harness around his chest, which allows him to lean back from the rope as he goes down. His face is now only a foot away from the granite overhang. He reaches out to touch the rock, but gently, so as not to induce a spin on the rope. The mountain air is clear and cold, with only a hint of a dawn breeze, enough to mask small sounds but not enough to disturb his body as he slips down the rope.

He's already come down sixty feet from the anchor point up above the overhanging bulge, and he's now at the closest point to the rock face. Ten more feet down and the cliff curves back in to become a sheer wall that descends into the morning mists above the river. It is just past morning twilight, that time of suspended animation when darkness retreats but then seems to make a comeback even as the stars begin to lose their definition. He can't be certain, but the cat should be back in its lair by now.

Two hours ago, he'd heard her shrieking attack on some desperately scrambling prey animal, whose ensuing death squeals punctured the mountain darkness like a hot knife, followed by a momentary silencing of all other forest sounds. If she held to pattern, she'd quickly consume the soft parts, hide the carcass, and take a part of it back to the den for her cubs. He felt like he knew her, her habits, all her mysterious moves. He should; he'd been tracking and watching her for ten days and nights.

The rock face is definitely withdrawing from his line of drop now, getting two, then three, then six feet distant, the striations of the ancient rock no longer visible as the forest remained still in anticipation of dawn. He concentrates on the oval of dark shadow below that is her cave and resists the urge to touch the Max 800 to make sure it's ready to shoot. He knows it is; of course it is. But the urge is strong after days of spoor casting and stalking, using binoculars by day, night-vision goggles by dark, and now that he's within thirty vertical feet of his objective, he wants to make sure he's ready.

He stops the descent and regulates his breathing. He thinks he can hear the tiny creaks of the harness and the sounds of his own heartbeat echoing off the rock wall, even though the granite is now a good ten feet away. The whole expanse of sheer gray rock is a blur in his peripheral vision. The loss of perspective isn't helped by the effort of having his whole body hanging, with his left arm locked rigidly in tension against the rope, but it's the only way to let his body weight do all the work and to keep his right hand, the critical trigger hand, free at all times.

Twist and release, inch by inch now. He detects a barely discernible sway in the rope and extends his free arm ever so slightly, trying to dampen the swing so that he and the rig don't turn into a pendulum. He imagines he can hear the rope rubbing up top, its synthetic fibers heating under the strain. He can't hear it, of course, but, with her supersensitive hearing, the cat might. Nature's sounds are random. Rhythmic sounds in the forest are a trip wire to an alerted mountain lion. The soft, regular breathing of sleeping prey, the steady footfall and puffing breath of a hiker climbing blissfully into a furious ambush, the whimpering mews of a fawn searching for its mother, the crunch of hiking shoes across pine needles, the repeated click of a walking stick on a rocky path— these are the sounds that bring those delicate tufted ears up and the cat's sharp senses to hunting pitch. He now looks up, half-expecting the cat to be up there, peering over the rim of the overhang, a tentative paw reaching for the rope, waiting for him to come back up. Now that, he thinks, would be truly interesting.

Squeeze and release, inch by inch, the concave rock face now a good twenty feet away and beginning to curve back toward the vertical again. The dark blur of the cave's mouth is coming into focus, its top edges more defined, the hollow darkness of the opening contrasting with the bright white bones littering the ledge in front. It's a surprisingly big cave, maybe ten feet across. He wonders how many and what wonderful kinds of beasts have sought haven there over the millennia.

He descends in tiny halting jerks, ignoring the pain in his thighs and the constriction of the harness as he controls his breathing, mouth open to make no sound, taking in small irregular puffs of pristine pine-scented air. He thinks the breeze, such as it is, is working for him, blowing across the face of the sheer rock and masking the steely smell of his own adrenaline, which makes his eardrums thump with each heartbeat. The rig's swivel keeps him from spinning away from his target. He's still desperate to put his hand on the Max 800, just to make very damned sure.

Trust your instinct, he reminds himself. You've made your preps. Focus. Twist and release; twist and release. Then he's finally in position, ten feet below the lip of the cave's front ledge. He locks the ring. For a moment, he just hangs there and listens to his own heartbeat, willing it to slow down, trying for biofeedback and not succeeding worth a damn. The Max is attached to his camo jumpsuit by a tiny tungsten wire so that he can't drop it, even if he should want to, because sometimes that happens if the fear becomes sufficiently intense. He's dying for a drink of water, but there's no time for that, not now, not here. He concentrates on that ledge and what he can see of the top half of the cave's mouth.

She's in there; I know she's in there.

So: Let's go. Let's do it.

Time to dance.

He drops below the ledge because now he has to get closer, and the only way to do that is to swing in toward the rock face. The swing will begin with him at the bottom of an arc. He has to get within eight feet of the ledge, which will happen at the top of the arc, because the Max is worthless beyond eight feet, and its short range is the whole point.

Keeping his eyes on the ledge, he reels up the Max and takes it in both hands. With his fingers, he tests the firing mechanism for resistance, assuring himself that it's cocked and ready to fire.

He takes a deep breath, lets most of it out, and then, barely inclining his body, initiates the swing. It takes surprisingly little effort, with almost eighty feet of rope rising into the gloom above him. His body is stiff with tension and resists the swinging impulse. He has to bend his neck and then his shoulders to get it going, moving back and forth, not in a circle, but straight at the rock face, slowly but steadily gathering speed and reach as he swings in toward the rock and up toward the ledge, then away, down, and out over the seemingly bottomless gorge. An uneasy thrill lights up in his belly as he senses the great height and all that empty air. The river courses invisibly below him, making a distant rushing sound.

Back in again, still gripping the Max in both hands and controlling the swing with his body mass. He brings the Max up closer to his face so he can sight properly, pointing it toward the cave while he amplifies the swing into and up toward the rock face, then away, down, and out over the void. His brain knows that the rope is plenty strong, capable of holding him and two others like him. But his gut knows that there's nothing but a couple hundred feet of air between him and the shattered scree below. He's been down there, sniffing through bones and other debris from the lair above, trying to gauge the freshness of the litter, confirming that this is a live lair.

Back and forth now, a human pendulum riding a silent arc, each time coming closer to the ledge, rising higher with each sweep, a little off target now, focus, concentrate, straighten it out, and watch the back of the Max's sight, watch for the flickering red light to turn green when he's achieved the preset range of eight feet.

He's cat-dancing for real now. He no longer has to worry

about remaining soundless in the rising light. Out and back, out and back, as the dawn's terminator line creeps down the eastern slopes of the mountain. Suddenly, there's something visible in the mouth of the cave. He catches only a quick glimpse at the top of the arc, seeing and then not seeing, imagining or seeing—which is it?—then down and out, then back, the light getting better, and then he knows. *This* swing, *this* arc. All his instincts are screaming, and then the cat's screaming, *right there,* gathering to leap right off the ledge as he swings in for the last time. Her front legs are twitching back under her belly, the muscles of her massive shoulders and haunches quivering, her fangs baring, her eyes blazing while she shrieks at him and he shrieks back as he raises the camera, sees the blessed ready light, and shoots and winds, shoots and winds.

And then it's rise, Lazarus, rise, as he swings back out again, away from that coiled tawny fury on the ledge. He raises his knees, bends in the middle, and then thrusts fully upright like a human inchworm, his hands together on the Jumars, climbing now in powerful lunges, kicking up with his legs. The sudden vertical surge of his body interrupts the rhythm of the arc, so that it diminishes with each powerful reach, while the cat shrieks again and races furiously back and forth in front of her cave; her whirling turns incredibly quick, her total outrage echoing across the canyon, creating an echo chorus of a dozen furious cats. He's well above the ledge now, reaching up and grabbing whole meters of rope and pulling hard, the little camera bouncing around on his hip. The cat and the cave disappear as he approaches and then scrambles past the overhang. He can slow down now, catch his breath, savor the moment, pull the precious camera into his hip pack.

I have a face.

I have a *face*!

Now the trick is to get to the top and get the hell out of there before she figures it out and comes sprinting up after him. He should be safe, because she has cubs. She won't leave the cubs. He hopes to God.

In his mind's eye he can see White Eye waiting back at camp, a tiny Primus fire glowing against a circle of sharp rocks by now, the battered coffeepot balanced precariously on two stones, three cups of cold mountain water, grounds, eggshells, and his damned pinch of salt. He'll be grinning, he thinks, just like I'm grinning, ear to ear, having heard that incandescent shriek transfix the morning air from the mouth of the cave, that feral "How dare you?" sound echoing down the gorge and over into the high pines, where White Eye's been waiting since midnight.

Waiting and wondering if, after four years of training, I could really do it.

Well, I *have* done it.

I have a face.

Now for the good stuff.

2

K-DOG IS RANTING. HEY, you know what, dude? We had the fucking thing done. The money was in my pocket, that clerk slapped down on the floor, a whole candy rack pulled over on top of his ass, our piece-a-shit rice-burner parked fifty feet away, pointed out at the street, the security cam bashed off the wall—and, shit, we even had its VCR smashed all to hell and lubricated with some convenient motor oil. That's why they called it a convenience store, right?

And then here comes this fucking minivan, mama bear and baby bear pulling into absolutely the wrong place at the wrong time. A hundred gas stations in this fucking town, and these civilians pick this one? This bitch looking over as she shuts down the van. I mean, it was fucking obvious she saw our asses as we came through the door. I could almost hear her makin' her statement, you know? "There were two of them, Officer. One was this sorta tall, skinny, scraggly-haired white boy in a sleeveless T-shirt and jeans. Dude had this huge gun in his hand? The other guy? Oh, he was this dumpy-looking black guy in baggy red sweats, a do-rag on his head, looking totally spaced."

And that's when we made our big mistake, man: We stopped. That was it right there. I just fucking know it. Stopped in the doorway when we saw her looking, and that's when that old Paki dude must have realized there was a problem. Because, like, next thing we know? Here he fucking comes, man, rising up out of that pile of candy and shit with his own damn gun, if you could *believe* that shit, rising up and booming away at us. I mean, there's shit blowing right off the door racks and busting out the glass of the door right in our faces. Flash, well, Flash, what can I say, man? Flash does his usual shit, goes right for the floor, yellin' about motherfuckers this and motherfuckers that. And me? Well, shit, you know, I'm like Mr. Cool when the heavy shit starts to fly. That's my rep, right? So I do what I have to do—you know what I'm saying? I get *my* ass down behind a newspaper rack, whip that TEC-9 around, and hose *down* that cashier's stand. That Paki dude's still shooting, I'll give him that, man, two hands, like they show on the TV. But dig this: He had his fucking eyes closed, man. Incredible. Then one of my rounds takes the side of his head off, and then, shit, that dude's all done.

But that wasn't the bad part, man. After I drop the geezer—okay?—I get up, but then I trip over Flash, who's still down there on the floor, got his fucking eyes closed, just like that Paki, and he's all, like, babbling this black street shit. Anyway, so I trip over his worthless ass and fall right through the busted-out door glass. Lucky I didn't get cut all to shit. I mean, my damn feet are *all* fucked up. I'm like trying to catch myself, but at the same time I forget to take my finger off that trigger, and that TEC's stitching up the pump island's roof, a couple of those big bright lights out there, and then, oh, man, the gas pump right next to that minivan. Soccer mommy was still sitting in the van, staring at me like I was from fucking Mars, man, until that pump island fucking lit up.

You talk about your fucking Fourth of July. That whole mess—the minivan, the gas pump, all that shit—had to have been fifty feet away, but I can still feel that fireball. Flash is up off the floor now and he fucking passes me getting out to the pickup. There is fire fucking *everywhere* now, and then we get another pump going up, and then some hose or some other shit breaks and then there's, like, these blue *waves* of fire coming across the concrete. Fucking Hell's Beach, man. I jam that rice-burner into big D and we peel the hell out of there, driving right over those waves of fire. I swear to God I can still feel that heat through the floorboards. That minivan is roasting back in there somewhere, along with the witnesses, so, you know, the whole fire deal wasn't a total fucking loss. I was just wishing that wad of cash in my pocket was a whole lot thicker, because both of us knew there was gonna be some serious hell to pay over this shit.

So, anyways, we go screech-assing all the way across the center line before I can get ahold of it. We almost head-on some asshole comin' the other way, and he leans on his horn while eatin' up a ton of my gravel. I hammered down to straighten that bitch back out and then got us down the road and gone. Big-ass orange glow taking up the whole rearview mirror, all the way to the first curve. And, oh yeah, there's my man Flash, the whole fucking time, sitting there with his eyes *still* closed, tears running down his face, those funny little hands of his banging against the dash while he says "Muhfuggah" over and over again. We called him Flash in the joint, but his real name is Deleon. Dee-le-on Butts. 'Tween you an' me? That brother ain't playin' with a full deck, you know what I'm sayin'? Anyway, we're boogyin' down the road. I gotta wonder why I hooked up with him in the first place. I mean, yeah, we'd shared a cell up in Rock City for three years, and, you know, since we both came from the Triboro area, it just seemed okay. Right now, though, man, I don't know if that was such a good move.

So, the next morning, like, late? We're holed up in this shitty little curry palace on the east side of town, about a half mile from 1-40, close enough so's we can hear the semis. Flash is either dead asleep or passed out on the other bed; it's always kinda hard to tell with Flash. He's got this mostly empty quart of bourbon sticking up between his legs like a glass hard-on. I'm only medium high. I've got me an elephant head and that camel-crapped-in-my-mouth taste, you know, whiskey, two garlic pizzas, and maybe a half case of beer? I've got two, count 'em, *two*—fucking cigarettes, going, and there's enough smoke in that room to set off the smoke alarm, 'cept it's hanging by its wires 'cause those Pakis never fix anything, you know what I'm sayin'?

I got the TV news on and there's some big-hair blonde going off about the minimart holdup. She's all excited, but they don't have shit on who the bad guys were. Po-lice "working several solid leads." Yeah, right. The gas station and the minimart burned to the ground. Three confirmed DOAs: the clerk, and the two civilians in the van. Little pickup, possibly white, seen "fleeing the scene." Got that shit right. But, shit, if all they had was a *possibly* white pickup truck, we were good to go, man. Had to be a thousand or so of those around Manceford County, right? So . . . too fucking bad about the civilians, but, you know, sometimes shit just happens. Bad shit for them, but good shit for us—no wits, right? So that was the good news. The bad news was that we got jack shit in the way of money out of this whole goat fuck, so we were *definitely* gonna have to go hit another one, and, like, pretty fucking soon, man. I was so glad I hadn't ditched that fucking TEC, man. Hid that puppy outside.

And then, while I was, like, sitting there, just trying to think, you know? Where we oughta go, what the fuck we should do next—the whole fucking world fell in on us. I've got my breakfast beer in the air, man, when the door fucking explodes backward off its hinges and about a million armored cops blast into the room. This *huge* fucking deputy comes right at me and flat-arms my skinny ass right off the bed. Then the rest of the meat, all of 'em these huge dudes with fat red faces, helmets, lookin' like fucking Star Wars storm troopers, man, they just pile on, twisting my arms behind my back to get those cuffs on, an' all the time screaming at me to *"get down, get down, get flat,* don't *fucking* move," like I could even twitch with all that sweaty meat on me.

Then this really big dude gets right down on the floor with me, and he goes, "You the mother*fuckers* torched the gas station last night?"

By now I'm, like, seein' red spots in front of my eyes and my arms feel like they're coming right out of their sockets, and even with all the noise, I can hear Flash cryin' again. I can't see shit, Flash is makin' like a fucking sheep, and there's ten dudes sitting on me. So anyway, the big cop grabs my chin, and he asks again, "You the *man,* asshole?" I mean, he's so close his spit's sprayin' in my face. My fucking arms are making popping noises now, so I think, Fuck it, they flat got our asses, right? So I go, "Awright, yeah, we fucking done it, okay? Now let me breathe, motherfucker!"

Civilians, man. You know this has to be all about those fucking civilians. Night clerk in a minimart? Dude's gotta know what the game is, what kinda shit can go down. And it's not like I *meant* to take 'em out or anything. But fuck: You see two dudes coming through the front glass at eleven o'clock at night with a machine gun? You don't sit there and fucking *watch*, man, you put your ride in fucking reverse and you get the *fuck* out of there, man. Like, *every*body knows that. *Fucking* civilians.

Say, man, you got any extra smokes?

3

IT WAS LATE MAY, and the building-management gnomes who decided such things had turned off both the heat and the air-conditioning to save money, so the courtroom was unusually stuffy. Steven Klein, the local district attorney, was droning through the motions hearing on the minimart case, while Lt. Cam Richter and Sgt. Kenny Cox of the Manceford County Sheriff's Office tried to stay awake in the back of the courtroom. The case was pretty much a slam dunk, what with the confession and the submachine gun, but with Justice Bellamy presiding, one never knew what was going to happen. And sure enough, the judge raised a hand to interrupt Klein. Cam knew that Steven hated that, and it showed immediately on the DA's face. What came next got everyone's undivided attention.

"Mr. Klein, I've been looking at the arrest reports for these two defendants. I see a problem here. A big problem, actually."

"Your Honor?" Kelin said, pulling his reading glasses down his large nose. He was in his forties, abundantly fed, and still annoyed that the judge had interrupted him.

"You've stated that Mr. Kyle Simmonds, alias K-Dog, confessed to the minimart holdup at the time of his arrest in the motel room. But I notice that his Miranda statement was not executed until the SWAT team had both defendants back at the district station. This was what—forty-five minutes after taking them into custody?"

"They were Mirandized verbally at the scene by the arresting officers, Your Honor. They signed their paper once the deputies got 'em back to the district office."

"Which arresting officer in particular Mirandized them?"

"Uh," Klein said, looking sideways and behind him at Detective Will Guthridge. Will had been the supervising detective sent out by the district office when the SWAT team went in to take down the two robbers.

"The deputies who hooked him up, Your Honor," Guthridge said. "It was a SWAT takedown. Really noisy in there."

"Which specific arresting officer gave them their Miranda warnings, Detective? As in, a name, please?"

"I'll have to find that out, Your Honor," Guthridge said, popping out a flip phone and punching up his phone list. Cam looked sideways at Kenny Cox, his number two on the Major Criminal Apprehension Team. Kenny had his eyes closed and was shaking his head slowly from side to side. Oh shit, oh dear, Cam thought. Guthridge was bent sideways in his seat, talking earnestly, probably to someone in the Special Operations section. Cam leaned his head toward Kenny. "Who was the honcho on SWAT that day?" he asked.

"McMichael," Kenny muttered. Cam groaned quietly. Then K-Dog took the opportunity to throw some shit in the game. He spoke up from the defendants' table. "Nobody said shit," he offered helpfully. "They knocked us on our asses, told us to stay down on the floor about a million times. They was all yellin' and shit."

"Ms. Walker," the judge said to K-Dog's court-appointed defense attorney. "Please instruct the defendant not to speak until I ask him to speak. Detective, what are your people saying? You understand I'll want a live arresting officer standing tall, right here, under oath, stating that he gave the appropriate warnings, right?"

Guthridge nodded vigorously at the judge and kept talking. Cam nudged Kenny and asked him if he could call somebody and get this thing right. K-Dog's motel room confession was all they really had on these assholes, because the fire at the gas station had eliminated both witnesses and any physical evidence. The crooks had also been smart enough to wipe down and then stash the TEC-9 behind an AC unit in the motel parking lot, so even though they could tie the gun to the crime scene, they could only tie it circumstantially to the two mutts. Even the probable cause to send the SWAT team in the first place had been something of a Slim Jim.

"They don't love you at Narco-Vice just now," Kenny said as he pulled out his own cell phone and hit a button.

Well I know, Cam thought. He saw Guthridge hang up his phone and turn around to look back at him. His expression begged for some cavalry on this one, which was definitely not an encouraging development.

"Detective?" Judge Bellamy was a good-looking woman in her forties, with snapping bright eyes and a notoriously healthy suspicion of cops and all their works.

"Still working on it, Your Honor," Guthridge said, punching up another number on his phone. Cam realized that too many Manceford County irons had gotten into this particular fire. If no one stood up, they were going to have a real problem.

"Recap, Mr. Klein?" the judge asked. "You had no witnesses to the actual crime, the security-camera system and any potential on-scene physical evidence are toast, and the victims are all dead. Now, let me see. Besides the confession and a weapon found near the motel, you had one witness who stated, in effect, that he had been driven off the road by a small pickup truck *resembling* the defendants' vehicle at the time of the fire in the gas station, correct?"

"Well, yes, Your Honor, but they admitted—"

"You see my problem, Mr. Klein?"

Klein pretended to be confused. "Uh, no, Your Honor, I—"

Guthridge closed up his cell phone again. "Detective?" the judge asked again, looking past Klein. Cam raised his eyebrows hopefully at Kenny, but he was shaking his head as he hung up. "That was Captain Wall at Narco-Vice," he said quietly. "McMichael is 'not available.' And he reminded me that there was a Major Crimes detective on-scene." He glanced over at the perspiring Guthridge. "He's guessing nobody in the room actually did Mirandize either one of them."

Cam grunted. The judge prompted Will Guthridge again,

but all he could do was shake his head. Klein was shuffling papers on the table and trying not to look at Guthridge.

"Detective, *you* were at the scene of the arrest. Did you Mirandize these defendants?"

"I did, Your Honor, but not until the SWAT guys handed them over to me."

"But it was a SWAT deputy who asked the all-important question, right?"

Will nodded unhappily.

"And you're telling me you cannot produce an arresting deputy who verbally Mirandized these defendants at the time of the takedown?" the judge asked. "*Before* the alleged confession?"

Cam didn't like the sound of that "alleged" confession. "Not at the moment, Your Honor," Will replied, clearing his throat. "But if I can have some time, I can reassemble the team, and—"

"The confession is out," the judge announced. Bailiffs, half a dozen reporters, the attorneys, and a fairly large crowd of spectators all went silent in a collective wave of shock. The deaths of three people in a gas station robbery had been beyond big news both in Triboro and in Manceford County. Klein burst out with an indignant "*What*?"

The judge looked surprised that anyone would be shocked by her decision. "Per the arrest report, they clearly got their Miranda warnings *after* the deputies took them back to the district office, but that same report says the confession was elicited at the scene of the arrest."

Klein raised his hand, as if he were in school. "Your Honor? This is ridiculous. They spontaneously confessed to robbing the store."

Spontaneously? Cam thought. Nice try, Steven. And, as Cam expected, the judge pounced.

"The Sheriff's Office report says the deputy asked and the defendant Simmonds responded. That's not spontaneous, Mr. Klein, especially if he was hanging by his thumbs at the time of the question."

"These two started that fire," Steven said, almost shouting. "Both of them. They robbed and shot the store clerk and then trapped two people in the van by shooting into gas pumps. I'm sure they were Mirandized. Every deputy in the county is trained to say those words any time he locks cuffs. It's SOP. Hook 'em up, you say the words. They'd do it in their sleep."

"They ain't never said shit," K-Dog piped up, sensing a real break here. "They was screamin' and yellin', 'Get down, get down on the floor, assholes,' stuff like that, but they ain't never said no warnin'. I know what that shit sounds like."

The judge glared down at him. "I'll just bet you do, Mr. Simmonds. But at the moment, your prior experience with being arrested is not the issue here. One more time, Mr. Klein: Can you produce the arresting deputy who warned these individuals *before* the confession was taken?"

"I'm sure I can, if I can have a short recess here, Your Honor."

No way, Cam thought, not with Annie Bellamy, who obviously knew what would happen if there was a recess. The deputies would go back to the station, get someone— anyone—on the SWAT team to do the right thing.

"Mr. Klein, this hearing wasn't exactly a spur-of-the-moment affair. I'm seeing this in the arrest report *you* gave *me*, right? Do you want to nolle?"

Klein's face was getting red. "Not yet, Your Honor," he said. "I mean, I just can't believe they didn't warn them."

K-Dog's court-appointed defense attorney finally woke up to what was possible here. "Your Honor?" she said. Here it comes, Cam thought. Here it fucking comes.

"Yes, Ms. Walker?" the judge said wearily.

"Motion to dismiss, Your Honor? No confession, no physical evidence tying either defendant to the gun—there's really no case."

There was another sudden silence in the courtroom, and then Klein popped up out of his chair. "Your Honor, a motion to dismiss is beyond ridiculous. We know these defendants committed this crime. We know—"

"Here's what *I* know, Mr. Klein," the judge said patiently.

"Per your own report, they weren't Mirandized before that confession. What you say you know is based on a confession that no longer exists." She prompted him again. "Nolle, Mr. Klein?"

Cam wanted to throw a rock at Klein. For God's sake, Steven, say yes, he thought. Bring it back under another charge. Don't get all hung up on this Miranda thing. But Klein was a mule sometimes, and today was apparently going to be one of them. He shook his head angrily.

The judge stared down at Klein for a moment, her own anger now evident. "Okay, Mr. Klein," she said finally. "Try this: I am dismissing all charges, due to lack of evidence. With prejudice, Mr. Klein, because I don't really think you had quality probable cause to make these arrests in the first place."

"Good God, Your Honor—" Klein began.

"This isn't church, Mr. Klein, so God has nothing to do with it. You should have pulled it when I gave you the chance—*twice*." Bang went the gavel. "Bailiff, this court is adjourned."

Cam was stunned. Charges *dismissed*? He was dimly aware that the entire courtroom was buzzing all around him. Toss the confession, okay, but remand until they could go back, dig up some more evidence. These two guys had long sheets and directly relevant priors. They had the submachine gun, and the vehicle, although the CSI people hadn't done much with either of them because of that confession.

But *dismissed*? Kenny looked like he wanted to go up there and rip the judge's throat out. Will Guthridge was also standing now, shouting something at the judge.

The judge, who had stood up to leave, reached for the gavel and started banging it on the bench to drown out the rising protests. Sit down, Will, Cam thought, before you get in any deeper. The two punks were looking at their court-appointed attorneys to see if they had heard it right, too.

"Order!" the judge shouted over the commotion in the courtroom. "Detective, get control of yourself!"

"Goddamn it, Your Honor, I—"

"Shut *up*, Detective. You're the one who screwed this up, so just sit down and be quiet for a minute." Guthridge sat down abruptly, his face bright red, much like Klein's. Still standing, the judge pointed the gavel at Steven like a gun. "Mr. Klein, you have something further?"

Guthridge started to get back up, and Cam winced when the gavel banged down yet again. The young detective slapped his notebook down on the table and subsided. Klein, who had also started to get up, sank back down into his chair.

"Mr. Klein, your principal evidence was tainted and is not admissible. Your probable cause was a Kleenex. Good enough for Judge Barstow, maybe, but not good enough for me. You want to appeal my ruling, you go for it, but in the meantime, I want these defendants released."

"Your Honor, these are career criminals," Klein protested. "They are most definitely flight risks. They—"

"They are released. The charges are dismissed. Evidence, Mr. Klein. That's what we're all about in here, in case you've forgotten." The judge swept the courtroom with those snapping eyes, as if daring anyone to challenge that principle. She saw Kenny Cox sitting in the back and glared at him. "You should have sent Sergeant Cox there. At least he knows how to rig an arrest report." She paused for a moment as Kenny met her eyes, then banged the gavel again. "You don't have any evidence, Mr. Klein. Now, like I said: We're done here."

The judge left the courtroom and Cam rubbed the side of his face as he sat there, considering the disaster. He deliberately did not look at Kenny, not after the judge's last remarks. Almost three years ago, Kenny had been accused of playing fast and loose with an arrest report to cover up a similar error, and the accuser had been Bellamy. The facts regarding the incident had been murky, but Bellamy had forced the sheriff to suspend Kenny for three months without pay, in return for not charging him with evidence tampering and maybe even perjury. It had been nasty in the extreme, and if today's case hadn't been so high viz, Kenny would never have shown up today, and certainly not in front of Bellamy. Kenny's hatred for Bellamy was palpable, and Cam could just about feel his sergeant's anger radiating.

His cell phone trembled in his pocket. That will be Himself, he thought, and now comes the fun part. He saw Will Guthridge talking earnestly to Steven Klein as some excited media types were shouting questions at them from the press box.

"Okay, let's go," he said to Kenny. "See if we can unscrew this mess."

4

THE MAJOR CRIMINAL APPREHENSION Team was a unique organization for a metropolitan Sheriff's Office. It consisted of four senior detectives, a sergeant, and a lieutenant who ran it. Their job was simple: Once one of the local criminals rose to a position of real prominence in the county's outlaw society, whether as a major drug dealer, an enforcer, or a gang chieftain, the captain who headed Major Crimes would hand MCAT his name. They would then spend all of their time and effort busting the guy's chops until they either provoked him into making a major mistake, one that could lead to real prison time, or made him so radioactive among the rest of the rat pack that *they* would take care of the problem. MCAT had essentially unlimited access to all of the resources of the Sheriff's Office, which were considerable. The sheriff was intimately familiar with the federal criminal asset forfeiture and seizure program, giving the Manceford County Sheriff's Office every modern law-enforcement toy out there.

What MCAT did was to direct all of those bells and whistles against one badass at a time. The team worked off the clock and around the clock if necessary. They followed the subject, wiretapped him, pulled in any and all of his close associates again and again, searched his crib and haunts, came up to him in public restaurants and bars to thank him noisily for his cooperation, planted false leads in the papers implicating the guy in the successful prosecution of someone else, and generally made his life miserable. All of this was done with appropriate court orders and warrants, of course. Most of the judges, if only in chambers, positively licked their judicial chops.

Cam's job was to provide adult supervision. With a license

to run outside the normal checks and balances of the field operations forces, the MCAT cops were under constant scrutiny to ensure they didn't become the modern-day version of the Untouchables of the 1920s. Cam made sure they had court papers backing up everything they did, and the sheriff interviewed the entire squad frequently, both to keep up to speed on what they were doing as well as to assess their level of professionalism. He once told Cam that they were his armored cavalry, substituting speed, surprise, and aggression for the more plodding nature of criminal investigation.

Sheriff Bobby Lee Baggett was on the phone, his back to the door, when Cam knocked and went into his office. The room was spacious, and the walls were covered with memorabilia of famous people or famous arrests made during Bobby Lee's nine-year reign as sheriff of Manceford County. Parked against the back wall were three silhouette targets from the gun range. The sheriff took great pride in the fact that he, too, qualified once a month, just like the rest of them had to. Cam dropped into one of the two enormous leather chairs stationed directly in front of the sheriff's desk and waited for him to finish up.

The sheriff, at forty-nine, was five years older than Cam. He was in his third term as an elected official, having come to Manceford County from the governor's personal staff in Raleigh, the capital of the Old North State. Once upon a time, he'd been a Marine Corps aviator, and he'd apparently never gotten over it. He was six one, hatchet-faced, lean-jawed, buzz-cut, extremely fit, and all business all the time. He addressed everyone under his command by their rank, and sometimes they all wondered if he knew anyone's first name. In turn, everyone on his staff was cordially invited to address him as Sheriff. Cam couldn't say that he liked the man, but he did respect him. He'd whipped the outfit into becoming the foremost Sheriff's Office in the state any way you wanted to measure it.

The sheriff hung up the phone and swiveled around in his chair. "So WTF, Lieutenant?" he asked in his gravelly voice. "They just *walk*?"

"What happened was that those two went to the minimart to rob the place," Cam replied. "It went wrong somehow, and now three people are dead and, yes, the do-er's are free to go."

He gave Cam his commanding officer look. "Your detective failed to Mirandize these suspects?"

Cam wanted to say that Will was hardly his detective, but he knew that Bobby Lee would simply look at the organization board, and there would be Will's name, most definitely parked in the MCAT block. "Detective Guthridge went in behind the SWAT front line," Cam said. "They did their usual monster mash. A Sergeant McMichael from District Three went eyeball-to-eyeball with the white kid, Simmonds, asked him if he did the minimart. Mutt said yes."

"While dangling from his dick, no doubt."

"SWAT, what can I say?" Cam replied. "We don't ask them to be nice. We do ask them to be professional."

"And where was Detective Guthridge during this interrogation?"

"It was hardly an interrogation," Cam told him. "They had the perps on the floor, and McMichael literally got down in Simmonds's face, popped the question. By the time Guthridge came through the doorway, it was all done."

"So SWAT hooked them up, not Guthridge?"

"Yes, sir."

"And did so without reciting their rights? I find that hard to believe."

Cam sat back in his chair and tried not to sigh. "I wasn't there, Sheriff," he said. "And I find it hard to believe, too. You click the cuffs, you say the magic words. But apparently no one on the SWAT team is willing to swear that he did in fact give the warning."

"The other thing I can't believe is that she dismissed," the sheriff said.

"It's not like she didn't give Steven the chance to nolle," Cam said. "He got all wrapped around the axle."

"He going to appeal?"

"I don't know, sir," Cam said. "I mean, I can see her tossing the confession, but dismissing the charges?"

The sheriff shook his head. "This—this was a big deal. Gas station burned up. Two innocent bystanders burned alive in their car. The store clerk shot and then cremated. I mean, damn, attaboy for finding these pricks, but aw shit for this mess. You know the rule."

It was another one of the sheriff's favorites from his days in the Marine Corps: one aw shit erased ten thousand attaboys. Cam thought it was time for him to defend his outfit. "This whole goat grab arrived in slices," he said. "The incident originally came in as a bad fire. The fire investigators didn't report bullet holes in the pump island until daylight. They had bodies from the fire, but nobody knew the clerk had been shot until the coroner called in *his* prelim. The district got the bullet holes repot from the fire department at about the same time as the street witness report filtered in, and then here comes the district, asking for a SWAT takedown. MCAT never officially rolled on it. In my view, Will Guthridge stepped into a Special Operations mess-up. It was Sergeant McMichael who popped the question without a warning, not Will."

"God help us, we train and we train, and now this," the sheriff muttered. "But why in the hell dismiss the charges? I mean, I know it was Bellamy, but damn!"

"Those shitheads are factory-programmed to screw up again," Cam said. "Or maybe Klein can get around it, reconstitute the case—it's not like we don't know who did it."

The sheriff stared down at his desk, probably calculating the degree of damage to his own professional reputation once Bellamy's decision got some traction in the media. Cam, on the other hand, had two years and some change to go for full retirement eligibility, although he could walk right now if he was willing to accept a little less pension money. He was pretty sure he would survive the gathering shit storm, although one never knew with Bobby Lee. The sheriff defended his people vigorously, but he also could be ruthless when it came to major mistakes.

The sheriff seemed to have made a decision. "You're right," he said. "A judge doesn't have to explain anything. Unfortunately, we do. Next Door is up in arms, as you can appreciate."

"Next door" meant Triboro's mayor and the city council, whose offices were in an adjacent building. Bobby Lee was always pointing out that he answered directly to the voters, but nearly two-thirds of those voters lived in Triboro. "The vultures were in the courtroom," he said.

"Which is why I have the victims' relatives in my conference room as we speak," the sheriff said. "I need them calibrated before the media gets to them, if that's possible." He gave Cam a meaningful look.

Perfect, Cam thought. Absolutely perfect. "Any suggestion on what to say?" he asked. "Like, we're going to work it some more? We're going to appeal? Or should I just say we're going to roll over, pat 'em on the ass, and just watch 'em go?"

"The charges are dismissed," the sheriff said evenly. "That's pretty final, the way I understand it. I assume Steven Klein is conferencing with the AG's office up in Raleigh right now, but, yeah, I'd say they flat got away with it."

"He should have nolle'ed," Cam said, exasperated. He wanted to hit someone as the enormity of the injustice sank in. He wanted to tell the sheriff what Kenny Cox had suggested: trail the two bastards, then tell the victims' family where they were. That dead woman's husband—he'd been really quiet after the judge's rulings. Cam hadn't been able to tell if it was total shock at the ruling or the ignition of a slow fuse.

"So, what do I tell them?" Cam asked again. "Because otherwise, I'm just going to lay it out for them. Tell the truth."

The sheriff shrugged. "Your box, Lieutenant. Paint it as you see fit." He looked pointedly at his watch. "You're not the only one with unpleasant duty—I've got to go Next Door."

5

OKAY, THERE'S NO WAY around it, Cam thought.
I'll just go in there and tell the poor bastards the truth. Answer their questions straight up. There's no official spin, so
I'll just tell them what we knew, when we knew it, what we
didn't know, and what we failed to do. If they took any of it to
the press, so be it. He'd been policing long enough to know
that telling the truth first time up was the best way to put the
media vultures off their feed, because the truth left them
nothing to uncover. Sounded good anyway.

As he left the sheriff's office and headed toward the conference room, he saw Kenny Cox chugging down the hall,
looking like the front end of a Peterbilt. Kenny was varsity
front-line large. He worked out daily with some of the more
extreme deputies in field operations and had the overlong
arms of a gorilla, although that wasn't feature a sane man
would point out to Kenny face-to-face. When he was happy,
he reminded Cam of a great big friendly bear. His game face,
on the other hand, brought to mind a picture Cam had once
seen of an East Berlin border guard, with that ruddy complexion, close-cropped blond hair, intense blue eyes under almost white eyebrows, a great beak of a nose, and a
down-turning mouth.

"Sally said you were teeing up to face relatives," he said.
"Want some backup?"

Cam smiled to himself. He could always count on Kenny
to know what was shaking down the hall. Kenny had Cam's
vote to step up to his job and lieutenant bars when Cam finally quit policing. The only fly in the succession ointment
was Kenny's run-in with the same Judge Bellamy who was

now making headlines. "Backup's good," he said, eyeing the piece of paper in Kenny's paw. "That the guest list?"

"It is," Kenny said. "James Marlor, fifty-six, husband of decedent victim Vicki Marlor, soccer mom, and stepfather of decedent victim Trudy Anne Marlor, age nine. He works for Duke Energy, something to do with forestry. His sister, a Mrs. Becky Thomason, is here to provide some family support." He frowned at the next name. "Jaspreet Kaur Bawa, thirty-five, niece of decedent victim Jasbir Chopra, the minimart night clerk. She's some kind of high-priced computer wonk, works down in the Charlotte area. Plus Jasbir Chopra's wife, Surinder Chopra, plus three more female relatives, whose names I can't *even* pronounce."

"Okay," Cam said. "And no lawyers?"

"Correct. The sheriff restricted this briefing to humans." Cam nodded in appreciation.

"Is there a party line?" Kenny asked, handing Cam the list.

"Nope," Cam said, and buttoned up his suit jacket. The .45-caliber semiautomatic in his shoulder rig distorted the fabric on his left side, indicating that perhaps he needed to forgo the morning doughnuts in the MCAT office for a while. On the other hand, it was well known that suits did shrink. "Let's do it," he said, exhibiting lots more confidence than he felt.

They went in and introduced themselves to all those tight white and brown faces sitting around the table. For the next half hour, Cam briefed them on the sequence of events since the incident at the minimart. Then he took them through the DA's current options, which weren't promising. When he was finished, James Marlor was the first to speak up. He, too, was wearing a suit, but he definitely looked like an outdoorsman, with large, rough hands, a weather-burned face, and a determined, jutting jaw. Cam thought he looked a little like Kenny; they were about the same size. It had been seven days since the incident, and he could see the strain of the past week written all over these people. He didn't feel so good, either, but he wasn't burying relatives. It was a shitty deal all around.

"Did the judge do something that was outside her judicial discretion?" Marlor asked.

The question surprised Cam. "No, sir," he replied. "I'm not a lawyer, of course, but a judge can dismiss the charges if he or she decides there's insufficient evidence to proceed. Normally, the judge would telegraph that opinion to the prosecutor, and then the prosecutor would pull the case and recharge it later."

"But not once the charges are formally dismissed?" Marlor was looking right at Cam, like a man who was making sure he understood the ground rules before he did something. Definitely more than just a run-of-the-mill country forester here, Cam thought.

"No, sir," he said. "Dismissed means it's over."

"The judge kept asking the DA about a no-lay, or something like that. Was that a hint for him to pull the case?"

"I think so, yes, sir," Cam said. "The term is nolle prosequi. It's actually something you enter in the court record, but, roughly, it means 'I won't prosecute now.' Doesn't mean he can't prosecute later, with new charges."

"Unless the underlying charges are dismissed, correct?"

He's like a dog with a bone, Cam thought. "Not unless he can get this ruling overturned."

"And you're saying you don't know if he's going to do that?"

"That's correct, sir." Cam didn't say what he was thinking—namely, that a successful appeal was unlikely. Kenny sat beside him, his bulky presence comforting. Kenny's face was a study in anger, but he also seemed to be watching Marlor.

The exotic-looking young woman at the other end of the table raised her hand. Cam had been trying not to stare at her; she was really striking, with that long oval face, the prominent Southwest Asian nose, glistening jet black hair, and luminous dark eyes. She was dressed in a rather severe-looking business suit, and her elegant long hands were devoid of any jewelry.

"Yes, ma'am?" he said.

"If I understand this situation, Lieutenant, my uncle is dead—murdered, actually—and the two individuals who did this thing are . . . free?"

To Cam's surprise, she spoke with a subdued British accent, modulated by the rising and falling tones of the Indian subcontinent. Her posture was upright and she appeared totally composed. Compared to her, the older Indian women sitting next to her looked dumpy and plain, although just as angry.

"Yes, ma'am," he replied. "For the moment anyway." He looked down at Kenny's list. "You are Ms. Bawa?"

"'For the moment'?" she said, ignoring his question. "In my uncle's country," she continued, "his family would see to it that appropriate justice was done for such a crime. We are Sikhs, you understand." The other women seated with her nodded approvingly. Cam didn't understand what she was getting at with the Sikh business, but he nodded, too. Marlor had a small spiral notebook in front of him on the table, and he was drawing a tight zigzag line on it again and again, pressing down hard. The Indian woman's remark about retribution got Kenny's attention, and he stared at her intently now.

"In this country," Cam said as patiently as he could, "the victim's family does not have the option of revenge, Ms. Bawa. If it's any comfort, these men are career criminals. It's my opinion that they'll die in prison, eventually."

She was not impressed. "'Eventually'?" she spat out. "They should be dead. Now. Just like my uncle and this gentleman's wife and daughter. They are animals. Crazed, drooling pariah dogs. They should be dragged by their genitals to the courthouse square and summarily beheaded."

Cam detected a faint twitch in Kenny's face, which meant he was in full agreement with this bloodthirsty woman. To tell the truth, Cam thought a beheading or two would do a world of good towards motivating their local criminals to seek the path of righteousness. "The Sheriff's Office is going to go back over the facts of this case," he said. "We're going to comb the incident trail, see if we can put together a package of evidence that doesn't depend on the one individual's confession at the time of the arrest."

"And then what?" James Marlor asked. His pencil was poised over the small notebook. The zigzag pattern was black and bold on the dented paper.

"And then we'll sit down with the DA and see what can be done to resurrect the case or bring new charges." Cam hesitated, but then he remembered he had promised himself he was going to tell them the truth. "In all honesty, I can't promise much, because there will be an element of double jeopardy in anything we try to do now to these two. But I personally feel obligated to make the effort. Those two individuals are guilty and need to pay for it."

"Especially after a police mistake," Marlor said.

"Especially because of that, yes," Cam said, facing him. "I'm truly sorry about that, but the police do make mistakes."

"Did the judge *have* to dismiss the charges?" he asked.

"I don't know, sir," Cam replaced. "I don't think the judge *had* to dismiss, but again, I'm not a lawyer. Most of the time, judges are constrained to make their decisions based on the law, not justice."

"Where are they now?" Ms. Bawa asked.

"The two suspects? They're still in police custody, but they'll probably be released this afternoon."

"Where will they go when they are released?" Marlor asked.

"I can't say, sir. They aren't on probation, so they can go wherever they please, I guess."

"Will you follow them?" he asked.

Cam shook his head, although he fully intended to keep track of them at least. "Once they're released, we can't do anything that might be construed as harassment."

There was a strained silence in the room. There were no answers for all of the other questions they desperately wanted to ask, and Cam was pretty sure they knew that. Finally, Marlor spoke up. "Thank you," he said, looking first at Kenny and then at Cam. "For being honest with us. I expected—well, I don't know what I expected."

Cam nodded at him and asked if anyone else had further questions. No one did, so he closed the meeting. Kenny called a desk officer down to escort them back to the security lobby. James Marlor appeared to be lost in thought as he left, his sister holding on to one of his arms above the elbow. The older Indian women gave Cam and Kenny venomous looks before they walked out of the room. Cam couldn't really blame them.

As they walked back to the MCAT offices, Kenny asked if they were really going to resurrect the case.

"I'm going to until someone specifically tells me to stop," Cam said. "This is awful."

"Fucking liberal-ass Communist judges—that's what's awful," Kenny said.

They arrived at the double glass doors leading to the Major Crimes Division's reception area and Kenny punched in the entry code. Cam asked him if he thought the husband, Marlor, might have some vigilante in him.

Kenny paused as the door buzzed open. "You know? He just might. I should probably pull the string on him. He didn't come across as some country boy."

"I hope that Indian woman was just venting," Cam said,

"I don't," Kenny replied with a disgusted look.

6

A DEPRESSING AND BUSY week later, Cam was going through the overtime logs when Tony Martinelli, one of the four MCAT detectives, stuck his head in and told him to come see who was on television. It was a Monday morning, and the whole MCAT squad was in the office for a change. The guys kept a small television going next to the coffeepot, and Cam found everyone watching newly famous K-Dog Simmonds, outfitted now in pseudo-*Matrix* black T-shirt, black pants, and a rumpled, draping black linen jacket, telling the hostess of the local sleazoid television talk show what it was like to be victimized by the "po-lice." The hostess was a big-haired blonde, with round, eternally surprised blue eyes and a mouthful of artfully capped teeth. She was hanging breathlessly on this shitheel's every word, and she was "shocked—*shocked*—" by how badly this heavily tattooed prison punk had been treated, so shocked that she could barely keep her shiny little knees together, to the point where Simmonds kept sliding his eyes sideways to look up her skirt. Their boy was fully on the strut, tossing off belligerent denials about any involvement in the minimart robbery but letting the smirk on his face declare that just the opposite was true and wasn't he a really badass dude to have gotten away with it.

"Hiawatha had it right," said Horace Stackpole, the oldest detective on the team. "Hang him by his nuts and cut his fucking head right off."

"She's an Indian princess, Stack," Kenny said. "Not a Native American."

"Give a shit," said Stackpole. "Hedge clippers would be the way to go. Dull hedge clippers. The manual kind." He made the motion. "Lotsa fucking chops. You could sell tickets even, dollar a chop."

"You'd need to sell rubber aprons, too," Tony offered. Tony was just a little bit weird.

"I hope to God the families don't see this obscenity," Cam said, going back to his desk. "They haven't sued us yet, but this would inspire even me to talk to a lawyer."

"Look at that little prick," Kenny said, "Right out of a trailer park's septic field and proud of it. Knows he's bulletproof, too."

"Thank you, Judge 'Let 'Em All Skate' Bellamy," Pardee Bell growled. He was one of two black detectives in the MCAT, the other being Billy Mays. Pardee was almost as big as Kenny, but not as tall, and he just loved to get in criminals' faces, especially black criminals, and severely "punk 'em out," as he was fond of saying. Everyone thought Pardee was on the team to provide some in-house muscle, but Pardee had a degree in computer science from NC State and could do some real damage with a desktop. Billy was called "Too Tall," for obvious reasons; he was six eight, the team's signals intelligence specialist and also a master at B and E. He had once shown up at a downtown gangsta-rap nightclub, decked out as a Masai warrior, complete with the appropriate edged weapons and pretending to be on a seriously bad ganja trip. He'd cleared the place out in one minute.

Earlier in the week, the state attorney general had told Klein to cease and desist with all his bitching and moaning, pointing out that if the perp had thought he was in custody, then he *was* in custody, and the Miranda would have had to precede any allowable confessions. Since the SWAT sergeant had asked Simmonds flat out if he did it, with two or more armed gorillas sitting on his chest, the AG thought the thing was open and shut. Mostly shut. Word in the hallways was that the sheriff was trying to figure out how to step hard on McMichael's neck without setting up the whole Sheriff's Office for a lawsuit.

Cam's plan to send the guys out to beat the bushes on the two robbers hadn't fared any better than Klein's protestations. The sheriff had shot it down as soon as he got wind of it. Trying to avert even more serious consequences, Bobby Lee had already taken disciplinary action against Will Guthridge, suspending him without pay for two weeks and demoting him off the MCAT. Will was home, feeling both guilty and picked on, and the rest of the guys were pissed off at Bobby Lee and talking about the bad things that were going to happen to a certain sergeant. Cam knew that the sheriff had really been trying to preempt public opinion. Everyone was feeling the heat.

Kenny stopped by Cam's desk. "I sent you an e-mail report on James Marlor, the husband?" he said. "Turns out he's a little bit more than just some timber cruiser."

"Couldn't you just print it out and let me read it?" Cam asked. He was not fond of computers and all their works.

"You gotta read your e-mail once in awhile, boss," Kenny said with a malicious grin. He had embraced the world of the Internet years ago and was a true adept. Cam promised Kenny he'd look at it. Kenny politely reminded him to turn on his computer first. Then he and the detectives all left for lunch. Cam retrieved his mystery-meat sandwich from the office fridge and then reluctantly booted up his desktop.

It turned out that James Marlor was not a forester, but a senior environmental engineer for Duke Energy. He was technically assigned to Duke's headquarters near Charlotte, but actually worked out of his home, which was in Lexington, between Charlotte and Triboro. He'd been born and raised in southern Virginia and had a bachelor's degree in forestry and a master's in environmental science. He worked in the power conglomerate's environmental-protection division. His specialty was the effects of coal-burning power plants on forest ecology. He'd done extensive field research, was the author of one book and two monographs on the subject, and also a candidate for a Ph.D. in environmental science at UNC–Chapel Hill. He'd been with the company for twenty-seven years.

The late Vicki Marlor had been his second wife, and the deceased child was hers by a former marriage. His first wife had died in a car crash, the victim of a drunk driver. Whoa, Cam thought. Now he's lost two spouses. No wonder there'd been no histrionics in the courtroom—brother Marlor had had some direct experience with grief. Prior to college and going to work for Duke Energy, he'd enlisted in the army and had attained the black beret of the Army Rangers. Tramping through the state's forests must be good for him, Cam thought. He's fifty-six, but he sure as hell doesn't look it.

Marlor had no criminal record, no tax problems, and no traffic offenses. And there was another surprise: he had been licensed by the state for fifteen years to carry a concealed weapon—the justification for this being that he had to go into some relatively primitive areas up in the Carolina mountain country. Got that right, Cam thought, mindful of some of his own experiences in them thar hills.

Of interest was the fact that Malor had requested early retirement from Duke Energy two days ago. Cam wondered how the hell Kenny had dug that up. Corporate personnel departments were usually pretty closemouthed unless there was a warrant on the table. He started in on his sandwich, trying not to get too much of it onto the keyboard. So now what? he thought. Here's a smart guy with a solid career suddenly shutting it all down after his wife and stepchild end up at the wrong place at the wrong time. Okay, he could see that. But what's he going to do now? Cam wondered. An ex-Ranger, an outdoorsman, and a man who carries a concealed weapon. How would a guy like that react if he happened to stumble on a rerun of that talk show and see that worthless white trash acting out?

Cam jotted down a reminder to talk to Kenny about doing a postincident follow-up with Mr. Marlor. He couldn't shake the intuition that Marlor might go after those two. There'd been something in his face, something about his demeanor at that meeting after the court decision. Cam also realized that some of his instincts were driven by bureaucratic necessity. If Marlor did go after those two, he wanted the record to show that they'd covered this base at least once.

Then he noticed that Kenny had sent two reports. He clicked

on the second e-mail without crashing his computer, and saw that this one was on the "Indian princess," as Kenny called her—Jaspreet Kaur Bawa, the minimart clerk's niece. She'd come to the United States as a teenager to live with her aunt and uncle in Charlotte. The uncle was more father to her than her biological father, who had remained in the Punjab. Now a naturalized citizen, Bawa had graduated from UNC–Chapel Hill in only three years, with a double major in mathematics and computer science, followed by a three-year doctorate program in computer science from the Steinmetz Institute. Thirty-five, never married. Lived in a condo/office in Charlotte and did expert consulting work in systems engineering for mainly corporate clients, both in the United States and abroad. Her consulting fee was two thousand dollars per day, plus expenses, and there was a waiting list. She also apparently worked for the FBI from time to time.

Not bad for thirty-five, Cam thought. Kenny had added some personal notes. Her hobbies included yoga, whitewater kayaking, and driving expensive cars. DMV records indicated that she drove a $115,000 BMW 760Li and had accumulated not a few speeding tickets. She was rumored to be a regular in the Blue Ridge Parkway night car-rally scene up in Swain County. Officially, the parkway closed at sunset, but the rally crowd would assemble on some secret signal on the segment of the parkway that ran through the Cherokee Indian reservation. They would then race for bragging rights.

That last bit gave him pause. "Rumored to be"? Where the hell was Kenny getting this stuff? He made a second note to ask Kenny that very question.

7

THAT NIGHT, CAM TOOK a wee dram of a boggy single malt out to his back deck to watch night fall over the Carolina Piedmont. He lived alone with his two German shepherds in the northern part of Manceford County. His home was in a leafy subdivision called Lakeview, which backed up to the Lake Brandeman reservoir watershed area. The house was a one-story rambler with a large walk-out basement facing the backyard, which, in turn, led down a fairly steep hill to a small creek. The hillside rising up behind his property was an abandoned farm. In summer, he could hear the creek but not see it because of all the trees. He'd picked this area many years ago, after his divorce, and bought three adjacent lots on a cul-de-sac at the back of the subdivision while the bulldozers were still moonscaping. He'd built on the middle one and planted groves of Leyland cypress on either side for privacy.

Cam would not have said that he lived alone, for the two shepherds offered amiable company. Frick was an American-bred sable bitch who would happily amputate the extremities of any intruder. Frack, the larger of the two, was an all-black East German model. He was something of a blockhead, and he had a disconcerting habit of sitting down and staring at strangers, instead of running around and barking his fool head off. He had wolflike amber eyes, and lots of people were more than willing to believe Cam when he told them that Frack really was a wolf. As any dog owner knew, deterrence was 80 percent of the battle.

With the notable exception of Kenny Cox and Tony Martinelli, the other MCAT detectives were married and apparently serious about it. Kenny was, by reputation, seriously devoted to the pursuit of any female who looked in his direction, much less smiled at him. Cam no longer pursued women, if, in fact, he ever had. He'd long ago discovered that pursuit could actually lead to catching one, and then life always got a whole lot more complicated—like when he had been married to the woman who was now the poster child for everything wrong with the criminal justice system, and the woman most hated by the Manceford County Sheriff's Office, SWAT teams, and MCAT: Judge Annie Bellamy.

His memories of marriage seemed more like a movie he'd watched as a teenager than as a sustaining personal memory. They'd both been young, on the make, and definitely on the move. Annie Bellamy had been an up-and-coming trial lawyer, and Cam a brand-new police sergeant with a college degree, a man who was going places in the Sheriff's Office. All anyone had to do was ask him. Fortunately, as it turned out, they'd agreed to forgo having children in favor of lots of flashy catalog toys, ample credit-card bills, and a studiously energetic sex life. Any married couple who'd been together for a while would have known they couldn't keep that deal going forever.

Cam had broken out of the street-patrol force in record time. That was the good news. The bad news was that his quick advancement to detective just about guaranteed a long stint in his new sergeant's rank, as older hands in the Sheriff's Office exerted their influence to make sure the brash young college boy didn't go too fast for his own, or their, good. And that had become the problem, or at least the *casus belli,* because his darling bride, all swishing legs, flashy smile, and that lightning quick litigator's brain, went very fast indeed. He was still a detective sergeant earning his bureaucratic bones in a district office by the time she had stepped up to a partner's office, and by then she had begun to move in very different economic and social circles. His boss at the time had been Connie Harding, a crusty captain of the old school, who was in charge of the district. He'd taken seven years to pin on sergeant stripes, and another five to make lieutenant. He'd pulled Cam aside one day and finally let him in on a secret, which apparently was no secret to anyone else—namely, that his wife was stepping out on him.

"You're the hotshot detective," Connie had said somewhat sadly, Cam now realized. "Go check it out, Cam."

So of course he did and she was, and that ended that. They parted stiffly. With her six-figure income, she took over their joint financial obligations and even offered to pay him alimony. Being a good southern boy, and not too bright in the bargain, he had considered his pride and said no. She then made the mistake of marrying her current boyfriend, another lawyer, who was also married at the time of their little affair. In a parting gesture of disaffection, Cam had generously made the observation that if the guy had cheated on his first wife, he would surely cheat on his second. Within four years, the lawyer proved Cam right. A few years after that, she'd married again, this time to a money manager, who was substantially older and even richer than she was. Then one morning, the moneyman was found floating in his swimming pool, the body discovered by a twenty-five-year-old "executive assistant" who had supposedly just come over from the office to see why he hadn't shown up for work. Except, of course, as things turned out, she'd been there all night—an apparently routine arrangement whenever Annie went on a business trip. Annie had been single ever since.

Cam had kept track of Annie, however. She'd hurt his feelings, but over time he'd grown beyond that, understanding that a marriage based mostly on lust was never going to be a long-term thing. Now that she had taken marriage off her life's agenda, too, they'd recently become friends again. Triboro was no longer the small southern town they'd started out in, but for people like Cam, who'd been there for most of his working life, keeping in touch with one's ex was a routine social phenomenon. In some divorce cases, of course, it was more a matter of keeping your friends close and your enemies closer, but it had worked out better for them the second time around. They'd gotten together a few times, and then more frequently over the past two years. Cam figured they both appreciated the fact that there was no longer any element of competitive boy-girl pursuit, implied or otherwise, and certainly no long-term commitments being sought or offered. Plus, there was a store of knowledge about each other that made the context as comfortable as they wanted it to be.

And then one evening—Cam wasn't sure why, maybe just mutual horniness—they'd tried out the bedroom again. It had been better for both of them than anything in between, or so they told each other, and they laughed about that for a long time. They'd gravely set some conditions: no talking shop, and no fixed routines—his place one night, her place the next, that kind of crap. If one of them felt the urge to see the other, he or she would just call. It would happen or it wouldn't. They didn't go out to restaurants or parties where the socially prominent people went, but it wasn't exactly some deep secret that they were seeing each other. They tried their best to keep it as private as possible, though. They'd solemnly agreed that if either one got bored with the other, they'd simply stop calling. Cam was beginning to think that in their own late-blooming fashion, they might be backing into the relationship they should have had when they were much younger. They both seemed to sense that the trick was not to talk about it, just to enjoy it. She'd even joked about putting Cam in her will, or if not Cam, then certainly Frick and Frack.

The phone rang in the kitchen and he went to retrieve the portable phone. Speak of the devil: It was Annie. "Hey," she said.

"Hey, yourself," he replied. "I was just thinking about you."

"Good or bad?"

"I was thinking about your legs, actually," he said, smiling into his scotch in the darkness. An owl called somewhere down along the creek. Another one answered. Frick woofed some criticism from a corner of the porch. "How they make that swishing sound when you wear tight skirts."

"Tight skirts are déclassé just now," she said, "especially at my age." But he could tell she was flattered.

"You ever sit on the bench with just your underwear on under those big black robes?" he asked. She had given up lawyering to become a judge about five years ago, although after two divorces and one agreeable probate, she was wealthy enough not to have to work anymore.

"Is there book on that across the street, Lieutenant?"

"Entirely possible, Your Honor."

"Well, you let me know when the odds are right and you're on the long side, and maybe I'll see what I can do," she said, laughing. Cam loved her laugh. It was throaty, bordering on a belly laugh tinged with the experiences of being an attractive woman for all of her adult life.

"But hopefully you didn't call to talk about my gambling jones," he said.

"No," said Annie. "I've heard some stuff around the halls of justice."

"Stuff?"

"Like detectives getting suspended and thrown off the MCAT, and a whole lot of political heat radiating from Raleigh, headed in our fair city's direction."

Now that surprised him. What she was supposed to have said was that she wanted him to come over. No talking shop. "You heard correctly," he said reluctantly. "Although that wasn't really an MCAT deal."

"Guthridge was your guy, wasn't he?"

Cam didn't say anything for a moment, taking a sip of scotch instead. Damn it, he thought. We had a deal. Plus, he wasn't sure he wanted to talk to her about this mess, in which she had a starring role.

"Technically, yes," he said finally, and then explained what had happened.

"I heard another rumor—that MCAT might be gathering a posse to revisit the minimart case."

Whoops, he thought. We definitely should have stuck to the rules. He wondered who her sources were. "Take the Fifth, Your Honor," he said, trying to keep it light. "I've seen no evidence of said posse. You remember evidence, right?"

"All right, all right, don't get picky."

"I won't if you won't," he said. "So back to the rules?"

"Yeah, okay. Back to the rules."

"So why'd you call, really?"

He heard her take a breath and release it. She always did that when she thought she was going to say something significant. Women.

"A girl's got needs," she said.

He couldn't help himself; he laughed.

"It's not funny," she said, but he knew she was smiling, too. They amused each other these days, which was almost as good as the sex. Almost.

"You gotta say the words. I'm a cop. Cops love their rules. Besides, you know what a busy social life I have."

She groaned, but then said the magic words. "Can you come over tonight?"

"Now we're talking," he said.

"Talking's not what I had in mind."

8

THREE MONTHS AFTER THE minimart case went off the tracks, Cam returned to his office from an interminable budget meeting and sent his notebook skidding across his desk and onto the floor, scattering papers like duckpins. Horace, recognizing the symptoms of bureaucratic overload, pretended to stare hard at his computer monitor, even though it wasn't on. Cam swore out loud as he dropped into his chair. Kenny came in from next door, pulled up a straight-backed chair, and sat down in it backward, ready to hear Cam's tale of fiscal woe.

"We lose?" he asked.

"We lost," Cam said. "Narco-Vice got the augmentation money." His phone rang. He picked it up and identified himself, listened for a moment, wrote down a string of letters and numbers on his blotter, and then hung up.

"That was Eddie Marsden over in Computer Crime," he said to Kenny. "Says there's something we need to see on some Web site. Here's the Web address." He turned his blotter around so Kenny could read it. Then Cam got up out of his chair so Kenny could get on Cam's machine and find the Web site. Every time Cam tried to surf the Web, his machine would bring up a string of porn sites, which Kenny said meant somebody had been screwing around with his computer. Kenny rattled the keyboard and made the screen dance through several images before stopping at a totally black screen.

"Oh, great," Cam said. "I recognize that. That's what I usually get. This is a joke, right?"

"Don't think so," Kenny said. "Says it's buffering a video."

The screen remained totally blank. "Speak English," Cam suggested. As far as he was concerned, buffering was what the cleaning crew did to the linoleum.

"Means it's downloading a video stream from a Web site. Like a movie, or a TV clip."

The screen remained black, but then Cam thought he could hear something coming from the computer's speakers: a hissing sound, with a deep bass note underlying the hiss.

"Still buffering," Kenny said, watching the screen. "It's big, whatever it is. Eddie say where he got it?"

"He said it was an attachment on an e-mail from the Bureau's Charlotte field office, but the Feebs say they didn't send it. Whoa—what the hell is that?"

A picture was forming on the screen. The video camera was obviously sitting on a table, pointing across a long, narrow, darkened room. Perhaps ten feet away, a crudely hooded figure was sitting in what looked like a barber's chair, or maybe it was a dentist's chair. Whatever it was, it seemed to be made of shiny metal, with footrests, armrests, and a barely visible metal pedestal. There appeared to be metal clamps binding the figure's forearms and bare feet to the structure of the chair, and there was a wide leather belt cinched around his middle. The deep humming sound grew louder, reminding Cam of one of those big pipes on a church organ. As the sound rose, another hooded figure appeared behind the one in the chair. Horace got up and came in to stand behind Cam's desk when he heard that deep humming sound. The second figure had the physique of a man, and he was wearing a dark windbreaker and a hood that had vertical eye slits. His clothes revealed absolutely nothing about the face under the hood or the man's size. Cam realized he was just assuming it was a man. Then an electronically distorted voice boomed out of the computer's speakers, startling all three of them. Cam hadn't been aware that his speakers were even capable of transmitting such a noise.

"All rise," the voice commanded, the sound loud enough to be heard around the office. A detective from Major Crimes stuck his head in the door and asked, "What the hell was that?"

The standing figure reached over the figure in the chair and lifted the hood, which Cam recognized was probably just a pillowcase. The video was a little jerky, but it was clear enough to see who was in the chair, and Cam grunted in surprise. It was Kyle Simmonds, aka K-Dog, of minimart fame.

"Well, looky here," Kenny murmured. "K-Dog, my man. What you doin' there, dude?"

K-Dog's tongue came out as he licked his lips for an instant and tried to look around. Then Cam saw the neck brace and realized that K-Dog's head was also immobilized.

"Watch carefully, Officers," the computer's speakers intoned in sepulchral tones. "This man slaughtered three innocent people. *You* let him get away with it. *I'm* going to rectify that problem. I'm going to send him to hell until the end of time."

K-Dog's eyes got very wide and he appeared to be trying to speak, but then they saw that there was something in his mouth, some soft, wet, bulky object that appeared to be held in place by two shiny metal clamps on either side of his mouth. He was wearing a white T-shirt and jeans, but no shoes or socks. Beads of perspiration stood on his forehead. They couldn't see his teeth when he opened his mouth and began making increasingly frantic mewing sounds while his hands turned red as he fought against the steel restraints on his wrists. The hooded figure standing behind the chair withdrew from sight, and for a moment nothing happened.

"Oh my God," Horace said. "You know what that is? That's a fucking—"

The deep bass note coming from the speakers was replaced by the unmistakable sound of high voltage, a lethally urgent throbbing sound that transfixed K-Dog's strapped-down body, making every one of his muscles suddenly visible and causing a sputtering cooking sound to come from his mouth. Cam found himself backing away from the computer screen as the electrocution gained in strength and ferocity, the volume rising now as K-Dog's eyes bulged out to the size of golf balls and then began to change texture from clear to something more like hard-boiled eggs. The sputtering from his mouth became the sound of fat roasting in open flames, and it was accompanied by a brownish vapor. His hair began to smoke and his arms and legs were jerking furiously against the restraints as the neurons in his body responded to the current's frequency, forcing every one of his muscles to expand and contract in time with some distant power plant's turbogenerator. Finally, visible flames crackled around K-Dog's neck and ears and his spine curved outward against the leather belt, bending his fuming corpse toward the camera as if in supplication, while an eerie blue aura formed around his extremities. Then came the sound of a huge electric arc, and all the sound stopped, along with the current, apparently. K-Dog's body slumped down into the chair as if his skeleton had been rubberized. His eyes were still wide open, but they were just brownish white balls now, with only barely visible irises.

Cam swallowed and exhaled noisily, as did the other men, unaware that they'd been holding their collective breath. And then, to their horror, the current snapped back on. This time, the body jerked around in the chair like a puppet on springs as the relentless amperes coursed through what had to be a very dead body for another ten gruesome seconds.

Then the screen slowly dissolved to black again and the speakers subsided into that original deep bass note. Just as Cam was clearing his throat, the spectral voice boomed out again.

"That's one," it announced.

Then the screen went gray and the humming sound stopped.

Kenny whistled softly and then started banging away on the keyboard again.

"Mother*fuck*!" said the detective standing behind Cam, who hadn't realized that all the noise had attracted an audience from the office next door. "I think I'm gonna puke."

"What are you doing?" Cam asked Kenny.

"Trying to get a fix on the real source of that attachment," he said, tongue between his teeth as he concentrated on the screen. The screen had turned blue, with white text and computer hieroglyphics scrolling down.

"Was that real or Memorex?" Horace asked.

"Looked real to me," Kenny said, still typing. "Hope so anyway."

The phone rang on Cam's desk. He picked it up, the execution images still vivid in his mind. "MCAT, Lieutenant Richter."

It was the sheriff, trumpeting on his speakerphone. "Lieutenant, I have Carol Hawes with me. Her office has been getting calls about a Web site that's purportedly showing an electrocution of one those guys who did the minimart fire. You know anything about that?"

Carol Hawes was the Sheriff's Office's public relations officer. "We just saw it," Cam said. "Puke city. Computer Crimes alerted us. I take it this is out there for the whole world to see?"

"I think that's why they call it the *World* Wide Web, Lieutenant," the sheriff said dryly. Cam's reputation for being something of a Luddite when it came to computers was widespread. "What are we doing about it?"

"Watching it?" Cam said, rolling his eyes. Like what in the hell could they do about it? And why was the sheriff calling MCAT? This was definitely one for Major Crimes. "Sergeant Cox is trying to do an Internet trace on the attachment, see what he can find out about it. We need Computer Crimes to do the same, I guess."

Cam heard a buzzer going off in the sheriff's office. There was a moment of quiet mumbling as the he took a call. Then he was back on the speakerphone. "Meeting. My office in thirty," he announced, and hung up.

Kenny swore as a black screen came up. He hit one final key with a dramatic flourish, which signaled he'd signed off for Cam, and got up from Cam's chair. "Nada," he said. "It was posted on one of those floating chat rooms. Kind of like a blog. Current events and shit. I Googled the name string from the attachment, found the site again, but on yet another floating box."

"Oka-a-y," Cam said. "I'm punching the 'I believe' button here. And?"

"No luck. I'd recommend getting the Bureau into this. Eddie's going to agree, I think. Goddamn, boss. You thinking what I'm thinking?"

It took Cam a moment. "Marlor?" he said.

As Kenny nodded, Cam suddenly realized he needed some coffee. Actually, he needed a drink, but he didn't keep booze in the office.

They had gone to see James Marlor a week after the media dust began to settle on the minimart case. His home was down in Lexington. His job required him to be on the road most of the time, so the company didn't care where he parked his family, and he'd chosen Lexington over the much larger and more crowded city of Charlotte.

Marlor had been reserved, attentive, and not terribly surprised when Cam finally broached the real purpose of their visit. Marlor had told them simply that he was not going to introduce more tragedy into his life by hunting down those two. He said they'd probably die in prison, as Cam had suggested, and that that was a better fate than a bullet through the eye. Cam remembered that particular image now as he mixed sugar into his coffee. Marlor would have to be a very cool customer indeed to have done this, if it was indeed real. And that was the larger problem: This could well be just some more digital fraud zinging away out there on the Internet.

"We'll have to look at him, I guess," he said. "It's been what—three months since we talked to him? He certainly has a motive."

"What do you think?" Kenny asked.

"I think we need to let the Computer Crimes guys do their thing, you know, see if they can find out how that little drama got onto the Web." He looked at Kenny. "Is that possible?"

Kenny fixed up his own coffee while he thought about that. "Again, that's probably a Bureau labs project. It would take a hell of digital studio to do that from scratch using just ones and zeros. Only real way to find out is to chase down K-Dog; see if he's still out there, alive and eating shit."

"If he's alive, that would settle it," Cam said. "But if we can't find him, we still don't know. What's your gut reaction?"

Kenny was nodding to himself. "I think it was real," he said.

"He said 'That's one,' right there at the end. That tells me he's going to do it again. That black guy—what's his name, Butts? He's gotta be next."

Kenny nodded again. "The media is gonna go to town on this thing," he said.

"Gosh, you think?"

"Worse, actually," Kenny replied. "Something like this can attain cult status on the Web, especially if he's promising to do another one."

"Maybe we should pick Butts up for his own protection."

"On what grounds?" Kenny asked.

"Hell, I don't know—show him the video?"

"And what would Commissar Bellamy say to that?"

Cam had no answer for that one.

"If we have to work on Marlor," Kenny said, "maybe you should let me do it."

"Why?" Cam asked.

"Because I'm more sympathetic to his cause than you are?"

9

AN HOUR AND A half later, Cam assembled the entire team in the office. Billy Mays and Pardee Bell had been on their day off and were not too thrilled, but having seen a rerun of the video, they now were at least interested.

"Okay, boys and girls," Cam said, sitting sideways on the edge of his desk. "I've just been to a stimulating meeting with Bobby Lee, Hizzoner, and the usual suspects from Next Door, subject: the electric horror show now playing on the Internet. We have orders."

"*Achtung!*" croaked Horace.

"Yeah, well, first: The sheriff wants MCAT to run with this one. It's not exactly what we were formed up to do, but this hairball is going to play across a lot of jurisdictions, legal and otherwise, and we do that every day."

"Internet is interstate," Pardee said. "This is a Bureau deal."

"Agreed," Cam said. "And the sheriff has already made the call to the Charlotte field office. But in the meantime, we urgently need to put eyes on the dynamic duo of Simmonds and Butts. Kenny, you got something for us on that?"

"Yeah, boss." He briefed the team on the usual hangouts of both individuals.

"And how do we know that?" Tony Martinelli wanted to know. "I thought Judge Red Banner put their evil asses off-limits."

"Well . . ." Kenny said, looking over at Cam.

"I had proposed to the sheriff that we rebuild a case," Cam explained. "Start from scratch, get a bag of circumstantial evidence, re-ring 'em. Sheriff said no, after checking with sister Klein. So instead, I had Kenny here do a little after-hours bird-dogging, mostly to establish where these guys hang out, known associates, daily routine. Just in case Bobby Lee ever changes his mind, or if we ever need to have a word. Like, for instance, now."

Tony acknowledged that. Bird-dogging was something Kenny did very well, and better solo than with a partner.

"Horace, you and Tony see if you can produce one K-Dog Simmonds. Billy, you and Pardee go find brother Flash. Don't apprehend. Just locate and report. If Simmonds is alive and drooling, then the Web show is bullshit and we can terminate this firefly."

"And if we can't find his ass?"

"I'm to report that fact to the sheriff, and then he'll have some more decisions to make. Like whether or not to apprehend and put into protective custody one Mr. Deleon Butts."

Horace cleared his throat and spat into a trash can. "Why bother?" he said, giving voice to a sentiment that they all felt to different degrees.

"Think of it this way, Horace," Cam said. "If the vigilantes dispose of all the bad guys, who needs us, right? So ride, cowboys, ride."

The group broke up and Cam joined Kenny back at his desk. "What else?" Kenny asked.

"We need to figure out who the executioner is. Which means, for starters, you and I are going to go see James Marlor."

"I already made a call; seems his phone's disconnected."

"That's encouraging. Does Duke Energy say where his retirement checks are going?"

"Direct deposit into a BB and T branch bank in beautiful downtown Lexington, right where his regular paychecks used to go. We'll need to paper up to find out if he's cashing them or if they're just piling up."

"Okay," Cam said. "Let's go see Steven Klein, find out what we'll need."

"We might as well get domicile and vehicle search warrants, too," Kenny said as they left the office to go next door.

"Why?"

"Marlor may not be there anymore."

Cam stopped in the hallway. "That's a point, but you know what? Before we go to all this trouble, why not call his sister, see if she knows where he is?"

"That's no fun," Kenny said.

10

JAMES MARLOR'S HOUSE WAS located in an up-scale subdivision outside of Lexington. The house was a *Southern Living* number, with a wide carport on one end. As they pulled up in an unmarked Crown Vic, Cam noticed that the lawn had been mowed recently and the flower beds along the front of the house were being cared for. It was apparently trash-pickup day, because there were green Herby Kerbys up and down the streets. They parked the car in Marlor's drive-way and got out while the driver of the Davidson County cruiser, which had led them to the house, parked out on the street. Cam lifted the lid of Marlor's trash can and discovered that it was full of what looked like junk mail. He picked up a couple of items and saw that the postmarks were fairly recent.

Marlor's sister had been unwilling to talk to them about her brother. Cam had been as polite and as persuasive as he could be, without revealing what was precipitating his call. She would say only that the police had done enough damage to the Marlor family and she wanted nothing more to do with any of them. Good-bye. Kenny had obtained the warrants to search Marlor's premises and vehicles. Steven had gone to Judge Barstow, which, given what had happened to him in front of Bellamy, made sense. Barstow gave them domicile, vehicle, and financial records, but he held back on their requests for an electronic sweep until a conventional look-see had been attempted. Cam had offered to show him a rerun of the execution scene, but Barstow, pushing seventy, declined. He said he did not object to capital punishment, but he told Cam he believed nothing that he saw on a computer.

Marlor's front door was locked, and no one answered the

bell. But Kenny had seen a couple of teenagers doing some lawn maintenance three doors down, and from them he learned that Marlor's next-door neighbor had a key. The neighbor turned out to be a retired schoolteacher. She'd been collecting the mail and putting it inside. She gave them the key to the front door once they showed the warrants.

"He's been gone for some time," she said. "Going on two months now. He asked me to look after the house, you know, heating and air-conditioning, picking up his mail and getting rid of the junk, paying the kids to do the yard."

"How are you paying them, ma'am?" Cam asked. She was in her sixties and seemed unconcerned that she was talking to Sheriff's Office deputies with Manceford County search warrants. They could hear a television going behind her.

"Believe it or not," she said, "he left me a checkbook. He said he was going to be gone for some time, that he had to get away from his life here for a while. He said there'd be money coming in direct deposit to the account, and so far, nothing's bounced."

"And you're on the account?" Cam asked.

She nodded. "He signed some of the checks in case anyone balked, but I'm on the card as joint, and, so far, the bank's putting everything through."

Kenny asked if he could look through the checkbook, and she produced it. He sat down at her dining room table and began leafing through it.

"He just . . . left?" Cam asked.

She nodded. "That's right. It's a wonder he didn't harm himself, all that tragedy. I knew her better than him—he was always gone a lot. We went to the bank for me to get a signature on the card, and then he packed up his pickup the next morning and just left."

"No contact numbers?"

"Nope. He said to write myself a check for two hundred and fifty dollars each month for my troubles. I'm a widow on school-district retirement, so I said yes."

"What do you do with any personal mail, as in something besides bills?" Kenny asked from the dining room.

She pointed with her chin at the house next door. "There hasn't been hardly any. I think he shut everything off."

"Does he have any relatives besides his sister?"

"He mentioned a brother once, but I've never seen him. His wife's relatives are all in California."

"And no indication of when he plans to come back?"

She shook her head. "I half-expect a realtor to show up any day now with a FOR SALE sign." She sighed. "It's a nice house. They were a nice family. And I hear those bastards got away with it."

Kenny gave Cam a look from the dining room, but he decided not to get into a discussion about just how those bastards got away with it. They thanked her, took the key, and then went next door. For the next hour, they conducted a general walk-through of the house. It wasn't really a search. They found that his wife and stepdaughter's clothes were still there, but not many of his. The house was clean and uncluttered, although dusty. The refrigerator was completely empty, but it was clean and running. The dishwasher was empty. Kenny wore rubber gloves, but Cam didn't bother. It wasn't a crime scene.

"He didn't rush out," Cam said finally. "Picked the place up, got rid of anything that could stink, arranged for someone to set the thermostat, pay the bills, and cull his mail. A totally planned departure."

Kenny nodded, looking around the living room. "I'm thinking all those memories caved in on him and he just had to get out of here," he said. "I wonder if he has another home, a cabin in the mountains or something."

"We'll have to get with his bank. See if this place is free and clear, and if there's another mortgage out there."

"Should we bring in a CSI team?" Kenny asked.

Cam shrugged. "No indication that anything bad happened to the guy," he said.

"Besides losing his wife and daughter to those slimeballs," Kenny said.

"Okay, besides that, yeah. Looks to me like he just wrapped the place up and left. I think we're going to need that electronic sweep after all, see if he's on the road somewhere."

Kenny sat down at the dining room table and began going through the small stack of keeper mail. "Most of this looks like first-class mail," he said. "But I think it's just disguised junk mail. And no bank statements."

"That's our next stop, I think. Find out which branch from the lady next door, go see how the money's coming in and going out."

Kenny looked up at him. "Who else would put K-Dog in an electric chair besides Marlor?"

Cam scratched his head. "What expertise would it take?" he said, ducking Kenny's question for a moment. "To put a thing like that out on the Internet in such a way that it couldn't be traced back to you? I mean, I don't know dick about it, but it seems to me that if you weren't a computer expert, you'd have to hire somebody to set that up. Otherwise, it would come back all over you. Wouldn't it?"

"He would have to know a lot," Kenny said, "*and* have access to a pretty damned good computer to do it by himself. Not to mention capturing K-Dog, holding him in some remote place, building an electric chair, getting enough power to run it, then filming it with a digital camera, *and* then formatting that for Web play."

Cam walked around the dining room, thinking out loud. "Marlor's an environmental-science guy. Plus, he's a doctoral candidate in science, which means he's done everything for his Ph.D. except his dissertation. So he has to be competent in terms of computers and Web research."

"I keep looking at motive," Kenny said. "Nobody else really has the motive."

"I'll grant you that," Cam replied. "Except maybe that bloodthirsty Indian woman. So, okay, let's work it that way— make the assumption it's him, then focus on the other two legs: opportunity and means. Unless, of course, Tony and Horace bring us word of a living, breathing K-Dog."

"I'm not holding my breath," Kenny said.

"If you're right, neither is K-Dog."

11

THE BANK MANAGER TURNED out to be a stunning redhead in her thirties. She did not look like any bank manager Cam had ever seen. Even Kenny, the professional pussy hound, was momentarily speechless.

"How can I help you, Officers?" she asked, slipping behind her desk and treating Kenny in particular to a dazzling display of legs.

They had called in advance, and now Cam produced the search warrant, which she actually read. Kenny had a barely disguised grin on his face as he studied her, and Cam could see that she was fully aware of Kenny.

"Okay," she said, "I brought up his records." She tapped a computer keyboard on her desk. "Savings account, checking account, some CDs, and just over a quarter of a million in a retirement account. Twenty and change in savings, and his Duke Energy pension is direct-deposited in his checking account on the fifth of every month."

"We're trying to locate Mr. Marlor," Cam said. "We've talked to his sister and the lady who's taking care of his house. What we get is that he just left for parts unknown. Can the checking account help us out?"

"What period of time?" she asked.

"He's been gone for about eight weeks. That far back."

She clicked some more and then studied the screen. "I don't think so. He's got the recurring bills on electronic bill payer. There's no mortgage. I see some checks signed by Mr. Marlor and then endorsed by Mrs. Watkins—a neighbor, whose name is on the joint account—and there're a few checks made out to other people. We autotransfer all but seven hundred from checking over to savings at the end of each month."

"Anything signed by him in that time frame?"

She scrolled through images of the checks. "Nope," she said. "He executed the new signature cards for the account almost . . . You're right—it was eight weeks ago."

"Where do his statements go?" Kenny asked.

She finally looked directly at him, and Cam saw Kenny give her his most winning smile. She blinked once before answering. Kenny had that effect on some women—okay, on most women—although this one was wearing both a wedding and an engagement ring. "The statements are generated but not mailed," she said, clearing her throat. "Our customers can arrange it that way if they want."

"Can they be accessed via the Net?" Kenny asked.

"That, too, has to be prearranged, but, yes, our customers can do anything they need to do electronically except for the signature cards."

"Okay, so has there been any electronic action on any of his accounts?"

She tore her eyes away from Kenny and went back to the computer. Kenny gave Cam a sly wink, which made him feel even more superfluous. "No," she said. "The last electronic transaction was five years ago, when he ordered up fifty thousand for a wire transfer."

Kenny stopped flirting. "Wired to whom?"

"A bank up in Surry County."

"Could someone there tell us who cashed it?" Cam asked.

"Good luck with that. It's a privately held bank—on the edge of the mountain country. People up there really value their privacy, if you know what I mean."

She gave them the bank's name and address, and Cam thanked her for her help. He and Kenny went out to the car, where Cam dialed the number for Tony Martinelli's cell phone. Tony reported that K-Dog hadn't been seen at his regular hangouts for a week to ten days. They were on their way to an old girlfriend's trailer. "Don't get any on you," Cam said, and switched off.

"Marlor's gone, and K-Dog's not to be found," Kenny mused. "So two and two make . . ."

"We've got a ways to go before we jump to any conclusions," Cam said, even though he, too, had already jumped to that very conclusion. "K-Dog may hole up once word gets out on Punk Street that the cops are really asking around. He's going to think that we're coming back about the mini-mart. Plus, I want to know what that fifty K was for. I'm thinking a cabin or mountain property."

Cam's cell phone rang. It was the bank manager.

"I just saw something you might want to know," she said.

"Okay?"

"Mr. Marlor withdrew thirty-five thousand dollars in cash a few days before he set up the new signature cards. I would have noticed it earlier, except that you were asking about electronic transactions. This was done in person, at the counter."

"Thirty-five thousand cash—that's fairly unusual."

"He had it to withdraw, so it wasn't as if we could say no."

"Thanks very much," Cam said. He hung up and told Kenny.

"Walking-around money?" Kenny said.

"More like off-the-grid money," Cam said.

12

AT 8:30 THAT NIGHT, Cam sat watching the electrocution scene again on his desktop in the office. The other detectives had all gone for the day. There'd been nonstop
meetings with the sheriff and the public relations staff late
that afternoon, the district attorney's office, and with the
MCAT detectives. They'd put the superstar of the month on
ice in order to work this execution thing, so the team was
spending a lot more time in the office than usual.

The bottom line was that K-Dog was not to be found. Tony
and Horace had looked under all the usual rocks, and a consistent story emerged that no one had seen his sorry ass for
about ten days. He'd been living with two women in a trailer
outside of Triboro, and they were emphatically glad to be rid
of him. His replacement, a Texan with one glaring eye, was
firmly in residence and threatening to "slap an entire can of
whup-ass on that punk" if he ever came back. The nature of
K-Dog's transgressions against the females had not been determined, although Tony allowed, having seen the two afore-
mentioned women, they were probably deserved.

Billy and Pardee had had better luck. They'd tracked
down Flash in about two hours. He was holed up at a crack
whore's squat one block back of Lee Street in south Triboro,
sustaining his various addictions. Said crack whore did not
know any ghost named K-Dog, so it appeared the dynamic
duo had finally split up. Kenny got the Sheriff's Office's PR
division to obtain a tape of the talk show starring K-Dog, and
then they ran it and the execution scene side by side to make
sure they were looking at the same guy. Everyone agreed that
it certainly looked like the same guy. Horace was happily
philosophical about it, saying, "Brag about getting away with

murder in North Carolina, someone's going to rise up and take care of business." Cam landed pretty hard on him for the comment. "You can think it," he'd said, "but you can't say it out loud."

The problem was what to do about it. The Web site showing the execution scene had made the local TV evening news and would surely go national pretty soon. The putative candidate for executioner, James Marlor, was not to be found. The voice had clearly said, "That's one," which meant that Flash was possibly in some danger. Everyone at all the meetings had had the same unvoiced philosophical problem: So what. The sheriff had finally come up with a reason to care. "Someone's eventually going to start throwing shit at the Manceford County Sheriff's Office," he'd said. "They'll point out that we screwed up the arrest and these shitheads got away with it, so now one of *us* has decided to take justice into his own hands. So keep your secret vigilante decoder rings in your lockers and go find out who's doing this shit." There'd been much rolling of eyes behind the sheriff's back, but Cam thought he had a valid point. The only thing saving them from a media rumble right now was the fact that no one knew for sure if the execution was real or staged.

The next question was whether they should pick up Flash and hold him in protective custody. Klein had agreed to go talk to Judge Bellamy in chambers. He'd called back while the team was going over their search plan for Marlor and tearing up a pizza. Bellamy, as expected, had said no. They were to pick him up, get him sober enough to show him the video, make sure he understood what he was looking at, and then turn him loose. If he then came back in on his own volition and asked for protection, then and only then they could place him in protective custody. But he had to ask, and do so a second time in front of her. They'd sent a deputy out to pick him up, but it was dark by the time they got there and he was no longer at the squat, nor was the lady of the manor. This was duly reported back to Klein, who said he'd tell the judge in the morning.

Cam clicked the little *x* on the top right of his screen and the execution scene disappeared. He smiled; making sites disappear was at the top end of his computer abilities. He sat back in his chair and rubbed his eyes. His fingers smelled of pizza sauce. We're going through the motions here, he thought. There isn't anyone in this office who gives a shit that K-Dog rode the third rail. James Marlor had lost one wife to a drunk driver and now another one, plus his stepdaughter, to blind bad luck and the depredations of two walking, talking sewer rats. Marlor's professional career was complete, if not over, his immediate family had been erased, and he was of an age where he might well have decided that he didn't care what happened as long as he took these two pustules off the streets forever. Cam could even see himself pulling the switch on a mutt like K-Dog. The only good news was that, once the story went truly national, the Bureau would be into it, and then maybe the Manceford County cops could sit back and let the *Übermenschen* from the Justice Department sort it all out.

His phone rang. He looked at his watch. Almost nine o'clock. He wasn't on duty. Did he really want to answer this? Had he learned nothing in twenty-some years about answering office telephones after normal working hours? He picked it up, and it was the desk sergeant, reporting they had Flash in the drunk tank.

"Great. How bad is he?"

"Fustier than most," the sergeant said. "Looks like the back side of a crack high, irrigated by some demon rum."

"Is he coherent?"

"You're kidding, right?"

"Okay, look. I need him mostly sober and reasonably presentable by around ten tomorrow morning. I'll need him breathalyzed before he comes upstairs, so we can prove later on he wasn't totally drunk when we interviewed him."

"It'll be close," the sergeant said. "Jumpsuit okay? Because the clothes he came in had a lapful of breakfast. If you want him clean, we'll need a fire hose."

"Yeah. We're not going into court or anything. Just us country boys."

He hung up, then called Kenny's office and left a message on his voice mail, reporting they had Flash. Now if only they could find K-Dog and Marlor, they'd be home free. Time to see-cure.

He was halfway home when his cell phone chirped. He chided himself for leaving it on, then realized it was his personal cell, not his police phone. It was Annie.

"Where are you?" she asked.

"Halfway home," he said. "What's the matter?"

"Can you come over?"

Her voice seemed different. "Sure, but what's the matter? You okay?"

"There's nothing wrong," she said. He thought he could hear ice tinkling in a glass. Horny, then.

"Look, I've had a long day," he said. "Not all of it successful. I need a drink, a hot shower, and something to eat."

"I can provide all of those things," she said, and hung up.

When he got to her house and knocked on the front door, she opened it immediately. She was wearing one of her better Slinky-toy outfits. "Lucky I wasn't the UPS man," he said.

"How 'bout we reverse the order?" she said with that certain smile, and when he couldn't think of anything clever to say, she pulled him through the door and kicked it shut with her foot. The rest of her was already busy.

Later, as they relaxed in the hot tub with a scotch for him and some vodka for her, she told him she'd seen the Web site. He frowned at her. Here we go again, he thought, talking shop after hours.

"I know, I know," she protested before he could say anything. "But everybody was talking about it. It was even on the news. I think I was the only one in the courthouse who hadn't seen it."

"Go through some Kleenex?" he asked.

"That's not funny," she said. "Surely you don't approve?"

He shrugged. "I wouldn't want to watch it over dinner, not unless I muted that sound of frying bacon."

"Cam!"

"Well, that little shit killed a woman, her daughter, and a

store clerk, probably for a couple hundred bucks, tops. For reasons understood only by you lawyers, he ended up getting away with it. And he was proud of himself. From the perspective of the blindfolded, bare-breasted lady with the scales in one hand and a sword in the other? Seeing that fuck ride the electric pony to meet the baby Jesus didn't exactly ruin my day."

"Someone not only murdered him—horribly—but filmed it, for God's sake. And put it out on the Internet for the whole world to watch. That's grotesque."

"So was his crime."

"Cam!"

"Glad we reversed the order, Your Honor," he said, reaching for a towel. "Yes, I'm upset that my guy screwed up and you had to let them go. I'm depressed about all the bad publicity and political heat that we've been eating, and that there's more headed our way. But I'm not displeased with the fact that Simmonds got the jolt. If in fact he did—we still don't know that. I think I'd better go."

He started to get out, but she raised a leg, hung it over his right shoulder, and pulled. As signals went, it was reasonably effective. Annie did an hour of tantric yoga every day, and she could and did surprise him in the most amazing ways. Even if she is kind of bossy, he thought. After round two, she went to fix them a steak while he went to find some more scotch and catch his breath. Over dinner, he told her in general terms what they were planning to do about finding Marlor and Simmonds. He pointed out that, for the moment, these were just his plans, and that the sheriff might have other plans.

"Lots of fingers going to get into this pie," he said. "Great steak, by the way."

"You never could cook, not even on the grill."

"That's right, now that you mention it. I married you for your cooking, didn't I?"

She laughed, and for a moment he envisioned the peaches and cream complexion, ash-blond hair, blue eyes, and endless legs of the woman he'd courted and married so many years ago. She saw the look.

"Every once in awhile, I get this terrible feeling we pissed away a good thing way back then," she said. She drew her terry-cloth robe around her shoulders as if to ward off a chill.

"I don't know, Annie," he said. "I think you would have had to make your run, one way or the other, and I would have just held you back. Look where we are now—this is pretty good."

She was still beautiful, with one of those faces that defied a lifetime of unfriendly gravity. She gave him a severe look. "Just *pretty* good?"

"We need more practice," he said with a comic leer.

She laughed again. "As if," she said, getting up to clear the plates.

"Was that a little wobble I just detected?" he asked.

"Shut up. I'll call Steven in the morning, get him in chambers, let him explain the current thinking. This time, I'll authorize PC for Butts, on the proviso there's no attempt to force a confession or anything else related to the original crime."

Cam nodded, more to himself than to anything she'd said. "Myself, I kept hoping we'd find K-Dog," he said. "Otherwise we're in for a long couple of weeks. We can't hold Flash forever, and then . . . 'That's one'?"

"I may have to keep my eye on Mr. Steven Klein," she said from the kitchen.

"How so?"

"You mentioned 'political heat.' You're not exactly the Lone Ranger when it comes to getting heat over this mess." She closed the dishwasher door and came back into the room. She could see he didn't understand, so she laid it out. "I've been the subject of some pretty hostile BS these past few months," she said. "Letting those little pricks off like that, et cetera, et cetera. You ever wonder why it was the *judge* who spotted the Miranda error in the arrest record, instead of, say, the DA?"

He had to think about that one.

"I mean, you cops work for the DA, not the court," she said. "I think it's entirely possible young Mr. Klein did see the problem and then decided to let it come to the hearing anyway. That way, I would be the one tossing the confession, not him, whose people had messed the thing up in the first place."

"Why would he do that?" he asked.

"Because he knew I'd catch it. Because he knows I read everything in the package, sometimes twice. And he knew I'd toss it because it would never survive trial, much less appeal."

"And his objective?"

"My term is for five years. I'm up for reappointment the end of this year. Enough political heat, I don't get reappointed. That's how vacancies on the bench occur."

"Why, Steven, you clever little devil," Cam said. "Who'd a thunk it? But, shit, I thought you judges had to die or go senile or something."

"Senility is not necessarily a disqualification," she said primly. "But death is, and so is pissing off the governor. Bet you don't hear any talk about liberal, pink-ass, Communist ADAs, do you?"

" 'Pink-ass,' " he mused, as if considering the notion. She grinned despite herself, and even blushed a little. Well, well, Cam thought. I've done one thing right today. He reached for her hand, and there it was.

13

AT 9:15 THE NEXT morning, Kenny Cox, Steven
Klein, and Cam entered one of the homicide squad's interview rooms. The room was built like a small conference
room, with a plain rectangular table, eight chairs, four on a
side, and a large television screen mounted just above head
height on one end wall. There was no one-way mirrored window. In its place was a microcam mounted just underneath the
television monitor, and there were four microphones mounted
flush in the ceiling. One place at the table had eyebolts to
which a prisoner's handcuffs could be secured. Flash was sitting at that place, although he was not handcuffed.

"They were callin' him 'Splash' last night down in the
tank," the escorting officer said as he let them into the room.
Cam wondered if Butts would be up to what he was about to
see, given his appearance. His normally dark brown face had
a grayish tinge and his eyes were bloodshot and jumpy. The
skin on his face was tight across protruding cheekbones, and
his county jail jumpsuit hung loosely on his wire-thin frame.
He was sniffing hard every thirty seconds or so, and shifting
around in his seat almost continuously, as if his butt bones
hurt. Cam thought he looked old, even though his record said
he was only thirty. He froze when they trooped in, looking
from one to another as if trying to determine which one of
them was going to start beating on him. He settled on Kenny,
who obliged him with a withering glare.

"Mr. Butts," Klein began. "Relax, okay? You're not in any
trouble with the law, and you're going to get out of here this
morning. You need a cigarette?"

Flash blinked as he tried to process this unexpected information, and then he focused on the offer of a cigarette. Flash

lit the cigarette with trembling fingers and sucked half its length into his lungs in one go. He was well and truly wired.

"Mr. Butts, I'm Steven Klein, the district attorney. Let me say at the outset that you're here because we're actually concerned about your safety."

Flash spoke for the first time. "Say what?" he said after a second deep drag on the cigarette. He inhaled every molecule of the smoke, then didn't exhale for almost thirty seconds. Cam found himself holding his own breath. They'd agreed that Klein would do the talking. Kenny continued to look at Flash the way one would look at a rat who'd appeared next to the family picnic hamper. Cam stared into the middle distance and pretended he wasn't very interested in what was going on.

"Mr. Butts," Klein continued in his most sincere voice, "do you by any chance know where Mr. Simmonds is? That guy they call K-Dog?"

That guy whom you helped to kill three people, Cam thought, but he kept his silence. He exchanged looks with Kenny, who, he could see, had the same thought. Butts was shaking his head.

"Me'n K-Dog, we split, man," he said. "Muhfukah's crazy."

"When was the last time that you did see him?"

Butts shook his head again and finished the cigarette in one final intense drag.

"Mr. Butts?"

Butts was thinking about the question, and it was painful to watch. "In the courtroom," he said. "You know, when the bitch let us go." He glanced over at the cops for the first time, a faint spark of defiance in his eyes until he saw the expression on Kenny's face. His eyes bounced off Kenny's venomous stare like a moth hitting a hot lightbulb. Cam tried hard to keep his own expression neutral. The man's a halfwit, a crackhead, he told himself. K-Dog's the one, not this cocaine-soaked idiot.

"Well," said Klein, nodding at Kenny. "Mr. Butts, we have something to show you." He explained what a Web video was, then said that what Butts was about to see might or might not be real. He might as well be speaking in Greek,

Cam thought, but then Kenny turned the television on. Butts turned in his chair to look at the television, his thin body making jerky little contortions in the chair. Cam could actually see the man's pelvic bones outlined against the back of his jumpsuit. Crack, he thought. For all too many impoverished black Americans, it was the new slavery, just like crystal meth was becoming for impoverished white Americans.

They all watched Butts's face intently as the drama played out. They saw his head jerk backward with a spark of recognition when K-Dog appeared in the chair, and his rising apprehension as the hooded figure rose from behind the chair and began to speak in that voice-of-doom tone. His mouth dropped right open when the electrocution began, and he unconsciously began to push his chair back, as if to get away from the television as the scene played out. He actually cried out when the second jolt hit. When it was over, he had backed his chair all the way against the wall and was gripping the armrests as if he was about to flee, his eyes flitting from them to the now-darkened television.

"Whutdafuck, man, whutda*fuck!*" he shouted, his eyes huge and his voice rising to a falsetto. "Y'all do that shit?"

"No, Mr. Butts, we did not," Klein said, speaking quietly, trying to calm the man down. Butts was looking over at the door again, obviously ready to bolt. "Like I said, we don't even know if that was real. That's why we wanted to know if you'd physically seen Simmonds and, if so, when."

Butts clearly didn't get it.

"We want to see if that execution happened or not," Klein said patiently. "If we find Simmonds, then that has to be a fake, okay?"

"Looked fuckin' real to me," Butts said, licking his lips but calming down a little bit.

"You agree that was Simmonds in the chair?" Klein asked.

Butts nodded. "Whut you want with me?"

"Did you hear what the man in the hood said at the very end?" Klein asked.

"Uh-uh. Heard that cookin' sound, thass all. That dude on fire an' shit."

Kenny leaned forward. "He said, 'That's one,' Flash. Know what that means?"

Butts shook his head, unwilling to look directly at Kenny. "I don't know *nuthin* 'bout this shit, man," he protested. "Whut you want with me? I ain't done *nuthin*."

"Whoever the man in the hood was, he electrocuted Simmonds in retaliation for what happened at that minimart," Kenny said. "At the end there, the man says, 'That's one.' But there were two dudes did that minimart, right?"

"Uh-uh," Flash said. "That was all K-Dog. He done the shootin', done all the crazy shit. This nigger wuz on his fuckin' hands and knees, man, jus tryin' to get the fuck outta there, man." Then it finally penetrated. His voice went back up to falsetto again. "You meanin' *me*? You sayin' that hood muhfukah be comin' for *me*?"

"That's what we think, Mr. Butts," Klein said. "He put K-Dog in the chair because of what happened that night. When he says, 'That's one,' he's clearly implying there's going to be a number two."

"And that would be you," Kenny said helpfully. Cam wanted to kick him under the table.

Flash's head looked like that of a string puppet as he looked at all three of them in quick succession. "You gotta stop this muhfukah," he shouted, tears appearing in his eyes. "I didn't *do* that nasty shit, man. K-Dog, he's the one who done it. I was along for the fuckin' *ride*, man. Hands and knees, man. That's what I was doin' that night. Shit, man. *Fuck!*"

"Calm down, Mr. Butts," Klein said. "Just calm down for a minute. We're not here to talk about the minimart."

But Flash was gone now, blathering away, protesting his innocence about what happened at the minimart, laying it all on K-Dog, who'd planned the whole thing—got the gun, got the ride, picked that station, everything. He became progressively more hysterical, until Kenny slapped a meaty palm down on the table. A paper coffee cup jumped clean off the table and startled Butts into sudden silence.

"Mr. Butts," Klein said. "Look at me. Look at *me*."

Butts had his head in his hands, and he peered out between splayed fingers at Klein.

"Mr. Butts, like I said before, we don't know yet if what you saw there was real. For the last time, do you have *any* idea where we can find him?"

Butts groaned and shook his head. "He gots this crib, over in a trailer patch. Said he had him two wimmens. Braggin' on it, havin' two. I seen one—that night we got out? Ain't nothin' to be braggin' about. Know what I'm sayin'?" He banged his own hands on the table. "Shit!" he said.

"Mr. Butts," said Klein. "If you want, we can place you in protective custody until we find out whether this whole deal is genuine or not."

Butts eyed Klein suspiciously. "You talkin' jail?"

"Yes, but—"

"Uh-uh. I ain't volunteerin' for no damn jail, no fuckin' way, man."

Klein explained that he wouldn't be hassled in the protective-custody area. He'd have three squares a day, a clean bed, television, no crap from the main-pop prisoners. "We think you'd be a whole lot safer in custody than you'll be out there on the street. Remember, out there, you're the prime candidate to become number two."

But Flash was no longer listening. He'd heard the word *jail,* and there was simply no way. He shook his head again. "Uh-uh. Y'all ain't been in jail. I have. I got me some places to hide. Know what I'm sayin'? Ain't nobody find me, I want to stay hid."

Klein looked at the two of them and raised his eyebrows.

Cam shrugged and got up, as did Kenny. "We'll turn him loose," he said. "Let him find out for us if this guy's real or not."

"Y'all *know* who's doin' that shit?" Butts asked Klein, but the DA had opened a flip phone and was making a call.

Cam answered him. "Nope," he said. "And like Mr. Klein here's been saying, that video may be bullshit." He pushed one of his cards across the table to Butts. "I suggest you keep this. You feel someone's setting up on you, you call us, hear?"

Butts frowned and then pocketed the card without looking

at it. Cam knew it would remain in the jail jumpsuit when they let him go. Butts's shakes had returned, and he was licking his lips almost continuously. "I can go now?" he asked.

Kenny stepped outside and signaled the escort officer, who took Butts downstairs to be outprocessed. Klein joined them in the hallway. "Well, we tried," he said.

"Real shame he didn't take us up on it," Kenny said. "*Real* shame."

"You think he knows where K-Dog is?" Klein asked.

Cam shook his head. "I think he knows his own name, and maybe where his next rock is coming from. We did tape that entire session, in case you were wondering."

Klein made a so-what face. "Lot of good that'll do us. Me? I'm betting on the hooded guy. You people any closer to locating Marlor?"

Cam shook his head. "We're initiating an E-sweep, but so far, we got zilch."

"How about Simmonds?" Kenny asked Klein. "Should we keep looking for him, too?"

"Truly?" Klein said, looking both ways down the hallway. "I don't give a shit. Suits me if they both fry; they fucking deserve it."

Kenny tried to suppress a grin as Klein walked away. "Took all that personal, you think?" he asked.

"Must have," Cam said, remembering what Annie had said about judicial vacancies. "But we'll keep looking for both of them anyway."

"Shame to waste the hooded guy, like Steven was saying."

"He was just venting," Cam said. "I mean, here's my real problem: What do we do if the next time he does the Mongolian barbecue, say with Brother Flash there, and then at the end he goes, 'That's two'?"

"Don't understand," Kenny said.

"What if he wants to make it a hat trick? Do the judge. Are we really up for that?"

"You'll have to speak for yourself on that one, boss," Kenny said with a rueful smile.

14

CAM HAD BEEN DREAMING something truly lascivious when his phone went off at 2:15 in the morning. "Richter," he growled while fumbling for the bedside light. "And it better be dead, bleeding, or burning." He was getting much too old for this middle-of-the-night shit.

It was the Major Crimes desk sergeant. There'd been an incident. "I just had me a hysterical mother on the phone, as in the mother of one Deleon Butts."

"And why do I care, exactly?" Cam asked, and then the name penetrated and it occurred to him why he might indeed care. But he was wrong.

"Lady reports her darling baby boy, Deleon, was crashing at her place for the night after a tough day with the 'po-lice.' According to her, Deleon came out on the front stoop at around midnight to commune with the local gentry and maybe score a rock. Said gentry report a pickup truck came around the corner an hour later, about zero one hundred. Truck stops suddenly in front of the house, guy drops the curbside window, sticks some kind of machine gun out the window, and goes to town."

Cam was fully awake now. Machine gun? Someone wanting to assassinate Flash? "They get his ass?" he asked.

"Seems all the homeys didn't stay around to find out, seeing as there was a sudden general interest in finding a direct route to China. Anyways, when the smoke cleared, brother Flash was MIA."

"MIA. But not dead on the sidewalk?"

"Just plain gone."

"Any blood on the steps?"

"No, but other leakages aplenty, if you catch my drift," the sergeant said with a chuckle. "But interestingly, no blood. And no Flash. One extremely drunk citizen claims he saw a hooded MFer jump out of the truck, snatch Flash off the sidewalk, coldcock him, physically throw his ass into the back of the pickup truck, and then boogie the hell out of there."

"And of course we have a full description of the truck, license plates, et cetera?"

"The consensus in that particular neighborhood is that all pickup trucks look alike to a black man, especially when there's a machine gun working."

Cam sighed. A hooded dude had abducted Flash. Here we go again, Cam thought.

"Lieutenant? You want me to roust the on-call detectives? Right now, the city cops have the scene."

"No, not yet," Cam said. "Abduction isn't homicide." Yet, he thought. "Have patrol collect what they can from the Triboro cops. I'll be down in a little bit. Then I'll make the call on whether we take it or leave it with the city."

"Should I call the sheriff?"

"Negative," Cam said. "I'll do that when I know more."

Cam arrived at the Sheriff's Office complex forty minutes later. The watch commander was Bud Winters, the lieutenant who ran the community policing program. He filled Cam in on what few hard details they'd been able to retrieve from the city cops. Most interesting was that, in addition to there being no blood, there were no bullet holes in any of the buildings or nearby cars.

"He shot the place up with blanks?"

"Those who were willing to talk all said the same thing—machine gun, looked military, spitting fire. Lotsa noise, big, kinda sideways muzzle flash. That's consistent with blanks. They have casings. Our ballistics guys will be able to tell."

"Son of a bitch. And Flash would have been paralyzed with fear."

"Paralyzed and incontinent. One among many, apparently."

"Can we believe this guy about seeing Flash getting tossed into the back of the pickup truck?"

The lieutenant consulted the patrol reports. "I quote:

'MFer done throwed the nigger in the MFing truck, turned that MFing gun on the whole MFing street one more time, and then peeled that MFer the F out of there.' Unquote. You interpret that as you will."

Cam grinned despite himself. "So, no description of the vehicle or the shooter?"

"Nothing that doesn't involve further and copious sexual interactions with various mothers," the lieutenant said wearily, closing the report folder. "This incident is related to your Internet Fry Baby hair ball, if I'm not mistaken?"

"I got it," Cam said reluctantly, taking the folder. "City still have the scene secured?"

"Yep," he said. "There's already book on whether or not this is number two, in case you're wondering."

Cam rolled his eyes. "I hate the crime, too, Bud, but in this case, if Simmonds was the teeth on that rabid dog, Flash here was the tail."

Bud was unimpressed. "He was there," he said. "And I'll bet he spent some of the money they took. This whole hot-seat idea works just fine for me."

He gave Cam a wry two-finger salute and went back to the watch commander's office. Cam drove himself down to the scene, talked to the street unit people, and then returned to the Washington Street complex. He went to his own office and cranked up the coffeemaker. Then he sat down and tried to figure out what the hell he was going to do next. The phone rang; it was Bobby Lee.

"What are you doing about this mess down in the projects?" he asked without preamble. "I understand you went down there yourself?"

"There really wasn't a scene when I got there," Cam told him. "Lots of yellow tape and two city patrol units, but by then the word was out that the gunfire was all bogus, and all the regulars had done their usual fade. I didn't bother with CSI."

"Was that wise?" Bobby Lee asked. "You did have an abduction. There could have been evidence on the street, something from the truck or the abductor."

"The scene was hopeless. The city cops bagged what they think is Flash's ball cap and what is presumably one of his shoes, plus some shell casings they want our lab to work."

"How do they know it's his shoe?"

"The shoe was full of urine, and it smelled a lot like the ball cap. The few people they did interview at the scene still had their shoes."

The sheriff hesitated for a moment. "If this is what I think it is," he said, "he won't be needing shoes."

Cam nodded to himself. He could still visualize Simmonds's bony feet being welded to the frame of the footrest. He wondered idly if the executioner would clean the chair up before doing Flash.

"Why screw around any more?" Cam asked. "Let's call in the Bureau, or the ATF, or both. This was a public abduction, a kidnapping, with a machine gun, even if it was shooting blanks. They'll get a twofer."

"You *want* to be sidelined on this one?"

"To be honest, Sheriff," Cam said. "I don't share the popular notion that MCAT caused this mess, so I feel no personal affiliation with this chair thing."

"Lieutenant, it was your—"

"It was Judge Bellamy who released them and dismissed the charges," Cam said, surprising himself by interrupting Bobby Lee, something deputies rarely did.

The sheriff went silent, and then surprised him. "Reasons to turn it over to the Bureau?" he asked.

Relieved that they weren't going to spend the morning squaring off like two male dogs, Cam laid it out. "We don't have the assets to track the Internet video. Kenny Cox is the best Webhead we have in MCAT, and he says this would take some heavy-duty computer expertise. The feds are all over that. They have that program that watches everyone on-line, so they can probably find the source. Plus, we now have a terrorist-style street abduction of a subject related to the guy who supposedly got fried. The Bureau does kidnapping cases. And finally, the Internet is, by definition, interstate. Crimes across lines also means the Bureau."

"They come in, they'll push you and your guys aside like so many annoying insects."

"I'm ready to be pushed aside," Cam said. "We're not getting anywhere."

Another silence. "Okay," Bobby Lee said. "I'll call 'em. Let's just hope we don't get act two in the meantime."

"For what it's worth, Sheriff, you might be all alone in that sentiment."

15

JUST BEFORE NOON, THE sheriff's secretary called to report that the FBI had arrived and that Bobby Lee wanted Cam down there. The unreasonably young-looking agent introduced himself as Supervisory Special Agent Thomas McLain. He shook Cam's hand with a hard, if restrained, grip. He looked to be in his late thirties, tall and rangy, with short black hair and piercing gray-green eyes. If he's a supervisory special agent, he has to be older than he looks, Cam thought. Or I am getting old. To his surprise, Jaspreet Kaur Bawa accompanied McLain. She nodded at him.

"Ms. Bawa," Cam said, turning to shake her hand. "We meet again. Are you in the FBI now?"

"No, Lieutenant, I am a consultant to the Bureau in their investigation into the execution video."

"Oka-a-y," Cam said, unaware until now that the FBI even had an investigation going on the chair video. Bobby Lee gave him a discreet "Thought so" look.

"Anybody need coffee?" the sheriff asked. "No? Okay. We were just talking about getting you guys into this mess, so let's hit the conference room and I'll let Lieutenant Richter tell you what we know and what we don't know. Mostly the latter."

It was actually McLain who led off, telling them that the Bureau had opened a case on the Internet execution video and that they wanted to collaborate with the Manceford County Sheriff's Office, since it appeared that the case had started there. He said he would appreciate any information they could give the Bureau. To Cam's vast relief, McLain projected none of the traditional "We're the G, step aside, small people" posturing. He was polite, professional, and willing to listen as Cam walked them through it, starting with the disastrous minimart heist. McLain had set up a laptop and used it to take notes, although Cam got the impression that whatever went into Thomas McLain's brain was being stored there in neatly bulleted outline fashion.

Cam then described the abduction incident of the previous night and said that in his opinion, K-Dog Simmonds had been the killer-diller at the minimart, while Flash Butts had been along for the ride, both mentally and physically. He noticed that Ms. Bawa curled her lip when he mentioned the killers. She was obviously still very angry about it.

"He saw the execution video and didn't want protection?" McLain asked.

"He saw it, freaked, but would *not* entertain the notion of jail as protection. He's a crackhead. Brain's gone."

"And we have no idea of where James Marlor could be?"

Cam noted the corporate "we" and saw that Bobby Lee probably didn't feel that way, based on his body language. The sheriff had always been fiercely protective of the Manceford County Sheriff's Office's prerogatives when it came to sharing cases. He suspected that the sheriff, like Kenny Cox, lived for the hunt.

"It looks like his departure was orderly," Cam said. "We found out that Marlor took out thirty-five thousand in cash money a week after the judge let the bastards go."

"Walking-around money, with no electronic consequences," McLain said.

Cam nodded. "We think so," he said. "And he's the guy with the best motive." Then he glanced over at the Bureau's consultant as if to say, and she's the one with the second-best motive. She stared right back at him, as if daring him to say it out loud.

"Ms. Bawa," Cam said, "I'm concerned that you're involved in this case."

McLain answered before she could speak. "Jay-Kay here is an expert consultant on the inner workings and hidden mechanisms of the World Wide Web," he said. "And since she's based in Charlotte, Washington authorized the Charlotte field office to engage her services."

"I would have thought the Bureau had its own assets for that," the sheriff said.

McLain nodded. "We do, but they're otherwise engaged these days. Mostly by the Department of Homeland Security.

"Also," she said, "I'm pro bono when I work for the Bureau. No cost to the government."

Cam gave McLain a look. Having the victim of a crime involved in the investigation was not kosher at either the federal or the local level. McLain understood. "She gets her tasking from us," he said. "And it's specifically related to Web stuff. She doesn't go along on any rides, and she won't have access to everything we generate about the case."

Then she shouldn't be here at this meeting, Cam thought, but he didn't want to piss McLain off. The Bureau was being polite, and that counted for a lot in his book. "Right," the sheriff said, "Your consultant, your call. How do you propose to work this?"

"I've been instructed to put the technical assets of the Bureau at your disposal and to offer professional advice on the course of the investigation whenever I see an opportunity to be helpful. It's your case, and it will remain so until and unless certain exigencies arise that trigger a wider national security interest."

That little speech sounded rehearsed to Cam, but the sheriff thanked McLain for the Bureau's offer of help, then suggested to Cam that the three of them adjourn to the MCAT office. Once there, Cam saw that Kenny was back. He called him over and asked him to get Ms. Bawa set up with a computer terminal. He took McLain into his personal office, took off his gun belt, and invited McLain to make himself comfortable.

"You have been bending over backward to be nice," Cam said without preamble. "I appreciate the hell out of it, but how come?"

McLain smiled. "First of all, we really do have a full plate these days with this antiterrorism mission. And second, now that Butts has been abducted, we think it's just about guaranteed we'll see a second execution."

"The first one was a grisly novelty," Cam said.

"Yes, but a second one is going to nudge the liberal establishment into high dudgeon. Inquiring minds are gonna want to know: Hey, you guys on this, or what?"

Cam laughed. "And that's what you meant by 'certain exigencies'? If the political shit storm reaches a critical mass, you guys will step up?"

"Something like that," he said with a smile. "Assuming it's real."

"Yeah, that's one of our problems," Cam said. "It could be a damn hoax."

"What's MCAT?" McLain asked.

Cam told him. "Interesting approach," McLain said. "You okay with us being here like this?" he asked.

"Hell yes," Cam said. "I was just telling the sheriff that we ought to hand this sick puppy off to the Bureau right now."

"He good with that?"

"Not entirely," Cam said. "He feels that since we—and that means a guy in my shop—actually lit the fuse on this thing with a screwup, we should be the ones to 'unscrew' it, as he quaintly puts it."

"I can understand that," McLain said.

Cam told him what the sheriff had said about a possible division of labor. McLain agreed immediately. "What's first?" he asked.

"We like James Marlor as the possible doer, and we've been looking. But of course now our urgent priority is to retrieve Deleon Butts. We have very little to go on, other than it was a hooded guy in a pickup truck, using an automatic rifle but shooting blanks."

"Yeah, blanks. We heard about that. Any leads?"

Cam shrugged. "The city cops have a full-court press going in certain neighborhoods, but you know how that goes."

"And you've found no trace of the other guy, Simmonds?"

"Only on the Web. And that's a problem, of course, because we don't habeas a corpus."

McLain frowned but didn't say anything. Cam switched to his problem with having Ms. Bawa involved. He told him of her sentiments on what should have happened in the courthouse square.

"She told me the same thing," he said. "Refreshing, isn't it?"

It was Cam's turn to smile.

"She's a piece of work," he said, "both technically and personally. She's worked for the Bureau before, with our counterterrorism folks. Technically, she's beyond good. She keeps a brace of mainframe IBM computers in her home office and connects to the Web with her own T-one line."

"English?" Cam said. "T-one?"

"That means a huge data pipe. The word *broadband* doesn't adequately describe it. She says she never deals directly with the Web. She interfaces with her mainframes— she calls them her 'tigers'—and *they* go out on the Web."

"Sounds a little scary. This is in Charlotte?"

"Right. She's a professional consultant. Adheres to Bureau guidelines and does what she's told. My boss is okay with this, despite the personal angle."

"As long as you and I can meet like this," Cam said. "I don't like civilians listening in on everything we do."

"Absolutely," he said. "But she'll need a liaison here."

"I put her with Sergeant Cox—he's the big guy you met out there. He'll handle Ms. Bawa's needs."

"Jay-Kay. Everyone calls her that," McLain said.

They sorted all the logistics out in about five minutes, then rejoined the gaggle of MCAT cops and agents back in the office. Jay-Kay, who looked positively sleek in a rose-colored business suit, was sitting at Kenny's computer and showing him something. Kenny looked at Cam over the monitor as he came back into the outer office. The sergeant rolled his eyes, as if to say she had long ago left him in the digital dust. Cam introduced the rest of the MCAT crew to McLain and then suggested they all go to lunch at a nearby cop bar, to be fol-

lowed by a joint planning session to see where the hell they'd
go from here.

Cam's heart sank when he saw that there was a message
from Computer Crimes when they got back. All it said was
that they should go to a particular Web address. He showed it
to McLain, who groaned. Lunch was about to be spoiled.

If anything, this one was worse than the first time. They all
knew what was coming, and Butts was totally terrified, because *he* also knew what was coming. The MCAT cops reacted differently to this one, too. There had been shock and
horror when they watched K-Dog die, but there had also been
an element of satisfaction: That punk had gotten what he deserved. This time, there was no crowing, nor any sentiments
of just desserts. They all waited in suspense for the important
bit—the final voice-over—and, sure enough, here it came.
"That's two," the electronic voice intoned.

The comradely buzz they'd developed over lunch evapo-
rated. Jay-Kay took a small handheld computing unit out of
her briefcase, connected it to her cell phone, sat down at
Kenny's desk, and went to work on that Web address. Cam
called the sheriff and gave him the bad news. McLain called
his office in Charlotte and did the same. The people there apparently already knew about it, and they told him to stand by
for additional instructions. Computer Crimes delivered a
videotape of the second execution a few minutes later, and
they watched it again, amid much speculation about whether
or not it was real.

"I've seen an official electrocution," McLain commented.
"Except for some details, this is pretty close."

"Details?" Cam asked.

"Yeah. I watched one at Marion, the big-lock pen in Illi-
nois. The prison chair there is actually made of wood, which
is nonconducting. The current path is into the skull and out
through an electrode on the guy's leg. They use five cycles of
current, not two. The current comes in through a metal skull-
cap, under which they put a vinegar-soaked sponge to ensure
conductivity. The current comes out via a leg iron to ground."
He pointed with his chin at the video. "This guy has put the

top electrodes in the victim's mouth and is bringing it out through the entire chair, wherever his skin touches metal."

Cam flinched just thinking about it. "An academic distinction once the juice comes on," he said, but he still felt a little creepy talking about it.

"But symbolically important," McLain said. "Whoever's doing this *hates* the people he's doing this to, putting the electrode in the guy's mouth like that. In my book, that strengthens your theory that this is Marlor. This is absolutely personal."

"I'm wondering where he's getting high voltage. Doesn't the state version of this use a couple thousand volts?"

McLain nodded thoughtfully. "Yeah, two thousand, I think. That's not available to a house. He'd need a generator and a sizable power transformer. Those are things we need to look for."

Kenny joined them and heard McLain's comment. "After Hurricane Hugo, half the people in this state have generators," he said. "Transformers, now—that's probably worth running down."

"Fifty milliamps of AC power can kill you," Pardee Bell said. "It doesn't take being connected to the Hoover Dam to do that."

The voice on the video made its pronouncement about Flash being number two.

So: Who was number three?

McLain had the same question. "Surely not the judge?" he asked quietly.

Kenny reached forward and turned off the VCR. "Either the judge or Will Guthridge," he said. "If there's going to be a three, that is. He's done the two shooters. The only choice left now is between the cop who supposedly screwed it up and the judge who let 'em go."

"That's easy," Horace said.

McLain grunted and went to see what Jay-Kay was accomplishing. Cam pulled Kenny aside. "Things are going to get crazy here in the next few hours," he told him. "I think the sheriff wants a division of labor that keeps us in the game:

The Bureau chases the executioner around the Web, and we find Marlor by using our superior local knowledge."

Kenny rolled his eyes at Cam's mention of superior knowledge.

"I know, I know," Cam said. "But for starters, I want to move on that fifty K he drew out five years ago. That bank in Surry County. See if we can get a line on what that was all about." He looked at his watch. "There're going to be lots of phone calls, hand-wringing, and spin doctoring here for a while, so let's go up there tonight. I'm going ask the Bureau to focus on the Web site."

"I'll be ready when you are," Kenny said.

Then Cam talked to McLain to see what they needed to do to circle the wagons. Jay-Kay needed to talk to their city government network administrator so that she could use their networks without tripping over fire walls. Kenny got one of the guys to come up from Computer Crimes, and he took her to see the administrator next door. Cam told McLain that Kenny and he were going to drive up to Surry County to run down a local lead on Marlor involving mountain property.

"Can't you just tap a statewide database on property ownership for that?" he asked.

"Yeah, but I lean toward face-to-face investigating," Cam said. "Given where this is, it'll be all good ole boys doing a little private banking in the Carolina mountains. They *might* be in the database, but then again, they might not."

McLain wanted to know if they should be in on that. Cam told him no, not yet, unless the bankers stonewalled. McLain nodded. "We have ways of dealing with bankers who stonewall," he reminded Cam.

Cam said he'd keep that in mind. Mostly, though, he wanted to get the hell out of there before news of the second execution gained some traction with the local media.

16

AS IT TURNED OUT, McLain asked if Kenny could stay behind to work with Jay-Kay, so Cam ended up hitting the road alone. He checked in with the Surry County Sheriff's Office in Dobson and then drove to a little town called Hanging Dog, up near the Blue Ridge Parkway.

The bank manager had started out being a little bit stuffy, so Cam had run the videotape of Flash's execution for him, after which the level of cooperation rose substantially. The upshot was that James Marlor had indeed purchased a small tract up in the mountains west of town. It took another hour to retrieve plats and establish the rough location of the property. The Surry County Sheriff's Office provided a deputy, who suggested they go in his cruiser. Cam thanked the sheriff for his help, and then they went up the state road until they crossed over the Blue Ridge Parkway. After that, Cam was really glad to have the deputy driving, because the road quickly deteriorated to a narrow lane, a barely paved affair with lots of one-lane bridges and some potholes capable of serving as tank traps. Heavily forested slopes rose on either side, making the road seem dark. The only signs of human habitation appeared along the road itself, and these ranged from neat little cottages to derelict trailers surrounded by rusting vehicles of every description. They had to stop short at a one-lane bridge to give way to an oncoming logging truck, whose brakes gave it the old college try but generated more smoke than stopping power. The driver gave the cop car a white-eyed look as he rumbled past, but the deputy didn't seem particularly interested.

They wandered through one long, fairly continuous valley for five miles or so, then climbed a hair-raising switchback for twenty minutes in second gear. When they arrived at the top, they were not at the top of the mountains, however, and they cut through a steep pass alongside a rushing mountain stream. Cam caught a glimpse of a lake in the distance and asked the deputy which lake it was. He said it was the Sinclair Reservoir, backed up behind a four-hundred-foot-high dam. They branched right out of the pass and the road turned to gravel and then finally to red dirt. Fortunately, it hadn't rained for a couple of weeks, so they could press on without four-wheel drive. There were no more signs of humans or their houses up here, but the road looked well used. The deputy explained that this was the access road to the hydro plant at the Sinclair dam.

They climbed some more, going between and occasionally across the face of increasingly steeper slopes. Cam couldn't really see the scope and extent of the mountains because their car was confined to the road, which followed the lowest points. Finally, they climbed another scary switchback and came out onto an overlook. Cam was very glad there'd been no logging trucks on that last bit. The deputy glanced down at the plat map and pointed with his chin at a vista of rolling hills, an expanse of unrelieved forest green, and three large mountains whose tops were sheathed in a blue haze.

"That way, yonder," he said. "Maybe eight miles in, and half of one up."

The deputy's "yonder" indicated a crumbling, brush-covered firebreak that led generally north and west into the wilderness. A set of high-tension lines snaked across the hills along the route of the firebreak. None of it looked suitable for wheeled vehicles. Tracked, maybe, but not wheeled. Cam asked if there was another way to approach the cabin's location. The deputy said there was an abandoned cattle farm on the back of Blackberry Mountain, on whose front slopes the cabin supposedly was located. He gave Cam driving directions.

That evening, Cam checked in with Kenny to see how the zoo was taking shape. Kenny reported that the rest of the day had turned into a whirl of urgent meetings, conference calls, more meetings, and no visible progress in locating James Marlor. "The Bureau's pulsed all their systems, and everything seems to end right about the time the neighbor says he beat feet. One gas card used a mile from his house around that time, and then genu-wine radio silence."

"Is it still our case?"

"McLain's been in with the sheriff, and he also met with the powers that be next door. I worked with Jay-Kay for a while, but then it became obvious I was way out of my league, so I just backed out and let her smoke the keyboard by herself.

"She get anywhere?"

"She says that each video clip was posted just once, and then the site it landed on forwarded it out to the world. Whoever did the posting came in via a secure server, banged it out there, and went back down. She's working on a way to uniquely identify some aspect of the original post, and then there's a govvie system that can lurk the Web and watch for that tag."

"How the hell can she do that if he only posts and runs?"

"She says it has to do with the configuration of the actual packets he posts," Kenny said. "At that level, it's by me, boss."

"What are the teams doing?" Cam asked.

"Still looking for K-Dog and Flash. Word's out on the street that they're real Internet movie stars now, so whatever help we might have gotten from the snitch network is drying up fast. Nobody wants to attract pickup trucks with hooded drivers."

"You get word to Will Guthridge that he might be a target?"

"I talked to him myself," Kenny said. "He's not sweating it."

It must be something they teach 'em at the Police Academy these days, Cam thought. Too many cops thought that the bad guys would always draw the line at doing a cop, because, according to Hollywood, that would spark a cop-killer frenzy and the heat wasn't worth what would happen next. Cam knew it wasn't true anymore, if it ever had been. Today's bad guy would ice a cop as soon as hit a dog in the road. It wasn't that they didn't stop to consider the possible consequences. It was more that they didn't associate consequences with anything they did, good or bad.

"Get to his district boss," Cam said. "Get him into the district house on admin duty somehow until we sort this thing out."

"Got it," Kenny said.

"And then there's the judge," Cam said.

"The Feebs are working that one. They're asking us to set up the protection loop. And that's a pity."

"You can think it, Kenny, but you can't say it."

"Yeah, yeah, I know. But in my book, she started this shit. I'm surprised he didn't start with her."

"Well, we don't want him to end it with her, either," Cam said. "Bellamy's a tough lady. She may need a talking-to, just like Will."

"You ask me—" he began.

"I didn't. I know how everybody feels about Judge Bellamy right now. I'll talk to McLain when I get back tomorrow."

"How about the cabin?"

"Round me up a state helicopter."

"You gonna take McLain along?"

"No," Cam said. "I'll evaluate the situation, then get back to the office and huddle with them. After Eric Rudolph, they should be right up to speed on rousting bad guys out of the Carolina mountains these days."

Kenny laughed at that one.

17

CAM GOT CLEAR OF Hanging Dog at eight o'clock the next morning and was back in the office by 11:00 A.M. He briefed the sheriff on what he'd found up in Surry County. Bobby Lee listened and then said he had some news.

"The Bureau's backing out," he announced, a glint of triumph in his eye.

"They are?" Cam asked, truly surprised. "Two people executed in an electric chair on the Internet and they're backing out?"

"*Apparently* executed," Bobby Lee said. "All we *actually* have are two video clips purporting to show two people being executed, said clips arriving on the Internet from an unknown and unverifiable source. Senior Bureau management in Washington is skeptical. No physical evidence—no crispy critters. They, on the other hand, are facing an unlimited supply of crazed Muslims. Basically, they will not deploy assets on this case until we 'show them the meat,' to quote Mr. McLain."

Show them the *meat*? Cam wondered who'd come up with that beauty. "The bodies could be anywhere," he said. "This isn't the Bureau I know—they get into something, they don't just withdraw, especially if it has a publicity tail like this one."

"Things have changed, Lieutenant," Bobby Lee said. "Ever since nine/eleven, the Bureau's been backing out of what they consider routine crimes and redeploying assets into the counterterrorism task forces. The bosses at the Hoover Building think our videos are some kind of hacker stunt."

"So where are Simmonds and Butts?" Cam asked. "And James Marlor?"

"I'm waiting for you to tell me," the sheriff said. "But basically the Bureau seems to be saying: Who cares?"

"Excuse me?" Cam said.

The sheriff told Cam to sit down. "Look at it from Washington's perspective: Two local hoods have disappeared, after having been let off by some Communist judge. Not believing their good fortune, they promptly get their ugly asses out of Dodge. And Marlor? He's now lost two wives, plus his stepdaughter. Perfectly logical for him to hang it up at Duke Energy and go somewhere—anywhere—as long as it's away from these unhappy parts."

"But how about the abduction? A white guy pulling into a black neighborhood at one o'clock in the morning and cutting loose with a submachine gun?"

"We don't *know* it was a white guy," the sheriff pointed out. "And there isn't a single bullet hole anywhere. Our only witness to Butts being abducted showed twice the legal limit for alcohol in his blood when he made his statement. And now *he's* not to be found anywhere."

"Why would a bunch of guys on a crack corner make all that up?" Cam asked.

"Because they're a bunch of crack-smoking, drug-dealing, bitch-slapping, booze-slopping no-loads with nothing else to do? Just like brother Flash?"

Cam didn't know what to say. "So what now—we just quit right here?"

The sheriff smiled his "Gotcha" smile. "Not at all. We work it from the physical-reality point of view, as opposed to the virtual-reality one. First, find Marlor, or find out what happened to him. Consider that your main bang. Second, keep someone looking for the two mutts, because if either of them surfaces, obviously we're home free."

"Well, hell, maybe the Bureau's right," Cam said. "Why do anything?"

The sheriff got up and started pacing around. "Because I can't afford to be wrong about this," he said. "And because of what the executioner said when he did the black guy: 'That's two.' Assuming this is real, I think he's going to do one more."

"And that would be Bellamy?"

He nodded. "I think so. Either way, Next Door feels, of course, that this whole mess has given Triboro a big black eye. They want it to go away, but they're terrified of what the voters will think if they do nothing and the judge shows up in lights, so to speak."

"Will there be budget money for a twenty-four/seven protective detail, and if so, for how long?"

"How long?" Bobby Lee said. "How 'bout until MCAT finds Marlor, or one of those two purported victims surfaces. I'm planning to use SWAT-qualified assets for the detail, and to rotate the requirement through the district offices. Starting with Sergeant McMichael, seeing as how he started this cluster fuck."

Well, there is some justice, Cam thought. But the sheriff had ducked his question. "That could be a very long time, Sheriff," Cam said, thinking of those vast, remote mountains he'd just visited. "It took the entire FBI four years to find Eric Rudolph, and actually, they never did—it was a local who dropped a dime on him."

"Way I see it," the sheriff said, returning to his desk, "if all this *is* real, he'll come for the judge. If it's not, you only have to find one of three people to prove the whole thing a hoax. Granted, finding Marlor might be hard, but K-Dog and Flash?"

Cam didn't say what he thought should be obvious: that they might never find any of them.

18

THAT NIGHT, CAM CALLED Annie from home. She must have looked at her caller ID, because the first thing she said was, "They're already here."

"Your baby-sitters."

"Yeah, my favorite people. Manceford County SWAT deputies."

"*In* the house?" Cam asked.

"Does it matter?" she said with an almost audible grin.

He thought for a moment. She was in lockdown for the night, and he sure as hell wasn't going to traipse over there for a quickie. "Consider it a refreshing break," he said.

She laughed out loud this time. "I would," she said, "except for *why* they're here."

"It's a precaution we have to take, Annie," Cam said, not joking now. "That guy pretty much guaranteed there'd be another one."

"He sure as hell has," she replied.

"What?" Cam asked.

"I've got mail," she said, imitating the AOL greeting. "Would you believe an E-mail message, complete with picture of a hooded guy sitting in that goddamned chair, pointing at me, the viewer?"

Cam sat up in his chair. What the hell was this? And why hadn't he known about it? "When?" he asked.

"Late this afternoon, on my workstation computer. In chambers, no less."

"God Almighty. I thought the courthouse system was really secure."

"Apparently not," she said "It was an attachment to an E-mail purporting to be from Steven Klein. Subject line was

'Simmonds Ruling Appeal.' Of course I opened it. We'd all heard that Raleigh'd told him not to bother. And for the record, no, Steven didn't send it. Nor did his computer."

"Son of a bitch! But how the hell did someone get that into the courthouse system?"

"Into the courthouse LAN *and* the state judiciary's very private wide-area network," she said.

"Your system administrator get on it?"

"Yeah, buddy," she said. "Plus some very nice nerdlings from your Computer Crimes division. They're baffled, or so I'm told. At first blush, the implications are not good."

"Shit, I guess not," Cam said, thinking immediately of the chair. He heard a click on the line.

"Gotta take this," she said.

He said good night and hung up. Maybe someone inside the courthouse system had sent the E-mail. And wherever James Marlor was, chances were he wasn't hiding out in the Manceford County courthouse basement—unless, of course, he had him some inside help.

The next morning, Cam ran into the sheriff and told him about the E-mail getting into the judges' network. Bobby Lee was quick to see the implications. He immediately started talking Internal Affairs, but Cam turned that off for the moment. "Let me get some facts, identify the technical parameters, and then I'll brief you," he said. That seemed to mollify the sheriff for the moment. The term *technical parameters* was one of Bobby Lee's favorites. No one in the Sheriff's Office understood precisely what it meant, but Bobby Lee was always willing to wait for those boundaries to be identified.

Cam met with Kenny in his office and asked why he hadn't been informed that the judicial network had been penetrated. Kenny said he hadn't gotten the word until earlier that morning.

"If Judge Bellamy's hate mail came from the Web," Kenny said, "it had to get past both the honcho server in the sky and its fire wall, and then past the courthouse LAN server and its fire wall, *and* he also had to know her address on the state judiciary network."

"She said the attached file format was improper, that it shouldn't have come through."

"Right," Kenny said. "The system is set up for official business only, so baby pictures, porn, streaming audio for your MP-three player—that shit gets stopped at the fire wall. Only the human system administrator can make exception to the rules, and that person has to be sitting at the honcho server's keyboard to make that happen when the message first appears."

"But this one just appeared in Bellamy's desktop terminal?"

"Yup," Kenny said. "So somebody inside the system had to know a lot, and fool all those fire walls."

Cam went to get some coffee. Even talking about computers gave him a headache. "What do the guys in Computer Crimes say?" he asked.

"Not guilty?" Kenny offered. "I mean, if anybody could do it, those guys could do it."

Cam looked at him. "You mean like some kind of sick joke?"

Kenny shrugged his shoulders. "Bellamy's not in any cop's top ten on the judicial hit parade just now," he said. "Could have been another judge, too, for that matter. Anybody who has access to their private little judiciary network."

Cam sat down in his chair and slowly rotated in place behind his desk. "So what's this all mean, Kenny?" he asked. "This can't be Marlor."

"Not likely," he said. "I'm leaning toward the 'sick joke' angle—somebody who knows what's going on, and who's really pissed off about what she did in the first place."

"Somebody who also knows that we have her under protection?"

Kenny sat down in the one chair Cam had in the office. "No, probably not. That just happened." He hesitated. "People are pissed, boss. She didn't have to dismiss. Klein showed his ass, she had a migraine, who the fuck knows, but when she turned those little pricks loose, that was definitely not righteous."

"What will it take to find out who did this?" Cam asked. "The sheriff wants the shooflies in."

"Mostly, it would take a lot of time and some really expert people," Kenny said. "Maybe we ought to go hire that Bawa honey."

"At two grand a day? I don't think so."

He told Kenny he'd talk to the sheriff some more, and he asked him to generate a memo covering what he had just explained about the networks.

"Technical parameters?" Kenny asked with a grin.

"Just so," Cam said. Horace stuck his head in and said, "The fling-wing is set up. Time on top at the Detention Center helipad is eleven hundred hours." Like Cam, Horace was ex-Army and loved his military lingo.

"Don't you think a police helo appearing overhead might spook the guy?" Kenny asked. "Especially if he's been frying guilty bastards?"

"Maybe," Cam said. "But if he runs, he's more likely to bump up against the grid, and then we'll know he's alive and operational. Right now, that's almost as important as finding him."

Kenny nodded slowly, a distant expression on his face. "You think he's dead?"

"I don't know," Cam said. "He could have flipped out. Living out there, growing a long beard, communing with the wildlife, and studying Buddhism."

"And if that's what he's doing . . ."

"Right," Cam said. "If that's what he's doing, then someone else is doing this shit. Someone a lot closer to home than Marlor. And I don't even want to think about that."

19

CAM WASN'T FOND OF helicopters, especially when they were of the two-seater variety, where you sat up there underneath those rotors, surrounded by what looked like semirigid Saran Wrap. Yes, you could really see; he'd grant you that. But his pilot for this little jaunt had flown warbirds of some kind in a past life and obviously missed it. Cam wasn't airsick. He was afraid, especially when the pilot would drop down to treetop level to enter a canyon, without possibly being able to know what happened to the available airspace at the end of said canyon. He guessed wrong a lot, so then Cam was treated to that nifty sensation one got as a roller-coaster car flattened itself in the valley and then went up and over the top of the next hump. Each time he did it, Cam's cranial helmet would drop down over his eyes. The pilot said he liked canyon hopping because that meant he would just appear over the target area without announcing that they'd been inbound for a half hour. That was when Cam realized the guy was doing this scary shit on purpose, and enjoying it.

They popped out of the final canyon after about fifty minutes of evading enemy missile sites and flared into a high hover over a patch of dense forest that stretched down the side of Blackberry Mountain. It was as clear a day as one got on the edge of the Blue Ridge, which was to say that it was clear where they were but not in the distance. The trees below were large and numerous, their foliage just beginning to turn to fall colors.

"Mark on top," the pilot called cheerily over the intercom. He pointed to the small circle on his chart, which corresponded with the position given in the plat. Cam looked down and then stretched in his straps to see if he could spot the cabin. He couldn't see a damned thing except more trees. The pilot obligingly tilted the aircraft, so now Cam was hanging sideways from his straps, but he could also see right below the aircraft. A small freshet sparkled through what looked like a crack along the face of the slope, and, yes, there was a structure of some kind down there in all those trees. But it wasn't big enough to be a cabin. An outbuilding? They were not directly on top of it, so Cam asked the pilot if they could drop down so he could see better through the trees—an entirely wrong choice of words, as it turned out.

"No problem," the pilot said, and then the helicopter dropped like a stone and flared out practically on top of the structure, sending clouds of leaves and other forest debris roiling through the rest of the trees as the chopper bounced gently from side to side, its rotors chopping frantically at the thin mountain air. There was a faint path leading from the structure, which looked now like a lean-to toolshed. At the end of the path was the cabin.

"See anyplace to land?" Cam asked. The only clearing he'd seen had the toolshed right in the middle of it.

The pilot nodded and then let the chopper sink sideways down toward the lean-to. When Cam thought they were going do a Cuisinart number on it with the rotors, the pilot halted the descent and reached over to release Cam's harness.

"I'll hold her right here," he said over the intercom. "Open the door and step out onto the skid. Then sit down, turn around, and hang on to the skid with your hands, and I'll get you close to the ground. Then let go and drop. Don't touch the bird and the ground at the same time. Keep your cranial on until you're on the ground. Put it back on when I come back to get you. Just wave, and I'll come back down. Okay?"

Before Cam had a chance to protest that that was the dumbest damned thing he'd heard in his life, the pilot unjacked Cam's intercom wire, stuffed the end of it in Cam's jacket, and pointed encouragingly at the handle on the hatch.

Cam discovered that it was harder than it sounded, especially when his sphincter muscle was trying to wrestle his entire intestinal tract out the back door. The noise was terrific, the down-draft from the rotors was even more terrific, and purposefully dropping off that metal skid felt like suicide. But once he was hanging like a deer ready for dressing in a hurricane, the pilot nudged the aircraft to the right and Cam saw that his feet were barely a foot above the ground. Amazing, he thought as he dropped, rolled, and then got rolled when the pilot lifted the bird back up. The aircraft elevatored back up to several hundred feet and then began to fly in a lazy pattern around the site.

Cam sat up and took an apprehensive look around. Apprehensive, because if Marlor was a bad guy who had been zapping guilty bastards up here in his mountain aerie, he'd certainly had plenty of time to go get his black hat and ten-gauge double-barreled Greener. Kenny may have had a point, he thought. When he'd asked the pilot if he could give him any backup if things went noisy, the pilot had lifted an MP-5 from behind his seat and nodded. But nobody seemed to be around besides a million diseased ticks and one terrified squirrel who was cursing him from the denuded remains of his nest in a nearby pine tree.

Cam got up, shook the pine needles out of his hair, checked to see that his trusty .45 was still firmly ensconced in its hip holster, brushed off his uniform, and then headed up toward the cabin. It was either one of those kit-made log cabins and had been dropped here a long time ago by a really big helicopter or it was genuinely old. It was a square box, with what certainly looked like hand-hewn logs, chinked with grayish petrified clay. The front porch sagged a good bit, and the one stone chimney seemed too big for the size of the cabin. Two small square windows flanked a stout-looking wooden front door, but there were none in the cabin's sides. Trees grew quite close all around, as did large clumps of mountain laurel and other shrubbery.

He stopped in front of the porch and called out, feeling faintly ridiculous after all the noise that helicopter had made. He walked up onto the front porch and knocked on the door, and then peered through a window, feeling increasingly certain that there was no one here. In one sense, he was relieved. In another, he was disappointed. It would have been nice, he thought, to have found Marlor at home, sitting on his rocking chair on that front porch. He could have just asked him flat out if he'd been cooking up some justice. From what Cam had seen of him, he thought Marlor would have said yes or no, and been done with it.

As Cam expected, the front door wasn't locked, so he opened it up and stepped inside. The first thing he noticed was a musty, faintly putrid smell, and he immediately thought of some murder scenes he'd been to. The light was dim because of all the trees and the tiny windows, but there was just a single large opened-ceiling room, with some rustic wooden furniture, a long kitchen table parked in front of a very large fireplace, and a single cotlike bed to one side of the fireplace. There were two antique chamber pots under the bed. There were lots of shelves, filled with canned food and some opaque plastic containers, which probably held boxed foods. Two doorless armoires held boots, stiffly dirty one-piece Carhartt jumpsuits, hats, blankets, two quilts, and two army field jackets. A stack of dusty dry firewood was racked up in a firebox, and there was a brass can next to it with slivers of what the locals called "lightered," used for kindling. There was another door which went out the back, and he could see an outhouse twenty feet or so to the side and slightly below the cabin. If there was a well, Cam couldn't see it, but there was that narrow, deep creek rushing down the hill right out front.

There was nothing to identify who the owner was, and no signs that anyone besides some mummified mice had been in the cabin in a long time. Everything was covered in a fine layer of brown dust, and several of the food cans had no labels because mousies had torn them off to shred the paper for their nests. Cam guessed that the lingering death odor must be coming from vermin that had died in the cabin over the months, until he looked up into the rafters and spotted the rope. Well now, he thought.

The rope was Manila hemp and about five-eighths of an

inch in diameter. One end was securely fastened around the lower ridgepole of the cabin. The other end had been routed over the top ridgepole and now hung straight down to just below the rafters. It had obviously been cut off, or sawn off, actually, because the three internal strands were splayed raggedly out at the end. The rope looked old, but the cut portion looked newer than the rope. Cam couldn't reach the end of it, and there was no ladder visible in the room. He checked out back but found nothing that could get him up to that rope. He could hear the helicopter boring holes in the sky nearby, and he wondered how much time he had left.

He checked the interior of the cabin again, looking for any signs that someone had been here over the past few months. Then he realized that the dust layer was not uniform. There were places where it was quite thick, and others where it was not. He knelt down on the floor, directly under where that rope hung, and inspected the planks. It looked like there were stains there, but there was so much dirt and so little light, he couldn't be sure. But what else would that rope be there for? Well, it might have served as a wintertime deer-dressing rig. Winter up here brought temps well below zero. If someone did winter over and killed a deer or some other large game for meat, he couldn't dress it outside without a chain saw. But why would the rope be cut through like that, then? He wasn't sure why he immediately associated the rope with suicide, beyond the fact that he'd seen other ropes like that, although they usually came with a black-faced human balloon dangling at the end and required a change of uniform afterward. More relevant, though, were the circumstances of Marlor's life over the past few months, plus his banker's remark that he seemed to be a sad but determined man on a mission.

He walked back to the front door, turned around, and studied the entire room, as if it could tell him something important. Unfortunately, it didn't. It was just a very lonely, very remote mountain cabin, and it depressed him just to look at it. He began to regret touching anything in the cabin, as this, unlike Marlor's house, might, in fact, be a crime scene. Maybe not a crime scene, but at least something worth a forensics look-see. He smiled at the thought of the CSI guys rappelling down a helicopter sling with all their fancy gear. But for the first time, he seriously began to entertain the notion that James Marlor might be dead. And he remembered his conversation that morning with Kenny: "You think he's dead?"

He took the next fifteen minutes to walk around the immediate vicinity of the cabin. He looked in the outhouse, which was a primitive one-holer. His nose told him that it hadn't been used in a long time, nor was there any toilet paper. There were no other structures in view, and no generator or electric chair, as far as he could see anyway. He then cut up the hill from the cabin to the edge of the woods and made a long circle around the cabin area, studying the ground. There were no visible tracks. All he could see were the steep, sloping hillside, dense trees and underbrush, and those long shadows in every direction, from which all manner of wildlife might be watching him with varying degrees of interest. The hills *are* alive, just like the song says, he thought. But is James Marlor still alive?

20

HE CHANGED TO A clean uniform once back in the office and sat down to write up a report of his visit to the Marlor cabin. Bottom line: They still didn't *know* anything. There was still no sign of Marlor or of the two cretins who'd done the minimart, but the absence of the three subjects didn't prove anything, one way or another.

His phone rang.

"This is Jaspreet Kaur Bawa," she said. "Do you remember me, Lieutenant?"

"Vividly," Cam replied.

"Oh dear. Why vividly? Did I offend you?"

"No-o," Cam said. "You didn't offend me. I just remember that look you gave me after I met with you and Mr. Marlor. Plus your recommendations for dealing with those two criminals."

"Mr. McLain told me that you were uncomfortable with my being involved with this investigation."

"Which investigation, Ms. Bawa? I understood the Bureau backed out. I assumed you had backed out with them."

"Please, call me Jay-Kay," she said, sounding about three degrees more friendly. "In America, Ms. Bawa sounds too much like Mizz Bow-Wow. And you should never make assumptions about what the Bureau is or isn't doing; surely you know that."

"Well, Jay-Kay, I'm only going on what they told us."

"I will be in Triboro this evening. I am giving a course at the Marriott tomorrow morning. Would you be my guest for dinner?"

Now this was a surprise. "Well, yes, I'd like that," Cam said, hearing the hesitation in his response. "What time and where?"

"The hotel dining room is quite good. Eight o'clock?"

"Okay, I'll be there. Shall I stay in uniform?"

It was her turn to miss a beat. "As you wish, Lieutenant. I never let men tell me what to wear, you know?"

Cam laughed, said he'd see her that evening, and hung up. Kenny, coming up behind him, said, "See who this evening?"

"A secret admirer," Cam said. "What's going on with our various searches?"

The short answer was not much. No hits on the electronic sweep on Marlor. No rumbles from the rat warren on K-Dog and Flash. Kenny looked a little tired. "Late night?" Cam asked.

He gave Cam a wry grin. "Baby-sitting duty at guess where," he said. "Midnight to six. But I'm still young and strong, so it doesn't show, right?"

Kenny Cox fancied himself an outdoorsman as well as an indoorsman of note. He went deer hunting every fall, turkey hunting every spring, and liked to push a bass boat sixty miles an hour way up into the back creeks and coves of the state's many lakes to kill a big fish in the summertime. Cam had gone with him a few times, but he thought Kenny was an impatient hunter, which also reflected his approach to policing. Kenny was in it for the action, all the time. Cam debriefed him on his trip to the mountains.

"That rope made you think suicide?" he asked. His eyes were definitely red-rimmed, and Cam wondered if he himself could still stay awake from midnight to six and be of any use the next day. He tried to picture Kenny outside Annie's house, looking in at the judge he despised so much, and wondered how Annie was bearing up under virtual house arrest at night.

"Yes, it did," Cam said. "Or a game-cleaning rig for winter use. But if suicide, it begs the obvious question."

"Yeah," he nodded. "Who cut him down?"

That night, Cam parked his personal vehicle, a twenty-five-year old stick-shift Mercedes 240D, which he'd owned for the past ten years, in the Marriott's parking garage.

Jay-Kay was perched attractively on a stool in the little alcove bar, having a desultory conversation with a guy who looked like a traveling salesman. She was wearing a gray silk pantsuit that clung in all the right places alarmingly well. Cam had changed from his uniform into a dark suit. He kept a ready-service suit, shirt, and tie ready to go in the office for just such situations as this. She smiled at him over the salesman's shoulder, nodded good-bye to the guy, and they went into the dining room. The maître'd took them to a table, seated Jay-Kay, dropped menus, took a drinks order, and left. It'd been an unusually warm fall day, so Cam ordered a gin and tonic for a change, and so did she.

"I didn't get a chance to say this before," he said, "but I'm really sorry about your uncle. I understand he meant a lot to you."

"He did indeed, Lieutenant," she said. "Do you remember his name?"

Cam had to admit he did not. He was bad enough with American names, and he hadn't really even remembered hers once McLain had said everyone called her Jay-Kay.

"His name was Jasbir Chopra," she said. "My aunt's name is Surinder Chopra. She who is now a widow."

Cam nodded. "I sincerely regret the fact that those two got away with it," he said. "Please believe me when I say that was never anyone's intention."

"Most big mistakes are not,' she said. "But thank you for your courtesy. My uncle was very close to me. He made it possible for me to succeed here in America. But I am no longer so sure they got away with it."

"You think those video segments are real?"

She nodded as the drinks arrived. They exchanged a salud, and then she explained. "I think they are real because the video is of such poor quality. If it had been done by pros, say someone like Industrial Light and Magic, they would have been of much better quality. This stuff was filmed on an inexpensive digital camera and then downloaded to a PC via a firewire, and then uploaded via a broadband connection to the Web."

Cam raised his eyebrows. "You know all that just by looking at it?"

"I *know* all that by analysis, Lieutenant," she said. "I suspected it once I took a good look at it. Do you remember my name, Lieutenant?"

"Special Agent McLain said everyone called you Jay-Kay. I remember your last name, Bawa, but not your other names."

"Jaspreet Kaur Bawa," she said. Cam repeated it. She smiled to show that how people pronounced her name was not of earthshaking importance.

"Mine's Cameron Richter," Cam said, since they were exchanging names. "Friends call me Cam for short."

The waiter returned to take their orders. "Is it true you run the Cherokee reservation's parkway segment in a hopped-up BMW?" Cam asked.

It was her turn to raise eyebrows. "You have been checking up on me, Lieutenant Cam?"

"A little bit," Cam said. "On you and James Marlor, both. He wasn't as interesting. I'm told you make two thousand dollars a day doing your computer work."

"Sometimes that, sometimes more," she said. He couldn't take his eyes off her face. Her light brown complexion was perfect, not a blemish anywhere, and that didn't seem to be the result of makeup. She still wore no jewelry, but he detected a faint hint of perfume. She had on a lot of red lipstick, but against her skin, it didn't seem excessive. Her teeth were very white and she had electrically alive dark brown, almost black, eyes. Cam couldn't begin to guess her age, even though he thought Kenny had told him.

"I am a highly trained and highly intuitive computer systems engineer," she continued. "Something your country used to produce before your school systems evolved into glorified day-care centers."

During dinner she told him about her upbringing in both India and, later, the States. They talked generally about education systems and the world of computer science. Cam asked how it was that she was so highly paid. She said that in one day she could sometimes solve a problem that had been vexing a company or a lab for several weeks, or even longer. That equated to big money, and she worded her consulting contracts in such a way that if she broke a problem quickly, she received a chunk of the savings. She said her Beamer had been given to her by the big BMW factory in South Carolina because she had unstuck in three hours a production-line problem that was costing them $200,000 a day. "I like fast, powerful things," she said. "Fast, powerful computers, fast, powerful cars. To me, they're the same thing: intelligent, highly reactive engineering systems. I suppose I'm a thrill junkie. The more extreme, the better."

"You said earlier that your analysis revealed several things about those execution videos. Is this analysis you did for the Bureau?"

She smiled again, but it was a crafty look, not one of seduction. "I was wondering when you would ask that, Lieutenant Cam," she said.

"If they've had you on the problem, then—"

"Yes," she said. "They think it's real, too."

"But when they backed out, they said it was for lack of physical evidence, that there was no indication one way or another that those videos were real."

"Yes, they did," she said, and waited for him to catch on. He still couldn't see what she was driving at. He'd understood and sympathized with their resource problem—terrorism versus local crime—and he'd also understood their position on the execution videos: They had lots of negative indications, but no positive proof that anyone had been harmed.

Or . . . there was another reason. He drank some wine while he thought about it. The waiter cleared the dishes away and went to get the check.

Cam put down his wineglass when he finally saw what she was getting at. She looked at him expectantly. "They think there's a problem in the Sheriff's Office," he said.

"Full marks," she replied. "Do you remember how you received the information about the first execution scene?"

"Yeah, Computer Crimes called me. Said I should go to a Web address."

"What else did they say?"

He thought back. "It came via an E-mail, which supposedly came from—"

"The Bureau field office in Charlotte," she finished. "But of course it hadn't."

"Right. And so—"

"And so I looked at your intranet fire walls that day I was there," she said. "They are set up to prevent the passage of anything faintly resembling a full-motion video file."

"But then how could I get on that Web site? I remember Kenny saying that the site was buffering or something."

"Yes indeed, and that's a separate problem. But there is no way your Computer Crimes section could have received that video file from the Web. Not on the Sheriff's Office intranet."

"So you're saying—what, that it originated *inside* the Sheriff's Office?"

"Logic would so dictate," she announced. "Have you had any other recent anomalies in your intranets?"

"No-o," Cam said, and then remembered Annie's threatening e-mail. Jay-Kay picked right up on his hesitation. "What?" she asked.

"The judge in the case, Bellamy? She received an e-mail on the private state judiciary network that said she was 'next,' in so many words."

"Did she, now," Jaspreet said. "Tell me—do you know if the judge ever accesses her office computer from her home computer?"

"No idea—I suppose she could."

"If she does, she creates a vulnerability within the secure intranet. I should take a look at that. Have you told the Bureau that she received a threat?"

"No," Cam said, looking around to make sure they weren't being overheard. The ornate dining room was nearly empty, with only three other couples present. The waiter returned with the check and she dropped a credit card. "The Bureau had backed out, so, no, we didn't send that on."

"Perhaps you should," she said. "Mr. McLain is fully conscious that the judge in this case might be a target. He also said that protecting judges is part of their 'bag,' as he put it. On the other hand . . ."

"Yeah, on the other hand, that would point yet another finger back to the Sheriff's Office." Good God, he thought, could *cops* be doing those executions?

"Are you there?" she asked, and he looked up. Her eyes were boring into his like an owl's, totally focused, zero parallax. It was a physical impact. He felt as if his brain were being scanned.

"This has all the earmarks of a political disaster, not to mention the criminal aspects," he said. Shit! She was a civilian. Why was he telling her this? Because she'd reached out?

She sat back in her chair and rearranged the remaining silverware on the tablecloth. "The Bureau is an interesting organization," she said after a minute or two. "The people there seem to weigh the political consequences of everything they do or know. It is their principal limitation, other than the sheer size of the Bureau."

"Meaning?"

"Meaning, that this is no different from the problems I engage in the computer industry. Software systems are the closest physical analogue to human societal systems. Every problem always comes back to a human error somewhere. You fix software by examining the underlying logic, something besides the raw ones and zeros. There are no political consequences in my world."

"Of course there are," Cam said. "If somebody screwed up the software, that somebody's in trouble. Just like our outfit. The sheriff isn't like a chief of police. He answers directly to the electorate. If some of his people have formed a death squad, he's finished."

"Not as finished as the people being killed by the death squad," she said.

Sounds just like Annie, Cam thought. He closed his eyes and exhaled.

"I'm prepared to help you," she said. "Especially now that those two thugs are dead."

Cam opened his eyes and just looked at her. She shrugged.

"I told you before what I thought should happen to them," she said. "So now justice has been served, after a fashion, hasn't it?"

"How could you help, then?" Cam asked.

"I can find out who sent that judge an e-mail and how they did it."

"She said it had been deleted."

"There is deleted and then there's deleted," she said. "Let me look."

He had to ask. "Why do you want to help—now?"

She thought about her answer for a moment. "Because in India we have had some experience with death squads. Inevitably, the executioners begin to like it—killing people, settling old scores. And then eventually they realize they need to clean up after themselves—take care of loose ends, people who might know too much."

Cam had this feeling she was thinking way ahead of him again.

"Someone like me," she said. "If they're operating on the Web, they would have to know that someone like me can probably find them." She paused. "And of course, someone like you, especially if you decide to look for them."

Cam hadn't thought of that, but then he hadn't thought about any of this. "How do you know I'm not one of them?" he asked.

"I don't, of course," she said. "But at that first meeting, you were embarrassed, not angry, that the judge had let them go. Some of those other officers, on the other hand, were very angry. As was I."

"We may yet turn up K-Dog or Flash," he said. "Or even Marlor."

"Let's hope you do," she said, looking at her watch. "I must go. I have to lead a technical seminar in the morning." She fished out a business card. "Call me, Lieutenant Cam. I think you need me right now."

21

ANNIE BELLAMY WAS NOT adjusting to the idea of house arrest very well. She wasn't technically under any kind of arrest, of course, but, come evening, the easiest place to protect her was at her home, which meant that she'd lost most of her privacy. Her great big silver Mercedes stayed in the garage until daybreak or further notice. Cam had called her before coming over, and also the operations shift supervisor. Matters to discuss with the judge, he'd said. The supervisor said he'd have to allow him that. All of this was in order to keep any visits or contact Cam had with Annie strictly professional. He wasn't willing yet to have everyone in the Sheriff's Office know they were actually seeing each other socially or otherwise.

She handed Cam a scotch and they went into her study and closed the door. The detail consisted of one deputy in the house, one on the grounds, and a cruiser coming by at random intervals for a street pass through the neighborhood. They also had some electronic helpers stationed around the eight or so acres of manicured grounds. Marriage, however emotionally deficient, had been kind to Annie from a real estate perspective.

She was wearing a knee-length skirt and a sleeveless blouse, and she looked good. Tired, but definitely good. "Enjoying your captivity?" Cam asked.

"Not a lot," she said. "I'd gotten used to the idea that divorce meant you didn't have a man hanging around the house all the time."

"We could detail more female officers," Cam said, sitting down in one of the big leather chairs.

"No, don't. They always want to talk." She went over to

the sound system and turned on some classical music, maybe
two notches higher than absolutely necessary. Then she came
over to the chair, sat down in Cam's lap, unbuttoned and
peeled off her blouse, and then lifted one long leg over so
that she was straddling his knees.

"Tell me you don't want to just talk," she said, reaching
back and undoing her bra.

As usual, she was right, Cam thought later. Judges are like
that, he decided.

They put themselves back together, and then he confessed
that he had come over to talk after all. She gave him a faintly
disappointed look, but not that disappointed. Fortunately,
there was more scotch in the study, so over drinks he told her
about his meeting with Jaspreet, the Web wizard, and what
she had suggested about a death squad.

"Has a pretty high opinion of herself, doesn't she?" Annie
said. She was sitting sideways at her desk, her bare feet on an
open drawer.

"If they're paying her two large a day, she must be worth
it," Cam replied.

"What's she look like?"

"Indian. *Exotic* is the word I keep coming back to. Mid-
thirties, nice figure, eyes so bright, they bounce around inside
your head."

She smiled, but it wasn't a very pretty smile just then.
"Would you like to sleep with her?" she asked.

Cam was ready for that one. Annie was nothing if not direct. "Let's see," he said. "She's female, has a pulse—yup,
vital criteria met. Absolutely."

"I've got friends in Immigration," she said, and then made
the sound of a cat hissing and spitting.

"I've got to pass this one to Bobby Lee," he said, getting
back to business. "I'm thinking of a letter, preferably mailed
from Greece or somewhere equally far away."

"Greece is good," she replied. "Ordinarily, that should go
to the Bureau, but from what you're telling me, the feds are at
arm's length and want to stay that way."

Cam shrugged. "He asks formally, they have to come

back in. The Internet's involved—plus computer crime and intrusion."

"They'll leak it."

"Then the killers will go to ground," Cam said. "If it's even true. I keep coming back to that. We have no physical evidence except absence. And cops are very adept at sniffing the wind. If there is a death squad of some kind, the cops involved would feel the police web tremble and submerge."

"And then where are you?"

"Two bad guys who confessed to the crime are possibly dead. And nobody really cares."

"People would care if cops did it."

Cam wondered about that. J. Q. Public's reaction to the chair had been the usual mixture of titillation and media twittering, but he hadn't heard a whole lot of "It's imperative that we catch the bastards who did this outrageous thing," not even from the usual liberal wets who seemed to have infested the Old North State over the past ten years. He told her what Jaspreet had said about death squads getting a taste for it.

The inside deputy knocked quietly on the study door. "Another visitor, Your Honor," he announced.

She said, "Okay," and then, sotto voce, added, "And one with impeccable timing, I do believe."

Cam got up, finished his drink, and patted his clothes to make sure everything had been put back together. She watched him with some amusement. "Should I open the windows?" she asked. She was actually blushing just a little bit.

"Might meet him at the front door," Cam suggested, which is what they did. The inside cop went back to the kitchen. They stood in the open doorway as a car drove up. Cam recognized it as a Sheriff's Office vehicle. He felt a little nervous to be standing silhouetted like that in a lighted doorway, until he saw that the driver was Kenny Cox.

Annie checked to make sure the deputy couldn't hear them, and then she said, "If I was looking for a candidate to run a vigilante group—"

He shushed her as Kenny got out and nodded to the deputy

in charge of surveying the grounds. He had materialized at the corner of the house when Kenny arrived.

"Your Honor," he said to Annie as we came up the steps. "Boss." He was in full uniform, complete with hat. "Thought I'd just check by, see if everything was okay."

"Great minds think alike," Cam said.

"Found any evidence that any of this is necessary?" Annie asked.

"No, ma'am," Kenny said, glancing from her face to Cam's and back to hers again. Cam found himself wondering what the sergeant knew. Kenny was one sharp investigator, and his ability to read body language was better than Cam's. "Still no signs of Marlor or the two movie stars," he said. "Everyone's in mourning."

"And we're looking really hard, are we?" Annie asked.

"Yes, we are," Cam said before Kenny could answer. "Finding either one of those guys is still the best way to call off your house arrest."

Kenny gave him a look. "Or we could pull our people off right now, Lieutenant," he said. "If Her Honor here doesn't believe there's a threat."

Annie rolled her eyes. "Lieutenant Richter, thanks for the update. I've got briefs to read. She nodded frostily at Kenny. "Sergeant."

She went back into the house and Cam closed the front door. "Let's take a walk," he said to Kenny.

They went out into the grounds surrounding the redbrick Federal-style house, which fell short of being a mansion, but not by much. There were eight beautifully groomed acres of lawns, gardens, and mature trees, and a big swimming pool with a pool house directly behind the main house. The rest of the property was surrounded by a brick wall on three sides and a ten-foot-high chain-link fence across the back, the latter hidden by a dense stand of cedars. There was a service alley running behind the property for garbage trucks. The front drive was rolled gravel, and it continued around one side of the house to a three-car detached garage that was perpendicular to the pool house. The front gates were ornate, wrought-iron panels that were electrically operated from inside the main house or via a dashboard scanner, which was now in the hands of the deputies on duty.

The outside deputy was dressed in modified SWAT gear, and his orders were to wander around the grounds, settling in for random periods of time in corners and shadows. He had night-vision gear and a MP-5 for business. He'd appeared again briefly when Kenny and Cam walked around from the front drive, but then slipped back into the darkness. There was no moon, but their eyes were adjusting to the darkness.

"So what the hell do we do next?" Kenny asked. "This shit could go on forever, especially if all the guy really wanted was to ice those two shit-heels. And since he's done them, this threat to the judge doesn't make sense."

"It makes her life miserable," Cam said. "If it *is* Marlor doing this shit, that makes some sense, especially if he can't bring himself to electrocute a judge."

"Depending on which judge, I could," Kenny said, glancing back toward the house. Cam had been about to tell him what Jaspreet had come up with, but Kenny's comment brought him up short. At that moment, there was a loud crash out behind the garage, followed by the sounds of a vehicle accelerating down the alley. The crashing continued, as if the vehicle was dragging a couple of metal trash cans behind it, and then the noise stopped. Cam saw a dark shadow move out from along the brick wall and trot back toward the stand of cedars at the back of the property.

Kenny had his weapon out and Cam drew his. They crouched down behind a large boxwood hedge. Behind them, the lights in the main kitchen flicked off, leaving only a yellow glow coming from the French doors that led from the central hallway out to the pool area. Cam knew that the two deputies should be in radio contact. Annie should be in her study, which was in the front of the house. Since he and Kenny weren't up on the tactical net, they needed to stay put.

"We need to stay between the alley and the house," Kenny

said softly, echoing Cam's thoughts. "Let the deputies figure out what the hell's—"

Something whacked solidly into a tree about fifteen feet away from where they were crouching, followed instantly by the boom of a high-powered rifle from out in front of the house.

"Son of a bitch!" Kenny growled as the sound of second vehicle roaring down the front street became audible. "We've been suckered."

They both stood up and ran back around the swimming pool, heading toward those French doors. A battery of motion-detector spotlights came on as they approached, momentarily blinding them both.

"On the back door," Kenny yelled as they double-timed up the wide back steps. "Sergeant Cox and Lieutenant Richter, coming in!"

"Roger that," came the deputy's voice from inside the house. The central hallway lights were off now, but the front portico lights were still on, so they could see inside the house. The deputy joined them as they came in, his weapon out in a two-hand grip.

"Where's the judge?" Cam asked.

"She was in the library when it started," the deputy said. "Fucking thing sounded like an elephant gun."

They walked quickly down the central hallway to the library doors, which were still shut. Cam knocked once and called out Annie's name.

"Can I get up now?" she asked.

Cam pushed through the double doors. Annie was crouching down on the floor behind her desk. The front drapes were still drawn, but there was a pile of broken glass spilling out onto the carpet underneath the heavy curtains. An antique mirror hanging slightly above head height on the back wall had a large starred hole right through the middle. Cam walked over and helped her up. She was putting on a brave face, but the grip on his hand indicated otherwise. He steered her toward one of the big upholstered chairs as Kenny got on the phone to Central Dispatch. Annie squeaked at something behind him, and he turned and saw that the outside deputy was standing in the doorway. He had his NVG headset pushed up on his forehead, but the black outfit, Kevlar vest, and the MP-5 submachine gun had its effect. He'd been running, based on the way he was puffing.

"One vehicle dragged some trash cans down the alley and then took off," he reported. "There was a second vehicle with the shooter at the front gates."

Cam could hear Kenny organizing a quick stop-and-search operation in the neighborhood, but he suspected they were too late. Both of the vehicles had had plenty of time to disappear into one of the many side streets in the area and get clear before the cops could converge.

"Looks like he knew where to shoot, too," Cam said, looking at the mirror. "What's behind that wall?"

"Pantry and storage area for the kitchen," the cop assigned to house duty said.

"See what we've got," Cam told him. Then he turned to the other deputy. "You get back outside and make sure there isn't a second shooter setting up on the house while we're all standing inside here with our thumbs up."

The deputy disappeared in the direction of the front door. Kenny hung up.

"They've got units working a grid," he said, but the look on his face showed that he, too, thought it was too late. Annie announced that she needed a drink. Cam fixed her a splash in a lowball glass from the bar. "What was that outside deputy doing inside the house?" Kenny asked.

"Fucking up," Cam said. He heard some vehicles screech to a stop out by the front gates. "Why don't you go organize all that," Cam said to Kenny. "You'll need one of the deputies to open those gates." Kenny nodded, pulled out his pocket tape recorder, and left the room. Cam knelt down by Annie's chair once he'd gone.

"Sorry about that, Your Honor," he said. "Looks like we're not just imagining things here."

Annie had finished the scotch in one go, and now her

cheeks were flushed. "Look at that trajectory, Cam," she said, her voice trembling. "They knew where the desk was."

"They certainly knew where the study was," he said, nodding. "But those drapes had been drawn since—"

"I work after dinner every night except Friday and Saturday," she said. "Guess who absolutely would know that?"

Cam just looked at her. "Every cop who's been on duty here?"

She nodded. "These guys seem so friendly, courteous. Concerned, even. I can't imagine . . ."

"They do a log every night. The log says where you are at all times. 'Had dinner in the kitchen. Went for a swim. Went to the library to work. Went to bed at ten.' Anyone who saw the log would know the pattern."

"But the house plan? Who would know the house layout well enough to put a shot through closed drapes, right over my head? I *felt* that thing, Cam."

Cam could hear the inside deputy coming back down the hall, so he stood up.

"Lieutenant?" the cop said, indicating he had something to show him. Annie, unwilling to be left alone in the library, went with them. They walked to the kitchen and then to the pantry area. Cam had his own tape recorder out now, ready to make notes. The round had blown the sheetrock off the interior pantry wall, gone through a box of dry cereal, which was now all over the floor, and then punched through the opposite wall and right through the outside brickwork. Cam remembered that solid whacking sound in the tree. He took the deputy to the back door and pointed at the tree. "Tell CSI to climb that tree—the round's in there," he said. The deputy stared at him. "I heard it hit, okay?" Cam said. "About twelve, fifteen feet up the trunk."

They looked around for a few more minutes, trying to spot any other damage, and then finally heard more voices out front as Kenny brought in some crime-scene people. Cam told Annie that one of them would take her statement. She gave him a worried look but then reassembled her brave face and went with the growing crowd of cops back to the study area, her judicial aura reestablishing itself. Cam wished he could hold her for a moment, just to reassure her, but they both had to act their parts right now. Cam thought it was a good time to get out of there, let the techs do their work. He also badly needed some time to think.

22

CAM MET WITH BOBBY Lee Baggett at 7:30 the next morning.

"Our ballistics lab identified the bullet," the sheriff said. "Would you believe point-four-six-five-caliber? Basically, a big-game rifle. Maybe an H and H," he added.

"If it's an H and H, it's a very expensive rifle," Cam added. He'd seen one of the Holland & Holland Company's express rifles get appraised for sixty thousand dollars on the *Antiques Roadshow,* and it hadn't been in mint condition.

"That's right," the sheriff said." So we're probably not talking some local asshole just out of the joint with a grudge against the judge, not if he's using a big-game rifle."

"Unless he stole it," Cam pointed out.

"Well, that gives us a starting point, then, doesn't it?" the sheriff said, looking at Cam, who guessed the MCAT was going to own this one, too. "Dealers, people who sell that caliber ammo, and, of course, anyone who's reported one stolen in the past five years."

"And we should talk to the ATF," Cam said, making some notes.

They kicked it around for another ten minutes and then gave it up. While the sheriff took a phone call, Cam determined from Bobby Lee's desk calendar that he was free for lunch. When the sheriff saw Cam standing behind his desk, he looked pointedly at his watch and raised his eyebrows. Cam peeled off the Post-it he'd written on and handed it to him. The note said "Meet me in the Marriott Hotel parking garage at 12:30." The sheriff started to say something, but Cam pointed to the ceiling and shook his head. The sheriff blinked, frowned, but then nodded.

They met on the top deck of the parking garage, the sheriff in his personal cruiser, which was parked next to Cam's antique Merc. Cam got out and climbed into the cruiser.

"WTF, Lieutenant?" Bobby Lee asked without preamble.

"I have reasons to believe three things," Cam said. "First, that this electric chair thing is real; second, that it's *not* James Marlor doing it; and, third, I think it's possible that we have us a vigilante squad going right here in the Manceford County Sheriff's Office."

"Great God!" the sheriff said, visibly shocked.

Cam took him through it. He told him about his meeting with Jaspreet and her take on the difficulty of getting access to the judicial network from outside the system. He mentioned how odd it was that someone would go down into one of the most dangerous neighborhoods in Triboro at midnight with a submachine gun full of blanks, which, by the way, were pretty hard to come by except in a police or military organization, which used them all the time for training. Cam told him even Judge Bellamy was wondering how someone would know precisely where she would be at that time of night—which room, where her desk was—especially since the drapes were drawn. He said there was a bunch of cops pissed off at her about those two mopes walking away like that. Then he explained how Jaspreet had alluded to suspicions at the Charlotte field office that Manceford County cops might be the real faces behind the chair. Finally, he said he thought it unlikely that Marlor had been able to enlist an accomplice to go shoot at the judge's house if he was indeed in deep hiding.

The sheriff closed his eyes and hung his head when Cam had finished. A big shiny SUV came grinding up the ramp. They were both in uniform, and the driver gave them a curious glance as he went past.

"Evidence?" the sheriff asked finally.

"Very damned little," Cam said. "We might get some evidence if we try to track the network intrusion from the inside instead of from the outside."

"But we'd have to use cops to do it," he said. "Our cops."

"Then let's get some federal help. Just say that our people have drawn a blank, and let the outsiders look from the inside."

"If there is a vigilante group, they'd rumble that in a heartbeat."

"Then they might back the hell off and quit. Maybe we can't do anything about the first two, but I'd sure like to prevent a third."

Bobby Lee looked Cam right in the eye. "Whom do you suspect?"

Cam shook his head. He had some thoughts, but he wasn't willing to name them yet.

Bobby Lee swore. "I've worked for nearly ten years to build the most professional, the most competent sheriff's office in the state. We were the first in the state to be accredited. We've won every major award in law enforcement. We have the best toys, the best lab, the best command and control systems. And now you want me to believe we've got cops killing suspects?"

His voice never rose, which meant that he was truly furious. Bobby Lee had never been a screamer. The angrier he was about something, the quieter he usually got. "You don't believe it," Cam said.

"No, I do not," he said. "I don't want to, and I don't anyway. There has to be another explanation. And I have to tell you, Lieutenant, that at this point, my instincts are to get someone else to handle this case. Except that you are, or ought to be, the best guy I've got for this." He paused to take a deep breath and exhale. "You never heard me say this, but for once in my career as sheriff of Manceford County, I don't know what the hell to do."

Back-off time, Cam thought. "We'll keep working it, then," he said. "We'll keep looking for Marlor and the two stooges. We'll keep a guard on the judge until I don't know when."

The sheriff stared out the window and started to drum his fingers on the window frame.

"I think you should call McLain," Cam said. "I want to get straight with him about what Jaspreet was saying. I want to hear it from him if he thinks we're involved."

"If the Feebs really think that, they'd never tell one of us."

"Then it's worth asking the question. A stone wall would be a pretty good indicator."

More finger drumming. "And maybe you should go down there to the Charlotte field office. Meet face-to-face," Cam told him.

"You mean no phones," Bobby Lee said.

Cam exhaled. "It's new territory for me, too, Sheriff," he said. "But, yes, that's why we're meeting up here in this parking deck." His beeper went off and he pulled it out. There was a text message: "Marlor on the grid." Cam told the sheriff, whose relief was visible.

"I'll go see what this is about," Cam said. "But I still think you should contact McLain. Ask for a meet."

Bobby Lee pointed at Cam's beeper with his chin. "Go work that," he said. "Then come see me. I'll decide then."

Kenny was talking to Horace and Purdy when Cam got back to the office. "Where'd he surface?" Cam asked.

Kenny brought over an e-mail from the manager at Marlor's bank. James Marlor had cashed a check for five hundred dollars at a drive-up window in downtown Winston. The teller there had called to confirm with Marlor's branch that the account could cover the check, and then she had given him the five hundred.

"I went over there and reviewed the security video of the drive-up. White Ford pickup truck, the right vintage, and the guy inside was big enough to be Marlor."

"No face shot?"

Kenny shrugged. "You know how that goes. Fuzzy black-and-white shot shows a white guy, ball cap, aviator sunglasses. The right kind of truck. Plus, he put two IDs—his driver's license and his Duke Energy ID card—in the tray for them."

Cam sat down at his desk. "When did all this happen?"

"Eight-fifteen this morning," Kenny said. "They called Marlor's bank to clear it. The teller who cleared it made a computer entry, and that sent an alert to the manager. She didn't get in until eight-thirty, and she sent that e-mail ten minutes later. I rolled on it right away."

"So he's alive, then," Purdy said.

"So it would appear," Cam said, although he wasn't entirely convinced.

Kenny caught the hesitation. "What?" he said.

"This guy pulls out thirty-five K in cash money just before he disappears," Cam said. "What the hell's he need an additional five hundred bucks for?"

That provoked a thoughtful silence.

"Maybe he paid a pro—you know, to take out the two mopes and the judge," Purdy said finally.

"How many hitters you heard of who use an electric chair?" Horace said. "And if a pro used an elephant gun, he'd have had a target in view, not a house."

"Okay," Cam said. "We have to follow this up. Refresh the BOLO system. Tell field ops to highlight the vehicle description, get it back up in priority with the state guys, too. Let's focus on that pickup truck if he's driving around town. Purdy, anything on the crispy critters?"

"Not a whiff, boss," Purdy said. "And you'd think—"

Cam just looked at him.

"Okay, anyways, I pulled Simmonds's prison records, talked to some of the jerkoffs he hung with in the joint, see if they could put a face on him. No joy. The CO's up there who knew him said K-Dog was not exactly a memorable guy."

"And Flash? Any south Triboro intel?"

"His mother admits he was a stone jitterhead," Purdy said. "Those are a dime a dozen down there. I've checked with the morgue a coupla times. No well-done John Does listed, here or anywhere in the state system."

"Okay, Kenny? What's the fallout from last night?"

Kenny retrieved a copy of the patrol report. Definitely two vehicles, neither one of them visually identified. Guy in the alley tied a clothesline to a trash can and dragged it a hundred feet down the alley, then cut the line. Garden-variety clothesline, available at any Wal-Mart. The guy out front parked long enough to leave a puddle of AC water, but no brass from the cannon, which fit with a bolt-action heavy-caliber rifle. No wits to anything. By the time patrol set up the sector sweep, no suspicious vehicles noted in that neighborhood.

"Which is not exactly a closed-off area," Cam said, remembering the posh neighborhood. There were lots of woods and small parks among the mansions, along with streams, trees, grassy median strips, and not many streetlights. Very private big houses set in a very accessible neighborhood. It occurred to him that if cops were doing this, they could have used cruisers, which the patrol screen would have ignored totally.

"We're exploring the rifle angle," Kenny said. "I know guys in the sporting-arms business here in the Triad, so I'll run that down myself." Cam nodded. Like many cops, Kenny had an extensive gun collection. It was mostly handguns, but included some deer-hunting rifles.

"Marlor had a carry permit," Horace pointed out. "Maybe he has a collection?"

"We didn't see a gun safe or anything like that in his house, but, yeah, that's worth checking, too," Cam said. "Check shooting clubs, local gun ranges in his area."

They were taking notes, but Cam didn't exactly detect enthusiasm. This team was used to doing one case at a time and executing a complex campaign plan when they went after a single individual. Searching for three MIAs was not their usual line of work. They'd turned on all the state and local find-the-subject machinery, and usually what happened next was a long wait. They looked expectantly at Cam.

"Yeah, well, I wish I had some brilliant ideas," Cam said. "The toasts could be buried in a farmyard somewhere, or puffing out plastic bags at some landfill. And as to Marlor, he could have done those guys and the shooting and then driven to Mexico."

"He'd need money," Horace said, and then frowned when he remembered the thirty-five thousand.

"He might have all he needs for right now," Cam said, "And the rest he can get at electronically anytime he wants."

"Let's freeze it, then," Purdy said. "He tries for his cash stash, we nab his ass."

Kenny said it before Cam did. "He hasn't committed any crimes. We can't do anything *to* him until we can prove he's done something. No judge would freeze his accounts. His only 'crime' right now is that he's gone off the grid."

"Well," Horace said indignantly, and they all laughed. Horace had a certain fondness for the idea of a police state, which was why it was probably a good thing he was retiring. They all knew that a police state was no longer entirely out of the realm of possibility.

"The fact is," Cam said, "we're stuck on this chair thing. We don't even know if it was real or Memorex. So let's concentrate on the shooting incident last night. Forget any connection to the chair, and make it a straight shooting incident. Redo the neighborhood canvass. That's a unique rifle—pull that string hard. Somebody check Marlor's credit cards going back for a couple of years for the gun."

"That'll take a warrant," Kenny said.

"Go ask Bellamy," Purdy said. "She'll probably say yes for a fucking change."

23

"Somebody who looked like Marlor, in a truck that looked like Marlor's truck, and with two pieces of Marlor's ID, cashed one of his checks for five hundred bucks at a drive-up window today."

"Or put another way," the sheriff said, "James Marlor cashed a check this morning."

Cam reminded him about the thirty-five grand he'd taken out before he vanished. The sheriff asked if there'd been any big debts paid off—like the mortgage—with that money. Cam said no. The sheriff swore when he saw the hole in his argument.

"The neighbor lady taking care of his house had the checkbook and her signature on the account card," Cam said. "I'm going to ask her to see if there are any checks missing."

"What will that prove, even if there are?" Bobby Lee asked. "Marlor could have taken one or two with him."

That was certainly true. It was Cam's turn to swear. Another damned dead end, but he was still going to ask the question.

"Okay," the sheriff said. "I'll call McLain on the secure videoconference line. Might as well clear the air."

"He's in Washington, according to the Charlotte office."

"Surely they have secure comms facilities in Washington," Bobby Lee said. "But I'm still not convinced that we've got some wrong cops here. You getting all the assets you need to find these three guys?"

Cam nodded, then told him what they were doing, which was mostly spinning their wheels.

"I'm going to ask for some help from the state on this

chair thing," the sheriff said. "In the meantime, no more meetings with that Indian woman. We don't know who she's really working for, and that always makes me uneasy."

"Last night, she was going solo, I think," Cam said. "She still wants someone's head for what happened to her uncle."

"Not for money, then?"

"Negative. She was pro bono with the Bureau, and she didn't come near asking me for money to help out. I think it's personal."

"Personal's not professional, by definition," he said. "Keep the investigation in the official loop for now. I'll let you know what I get from SBI."

Cam thanked him and went back to his office. Going to North Carolina's State Bureau of Investigation might be a good move. The SBI existed to provide state-level assets to local law; all a sheriff had to do was ask. North Carolina's SBI agents were good people; Cam's guess was that Bobby Lee might also broach this other problem with their Internal Affairs experts.

In the meantime, his people were supposedly all in motion finding their three targets. But if this was a vigilante problem, some of them might be just going through the motions. Especially one.

With a great deal of reluctance, he kept coming back to sergeant Kenny Cox. Kenny was eight years his junior, and, as his deputy, the logical choice to take over MCAT whenever Cam hung up his gun belt. He was originally from southern Virginia, raised in a farming family, and had a degree in criminology from a junior college. He'd served in the army and had achieved the Ranger designation before transferring to the Provost Marshal Corps. He'd done one and a half hitches and then gotten out, for reasons never clearly explained in the time Cam had known him. He suspected it had something to do with Kenny's growing impatience at having to take orders from shavetails with zero military police experience but with plenty of instant authority over him.

He'd ended up in Triboro in pursuit of a young lady, or so he'd said, and that aspect of his nature hadn't changed one bit. He was reportedly a world-class skirt-chaser, but disarmingly up-front about it, and the women to whom he paid attention seemed to sense that and go with it. Cam had once asked him if he was ever going to get married and settle down, and he'd asked Cam to name one good reason to do that. Cam told him for the comfort of his old age, and Kenny allowed as to how old age wasn't something he was going to plan for. His parents had both died in their late fifties from lung cancer. Kenny was a smoker himself and positively defiant about it whenever the subject of smoking and health came up. He once said that one of the advantages of being a cop was that there was a ready-made solution to the problem of a long-term wasting illness.

He affected a cowboy attitude, but he was actually a highly competent detective who embraced technology in the pursuit of bad guys. He was also a natural leader. Some of that had to do with his imposing size, but he had a force of personality that tended to put him out front anytime something got going. He'd been involved in three shooting incidents during his career, all cleared as righteous. That was higher than average in the Manceford County Sheriff's Office, but not unheard of, especially for someone who was SWAT-qualified. There'd been an equal number of incidents in which Kenny personally had talked a barricade subject down, and one where the subject had given it up the moment he saw Kenny, in full SWAT gear, step into the house and look at him.

He was something of a legend among the younger single guys in the sheriff's office, but not because he went around telling tall tales. In fact, he took the opposite approach, letting other people tell the tall tales and then just grinning innocently about it. Cam happened to know that he wasn't much of a boozer and that he was a master of discretion when it came to his love life. Once in awhile, the MCAT crew would retire to one of the cop bars in the area, and Kenny was always the first to leave, usually hinting that he had some sweet young thing waiting. Maybe that was all true, or maybe it was just Kenny's way of keeping the legend alive. The one and only time Cam had seen him really drunk was after one of his deer-hunting buddies had been killed in a SWAT operation. Kenny hadn't been on the run that day, but the guy who'd shot his friend was a three-time loser who'd been let out on bond by none other than Annie Bellamy, as a matter of fact, once again because of a procedural screwup.

The county cops had gathered down at Frank's Place, a bar and grill favored by the Manceford County deputies over on the western edge of town. Cam had found Kenny drinking alone in a corner booth, and despite some warning looks from some of the other guys as he approached, Cam joined him. Kenny had been drinking Jack Daniel's and had more than his load on, to the point where Frank had already picked up Kenny's keys. Anyway, that was the first time Cam heard Kenny really unload on the subject of lawyers, judges, the criminal justice system, and the simplest cure to the problem of rising crime—namely, regular doses of twelve-gauge justice, preferably delivered from a darkened cruiser late at night.

Cam knew Kenny was drunk, sad, and furious all at the same time, but this was a side of his deputy he'd never seen. Kenny's face and voice revealed a potential for homicidal violence that was entirely consistent with both his size and aggressive nature but not with his being a supposedly mature and professionally seasoned cop. The booze overload finally propelled him out into the back parking lot for some purgative relief, after which Cam ran him home. Kenny had sat in the right front seat of the Mero, his head hanging out the window. Kenny lived alone on an old farm place on the banks of the Deep River, southwest of town, and they'd spent the remainder of the night drinking coffee and solving the problems of the world. By the time Cam left at dawn, the Kenny he knew was back and the murderous red-eyed monster who'd wanted to soak every single one of those wet-brained, creeping Jesus, Communist do-gooder, robe-swishing, gavel-wielding sons and daughters of diseased whores in vats of battery acid had slouched reluctantly back into its lair.

Cam had entertained some similar sentiments from time

to time. He'd once toyed with the idea of getting a law degree to improve his résumé, so he went over to UNC and took the L-SAT exam, which he failed miserably. He made an appointment with one of the law professors and asked what had happened. "Simple," the professor had said when he looked at Cam's test report. "You don't think like a lawyer; you think like a human." The test was rigged to allow the applicant to find either the just solution or the legal solution. Cam had gone for justice every time, which meant that he would never make it through law school. "The test did you a favor, young man," the professor said.

And that had been Cam's problem with lawyers ever since: They examined criminal incidents from the perspective of the law, as they were supposed to. They applied their abundant intelligence, a body of complex ancient law, elaborate procedure, and the nicest sense of professional ethics to people who were hatched out on the margins of civilized society, hadn't the first idea of right and wrong, and whose total intelligence manifested itself in cunning. The lawyers were never present when the cops caught these *things,* often still awash in the blood and gore of their victims, a sticky knife in one hand and blood lust glowing in their beady little eyes even as they were trying to figure out how to get out of the corner they were in yet again. That was when every cop out there, at one time or another, looked around for a club.

Senior cops would tell junior cops just to put it away, saying that they didn't want to get down there in the blood gutters with the animals. But the truth was, the longer one was in the cop business, the more one realized that the stinking killer cuffed in the backseat was going to get hosed down, cleaned up, and dressed in the first clean clothes he'd *ever* seen. Then he'd be taken into the cathedrals of The Law to appear before all its high priests, with a fair chance of getting away with whatever heinous crimes he'd committed, depending not on what the little monster had done but on how good or inept the opposing lawyers were when they eventually played their intellectual game.

So, what to do next? His personal style would be simply to

ask Kenny if he was running a vigilante squad, but that obviously wasn't on, given the notoriety of this case. Internet service providers around the world had embargoed the original execution scene postings, but enough people had downloaded the video clips to keep the thing very much alive in all sorts of chat rooms. Assertions by police and other authorities that the execution scenes weren't real rang increasingly hollow each day the two minimart heroes remained missing, and it was only a matter of time before one of the big news organizations ran a special, putting the videos together with the shooting at Annie's house. Cam could still hear that voice from the crypt saying, "That's two."

The sheriff's secretary called and asked that he come down to the secure communications room for a video teleconference. Steven Klein was already there when Cam arrived, and Bobby Lee came in a moment after Cam did. They took their places in front of the camera bank, and then Bobby Lee explained to Steven what he was going to talk to the FBI about. Steven was appropriately horrified, as this was the first he was hearing about it.

"Well, it's more of a possibility that we're exploring," Bobby Lee said. "Lieutenant Richter here gives it better legs than I do right now, but since he's had indications the Bureau people in Charlotte think we have a problem, I'm on with special agent McLain in"—he glanced at his watch—"three minutes. He'll be speaking from Washington, apparently. Lieutenant, fill Mr. Klein in, please."

Cam went through it with Steven, who just sat there and listened. He was an inveterate note-taker, and the fact that he wasn't writing any of this down showed that he knew how explosive it was.

"That's all so circumstantial," he said when Cam was finished.

"This whole mess is circumstantial," Cam said. "The Bureau's public position remains that there's no physical evidence that the Internet executions are real. But that big-game rifle at Judge Bellamy's house, that was real."

Steven shook his head. "We have plenty of nut jobs right

here in the Triad who might want to do that. How do you tie this shooting to the chair thing?"

Cam started to explain, but then the video circuit came up and they saw Special Agent McLain materialize on the forty-eight-inch main display screen. The red lights on all three face cameras came on, and the technician who established the link announced over the speakers that the connection was secure and that he was isolating the room.

"Gentlemen," McLain said, looking a little stiff in his suit and tie. The camera shooting him focused on the top third of his body, so if there was anyone else in the room, they weren't able to tell. It being the Bureau, they were probably taping everything.

The sheriff introduced Steven and Cam in case McLain had forgotten their names, then got right to it. "Mr. McLain, we're hearing that the Charlotte field office thinks there might be a vigilante problem here in the Manceford County Sheriffs Office," he said almost pleasantly. "Naturally, that disturbs me, so I thought I'd clear the air, one way or another."

"May I ask where you got that, Sheriff?" McLain asked. Bobby Lee looked over at Cam expectantly.

"I had dinner the other night with your computer consultant, Jaspreet Kaur Bawa," Cam said. "She voiced the opinion that, contrary to published Bureau opinion, you all felt the execution videos were real, and that because of the way the threat was sent to Judge Bellamy, someone inside our system either sent it or provided the access. This was before the shooting incident at Judge Bellamy's house."

"Whoa," McLain said. "What shooting incident?"

Bobby Lee got an annoyed look on his face. "I assumed that had been reported to your field office," he said.

"I'm on temporary duty in Washington, Sheriff," McLain said. "It may have been reported. What happened?"

The sheriff gave him the essential elements. McLain nodded when the sheriff was finished. "I think Ms. Bawa over-heard a conversation," he said, "rather than an official statement of Bureau policy. People are of two opinions on the execution videos, as I suspect they are in your shop, Sheriff. The *policy,* on the other hand, is that without physical evidence, the Bureau will not proceed."

"Okay," Bobby Lee said calmly. "What's behind all the conversation, then?"

"Our computer-lab types talked to your Computer Crimes people," he said. "To get a system description on your security hierarchy. Ms. Bawa was part of that discussion. The consensus was that your system is reasonably effective, so logic would dictate that the E-mail came from inside the system. Actually, based on the password setup, probably from another judge. In our opinion."

"In your opinion," Bobby Lee prompted.

McLain shrugged. "One could argue it wasn't much of a threat," he said. "And if judges want to snipe at judges, that's their prerogative. No crime, for one thing, and judge-to-judge communications are privileged. That's why we didn't share our opinions. Any signs of the two purported execution victims, by the way?"

"Nope," Bobby Lee said. "Nor any sign of our prime suspect, James Marlor, either."

What about the check? Cam thought, but then decided to keep his yap shut for a change.

"Well, that's a pisser," McLain said. "I happen to be in the 'Maybe it's real' camp, but I must reiterate—we won't get into it until there's physical evidence of a crime. Bodies, I'm talking about. And even then, we might not take it on. Washington headquarters has a point: We spin up on this one and we'll create a cottage industry of Webheads generating drama for our investigatory pleasure. Did you say you have that judge under police protection?"

"That's right."

"Well, I'd suggest that's where you need to start, Sheriff. Make the assumption that it was cops doing that, or not—that's your call, of course. You said you flooded the area with patrol units right after the shooting. Canvass the neighborhood—see if there were cop cars out there *before* the shooting. Like that."

"Believe it or not, we're already doing that," Bobby Lee said somewhat heatedly.

"No offense intended, Sheriff," McLain said, but Cam noticed he wasn't smiling. "Your office has the highest reputation. But the hard part is that initial assumption. As I remember from my visit there, your rank-and-file people were really pissed when that judge let those subjects go. If you're nervous about lighting that fuse, maybe get the SBI into it?"

"I've got that in motion, too," the sheriff said. That was quick, Cam thought.

"Look, I've got a meeting," McLain said. "Anything else to talk about?"

"Nope," the sheriff said. "Thanks for your time. Goodbye." He hit a button on the table before McLain could say anything and the connection was broken abruptly. The screens went dark.

"Arrogant sumbitch," Bobby Lee grumbled.

Steven disagreed. "No, they're just staying at arm's length," he said. "Bureaucratically, that's the smart thing to do right now, and in that outfit, Washington sets the policy, not the field offices."

"But that doesn't mean Charlotte's not working it," Cam interjected.

"Explain that," the sheriff said, a suspicious look on his face. His jaw was set, which meant he was still angry at McLain.

Cam leaned forward. "He didn't react when I said his consultant had been talking out of school. I'm thinking he sent her to put us on notice. He knew I'd bring that back to you. As in 'Officially, this electric chair thing is your problem, but we're watching your local yahoo asses.' "

"What about that 'judge-to-judge' business?" Steven asked. "That bothers me more than their speculations on the chair thing."

"Based on what Computer Crimes told me, it could just as easily be someone with access to another judge's computer," Cam said. "Not necessarily one of the celestial beings themselves. Once it goes over the Internet, they can trace back to an address, but not to whose fingers were on the keyboard."

"But isn't that just their point?" Klein asked. "That message to the judge wasn't on the Internet in the sky. It was on the intranet. The judicial intranet."

"Whatever," Cam said. "But I think he had one good point: Let's focus on who's behind the shooting, where we do have some tangible evidence of a crime. That might be more productive than this endless search for Marlor, Simmonds, and Butts."

"Not so fast," the sheriff said. "It might be productive, but it can also be very dee-structive. I don't want to start any wildfires in the Manceford County Sheriff's Office based on one dinner conversation, Lieutenant, and that with a civilian consultant, I might add, who works for a federal agency."

"She called me, Sheriff," Cam said.

"Okay," the sheriff said. "Enough of this shit. Lieutenant, you keep MCAT looking for Flash Gordon and his pal. And for James Marlor. I'll think about this other business. I do *not* want you to start any internal investigations, disrupt the whole damned Sheriff's Office, until I've had time to think it through and talk in detail with SBI. Steven, you and I need to talk."

That was a clear signal for Cam to go away, so he did. He went back to the office, which was empty. He called Marlor's neighbor but only reached her answering machine. He asked her to see if all the checks were accounted for, especially one numbered 2499. That number sounded like the last check in a series. Then he took advantage of the fact that the rest of the crew were out of the office and called the field ops center and asked for the dispatch supervisor. He asked her to generate a list containing the names of every deputy who'd been signed out to a cruiser at the time of the shooting incident, and the call number of each cruiser. Being a cop, she asked what was going on, and, mindful of Bobby Lee's warning about starting shit, Cam told her the MCAT needed to recanvass the neighborhood where the incident occurred. She said she'd send it by e-mail.

The next call would be cutting closer to the line, but he decided to go ahead anyway. He called the district office's three garages, and spoke to the maintenance supervisors. He asked each of them to generate another list, this one indicating by call number any cruisers that had been in for maintenance during the last twenty-four hours. The supervisors were all civilian employees, so none of them asked any questions and all three promised him their lists in the next hour, again by E-mail. Then, using his own computer, he printed out a list of all the vehicles owned and operated by the Sheriff's Office. He crossed off the special-use vehicles—such as the war wagon for the SWAT teams and the mobile-lab vans—and counted up all the cop cars.

With this list and the ones he'd requested, he would have the numbers of every cruiser in the Manceford County Sheriff's Office that had been available for street duty at the time of the incident. He could subtract the assigned cruisers and the ones in for maintenance from the master list. That should leave only half a dozen vehicles. He could then go check to see where they were that night, and who'd been using them. He knew it was possible that street deputies could be involved in something like this, but it would more likely involve senior people, sergeants at least.

He heard voices out in the main MCAT office, so he put away what he was doing and locked his desk. It gave him a strange feeling to be looking inside the Sheriff's Office for criminal activity, but the more he thought about it, the more he had the feeling that it needed to be done. Especially since one of his own people might be involved. He knew he had to be very careful—Bobby Lee kept his finger on the pulse of the entire Sheriff's Office better than anyone he knew. The sheriff had to be looking at him, too.

24

CAM WAS AWAKENED IN the night by the phone. It was Kenny Cox. Cam could hear the sounds of a crime scene in the background: tactical radios, vehicle doors opening and closing, people talking about setting tape, portable generators humming urgently.

"The chair is real," Kenny announced.

"What've you got?" Cam asked, turning on the bedside light and squinting at the clock, which read 4:30. Of course.

"I'm at the petroleum tank farm down by the rail yards, south Triboro. What we've got is a makeshift body bag. They decided to draw down a zillion-gallon diesel tank, and the pumps shut down due to a blockage when it was almost empty."

"And?"

"They did a gas-free certification and then an open-and-inspect. Found a bag. Looks like one of those big commercial laundry bags, about ten foot long. Plastic of some kind, nylon twine at the top. Only this one had K-Dog Simmonds inside."

"Oh boy. Sufficiently preserved for ID?"

"Absolutely. Diesel cleans metal parts and apparently preserves human tissue just fine—even very badly burned human tissue. It's him. You want to come down here? No media yet, but the night's still young."

Cam did his standard morning ablutions and made it to the tank farm about forty-five minutes later. Since it was an industrial area, he drove his pickup truck. A city cherry picker was parked next to the tank, and there were several hard-hatted union workers in evidence, doing what they did best—standing around. The crime-scene crew had a small area taped off around the base of the tank, and Herman Yarnell, the Manceford County medical examiner, was there, making his usual profound observation: "That guy's dead, all right." A lengthy immersion in number two diesel was masking what should have been a perfectly awful stench, although not entirely.

Cam saw that it was Simmonds, and he had most definitely been southern-fried. K-Dog's face perfectly matched the image imprinted into Cam's memory at the end of Simmonds's starring role in the first execution video. Cam felt a little bit sorry for him, but only a little bit. He was guessing that K-Dog now looked somewhat like those two people in the minivan when he and Flash got done setting *them* on fire. He wondered if he should call Jaspreet and let her come get some morbid satisfaction. But then, she'd already seen him die, and she'd been a believer right from the beginning.

"What's the estimated time of death?" Cam facetiously asked the elderly ME, who just stared at him blankly until some of the other cops started laughing. "You don't know who this is, do you?" Cam said.

He did not, so Cam explained it. He still didn't get it. Cam gave up, remembering that county pathologists don't get out much. That was especially true of Herman, who was rumored to really like his morgue.

"Anybody check to see if there were two of them in there?" Cam asked Kenny.

Kenny started to answer, but then he went over to talk to the visibly upset manager of the place to ask the same question. Minutes later, the workers bestirred themselves moving over to the cherry picker to take another look into the bowels of the big tank. Kenny came back over and Cam indicated that he wanted to speak privately. They moved away from the crime-scene technicians.

"Now what?" Kenny asked.

"Well, like you said, it's real. The chair, I mean. That has to be Simmonds."

"I suppose we have to wait for forensics, but, yeah, that's him. And something definitely cooked his ass."

"Stick with some*body,*" Cam said, looking right at him.

"The only question now is, Who?" If Kenny understood Cam's challenging stare, he gave no sign. It was still just the two of them, sweeping against the entire criminal tide.

"I give up," Kenny said. "Who?"

"Somebody with motive, opportunity, and means," Cam said, reciting the standard murder formula. "My bet is still Marlor."

"I'll grant you motive, and maybe means. But tell me about opportunity. How would a guy like Marlor even find a hump like K-Dog?"

"Money," Cam said promptly. "You know, stage something. Put the word out that he's a—I don't know. Publisher? Producer? Journalist? He's offering to pay for K-Dog's story. If it were me, I'd have called the producers of that show he went on and told them. They'd tell Simmonds, he and I would meet, and I'd show him some of that thirty-five K. Then we'd go someplace to do the deal and I'd bag his ass."

Kenny was shaking his head. "It might have been money," he said. "But I don't think scientist Marlor is the kind of guy who could do this by himself. Fry a guy and then get him into an oil tank? He had to have help."

The cherry picker's engine revved up as the basket went high over the tank. A tank diver in a white plastic suit with an air-tank respirator was riding in the bucket with the operator.

"Yeah, maybe," Cam said, watching the bucket as it jerked its way toward the access plate. "But how many hit men come equipped with an electric chair? Three-tap with a silenced twenty-two Mag's more like it."

"But how would Marlor get a commercial dry-cleaning bag?" Kenny asked. "And how would he get the body into that tank? You saying he rented a cherry picker? Came down here in the dead of night, unbolted that dome cover and then the access hatch, and dumped a hundred-plus-pound bag into an operational fuel tank?"

"You see any surveillance on this place?" Cam asked, looking around. "Cameras? Random vehicle patrols? A fence, even?"

They both looked around, and Kenny had to admit Cam

was right. There were lights, but the tanks were huge, maybe a hundred feet in diameter and at least fifty feet high. The tops of the tanks were above the sodium vapor lights standards, so somebody climbing around up top would not be in the cone of light. There were wide gravel lanes between the rows of tanks, and a circular raised berm around each one, big enough to contain a small to moderate leak. But neither of them saw any video cameras, not one, and there was no fence around the tanks, either. There was a railroad siding on one side of the complex and a highway on the other. A string of tank cars was parked on the siding. The only fence was on the other side of the railroad tracks. Cam didn't know how easy it would be for a pickup truck simply to drive into the tank farm, but if there was a checkpoint, it might not be a twenty-four-hour-a-day checkpoint.

"Okay," Cam said. "Those are all strings to be pulled." The medical examiner walked over to where they were standing. "When can we get an autopsy report?" Cam asked him.

"When it's done," Herman said amiably.

"We think this individual was electrocuted intentionally," Cam said. "As in executed in an electric chair. I'd like an opinion on what kind of current did this—AC or DC—and how much, if that's possible."

The ME scratched his head with his ungloved hand. "I'll have to do some research on that," he said. "Not sure there's a difference. Cooked meat is cooked meat. You say there's a video of this?"

Cam told him there was.

"I'd need to see that, then," he said. "AC and DC produce a slightly different arc color. This video in color?"

"Oh yes," Cam said. "Vivid color."

"Okay, then. Since this isn't really the murder scene, I'm releasing him to transport."

Since Kenny was technically in charge of the scene, Cam looked at him for approval and he nodded. He already had a crew line-walking the area around the tank, and of course the thing lying on the ground was now of interest to only the forensic pathologists. Cam spied a white TV van being stopped beyond the perimeter by a deputy.

"Time for me to boogie," he told Kenny. "I'll get the word to Bobby Lee." He looked back at the body and sighed. "I was really hoping these two humps were out in LA somewhere, where they belong."

"He's exactly where he belongs," Kenny said. "In hell. Precooked even." Cam definitely heard a note of triumph in his voice. I'd also better tell Annie, Cam thought.

25

ANNIE WAS SITTING AT her office conference table with her clerk when Cam knocked on the open door and went in. They finished up and the clerk closed the door behind him. Annie pointed to the liquor cabinet secreted in the bookshelf and Cam fixed them each a scotch. They sat together on the couch. The light outside was beginning to fade toward evening, and the lingering glare through the windows revealed some lines and shadows Cam normally didn't see on her pretty face.

"So how's the house arrest going?" he asked.

"Long," she said. "Especially now that this chair thing is real."

He nodded. "Seems so," he said. "The pathologists may have a different opinion, of course, but I saw the body."

"Great," she said, and stared out the window. "So now what?"

He moved closer to her and rubbed the back of his hand across her cheek. Her skin felt faintly powdery, but the small bones of her face were tangible, which meant she'd lost some weight. "I wish I could go over there and just let you sleep in my arms," he said.

She folded her face into his hand and nodded. "I'm being the big brave judge," she said, "But I'm also scared." She turned to look at him. "Was that a cop who fired that cannon at my house?"

"I don't know," Cam said. "And Bobby Lee doesn't care much for my theories along that line."

"You've talked to him?"

"He's the Man in this outfit. He's not anybody's friend, but I believe he's honest. I can't see him condoning vigilantes in his bailiwick, but just the whisper of an accusation like that would tear the place apart, so I've talked to him and only him." As he said it, Cam realized that wasn't entirely true. He'd also talked to Jaspreet Kaur Bawa. As usual, Annie read his feeble mind. "What?" she said.

He told her in greater detail about his dinner with Jaspreet and the vibes bouncing around the FBI's Charlotte field office. He also told her about their teleconference with McLain, and that the sheriff was talking quietly with the SBI.

"Too many people talking," she said. Your secret won't be a secret for very long. Look—I have to get home. The FBI is sending your fancy computer expert friend to take a look at my computer. Apparently they think I compromised the judicial intranet and that's how bad E-mails are getting through."

"You do access it from home?"

"Of course—we all do. It's supposed to be secure. How 'bout an escort?"

Cam went to get his car while she closed up chambers and retrieved her car. He followed her back to the house and they continued the conversation in her study. "What's really worrying me," he said, "is the fact that we can't find this Marlor guy."

"What's worrying me is that someone might be trying to kill me," she said, matter-of-factly, ever the judge. "Either some guy the whole world can't find or some cops who are right now just biding their time, waiting for the heat to dissipate or the budget people to pull off the watchers."

"Can't you take a vacation? Go to Europe or something?"

"And what—postpone the inevitable? Whoever killed those two men went to extraordinary lengths to do it—an electric chair, for God's sake! And then put at least one of the bodies in a place where it had to be found, instead of burying it up in the mountains somewhere."

"I don't know, Annie," Cam said. "Say it *is* cops. They've iced the two perps who did the crime, not to mention putting the fear of God into you. Sent you a threatening E-mail via a supposedly safe circuit. Fired a big rifle into your house. They'd have to know you're scared—the deputies stationed here have to be talking about it at the district office, in the cop bars."

"Wonderful," she said.

"But here's what I'm saying: it's a huge step to go from harassing a judge to killing a judge. If it is cops, they'd have to know that the entire federal and local law-enforcement machine would turn on them, find them, and execute them, in this state. If they do nothing else, they've achieved their warped sense of justice already. I just can't see it going past harassment."

She turned to look at him. "And for how long do the elephant guns through the windows go on? Until I resign from the bench? Is that what they want?"

Cam threw up his hands. "I don't even know if 'they' exist. Some kind of cop vigilante squad, I mean. It could be Marlor doing this stuff." He told her what McLain had said about another judge sending her hate mail. But she'd hit on something there—if it was cops, getting her to resign from the bench would be a victory in some quarters of the Sheriff's Office. Kenny Cox, for one, would be elated.

"Well, whoever's doing it can forget that shit," she said, finishing her whiskey. "I'm not going anywhere. Bobby Lee issued me a carry permit yesterday and I'm packing a three fifty-seven from now on. Any more shit starts, I'm shooting back. You can put *that* word out in the cop bars if you'd like."

"I don't go to cop bars," Cam said. "And what do you know about shooting a Mag?"

"You showed me, remember?"

"That was many years ago," Cam said. "I'm not even sure I could handle a Magnum pistol right now. My hands are getting old. This forty-five is a handful as it is."

She got up, went to the desk, and pulled out a shiny Smith & Wesson, took a fair to middling two-handed combat stance, and pointed it at the study door, right at the very moment the outside deputy knocked and opened it. His expression became quite interesting; if Cam hadn't started laughing, the deputy might even have fainted. Annie lowered the gun, apologized, and shook her head.

"What, Deputy?" she said in an embarrassed voice.

"Um," he replied, probably wondering about the state of his underwear, "There's a delivery for you, Your Honor."

"What kind of delivery?" Cam asked. He hadn't heard any vehicles.

"FedEx. He said he didn't need a signature."

Cam got out his trusty pocket tape recorder and turned it on. "Sure it was a FedEx truck?"

"Yes, sir, a white van. You know the kind, had the FedEx sign on the side. Guy brought the package to the front gate, did his scan thing, and handed it through."

"You expecting FedEx?" Cam asked Annie. She shook her head.

"Describe it, Deputy," Cam said, making sure the voice-activated recorder could pick up the deputy's words.

"Box of some kind, wrapped in brown paper, about the size of a shoe box, maybe a little bigger. Heavyish. Brown plastic tape. I didn't look at the address label." He pointed behind him. "It's right out here, on the—"

"In here," Cam said, motioning for the deputy to come all the way into the study and close the door. "Okay. We're going outside right now, through these French doors. Where's the inside guy?"

The deputy told Cam he'd switched stations with his partner, who was now covering the gate.

Once they were all outside, Cam had the deputy call into operations and give the code for a possible explosive device and then the code for Annie's house. Then they moved to the other end of the swimming pool complex. Cam told the deputy to come up on his secure radio circuit and describe in detail to operations what they had, and then he gave the deputy his pocket recorder and had him describe everything he could remember about the FedEx truck, the driver, and the package in case it went boom in the night. The deputy said the driver had been a white guy, medium, medium, tinted glasses, FedEx ball cap, white shirt with FedEx logo, dark pants, no distinguishing scars or marks. The guy had been in a hurry, didn't say much.

Annie asked Cam discreetly if maybe he was overreacting. "It might just be a FedEx package, Cam."

"It's well after six P.M.," Cam said. "The FedEx guys, the UPS drivers—they're all back at their stations, filing the day's reports. Anybody could make a magnetic FedEx sign, slap it on a white van, and nobody'd pay it any mind. So we play it safe."

The bomb squad got there in twenty minutes, during which time the four of them waited outside, swatting at late-season mosquitoes. Finally, Cam told the deputy to resume his patrol of the grounds. He figured that if it was a bomb, it would trigger when opened and not by some timer, unless the deliveryman had pushed a button inside the package when he'd handed it over at the gate. Cam wasn't going in there to find out. They continued to wait outside while the explosive guys did their thing, which ended when they launched their recovery robot into the hallway to grab it up and take it out to the transport truck, which hauled the object away.

While they were standing there, Jay-Kay Bawa and a man who looked like an FBI agent came around the corner of the house. Cam introduced her to Annie Bellamy, and then the two women stepped aside to talk. Cam asked the agent if he'd been told what was going on; the man replied that they'd been out front for awhile, and that he'd made a report back to Charlotte.

"We couldn't get through the perimeter cops. It was Jay-Kay there who talked her way in and then came and got me." He looked around. "They think it's real?"

The bomb squad's supervisor, perspiring in his body armor, came out to where they were waiting.

"Sure looks like one," he said, "Although the sensor pack didn't alarm on nitrates or anything. But it's heavy enough, and there's no FedEx bar codes on the package. If it doesn't go boom when they take it out to the range, we might get some decent forensics off that wrapping tape."

"The deputy said the driver scanned it," Cam said.

"Then he was acting," the supervisor replied. "No bar code there to scan."

"Did you sweep the house?" Cam asked.

"Yep," he said. "Nothing overt."

"Because there was no one in there for twenty minutes, and for at least some of that time I had both deputies outside."

"One of your guys had to come open the gates for us," he said.

"Your Honor," Cam said to Annie, "It's safe for you to go back in the house. Can I ask that you and Deputy Arnold here do a walk-through, see if anything's out of place or disturbed?"

"Just me, Lieutenant," she said. "If that was a bomb, I'm very much disturbed: Ms. Bawa, come along. You can look at my computer while we do a walk-through."

Cam told Annie sotto voce to come to his place once all the noise subsided. Then, since he couldn't think of anything else to contribute, he went back to his office to write it up. He called the sheriff at home later that evening to report on what the bomb squad had discovered. It hadn't been a bomb. But it hadn't been a legitimate FedEx package, either. FedEx had no record of a delivery to Annie's address, and Cam had been right about when the deliverymen returned to their stations for the day. The bomb squad had taken the package apart with their disassembly robot out at the bomb range, which was equipped for night work. They found a common cardboard box inside, and that contained a brick wrapped in bubble wrap. There were no wires, trigger mechanisms, or clocks. There was nothing unique about the brick or the box, and the brick had apparently been washed in diesel oil to get rid of any traceable elements. No prints on the package, tape, or the bubble wrap. But someone had inscribed the outer layer of bubble wrap with the roughly drawn letters *BFB* in permanent ink.

"And you can guess what that stands for, right, Lieutenant?" the bomb squad supervisor had said to Cam.

Cam absolutely could. Could have if he'd wanted to, that is. "Send me a report," he'd said. "And we need some internal discretion on this, for reasons I can't discuss right now."

When he'd heard the story, the sheriff said for Cam to get a report off to the Bureau office in Charlotte first thing in the morning.

"They already have it, Cam said. He told Bobby Lee about Jay-Kay's being there at the house, and the fact that her escorting agent had made a report.

"How'd our favorite judge cotton to somebody from the Bureau poking around in her computer?" Bobby Lee asked.

"The judge is a lot more frightened than she's letting on," Cam said. "This bomb shit, even if it was a fake, scared her even more. She had no problems letting the Bureau take a look."

He told the Sheriff he'd send a preliminary report to Charlotte before he went home, and follow that up when he had the formal paper in from the bomb squad. Then he called Kenny Cox at home, but he wasn't in. Out on yet another hot date, or ditching a white van somewhere down in south Triboro? Cam was tempted to beep him, but since there'd been no bomb, he figured it could wait until morning. The district had put a three-district call out for any white vans sporting a FedEx logo, but that was pretty much a hopeless endeavor. The driver had had at least a half hour to pull in behind some strip mall, take off the signs, and get on down the road, having nothing to worry about except an unlucky traffic stop.

Cam generated a summary report for the Bureau and sent it down to their secure communications facility. Then he checked his voice mail and listened to a message from Marlor's neighbor down in Lexington. She'd looked in the checkbook, and, yes, there was one entire page of checks missing from the very end of the current series. She hadn't noticed because she was still using checks in the front of the book, as she was writing only a few checks a month. The check numbers missing were 2497, 2498, and 2499, the last three in the book.

She had notified the bank, which informed her that number 2499, a check in the amount of five hundred dollars, had been cashed in Winston and that they would issue a stop-payment order for the other two checks—for a standard fee, of course. Cam decided to go out and get something to eat. He'd tackle all this in the morning. But first, he wanted to swing by Annie's house to make sure she was all right and to see what, if anything, Jay-Kay might have found in Annie's computer. He'd made it out to the parking lot and was fishing for keys when his beeper went off. It was a message from field operations. "Call home, E.T.—911." Those last three digits blinking on his pager meant something very bad had happened.

26

CAM UNLOCKED HIS CAR, slid into the driver's seat, and used his Sheriff's Office cell phone. The operator patched him through to the operations supervisor, who informed him that there had been two bombs at Judge Bellamy's place after all. The second one had worked like a fucking charm.

Cam was struck speechless as a cold wave of acute nausea swept through his midsection.

"Lieutenant, you there?" the sergeant asked.

Cam found his voice. "Yeah, I'm here. The judge—is she . . ."

"Oh, yes, sir, she, her car, and her garage. Apparently, it was a big fucking bomb. I'm fixing to beep the sheriff right now. You going on-scene?"

Cam nodded, and then realized the sergeant couldn't see that. "Affirmative," he croaked, and hung up. BFB—just like the brick package had promised.

His hands were shaking and suddenly he couldn't see all that well in the semidarkness of the police lot. He sure as hell couldn't drive right now, so he called back into the operations center and asked for a cruiser to take him out there. He met the car out front on Washington Street and they headed out to Annie's neighborhood with sound and lights going. The deputy driving took one look at Cam's face and tended to his driving.

Annie was dead. Just when it seemed they might be able to get a life going again, now this. He couldn't organize his thoughts or his emotions. He was just cold inside now, anxious to get to the scene, to do something. An image of the chair flashed through his mind.

It was a blue-light circus out there by the time they pulled up. Cam badged through two perimeters and three different sets of scene-entry logs. He could smell the disaster over the wall before he could see it. A heavy pall of smoke still hung in the air, polluting the beautiful ambience of the grounds and shrouding the smaller trees. It looked like every light in the house was on, but then he realized that every window on the garage side of the house had been blown in. The main crowd was back at the garage, or where the garage had been, because it wasn't there anymore. Only one end wall was standing, and not much of that one. There were crime-scene people, the bomb squad again, the fire department, of course, two ambulances, one with lights going, one with lights dark, and several deputies milling around with flashlights. It looked like the medical examiner's people were working at the darkened ambulance, while the EMT boys were swarming around the one whose lights were still spinning. One injured, one dead. Not too hard to figure that out.

The on-scene boss was the Sheriff's Office watch commander for this shift, Lt. Frank Myers. Frank worked in the Major Crimes division. He was a big guy, also ex–Marine Corps, but he was of the gentle giant persuasion and well liked in the Sheriff's Office. Cam headed toward him and found himself crunching through a thickening debris field as he crossed the dark lawn. His mind was in neutral, and the feeling of dread and nausea was returning. Part of his brain told him that he didn't belong here just now, but he ignored that, pressed ahead, and got to where Frank was talking on a cell phone. The remains of Annie's silver Mercedes smoldered in front of the garage foundations. Frank recognized Cam and cut off his conversation abruptly.

"Jesus, Cam, I'm sorry as hell about this," Frank said, which surprised Cam. It was not something that the officer in charge on the scene of a bombing would say to the chief of the MCAT, and then Cam saw that several other cops were looking his way with expressions of real sympathy, as was Frank. It struck him then that his and Annie's little secret may not have been so secret after all. He was overwhelmed for a moment, but then the situation intruded. Fuck it, he thought, taking a deep breath. Let's get this over with.

"Where is she?" he asked as quietly as he could, and Frank immediately pulled him aside. The other people were getting back to what they had been doing, but Cam noticed that there was a growing circle of space around the two of them out there in the ruined yard.

"The judge's remains are in that dark ambulance over there," he said. Cam immediately turned in that direction but found that Frank had a hold of his arm and wouldn't let go. Cam had to stop before he pulled himself off his own feet. He looked at Frank, who shook his head. "Don't go there," he said. "Keep what you got, Cam."

Cam tried to pull away again, but Frank was a big man, so then he just quit, which is when Frank let go of his arm and put a big paw around his shoulder. Cam felt tears streaming down his face. He didn't know what to do, and Frank turned him gently away from the crowd of cops and lights and walked him out into the darkness of the lawn, still stepping through broken bits of wood, glass, and even metal—and possibly bits of Annie, Cam realized.

Big fucking bomb.

After a minute or so, he got control of himself, sort of, took several deep breaths, and asked what had happened.

"Those FBI people left and then the judge decided she wanted to go out for a drive," Frank said. "All of a sudden. Said the house was giving her the creeps, all this shit going on. The inside deputy informed the outside guy and central ops, said he'd go get the car. She said no, she'd get it, told him to meet her at the front gates."

"So he didn't actually go with her?"

Frank shrugged. "It was Arnold. He's a second-year probationer, just off his tour at the LEC. She was a judge. He did what he was told."

"And then?"

"The outside deputy was Merriweather. He got the word, saw the backyard spotlights come on, saw the judge walk across the drive, heading back toward the garage. He said his night vision was shot to hell by all the spots, so he drifted back toward the front wall to get some trees between him and the house. Heard the garage doors go up, thinks he heard the car start, then doesn't remember anything after that. The EmTs say he got hit with a piece of the roof. They're fixing to transport him now."

"Badly injured?"

"Whacked in the head," Frank said. "Who the hell knows."

"And Arnold?"

"Physically, he's fine," Frank said pointedly, giving Cam a look that said, Don't go out there and beat up on him for not going with Annie to the garage. Because if he had . . .

"Okay, okay," Cam said. "He didn't do anything wrong."

"Yeah, that's how we see it right now. If anything, they should have had the outside guy go look in the garage, make sure there were no bad guys lurking in there. Of course they'd never have seen this coming."

"I should have," Cam said. "They did this before."

"'They'? 'What're you talking about?"

"Diversion. The night they shot up the house. One guy in the alley, making noise, while the shooter pulls up front and pops the real cap. Same deal here. They deliver a fake bomb, we go off on it, find out it's a fake, stand down. Then the real deal. Plus, the bomb squad swept the house, but none of the other buildings."

"I don't know, Cam," Frank said after a moment. Cam thought Frank was being obtuse, but then he realized that he was still looking for someone to blame—that is, besides himself. "Whoever did this couldn't have known she'd want to go out for a drive on the spur of the moment."

"Depends on who it is and how well he knew Annie," Cam said. He'd meant to say "the judge." He hesitated, but Frank was a totally straight-ahead guy. "I—we—thought we were keeping what we had going . . . well, something of a secret."

Frank looked down at the grass for a moment. "Probably not, Cam," he said. "This ain't the LAPD, you know? I mean, hell, there was nothing improper about it. You'd been married before. Most of your friends thought it was probably a good thing—for both of you."

"You think this"—Cam pointed with his chin to the smoldering remains of the three-car garage—"was about her decision to dismiss on the minimart?"

Frank's face settled back into a professional mask. "I have no fucking idea what this was about, Cam," he said. "You do understand that you can't work this one, right? Plus, this is most definitely for the feds."

Cam nodded. Then he said he needed to go over to that darkened ambulance. Frank gave him an appraising look and then nodded, but they went together.

The ambulance's emergency lights were dark, but the medical examiner's staff people were there. One of them recognized Cam and nudged the other people. They closed the back doors and stood back as Cam approached. Hell's bells, he thought, who *hadn't* known?

They reached the side of the vehicle and Frank left Cam alone after signaling the ME's people to back on out. Cam knew he wasn't going to open those back doors. The lights were on inside the unit, but he didn't dare look inside, either. Keep what you got, Cam, he told himself, remembering Frank's words. He just stood there for what seemed like a very long time, leaning his head on the boxy white sides of the ambulance. The metal was cool against his forehead, and the sounds of the crime-scene activities faded behind him. A part of his mind sensed that he might be going into shock. Then suddenly, Bobby Lee was there, putting his arm around him and walking him firmly away from that ambulance and the mortal remains of Annie Bellamy.

27

THEY TOOK CAM HOME about two hours later. One of the county hospital doctors who tended to the Sheriff's Office gave him some pills, and Bobby Lee stood there to make sure that he took one, and only then did he allow Cam to be driven home. There were no lights on in the house when they arrived, and the deputy offered to go in and light the place up. Cam told him no, he preferred darkness right now. He let himself in, thanked the guy for the ride, and was shucking his tie when he discovered that Kenny Cox was sitting there in his darkened living room, the two German shepherds flanking his chair comfortably. Cam realized then that he'd seen Kenny's pickup truck out front when the cruiser dropped him off but that it simply hadn't registered. Not much was registering right at the moment, and he knew that pill was beginning to take effect.

"I take it you heard," Cam said, peeling off his gun belt and turning on some more lights. There must have been something in his voice modulating the combination of fatigue, hurt, loss, and whatever meds the doc had given him, because Kenny didn't get up. Cam thought he saw the glint of a glass in Kenny's hand, and then he heard the tinkle of ice cubes. Cam wanted a drink right then, too, but the doc had told him in no uncertain terms: no booze with these pills. He flopped down into one of the living room chairs and stared at nothing.

"I came to make sure you were okay," Kenny said.

"I'm not okay," Cam said. "Not even close, although this pill is starting to work. Surprised the hell out of me, to tell the truth." The two shepherds, well used to Kenny, heard the pain in Cam's voice and quickly surrounded him, pressing noses into his hands and making small noises.

"Didn't know you loved her."

Cam smiled in the darkness and told his dogs to lie down. "*Love*'s too strong a word," he said. "But—"

"Yeah," Kenny said. " 'But.' I hear you."

"I hear myself," Cam said. "It's baffling the shit out of me."

"Another thing I've heard," Kenny said finally, "is that you think cops are doing this shit."

"Doing what shit?" Cam asked somewhat disingenuously. There was a warm fog at the edge of his brain. C'mon, fog, he thought.

"The chair. The threatening messages to the judge. Now this bombing. Killing Annie Bellamy."

Fucking Kenny, Cam thought. The consummate ear to the ground. Calling her Annie, too, like they'd been big buddies. He closed his eyes and didn't say anything. He realized he was that tired, and, in addition, the blessed fog was gaining ground.

"Do you?"

"It's possible, Kenny," Cam said. "The threats, the bombing—all that would require access, the kind of access cops have."

"You think maybe I'm one of them?"

"Of course not," Cam said quickly. Maybe too quickly, he thought. "It's been a bad night, Kenny," he said. "And I've got no evidence. Besides, you of all people are too smart for that kind of shit."

The ice cubes tinkled again. "I hated that woman," Kenny said. "No, that's not right. I didn't really know her, not in a personal sense. I hated what she stood for. For what she did in the courtroom—to me and to other cops. That's what I hated."

"But not enough to screw up your whole life."

"Killing a judge? No, even I'm not that stupid."

"I didn't think so." Cam sighed.

"Glad to hear it, boss," Kenny said evenly. "But you still think it could be cops?"

Cam leaned back in his chair and closed his eyes. At the moment, he didn't give a shit about anything. He opened his eyes when he heard Kenny's truck start up outside, but then he closed them again and let the world go away.

He awoke the next morning with a neck ache. The shepherds were nudging him, still worried. He looked at his watch. It was 1:15. He looked out the window. There was daylight. Okay, so it wasn't morning. Good pill, that. He was still slumped in the living room armchair, hence the aching neck, and the phone was ringing. Answering the phone wouldn't bring Annie back, nor would it cure the neck ache, so he decided to ignore it. He fed the dogs and shooed them outside through the dog door, then shuffled down the hall to his bedroom, stripped down, and took a long, hot shower with the nozzle pointed at the side of his neck that hurt the most. He shaved while he waited for the hot water to do its magic. It seemed to work right about the same time as the hot-water heater admitted defeat.

He got out, dried off, and then the phone started up again. Fair enough. Time to rejoin the human race. It was Bobby Lee. He asked how Cam was doing. Cam told him that he was alive, had just awakened, and needed coffee. The sheriff said he was sending a car and that then they were going to meet with Special Agent McLain, if Cam was up to it. Cam dutifully said he was. Bobby Lee didn't sound convinced, nor was Cam, but it would probably beat sitting around the house. He went to make coffee and then find a fresh uniform.

When he got to the office, McLain was already there, along with the sheriff, Lt. Frank Myers of Major Crimes, and the supervisor of their bomb squad. A captain was there from the State Bureau of Investigation.

McLain led off by reciting the standard formula that they were there to help. Everyone dutifully nodded. The feds were always there to help. He said no decision had yet been made to take over federal jurisdiction in the bombing incident at the judge's home, although they probably would. The sheriff said that he fully expected the federal authorities to assume jurisdiction, and that his office was ready to cooperate in any way it could. McLain announced that terrorism was probably not a factor in the fatal bombing, and everyone nodded sagely. The next ten minutes were occupied with similar pronouncements. Cam mostly just sat there. He was thinking about Annie, and repeatedly telling himself that she had never known what hit her. One moment, she'd been starting the car; the next moment, there'd been nothing but a lingering echo.

"Lieutenant?" the sheriff said, and Cam realized he'd missed a question.

"Sorry," he said, not sure who had asked it. "It was a long night. Say again, please."

"I said," McLain repeated, " 'do you believe the bombing is linked to that minimart case and the subsequent executions on the Internet?' "

"Yes," Cam replied.

"Why?"

"She shouldn't have dismissed those charges."

That provoked a moment of uncomfortable silence, and Cam realized that he needed to dress that comment up a little.

"Four significant things happened prior to this bombing," he said, "Simmonds disappeared, and we now know he was executed. Butts disappeared, and we know he was at least abducted. Given the video, he, too, presumably was executed."

"Why 'presumably'?" McLain asked.

"We have K-Dog's body," he said. "We don't have Butts's." McLain nodded and made a note.

"The other two things were the 'You're next' message to the judge via a supposedly private and secure judicial network, and then the shooting incident at her home. So, yes, I think the bombing is the culmination of a revenge effort."

"On the part of this James Marlor," McLain said.

Cam hesitated and saw Bobby Lee giving him a warning look. "That's been our assumption. Marlor's gone completely off the grid, with one exception—a hit on his checking account a couple of days ago."

"Is it possible that Marlor has had some help?" McLain asked.

The sheriff jumped in on that question. "As in?"

"As in some local police," McLain said. Cam saw that the sheriff didn't seemed shocked at this suggestion, which told him they had already kicked the notion around before he got there.

"Possible, but not likely," Bobby Lee said. "I mean, we're

talking abduction, murder, obstruction, a hit on a judge. That's a big step for any cop to take, no matter how pissed off he might be about a judge's ruling."

"Your people get pissed off at her ruling?" McLain asked.

"You bet your ass they did," Bobby Lee said promptly. "So did I. She was way off base, as far as I'm concerned. But of course that's not our call. And once the AG blessed it, the issue became moot for us. My cops will bitch about it, but that's about it."

McLain nodded and looked down at his notes. "Lieutenant Richter, I understand that you had a personal relationship with Judge Bellamy?"

"Yes, I did," Cam said.

"What was the nature of that relationship, if I may ask?"

"Personal," Cam said.

Bobby Lee made a face. "They were married many years ago, Special Agent," he said. "When the lieutenant was just starting out as a cop and Bellamy was just another lawyer. They got a divorce, and lately they got back together. She'd been through two husbands in the interim."

"What's the relevance of this?" Cam asked. "You think I set the bomb?"

"No, Lieutenant," McLain said. "But we've done some initial checking. You know, basic stuff. Like who might benefit if the judge died."

"You mean pending cases?" Cam asked, puzzled.

"No, Lieutenant. Who might benefit *personally*." He looked at Cam to see if he understood. Cam, clearly baffled now, looked at him and then at the other people in the room.

"Yeah, and?" he said.

McLain leaned forward. "Actually, I called her attorney. Asked about her estate. Did you know what was in her will, Lieutenant?"

Cam thought McLain was starting to sound like an Internal Affairs officer. He shook his head. "She went through three husbands, including me," he said. "She divorced two and one died. She never had children, and she was an only child. I have no idea of what's in her will. Why would I?"

"Because you are the sole beneficiary of her estate," McLain said with a thinly disguised note of triumph. He looked up from his notes. "You, Lieutenant, are now a millionaire." He paused to let that news sink in.

Cam blinked. He didn't know what to say.

"Literally a millionaire," McLain continued. "And this is news, I take it?"

"Sure as hell is," Cam said. He shook his head in amazement. "I never thought about it. I guess I assumed . . ."

"Assumed what, Lieutenant?"

Cam shrugged. "I never really thought about her estate or her money. When we split, she was making a lot more than I was as a detective, so we just split and that was that. Actually, she offered to pay me alimony, but I declined. But money, wills, estates? That never came up between us."

"Something north of ten million," McLain said, consulting his notes again. "You see our problem, Lieutenant?"

"No," Cam said. "I don't. What is your problem?"

"Motive, Lieutenant," McLain said. "James Marlor had a motive to kill the two suspects who burned up his family. He had somewhat less of a motive kill the judge, although one can make that case. There are indications that someone inside law enforcement might be playing in this game. So who might that be? Who might also benefit if the judge dies?"

"And that would be me?" Cam asked in astonishment.

No one said anything. Cam looked at Bobby Lee, who mouthed the word *lawyer.*

Cam shook his head angrily. "Look, Special Agent, you're way the hell off base with this. Annie Bellamy and I were seeing each other. I'd best describe it as an extended experiment. There were no rules, no deals, no promises." He paused for a moment. "The only special thing about it was that we were all each other had in the way of a personal relationship. I don't date, nor did she. It was kind of—I don't know—a relief not to have to do the dance every time, like you might with a brand-new person."

No one said anything for a moment, and then Bobby Lee leaned forward. "Do you think you two might have made it permanent?" he asked. "I don't mean marriage, but—"

"Hell, I don't know," Cam said. "And now I guess I never will. But to answer your question, Special Agent, no, I did not kill Annie Bellamy. I don't have expensive tastes or habits. I've basically got all the money I'll ever need, and no one to support or leave it to. I drive a really old car and a used pickup truck. I live in a modest two-bedroom house out in the burbs. I don't gamble. I don't do drugs. I don't lust after young boys or farm animals. The best part of what Annie and I had going was that that was all we had going, understand?"

McLain nodded slowly, and Cam saw the other people around the table relax. "Then we have to find out who did do this thing," he said briskly, as if everything was settled. "Okay. I've talked to ATF—they'll probably take the lead in the bombing investigation. Sheriff, we'll need your statements, the evidence bucket—you know, the usual."

Bobby Lee said they'd get any support they needed. McLain offered to merge his information with theirs, because in his opinion, Marlor was still the main suspect. Cam just sat there, bemused at how quickly McLain had moved on to other things after putting him through the wringer with a virtual accusation of murder. Bobby Lee gave him a signal and the two of them excused themselves and left the others to talk. They stepped out into the anteroom.

"Sorry about that shit," he said. "McLain told me they'd talked to the lawyer, and that he did not know you. He wanted to see how you'd react. If it makes you feel better, he did say he thought it was bullshit, but he felt obliged to go through the motions."

"Interesting," Cam said. "He almost had me convinced. What do you want MCAT to do now?"

"Let's do this: We'll let the feds start their investigation, give them all our information, and make sure everyone knows they've got the ball. Then maybe we'll work something out."

Cam nodded. He knew they each had a big stake in what happened now. Cam's was personal, the sheriff's professional.

"Who's going to arrange her funeral?" the sheriff asked.

Cam blinked. "I guess that's on me," he said.

28

A WEEK AFTER ANNIE'S funeral, Cam met with her estate lawyer, a Mr. J. Oliver Strong, who confirmed that she had indeed left all her assets to him, minus a few bequests to charity, her church, and her housekeeper. Cam asked how the process worked. Strong told him that as her executor, he would liquidate all the assets and eventually send Cam a check, less legal expenses and the taxes. It would take awhile—perhaps several months—to repair and then sell the real estate, but she had made a lot of money and had turned it all over to professional money managers, so the real estate wasn't actually the biggest piece of the pie.

He asked if Cam wanted to get involved in the liquidation process, or if Cam wanted him to handle it. Cam said he did not want to get involved. He had only one question: When had this will been executed? Strong had apparently anticipated to his question, and the answer surprised Cam: The will had been executed a year after their divorce. The only changes since then had been the charitable bequests and the bequest to the housekeeper, and those codicils had been added three years ago. Otherwise, she'd never changed the will she'd made when she was first married to Cam. Strong said she'd also made a provision that when Cam retired from police work, he would get an income stream from her holdings. She had told Strong once that this was the alimony she should have paid a long time ago. Strong felt this provision was still operative even though she was dead.

As Cam drove back to headquarters, he wondered if he ought to tell the feds about the time line relative to the will. Screw, he decided; they probably already knew. But it sure as hell wasn't as if he and Annie had gotten back together and then she'd changed her will to benefit him. Maybe this had all been Annie's way of making up for her original infidelity. He tried to put that history out of his mind. One day, he'd get a check in the mail and that would be that. He suspected taxes would take a lot of the heft out of his windfall, but either way, he still would rather have had Annie back than any sum of money. The depth of that sentiment still surprised him. Past-due alimony. That was rich.

He stopped in a men's room on the way up to his office and walked into a stall. He was getting ready to come out when two men came into the bathroom to use the urinal. They were talking as they walked in—about him. He recognized one voice as that of Lt. Frank Myers. He didn't recognize the other man's voice.

"Ten million fucking dollars?" the other man said.

"That's the number I heard," Myers said. "That Communist witch left him everything. Just like that. House alone is worth a couple mil, even with the new air-conditioning arrangements for the garage."

"I thought she hated all of us, big and tall, fat and small."

"Not Richter, apparently. You know they'd been married a long time ago, right? Story is, she'd played around a bit when she started making real lawyer money; he found out and dumped her."

"Least he could do, I guess. She pay *him* alimony?"

"Who knows. She has now, though."

There were sounds of flushing and then water running in the sinks. Paper-towel dispensers clattered.

"He ought to just pack it in, you know?" Myers said. "I was there that night. Whatever her public face was in court, she meant a lot to him, and now she's in the ground. Fucked him up, I think. Maybe more than he knows."

"Yeah, I hear some of the guys in MCAT are saying the same thing. Walking wounded. Goddamned women can do that. But he'd lose his pension, he resigned now."

"And why would he give a shit about a Sheriff's Office pension? He's got real money coming. The annual interest alone on ten mil would be—what, seven, eight times his pension? And from what I'm hearing, MCAT is adrift anyway."

"MCAT ought to get *taken* apart," the other man said. Cam finally recognized the voice. It was Sergeant McMichael, of SWAT and Miranda fame. "Buncha fuckin' cowboys, going around in civvies all the time, driving hot cars, soaking up all that overtime money. Pisses people off. All that flash, and usually just one perp in the crosshairs. What the fuck good is that?"

Cam didn't get to hear Myers's answer as they banged out the bathroom door. He sat there for a moment. The idea of quitting had never crossed his mind. He'd just assumed he'd go back to work, back to being the boss of MCAT, back to chasing bad guys. He was a cop. That's what he did. What else would he do? But Myers was right about the money of course. Financially, he could walk out of here tomorrow and never look back.

He came out of the stall and washed up. He stared at his face in the mirror. He'd lost a little weight over the past two weeks and his face was still haggard. He needed a haircut. His uniform wasn't as crisp as it should be. He'd been doing a lot of sitting around and staring into space, and he knew his people had been tiptoeing around him. Even Kenny had been keeping his distance, which was like losing a second friend. Cops weren't supposed to have friends, but they did, in the sense that they came to depend on one another and to meld their minds and reactions, especially in dangerous situations. If friendship was trust, then cops had friends. But he still thought there might have been cops involved in what had happened. Not Kenny, of course, and certainly not in the bombing. But in the executions of those two robbers? He finished drying his hands, pulled out his cell phone, and put in a call to the estate lawyer.

"Is this thing really going to be worth ten million dollars?" he asked.

"More than that, I think, depending on how we come out with the real estate," the lawyer said. "You weren't married, so the IRS and the state are going to claw back a pretty big chunk. Still . . . we'll see four and half, five mil net, probably, or maybe more, depending on where the market is."

We, Cam thought. Our money now, is it?

"You thinking of resigning?" the lawyer asked.

Jesus, Cam thought. Everybody's talking again. He began to feel a little ridiculous, standing in an empty men's room, talking on a cell phone. But at least it was private. Or was it?

"Well . . ." he said.

"I would," the lawyer said. "Let me tell you something, Lieutenant. Lawyers have a grapevine, too, you know? We gossip just as much as cops do."

No shit, Cam thought. "And?"

"And, well, I've heard some rumors that maybe police officers were involved in those executions that showed up on the Internet—that electric chair stuff."

"You're a lawyer," Cam said. "Surely you don't put much stock in rumors, do you?"

The lawyer laughed. "Of course we do, just not in court. But I have to wonder. Smoke and fire stuff . . . That chair thing was new and sensational, but there've been stories about Sheriff's Office cops taking care of business before this."

Cam had heard the stories, but he had always dismissed them as perp chatter: "I'm totally innocent, Your Honor. These cops framed me." But now he wasn't so sure.

"And you think that would extend to what happened to Judge Bellamy?" he asked Strong.

"She was not exactly beloved by the law-enforcement community, and I can also include more than a few lawyers in that community."

"That's total bullshit," Cam said reflexively.

"About Bellamy and her hate-hate relationship with law enforcement?"

"No-o, I'll spot you that one. She didn't have a lot of respect for cops." Or for criminal defense lawyers, either, Cam thought. Called them shit-eaters.

"To say the least," the lawyer said. "We've got three partners here in this firm who do criminal defense work. Now, *they* loved her. We had another lawyer here who went to work in the DA's office. He did not love her. But that's not what I was getting at."

Cam was getting tired of this, especially since what he felt required to say to this guy didn't exactly square with what he'd been thinking. "Which was?" he asked.

"Don't get pissed off, Lieutenant—I'm trying to help you. Consider this: If cops are doing this shit, and they had enough hair on their ass to blow up a sitting judge, who's the next logical target, assuming there is one?"

"I give up," Cam said.

"That would be you, Lieutenant, wouldn't it?"

Cam blinked in surprise.

"Because if cops *are* involved," the lawyer continued, "they'd have to expect you, of all people, to come after them. They killed someone who was close enough to you to leave you her fortune. That makes it extremely personal."

"The money didn't make this personal," Cam said.

"That's not what I meant," the lawyer responded.

"We don't pursue any personal agendas here in the Sheriff's Office," Cam said. "Bobby Lee would have our asses on a pig grill for that. Besides, we're too busy."

"C'mon, Lieutenant," Strong said. "I know you're required to say that, but we're both southern boys here. You've never seen cops get personal? I find that really hard to believe. My wife mouthed off to a state trooper a year ago, racked up five tickets over the next three months—all from other state troopers. It was like they had a list or something. If there are cops behind those executions, they'd have to be worried about you right now."

"Unless, of course, I'm part of this hypothetical vigilante outfit," Cam said, determined to shut this off now.

"Jesus H. Christ, Lieutenant—I don't even want to hear that."

"Precisely," Cam said. "Because it's all bullshit. This is a rumor started by the feds, because they're getting nowhere in finding the prime suspect. Look, any cop knows that killing a judge brings a federal posse. Those guys are pretty good when they want to be, so the chances of getting caught are also pretty good. Premeditated murder carries a death sentence in this state. Or, at the very least, life without parole. And jail for a cop? The needle would be preferable. It doesn't compute. It just doesn't. They may hate her, but no cop I know would take that chance."

"Okay, Lieutenant, I hear you. But if I were you, I'd think about a yearlong trip around the world. Hell, take a leave of absence if you don't want to resign. But get your ass out of town for a while. That's what I would do, I were you."

"You're not me," Cam said as pleasantly as he could. "But thanks for your concern."

He snapped the phone closed. Another lieutenant came into the men's room, nodded to Cam, and mumbled the standard formula about being sorry about Cam's loss. Cam thanked him and headed for the MCAT office. He asked Sue to get him on Bobby Lee's calendar. He'd said what he had to say to that lawyer, that the whole story was crap. He had some reservations about that, but he'd keep those to himself right now. And the lawyer had come up with one good idea Cam had not thought of: a leave of absence. There were miles to go before Annie's estate would be settled, and a whole herd of government leeches who would be trying to latch onto her estate. A leave of absence might cover all his bets.

Sue called and said the sheriff could see him in fifteen minutes.

"We've got a prelim report in on the bombing," the sheriff said grimly as Cam sat down. "BFB."

"We knew that, I think," Cam said, remembering the scope of destruction.

"Yes, but it was a bigger bomb than it had to be, which means that the guy planting it didn't know what he was doing. C-four, apparently, and a relatively old batch, probably stolen from some National Guard armory as long as ten years ago."

"How do they know it's that old?"

"They've been putting trace materials in modern military explosives for the past ten years, so that the residue can be identified as to source. This bomb didn't have any. The ATF lab said the guy used five times more C-four than was necessary, which makes him an amateur."

Or a very angry bomber, Cam thought. "A distinction without a difference to the judge," he said.

The sheriff nodded his acknowledgment. "You called me," he said, glancing at his watch.

"I'd like to request a leave of absence," Cam said.

The sheriff raised his eyebrows. "How long?" he asked.

"A year?"

The Sheriff jotted down a note on his ever-ready pad of legal paper. "If it's a real leave of absence, as opposed to my sending you off to training or some such, it would have to be without pay," he said. "Plus, I couldn't guarantee your slot as head of the MCAT would be waiting for you when you come back."

Cam nodded. He'd anticipated all that. "I'd stay until you pick a successor in MCAT, of course," he said. "So I can do a proper turnover."

"That's probably not necessary," the sheriff replied. "You've had Kenny Cox on the recommended list for lieutenant for some time now. Isn't he the logical candidate?"

Cam nodded. Of course he was. And his nemesis was no longer present for duty.

"Let me ask you something, Lieutenant," the sheriff said. "Are you doing this because of all that money coming your way?"

Cam shook his head. "Not exactly," he said. "Besides, the lawyer says it'll take months to settle out. So, no, this isn't about money."

"Then I'd recommend you go give this some more thought," the sheriff said. "And I say that because you're a cop through and through. A very good one, I might add. I can't imagine you gardening in the backyard, teaching at the local JC, or selling real estate. You've been a cop for a long time, and if you just quit like this, you're going to wonder who and what the hell you are, and that too often leads to a Smith and Wesson sandwich."

"I'm not quitting," Cam said defensively. "I just need some time. And my people deserve a full-time boss, an undistracted lieutenant. That isn't me right now, and I can't predict when it will be. I'm sorry, but that's the truth of it."

"That woman hated cops," the sheriff said. "I'm having a hard time reconciling the depth of your feelings with how she treated us. All of us."

"Maybe that was her public persona, her lawyer act," Cam said. "That's what she'd become famous for, so she stuck with it."

"I didn't mean to pry," the sheriff said hastily, putting up his hands. "It is absolutely none of my business." He paused. "Except when it affects my officers' performance of duty."

Cam nodded. Annie's sudden death most certainly had affected him, although his initial sense of loss was hardening into a cold anger and an even colder determination to find out who'd done this thing. Bobby Lee seemed to read his mind.

"I also have to tell you that you can't go out and play Lone Ranger here," he said. "You go on leave of absence, you and the Sheriff's Office split the blanket, formally and even informally, until you check back in. Your sidearm and credentials stay with me. That's how it has to be."

"Yes, of course," Cam said, telling his first lie of the morning.

The sheriff studied his pad of paper for a long moment. "All right," he said. "Then I think I will act on your request now. Put it in writing—something simple, no speeches, just say 'for personal reasons.' Get it down to me by close of business today."

"Yes, sir."

The sheriff hesitated. "You have your own personal weapons at home, right?"

Cam nodded. What cop didn't?

"Okay, then," the sheriff said. "Don't want you naked out there."

"You think I'll need weapons?" Cam asked.

The sheriff seemed to pick his words with great care. "If you're at all right about there being a vigilante group here in town, you might," he said. "But I'm going to look into that in my own way and in my own time."

"In other words," Cam said, "I should watch my back."

"And your front, Lieutenant."

As easy as that, Cam thought as he walked back upstairs. But what had the sheriff meant by that last bit—"in my own way and in my own time"? Suddenly, he thought he knew.

By 7:30 that evening, Cam, dressed now in jeans and a sweatshirt, was sitting out on his deck with a scotch, a free agent. The two shepherds were across the creek in the back chasing rabbits up on the abandoned Holcomb farm behind his place. The sheriff had been right about one thing: He'd felt positively naked walking across the parking lot to his car, still in uniform, but without his sidearm, badge, and credentials case. Technically, he remained a Sheriff's Office employee, but he was definitely no longer an operational cop.

Now for the interesting part, he thought. The sheriff had told him he couldn't go poking around into the Internet executions case or the bombing incident. Okay, he wasn't going to do that. The feds had the lead, and they didn't like outside interference one bit. What he was going to do was look hard at how a few cops might decide to get together and form a vigilante group. And if that was going on, how long had it been going on? He wasn't breaking any promises. It was more like an academic inquiry. Right.

He scanned the darkened hillside for the mutts and then heard a board on the porch creak behind him. He turned around to find a large man wearing the uniform of a sheriff's deputy and oversize sunglasses stepping out onto the porch with an equally oversize .45 in his hand.

29

"EVENING," CAM SAID AS calmly as he could while keeping his hands visible. He wondered why the deputy was keeping his sunglasses on when it was almost fully dark, but then he realized why when the big man pointed that .45 at him.

"What the fuck, over?" he said finally.

"Listen to me," the man said. He had an educated voice, one with a quiet tone of authority. "Your leave of absence? You need to take that on the road. Somewhere far away from here. Europe would be good. The Far East would be even better. But away." He paused. "You listening, Lieutenant?"

"I understood what you said," Cam replied, keeping his hands still, even though the nearest weapon was in the front hall closet. "But not why. Who the hell are you? What's this all about?"

"This is about your going away on a long trip," the man said, keeping his voice steady, entirely matter-of-fact, as if holding another cop at gunpoint was routine. "You're rich now, so you can go anywhere you want. An ocean cruise, maybe. A long one—around the world. But mostly you have to leave. And sooner is better than later."

"And if I don't?" Cam said.

"Not an option, Lieutenant. You have only two options. One is to leave. The other involves everyone getting into dress uniform, a parade, a bagpiper. I'm sure you get the picture."

"This is because I suggested that cops might have killed those suspects? Cops doing that electric chair business?"

"They said you were smart. Now prove everybody right. Go away."

"Who are you guys anyway?"

The man made a click of disappointment. "Now you're

proving everybody wrong. Maybe you're not smart at all. Think about it, Lieutenant. Use your ass. You've got a ton of money coming to you. You don't have to work anymore. You don't have to be a cop, get your hands all sticky with the pond slime, sweeping the shit off the streets night after night. You can do anything you want. Go anywhere you want. Get any woman you want. A new woman every night. Get yourself a brand-new Merc, instead of that antique you drive around in these days. The one with the green ignition wires? What do you care about law enforcement in Manceford fucking County anymore?"

"Murder is murder, Sergeant," Cam said, noticing the stripes for the first time. But he wasn't from Manceford County—too much belly on him. Bobby Lee would have had this guy going for five-mile runs with him. He also didn't think the man would just shoot another cop. He'd been sent to warn him off. Sure about that? a little voice in the back of his head asked.

"Murder is what happens to decent human beings, Lieutenant. To individuals in good standing with the rest of the human race. Not to landfill seep like those two assholes."

"Judge Bellamy was hardly street trash," Cam said. He wanted to keep the man talking, memorize that voice and soak up what facial features he could see around those glasses. Something about the face was wrong—it was too white, an inside face, not a working deputy sheriff's face.

"Judge Bellamy was a facilitator, Lieutenant," the man said. "One of those judges who makes life on the street possible and profitable. She let two confessed murderers walk out of her courtroom, and she was proud of it. And you know what they say about pride, right? By the way, word on the street is that the feds are taking a look at you for the bombing. All that money. That true? They doing that?"

"Who knows," Cam said, becoming increasingly uneasy. He remembered what he'd said about Will Guthridge and making assumptions about the immunity of cops. "As you can see, I'm still here."

"And that's the problem, Lieutenant. That *is* the problem. We want you gone. Easy way or hard way."

"Who's 'we,' Sergeant? You leave your robe and hood home tonight?"

The man just laughed. "Listen," he said. "We don't want to mess with you, Lieutenant. We're sorry for your loss and all that happy horseshit. But in the meantime, take that trip, why don't you? Make it a long one."

"As in, go the fuck away and live a lot longer?"

"There you go," the deputy said. His gun hand twitched and Cam heard the .45's slide rack forward and lock. He hadn't been aware that the gun had been racked open. He'd mostly been concentrating on that great big hole at the business end. Now it was chambered and cocked and pointed right at him.

"Everyone will understand," the big man said. "Your woman's dead, all the fun's gone out of policing, and you suddenly have more money than God. You fold your tents and steal away into the desert night and that will make perfect sense. And here's the thing, Lieutenant: Either you can arrange it or we can arrange it." He stopped talking for a few seconds, then said, " Bye now."

The man stepped back into Cam's house. Cam heard the dogs barking up on the hill and mentally swore at them. He waited until he heard the front door shut and then hurried through the house. He heard a powerful engine start up outside. He swept aside the curtain and saw what looked like an unmarked police cruiser headed up the cul-de-sac. He tried to catch the plate or the county letters, but the plate light had been turned off. There were no white dazzle side numbers visible as it drove under the streetlight.

Okay, he thought, definitely not Manceford County. But had he been a real cop? Anybody could doctor up a Crown Vic.

As he walked back into his house, he realized his heart was beating at twice the normal speed. Then he heard the phone ringing and grabbed it.

"Good evening, Lieutenant Cam," Jaspreet Kaur Bawa said. "I hope I am not disturbing you."

You're hardly as disturbing as the past few minutes have been, he thought. "No, not at all, Ms. Bawa. Jay-Kay, I mean."

"Oh, good. I always hesitate to call police officers at

home. Although I understand you will be spending more time at home."

"Looks like it," Cam said. "I'm on a leave of absence. But I suppose you already knew that."

"I had *heard* that, Lieutenant Cam," she said. "What will you do, then? Take a trip perhaps?"

"Not you, too," Cam said.

"Pardon?" She sounded genuinely confused, and Cam realized she had probably just been making polite conversation.

"How's the electric chair investigation going?" he asked. "Or are you even still involved? Do you work with ATF, too?"

"I work for the Bureau only," she said. "But the Charlotte field office is, in fact, working closely with the ATF. They know what the explosive was, but there is still discussion about how it was set off."

"Well, I'm out of that loop right now," Cam said. "I think the whole Sheriff's Office is out of that loop, actually. And to answer your question, I don't know what I'm going to do. It won't involve police work, though."

"That was a terrible thing that happened. And the agent and I had only been gone for, what, an hour? I was frightened, actually."

"I can understand that. Dodging a bullet doesn't make the fact of the bullet go away."

"Are you sad, I mean, that this woman was killed? I understand that you knew her other than as a judge?"

Cam explained the history between him and Annie Bellamy. "So yes, I am sad. I think we had a shot at something permanent."

"I am sorry," she said. "I was very angry with her for letting those two killers go free. But I understood there were legal issues. And this country is obsessed with legal issues, isn't it? The story is that you will inherit a great deal of money."

"So it would seem," he said. "That was all news to me, though, and I think it will take some time. Lawyers. Real estate settlements. Taxes. Is this all they talk about around the coffeepot in Charlotte?"

She laughed. It was a pleasant sound. "It made for an interesting bit of gossip, I'm afraid," she said. "The drama of the bombing, the possible connection with the Internet executions, and then your 'surprise' inheritance. Much more interesting than hunting down the latest terrorist alert. But some of the talk was perhaps more serious, Lieutenant Cam."

"You can call me just Cam if you'd like. I'm a paper lieutenant right now."

"Very well, Just Cam," she said. It was his turn to smile.

"So what are they saying?"

"That the motive to execute the two robbers was much stronger than the motive to kill the judge. Until they found out about the will."

"Cui bono," he said.

"Pardon?"

"Cui bono. It's a Latin term that means, roughly, 'who gains'? It's a first principle in homicide investigations. Who stands to gain by the victim's death. Apparently, that's me."

"Yes," she said. "I think that was the thrust of the conversations. Mr. McLain did not take the notion all that seriously, but the ATF people apparently still do."

"Glad to hear I've got McLain on my side," he said. "So, Jaspreet, is that why you called? To warn me that I might be a suspect in the Bellamy bombing?"

"Well, yes," she said.

"Not to worry. I didn't do that. I had no knowledge of any will or inheritance, nor any reason to expect to benefit in any way from Annie's death. Just the opposite, in fact. But I appreciate your concern."

"Well, someone did this terrible thing, Just Cam," she said.

"Yes, someone did, Jaspreet. And I have every confidence that the combined resources of the Bureau and the ATF will find them and get them. Don't you?"

It was her turn to hesitate. "I'm not so sure," she said. "There seems to be more going on with this investigation than a search for one person. But of course I'm only a consultant, so there is much I am not privy to."

"Unless, of course, you turn loose those big mainframes and start reading other people's E-mail," he said.

She laughed again. "I must confess to letting people think I can do much more than I really can do," she said. "Federal ciphers are provided by the NSA. No one breaks NSA code."

"Unless they let you into the office," he said. "And then let you open up a workstation to examine office fire walls and other security devices. Like we did in the Sheriff's Office. And at the courthouse."

"Sometimes that level of access is necessary if I am going to help my clients," she said primly.

"And your computers never forget a line of code, do they?" he asked.

"That is their nature," she said.

"You be careful, Jaspreet," he said. "Like you said, the feds have really big computers these days, and they're looking at all of us now. If they look your way, they'll see you."

"I am always careful, Just Cam," she said. "And I have every respect for this government's computers. But perhaps less for the people who operate them? Anyway, you, too, should be careful, I think. Stay in touch?"

"As best I can, Jaspreet," he said. "As best I can. And I may be hitting the road for a while."

"Take that Dell portable with you, perhaps," she said. "The one you bought two years ago?"

He chuckled. She was showing off now.

"Let me ask you something," he said. "Have *you* looked for James Marlor?"

"I have not. Would you like me to try?"

He told her about the cabin. "I couldn't tell if it had been used recently or not. But it seems the perfect place to lay up."

She asked if he could give her a precise location. He retrieved his notebook and gave her the GPS coordinates they'd given the helo pilot.

"You have a good night, Just Cam," she said. "And stay in touch, yes? Of course you will. Bye."

After he hung up, he remembered that he'd meant to ask her what she had found in Annie's computer, if anything. On the other hand, that was probably a moot point right now.

30

THE NEXT MORNING, HE inspected the Merc, looking for signs of intrusion in the electrical and ignition systems. He looked underneath, checked the brake lines, fluid reservoirs, the locking gas tank cap, the fire wall, and the entire interior of the vehicle. Then he checked for surveillance tracking devices behind the license plate frames and all the other places where he and his people routinely put such devices.

Then he pulled out the Blaupunkt radio and examined it for "extra" features, such as a second antenna or an additional tiny circuit card. A car's radio was a favorite place to put a locating transmitter, because it had constant internal power and was hooked to an antenna. He found nothing out of the ordinary. Then he checked the permanently mounted cell phone, but that also looked undisturbed. The police radio was a multichannel transceiver, but it could not access the Sheriff's Office secure communications system without someone entering a code that changed daily. Because it was a crypto device, it was a totally sealed unit, and there were no signs of intrusions there, either. He checked all the external antennas, looking for extra connections or splices in the antenna cables. Still nothing. He checked the front and rear frames for signs of recent towing. His guys had done that once—picked up a target's car with a platform tow truck in the wee hours of the morning, taken it to the lab for installation of a surveillance system, and then towed it back to the street lot where the crook had parked it. There were no marks on the attachment points of his car.

He then ran all the same checks on his pickup truck, which was a full-size four-wheel-drive Ford with close to eighty thousand miles on it. When he was done, he sat in the truck's front seat and thought about what he'd been doing. No signs of anyone screwing around with his rides, unless it had been a really sophisticated job. So that "deputy" talking about his ignition system? That had been a threat, pure and simple. Bellamy's car had blown up when she'd started it. Yours can, too, partner, he told himself. On the other hand, the ATF report had said they'd found the remains of a timer in Annie's yard. Their opinion was split: Either the timer had been the ignition device or it had been put into the car to deceive those who'd be doing the subsequent investigation. Some of their people were convinced that starting the car had set off the bomb. In their favor was the fact that the bombers couldn't have known Annie would go down there at that particular moment. More important, the word circulating in the Sheriff's Office was that it had been in the ignition circuit. The man last night had kept urging him to take a trip. Okay, maybe he would. There'd been no calls from Kenny Cox asking for details about this case or that, so if there were any loose ends, Kenny was handling them. And like his visitor had said, he was free to go anywhere. The round-the-world cruise might have to wait, but there was no sense in sitting at the wrong end of a shooting gallery, waiting for something bad to happen. He rubbed his chin and felt the beginnings of a heavy beard. He decided to let it grow out—a small statement of his newfound independence. There were no beards permitted in Bobby Lee's Sheriff's Office. And he'd stop getting a haircut every ten days, too. Enough of this Marine Corps stuff. He thought about taking up tobacco again, then smiled. It had taken him two years to quit, and there were some fires too dangerous to play with. But first he'd make one important change. He went back in the house and called his local Ford dealership to find out what they had in the way of new pickup trucks.

Just after sundown that day, Cam sat in an old rocking chair in the shadows of Kenny Cox's front porch. It had cooled off considerably, and he was wearing jeans, a red flannel shirt, his black mountain man hat, and a bulky hunting jacket. He'd driven the old Merc, not willing to let anyone who knew him see him in his new truck quite yet. And his Mercedes was known. He'd passed a Sheriff's Office cruiser set up as a radar trap while leaving Triboro, and the deputy had waved at him. Just for the hell of it, he'd deliberately misspelled his name on the new truck's registration papers, hoping to evade the web of curious computers.

He'd brought along his favorite sidearm from his small collection, a replica single-action army Colt .45. He knew that a single-action revolver would not be very useful in most tactical police situations, but he'd been taught to shoot at a Marine Corps school, which stressed the efficacy of well-aimed fire over the fire-hose approach. Having to pull back the hammer for each shot forced the shooter to slow down and take careful aim. The only things it required when some hopped-up bad guy was shooting at you were a steady hand and unblinking courage. Right now, the big Colt made a heavy, comforting lump in one of the coat's roomy pockets.

He'd parked the car right where Kenny usually parked his own pickup truck—on the circular gravel drive in front of the house. He wanted to talk to Kenny, not surprise him. There was a sliver of a moon out, and silvery gray clouds were blowing across it in the night sky. The farm consisted of almost fifty acres, most of it bottomland along the banks of the Deep River. The two-story farmhouse was on a small knoll at the back of the property, surrounded by aging oaks and within earshot of the river when it was up and running. Kenny maintained the yard around the house, but the fields and fences had long ago reverted to nature. He could just make out the silhouette of an ancient tractor that was turning into a pillar of rust out in one of the fields.

The house itself was set back nearly a thousand feet from the county road, which gave Cam plenty of warning when Kenny finally pulled into the driveway. The truck's high beams fully illuminated him on the porch for about five seconds before they were turned off. Kenny got out, closed the door, and came up the porch steps. He was in uniform.

"You didn't tell me about all the meetings," he said, stopping on the top step.

"Bureaucratic popularity," Cam said. "Comes with the private cube and all that extra money."

Kenny sighed. "You want a drink?"

Cam stood up and followed Kenny inside the house. They went straight back to the kitchen, where Kenny turned on some lights and retrieved a bottle of single malt. He poured them each a measure, handed one glass to Cam, and then hooked a chair out from under the kitchen table. Cam sat down and put his hat on the spare chair.

"One day and you already look different," Kenny said.

"So do you. Congratulations on the promotion."

"Very temporary," Kenny said. "I hope."

"Maybe not," Cam said. They both drank some whiskey and stared off into the middle distance. Cam thought Kenny looked tired.

"About the other night," Cam began, but Kenny waved him off.

"I was out of line," he said. "You'd just been kicked in the teeth. I had no business being there, or bringing up that . . . other stuff." He looked over at Cam. Even sitting at the table, he was still big enough that he had to look down to make eye contact.

Cam nodded for a moment, not trusting himself to speak without saying something stupid. "What's the word on the bombing?" he asked.

"Can't say," Kenny replied. Cam raised his eyebrows.

"Sheriff told me you were on LOA," Kenny explained. "One of the conditions of my taking over was that I wasn't to tell you anything about anything."

"What else did Bobby Lee tell you?"

"That if I did talk to you, it probably wouldn't be a big problem, on account of the fact you'd be leaving town directly."

"He say that?" Cam asked, trying not to show his surprise.

"What's that you got in your jacket pocket there?" Kenny asked.

"Peacemaker," Cam replied. "Replica."

Kenny snorted. "Why bother?" he asked. "Single-action revolver—that's useless."

Cam shrugged, and in the process he palmed the revolver into his right hand and brought it up. Kenny stiffened when the gun appeared. Cam pretended to admire the heavy weapon. "Bobby Lee said I had to hand over all of my Sheriff's Office gear," he said. "But then he made sure I owned some personal weapons. I took that as a hint. So this is what I carry these days. I can still group pretty good at fifty feet." He turned the gun over, half-cocked it, and spun the cylinder. He was careful not to point it at Kenny, whose empty hand was no longer visible, he noticed. Cop instincts. He let down the hammer on the one empty cylinder and slid the gun back into his jacket pocket. By then, both of Kenny's hands were back on the table, and they sipped some more whiskey.

"So what *are* you going to do?" Kenny asked.

Cam shrugged again. "Don't know yet," he said. "Part of me wants to go digging around in this bombing case, but I know that would just piss everybody off."

"Feds would grab your ass up for interfering," Kenny said. "Especially the ATF broomhilda they have on this case."

"Yeah, I do know that. I may just take that trip everyone keeps talking about."

"Sounds like a good idea," Kenny said. "Remove yourself from temptation."

"It's hard, though," Cam said. "So much unfinished business."

"That's our problem now," Kenny said, finishing his scotch. "I think all we have to do is find Marlor, and then this whole mess—that chair, the bombing—will unwind for us."

Cam nodded. "About that other theory," he began. Kenny didn't shut him off this time.

"One guy couldn't pull all this off," Cam said. "So it would have to be a small cell, people who trusted one another implicitly. I'm talking experienced people. Veteran cops."

"Someone like me?" Kenny asked.

Cam didn't reply.

"Or someone like you?" Kenny said with a grin.

Cam stared at him, wondering if this was perhaps an oblique invitation.

"I mean, hell," Kenny said, "don't tell me you've never thought about it."

"In the heat of the moment, maybe," Cam said, remembering one street fight he'd been in as a young cop, where the situation would have justified his just blasting one meth-eyed suspect to hell and gone. Instead, he'd shouted the kid into submission. "But if someone had proposed organizing a squad, no. For one thing, it would be very hard to do."

"Would it?" Kenny asked.

"Hell yes," Cam said. "They'd have to have some kind of initiation process. A new recruit would have to do something way out there that would give the rest of the cell a lock on him."

Kenny nodded thoughtfully.

"And they would need a secure comms system," Cam continued, watching Kenny carefully, looking for some sign of acknowledgment. "A system within a system, maybe," he said. "Some sort of code that could be overlaid on the existing secure comms. And a way to get around without calling attention to themselves."

"I suppose it's possible," Kenny said, his face revealing nothing. "Although what we would see as simple justice, the law would call murder, straight up, every time."

"Damned right, but being cops, they might think they were invulnerable, that being inside the system was such an advantage, they'd never be caught."

"I don't know, Cam," Kenny said. "You know everybody in the Sheriff's Office. We all talk trash about doing bad guys, but no one I know would jeopardize his job and his pension, not to mention his personal freedom, for a moment of satisfaction."

"Business before pleasure, huh?" Cam said.

"Yeah, exactly. I mean, who wouldn't like to pop some lowlife right in front of his mother? But, hell, Cam, get real. Ain't a cop in the world who wants to go inside for that."

"The only thing that could really threaten a cell like that would be another cop who got curious," Cam said carefully. "He or she would have to be dealt with."

"Yeah, and?" Kenny said, listening intently now.

"And maybe that's the initiation fee," Cam said. "A warning maybe, and then some direct action."

"A warning like that would go a long way to proving that the cell exists," Kenny said. "They wouldn't be that dumb."

"Unless they'd already made the decision to solve their problem."

"But we haven't lost any cops that way," Kenny pointed out. "Every line-of-duty casualty we've ever had was thoroughly investigated. No mysteries. Not one."

Cam nodded, no longer looking at Kenny. He was almost afraid to because of what he might read from Kenny's eyes. They went way back. Plus, he'd been expecting Kenny to dismiss the whole notion, to call it all total bullshit. But that was not what was happening here. He decided to change tack.

"I can see one guy being able to take out the two minimart robbers," he said. "But the incidents at Annie's house—that would have to have been organized. Not one guy carrying a grudge, acting on sudden impulse."

"Not one *cop* carrying a grudge," Kenny said carefully. "She was universally despised in the Sheriff's Office. You were probably the only cop in town who felt something besides contempt for her."

Cam stared at his scotch. He knew that Kenny was a lot more complicated than his skirt-chasing, cop-as-cowboy public persona indicated. "It wasn't love," he said. "I think it was more like comfortable companionship."

Kenny sniffed and made a face. "Well," he said, "you know my history with her. She went after other cops, too. Don't know who appointed her God, but that's how she acted."

Cam felt a surge of anger, but he hadn't come here to fight, he reminded himself. He wanted to leave Kenny at least neutralized, so he didn't point out that it was Kenny's own actions that had brought the court's sanctions. "Our relationship was a lot of things," he continued. "Some old, some new, some just spur of the moment. You should also know that she wasn't exactly happy the way the minimart case came out. But that was business, and, if you remember, more our fuckup than hers."

Kenny grunted. "SWAT's fuckup, you mean, and there was a lot more history between her and us than just that case. But either way, this has to be James Marlor. I'm sure of it. Occam's razor: The simplest solution is usually *the* solution. Cop vigilantes don't make sense, especially when there's a perfectly good suspect right there. All we have to do is find his ass. Then it's over."

"I suppose," Cam said. He wanted to leave it on an agreeable note. A disarming note, just in case. "I guess I do need to just get on with the rest of my life."

"And your coming inheritance," Kenny pointed out. "Assuming the feds let go of that."

Cam wondered if that remark was a subtle threat, a little hint that the tables could still be turned. He smiled as he stood up. "Don't have it yet," he said.

"The taxman won't take it all."

"They'll try," Cam said. "Remember what you get when you put the words *the* and *IRS* together."

"Enjoy your time off, then," Kenny said. He remained seated at the table. His face was an interesting mixture of friendliness and quiet satisfaction. He chuckled. "Although the guys're making book on how long you'll stay away."

"I may surprise you there," Cam said, rubbing his stubbly beard. "Might grow to like it."

Kenny tipped his empty glass up at him. "Happy trails, then," he said. "Just remember—if you're going to make the break, make the break. Don't look back. And if we've got a vigilante problem, trust me, we'll take care of it."

"I'm sure you will," Cam said, and then walked out of the house. And that was that, he thought.

From his car, he could see Kenny's face in a front window as he backed out and then drove down the long drive toward the blacktop. He had come out here expecting vehement denial and some good arguments as to why he was all wet about a vigilante problem. Instead, he'd gotten—what, exactly? Kenny had brought up a disturbing possibility—that the investigation might well indeed turn around and focus on the man with all that newfound money. And the sheriff had been awfully quick to accommodate his leave of absence. If they couldn't find Marlor, they very well might come after someone besides Marlor for all three murders.

"If you're going to do something, you better do it quick," he said aloud.

His personal cell phone rang. It was Jay-Kay. "I have good news, "she said. "A Lexington-area cell phone was used four miles from that place in the mountains you are interested in. Do I need to amplify that?"

"You do not, and thank you very, very much."

"Be careful, Just Cam. I may not be the only one who knows that."

31

AS HE DROVE BACK toward Triboro, he received a message from dispatch to meet the sheriff at the Triboro Arboretum. He got there twenty minutes early. The front gates were closed, but the service road on the back side didn't have any gates. The place was a combination arboretum and botanical garden out in the middle of a high-end residential district. Right now, it was more garden than arboretum, courtesy of an ice storm that had taken down about 60 percent of the trees a year ago. He parked toward the back in the staff parking lot, turned off his lights, and waited. There was a single amber streetlight illuminating the entire parking lot. Security wasn't a big issue at an arboretum.

He saw a cruiser with just its parking lights on coming up fast through the service entrance, and a moment later Bobby Lee was getting into the passenger side of the Merc.

"Sorry for all the cloak-and-dagger," he said as he closed the door.

"Me, too," Cam said. He wondered if the sheriff knew how the entire operations department tracked him from street sighting to street sighting. What they called him on the net. He probably did.

The sheriff gave Cam's face a once-over. "You need a shave, Lieutenant."

"Might be growing a beard," Cam said.

They sheriff rolled his eyes. "You're taking this leave of absence far too seriously, I do believe. Look, I've been thinking about what you said."

Cam didn't have to ask what they were talking about.

"I do want you to take a look. See if you can develop

something besides bull-pen rumors on these incidents, or even past incidents. Something substantial."

"Like evidence."

"Yeah, evidence would be nice."

"I'd need computer access," Cam said immediately.

"For?"

"To look into back cases. See if there have been any other suspects who've been evened out."

"Okay, but how would we get you in without people like the system administrator knowing?"

Cam shrugged. "I don't know, Sheriff," he said. "But I know someone who probably does."

The sheriff looked at him blankly for a moment, and then he remembered. "But she works for the feds," he said.

"That was my second consideration," Cam said. "The feds would have to know that I was doing this officially. Otherwise, we cross paths—"

"And they'd freak. Right. Can you trust that woman?"

"With my personal safety? No. But she would be a reliable channel back to the feds."

"How does that help us?"

"Shows them we're looking into our possible problem. Here's what I suggest: You go directly to Jay-Kay. Tell her I'm working undercover. Then you hire her on some pretext. She invents a fictitious consultant or associate, who would be me, and I'll do my thing as I need to, using her for the computer side. That accomplishes two things: It covers my ass, because I'm official, and covers yours, because you're taking proactive steps to see if there's anything going on."

He didn't add the third consideration: If he was working undercover, it would neutralize any federal efforts, and Kenny's, too, for that matter, to pin something on him.

The sheriff nodded thoughtfully. "Yeah, that computes. The problem is that I'd need to leave you on LOA to maintain the cover. Administratively, I mean. That means no paycheck."

Cam smiled. "I'll take it as back pay when we bag the bastard."

The sheriff grunted.

"How will we communicate?" Cam asked.

"I'll get us some pagers," Bobby Lee said. "We talk only when we can meet. No phones, and no damned E-mail."

"And nobody in the Office but you in the loop?"

The sheriff nodded. "Not my preference, but for something like this . . ."

"How about Steven Klein?"

"I'll think about it. Steven likes to showboat sometimes, impress people with what he knows. Especially at dinner parties."

Cam thought about the Sheriff's Office own Internal Affairs people, but then he discarded the idea. "What changed your mind?" he asked.

The sheriff looked over at him. His face was drawn in the amber light and he looked older than Cam had remembered.

"The feds have stopped talking to us," he said.

"Well, I've been talked to," Cam said, and he told the sheriff about his night visitor. The sheriff swore when Cam was finished.

"Could you tag him from a picture?" the sheriff asked.

"Probably not," Cam admitted. "That forty-five had most of my attention. I was just surprised all to hell when he did that. Definitely an older cop. Of course the uniform and the car could all have been a fake, too. Somebody buying an old cruiser from a Sheriff's Office auction."

"Looked and sounded real, did he?"

"Yes, sir, he did."

"And he admitted doing the two shooters and the judge?"

"No-o, he didn't," Cam said. "He was just there to tell me to get out of town."

"Son of a *bitch*. Then it's true."

"He wasn't one of ours, Sheriff," Cam said.

"That's small consolation. I've got to report this to the feds."

"If they're not talking to you, why talk to them?" Cam asked. "Start your own internal investigation, within the county sheriff's network. At some point, they'll want to trade information, and you'll have something to tell them."

"And meanwhile?"

"Meanwhile, I have to make it look like I got the message," Cam said.

32

TWO DAYS LATER, CAM was walking steadily up a ragged trail on the north side of Blackberry Mountain. The Sinclair Reservoir glinted across its two thousand acres to the northwest, casting the trees behind him into black silhouettes in the morning's hazy glare. His two shepherds ranged ahead of him, crossing and recrossing the winding trail, noses down and tails wagging enthusiastically. There was a mist lingering across the tops of the ridges, and the heavy air made his footsteps seem unusually loud. A light breeze flowing down from the heights couldn't make up its mind as to whether it wanted to be warm or cold. Since it was officially bow-hunting season, he wore a bright orange nylon vest over his lumber man's jacket. He carried a six-foot-long yew walking stick, and he had the big Colt in one jacket pocket and a thin can of pepper spray in the other. He was toting a small backpack on his upper back. He didn't plan to stay out overnight, but he never went into the woods without a pack continuing a minimal amount of survival gear, especially in the fall. The western Carolina mountain weather could change seasons on a hiker dramatically in just a few hours, and there were dark clouds gathering over the Blue Ridge to the west.

Cam was no stranger to mountain trails. He went up into the hills and mountains just about every weekend, usually taking his dogs, and had been doing so for many years. Today, the shepherds were wearing their bark collars. He wasn't exactly trying to sneak up on Marlor's cabin, but he didn't want the dogs to give Marlor a half hour's warning that someone was coming, either. Sound carried on these wooded slopes. He climbed steadily, although not in any great hurry. This was probably also a trail used to gather ginseng root, based on some occasional digs he'd seen. More than a few impoverished mountain people supplemented their welfare checks by gathering roots up in these hills.

He'd followed the same route as the Surry County deputy had taken to the abandoned farm on the north side of the mountain. After a half hour's search, he'd discovered what he believed to be Marlor's pickup truck hidden in a ramshackle tractor barn. The doors had been locked, so he hadn't been able to get in to make sure, but he'd cast the dogs out to find a trail, and they'd promptly discovered a small footpath leading up and across the northern slope. He consulted a handheld GPS unit from time to time to make sure he was headed in the right direction. He was watchful as he climbed, aware that sometimes there might be other beings watching him. There were some folks up here who enjoyed startling the flatlanders by standing motionless next to a big tree right off the trail and not moving or saying anything until the hikers were within five feet of them. That was one reason he'd brought the dogs—they would spot any human and most game animals long before he ever would. Otherwise, he'd feel obliged to do his hiking Indian-style: move, stop, look, and listen. It was interesting to do it that way, but not if you were trying to get somewhere and back before full dark descended.

He'd gone to a phone booth and talked to Jay-Kay via a landline to find out how she'd sniffed out the cell phone. With the phone company's help, she'd located the single tower that would serve any cell phone that was activated within five miles of the cabin's GPS coordinates on the south side of Blackberry Mountain. Then she'd located two other towers within line of sight of the cabin, but much farther away, one to the east and one to the west. Atmospherics aside, there was a higher probability that a signal from a cell phone activated up at or near the cabin would hit the first tower, while being rejected by the other two. But if all three towers recorded a hit, even a rejected hit, the topography of the south slope made it likely that the signal was originating on the mountain. Then she had her tigers initiate a continuous scan of the towers' servers for a Lexington-area phone meeting these criteria. There had been only one hit like that, and she'd called him immediately. There was always the chance that it had been an itinerant hiker from Lexington, but it was better than the nothing they'd had for days.

By one o'clock, he'd followed the trail to the edge of the woods behind Marlor's cabin. He'd called the dogs to heel a half hour ago, and now they flopped obligingly down on the pine needles while he studied the cabin for signs of life. He thought he could smell stale wood smoke in the air, which told him that he might be in luck this time. He fished in his back-pack for a couple of sandwich bags filled with dry kibble and fed this to the two dogs. He fished again and pulled out a mushy PB&J sandwich for himself, which he ate while studying the cabin and its surroundings. The woods were now perfectly still and he could just barely hear the brook that ran down the front side of the cabin. The temperature was beginning to drop and the breeze had made its decision after backing fully around to the north. He looked up and confirmed that the sunlight was fading, all of which meant he might be walking back through some snow. The good news was that the trail had been clear and had brought him right to the cabin. The bad news was that his GPS wouldn't be worth much in snow, but unless there was a whiteout, he should be all right getting back.

He heard sounds from the other side of the cabin, and the dogs' ears came up. He saw James Marlor appear at the corner of the cabin briefly and then trudge down out of sight, having headed in the direction of the privy. Cam smiled, pleased that his hunch had worked out. Perfect timing, too, he thought. When Marlor emerged from the privy, buttoning up his clothes, Cam was sitting on the front porch of the cabin with the two shepherds, his backpack on the floor in front of him. Frick lay down on the floorboards and casually eyed Marlor as he walked back to the cabin. Frack sat up, as usual, doing his wolf imita-tion, staring at the approaching man with those close-set amber eyes, but Marlor didn't seem impressed by the dogs. He trudged back up the slope, ignored the two dogs, nodded at Cam as if he'd been expecting him, and stepped inside the cabin, leaving the door open. Cam stayed in his chair but put a hand on his revolver. He heard water being poured into a basin, the sounds of washing, and then Marlor came back out with a bottle of Booker Noe's small-batch bourbon tucked under his arm and two tin cups in his left hand. In his right hand was an old government-issue .45-caliber semiautomatic.

He kicked the other rocking chair around so that he could face Cam and then sat down. He put the big gun in his lap and then poured himself some whiskey.

"Drink?" he asked.

Cam looked pointedly at the .45 in Marlor's lap. Marlor just looked back at him patiently. "No thank you, sir," Cam said finally.

"I'm going to be dead tonight," Marlor announced in a totally matter-of-fact voice. "You can have a drink with me."

Cam tried not to blink. "Put it that way, I guess I will," he said.

Marlor poured him a splash and passed him the cup. He leaned back in the rocker, tipped his cup in Cam's direction, and they both drank. A tendril of damp, cold wind came searching for them around the corner of the cabin, confirming Cam's suspicions of approaching snow. The Booker, at 126 proof, cleaned his sinuses right out.

"Nice dogs," Marlor said. "I had a shepherd once, but she was nuts. Hyper all the time. Chased cars. Caught one."

"They get that way sometimes," Cam said. "Usually, it's the human's fault. They feel it's their duty to be with you, herding you, full-time. If you go away to work all day, they can't do their duty. Drives some of them nuts."

Marlor nodded, and Cam decided just to be quiet. He wanted to see what Marlor would do. For some reason, he wasn't too worried about the gun anymore. It had taken a few minutes, though. Frick was dozing; Frack had his eyes on a squirrel that was tempting fate out in the yard.

Marlor's face was gaunt, indicating he hadn't eaten in awhile. He had aged since the meeting, and his eyes were more intense as he stared at nothing down the front slope, probably thinking that he was going to be dead tonight. He had an unkempt black beard and he needed a haircut. Cam could smell the wood smoke in his clothes. He looked like that portrait of Robert E. Lee painted after the War, with those haunted, defiant eyes.

"Why are you here?" Marlor asked him finally.

"Wanted to talk to you."

"Which way'd you come?"

"I came by helicopter the first time," Cam said. "Nobody home. This time, I hiked in from the north side."

"What brought you back?" Marlor asked.

"I believe you used a cell phone from up here," Cam said.

Marlor sighed and nodded. "I wondered. You guys must be pretty good."

"I wish we'd been better when we arrested those two bastards who destroyed your family."

"Your people screw that up?"

Cam shook his head. "Not mine, directly, but our Sheriff's Office. I remain very sorry for that."

"You come alone?"

Cam smiled. "Here's where I'm supposed to say I have lots of backup out there in the woods. Snipers in the trees. Helicopters on call. SWAT guys suiting up."

Marlor grunted. "I'd have heard all that, I think," he said.

"You never heard me," Cam said.

"True," Marlor admitted. "You're comfortable in the woods, then."

"Very," Cam said. "Look, I'm not here to arrest you."

"Got that right," Marlor said, patting the gun in his lap.

"I really just want to talk."

"Okay," Marlor said, reaching for the bottle again. "So talk." He poured and drank with his left hand; his right hand stayed casually in his lap.

"We found Simmonds," Cam said.

Marlor nodded. "Okay."

"We haven't found Butts, though."

"Probably won't," Marlor said. "Unless you do have a cast of thousands out there. Then you might."

"I'm curious. What kind of gun did you use when you grabbed up Butts?"

"M-sixteen-A-three, with a plugged barrel."

"Plugged?"

"Not enough recoil from blank rounds to cycle the action on an M-sixteen unless you plug the barrel."

"That's a pretty tough neighborhood for a white guy to go into with a load of blanks."

"They didn't look very tough to me," Marlor said. "Of course, all I saw were assholes and elbows."

Cam grinned. "Yeah, we heard."

"I believe some of those tough guys leak a bit when they get motivated," Marlor said. The sunlight was almost gone, the remaining light more a metallic glare than real sunlight. What could be seen of the sun had a ring around it in honor of the approaching front.

"You were a Ranger?" Cam asked.

Marlor eyed him over the tin cup. "Still am."

Cam believed it. "I was army, too, way back when. Worked for an engineer battalion."

"What was your MOS?"

Cam gave him the military occupational specialty code for sniper scout. Marlor, apparently recognizing it, grunted. "What'd you shoot?" he asked.

"Barrett fifty."

"Fine weapon. Army school or marines?"

"The Corps."

The wind picked up enough steam to start the pines moaning. "What was it you wanted to know?" Marlor asked.

Cam decided to go right to it. "We're all curious—how'd you put those executions up on the Internet without being traceable?"

"Went down to an Internet café in Charlotte. Signed on to AOL, took out a free trial membership. Used a fake name, fake everything—they don't care until it's billing time, and you get a couple hundred free hours to start with. Then I created a second screen name, sent the video clip out to a blogger as an e-mail attachment. I just assumed he would put it out there for general entertainment. Then I walked away from the AOL account."

Cam remembered seeing the ubiquitous AOL discs. "We never found any blogger."

"You wouldn't. He could clip the video attachment, post it out there anonymously on the hot-chat site du jour. First guy who saw it would forward it. Something really interesting gets out on the Web, it can spread like wildfire. Think geometric progression. Did the same thing with the second one. You can be anybody with one of those free discs, for a little while anyway."

"Still, I'd think the feds could have traced it back."

"I've heard they're pretty good at that," Marlor said. "Maybe they did but just didn't share. Either way, the best they could do was Charlotte. All *I* know is that it was out and running in about two hours."

"To mixed reviews, of course."

"Not from anyone who knew what those bastards did," Marlor said. He eyed Cam curiously. "What'd you cops think of it?"

"I'm in law enforcement, Mr. Marlor. We frown on citizens taking matters into their own hands."

"I asked what you thought of it. Say, in terms of justice."

"That's a separate question," Cam said.

Marlor grunted again, but he didn't say anything.

"What did you do with Flash?" Cam asked.

"Fed him to the turbines at a hydro plant," Marlor said.

Cam was silent for a minute. Then he had another question. "You said, 'That's two' at the end of the second execution. Like there was going to be a third."

Marlor sniffed and shook his head. "Thought about the judge," he said. "It's one thing to snatch up street trash. But a judge? With police protection?"

"How'd you know she had protection?"

Marlor smiled but didn't answer. Cam considered pursuing that question. Either Marlor had done a drive-by or someone had told him that there were cops on Annie's door. Someone inside the Sheriff's Office?

"Besides," Marlor continued, "I concluded she was just doing what she thought was her job. Unlike the two shooters, who didn't think twice about slaughtering my family."

"She did have other options," Cam said.

"So you said at that meeting," Marlor replied. "So what the hell was she doing?"

Cam hesitated. "We think her decision was aimed at us. She didn't exactly hold most cops in high esteem."

Marlor raised his eyebrows. " 'Didn't hold'? Past tense?"

"Somebody put a bomb in her car the other night," Cam said. "She's dead."

Marlor frowned and pursed his lips for a moment. "I didn't do that," he said finally.

Something in Marlor's overall demeanor made Cam believe him. Here was a man who'd as much as said he was going to commit suicide tonight. He was calm, relaxed, even peaceful about it. Cam believed that if Marlor had planted that bomb, he'd admit it. "How'd you find Simmonds and Butts in the first place?" he asked.

"Got an E-mail," Marlor said. "I assumed it was from somebody inside law enforcement. Didn't much care as long as the information was reliable. It was."

"And that M-sixteen?"

"Mine from a prior life."

"And the blanks?"

"In the mail."

"You mail-ordered blank ammo for an M-sixteen?" Cam asked incredulously.

"No." Marlor said, giving him a look that said he wasn't going to elaborate. Cam waited. "I guess you could call it a gift," Marlor said finally.

"From the same people who sent you the E-mail?

"Maybe. Don't remember."

Cam nodded. Didn't remember, or wouldn't. He wondered if they could find Marlor's computer. "That electric chair still out there somewhere?"

Marlor nodded. "I left the welding machine there, too," he said. "Should anybody want to use it again."

"Welding machine," Cam said. "We didn't think of that. We kept looking for power transformers. Or a generator."

"You were assuming two-forty AC. I used direct current.

Much simpler. Takes a little longer, though." He made a sarcastic clucking sound of faux regret.

And longer was what you were after, wasn't it? Cam thought. The wind puffed up again and he wondered if he'd brought a heavy-enough coat. The dogs noticed it, too, and were sniffing the air. Marlor finished his whiskey and put the tin cup down on the floor. He leaned back in the chair and grimaced, as if an old injury was bothering him. "Are we finished here?" he asked. "I've got places to go, things to do."

"How about the location of that electric chair?" Cam asked.

"I sent a reply to that anonymous E-mail—the one that told me where I could find those two killers? Whoever that is, he knows where the chair is." He gestured at the sky with his chin. "You'd best be getting back. That trail won't be visible if this gets thick."

"Dogs will get me back," Cam said. "Should I try to talk you out of what you're going to do?"

Marlor shook his head. "I killed those two bastards," he declared. "Not your precious judge. I lost my first wife to a drunk driver, who got off with two years of probation because, as the judge observed, it was his first offense. That made it okay, I guess. Justice for my second wife and only child was given away by the so-called justice system. Now that I've squared accounts, it's time for me to wrap it up."

"I guess I could try to stop you," Cam said. "For your own protection."

Marlor snorted. "You didn't come here to arrest or protect me. And I am *not* going to any damn prison."

Cam nodded. Actually, what Marlor intended to do seemed pretty reasonable to him. He'd probably do the same thing. "Anything I can do for you?" he asked. "Anybody to see later?"

"My sister will never understand it," Marlor said. "Tell her something nice, if you want to." He looked out across the slope, frowning. "Where *is* all your backup?" he asked, looking over at Cam. "You guys don't work alone, but I don't sense anyone else out there in the woods." He eyed Cam. "You're a lone ranger on this, aren't you?"

"Meaning what, exactly?" Cam said, trying to deflect him.

"Meaning you're here on your own. You're not in uniform. Those are your dogs, not police dogs."

Amazing, Cam thought. Maybe the approach of death was sharpening Marlor's intuition. What the hell, he thought. Tell him. He explained his situation, and why he was on leave of absence. He also described what he suspected was going on in the Sheriff's Office.

"You and that judge were in a relationship?" Marlor asked.

"Yeah," Cam said. "It was complicated."

Marlor didn't say anything for a minute. "When is it not complicated," he said finally.

"I actually thought you'd just gone away," Cam said. "That maybe some vigilante cops had done the executions. Except for the fact that you absolutely disappeared. Nobody just does that."

"That took some planning and doing," Marlor admitted. "But, no, I did those two bastards. The judge, now, you may be right. About cops, I mean."

"That's why I need to know about that E-mail," Cam said. "The one locating Flash and K-Dog for you."

"Can't help you there," Marlor said. "First, I really don't remember, and frankly, I don't care. In my book, cops taking care of business aren't necessarily bad cops."

"Yeah, they are," Cam said. "Because once that starts, it only gets worse. Especially once they get a taste for it. Then they become like any man-eater."

"Still don't care," Marlor said, rubbing his face with his hands.

"Did you cash a five-hundred-dollar check recently?"

Marlor shook his head. Then he looked over at Cam. "You ever married?"

"Briefly," Cam said. "Didn't work out." Until recently, he thought.

"Any particular reason why you didn't try again?"

"The job seemed enough," he replied, although even as he said it, it sounded lame.

"Then you have no idea of what I've just lost," Marlor said.

"Tell me."

Marlor blinked, poured himself some more of the whiskey, and then started talking. Starting slowly but building in passion, he described every one of the good and valuable things that had been ripped from his life by the holdup. Cam listened to a rushing litany of the individually mundane but collectively seamless and even glowing elements of a good marriage and a solid, loving family: dependent, striving, caring, forward-looking, optimistic about the future, fully participating in the stream of life—rocks, shoals, and all. Cam saw tears on Marlor's face when he finally ran out of steam and words. Marlor was right: He had had no idea.

Marlor finished his whiskey. "Obliterating those two was the least I could do," he concluded.

All Cam could do was nod. This man had abducted those two petty thugs and then broiled them alive in their own juices. And after what he'd just heard, it all seemed perfectly justifiable. He knew this was all wrong, legally, but he was damned if he could marshal any good arguments just now.

"You seem pretty reasonable, for a cop," Marlor said. He paused, as if trying to make up his mind. "I spent a lot of time up in the western Carolina mountains," he continued. "My company gets blamed for a lot of tree damage from its coal plants. My job was to prove that plants in Tennessee and Kentucky were doing the damage, not Duke. The evidence for that is in the Smokies."

"I've been there," Cam said.

"You ever hear of the cat dancers?"

"The what?" Cam asked.

"The cat dancers."

"Nope."

"You should probably check that out. Start up in Haywood County, around the Cherokee reservation."

"What's a cat dancer?"

Marlor ignored the question. "Ask around for a man called White Eye Mitchell. Haywood County. Swain County. Out there on the eastern edge of the park."

"What's a cat dancer?" Cam asked again.

"The answer to some of your questions, I think," Marlor said.

"That's not an answer," Cam replied.

"That's your problem, Lieutenant," Marlor said, looking pointedly at his watch. "Right now, I'm all out of time."

It was obvious Marlor wasn't going to tell him any more, and it was equally obvious that Cam had no real leverage on this man. "We going to find you?" Cam asked.

The sky was starting to get seriously dark. Cam could barely see Marlor's eyes in the shadows of the porch. "I wouldn't think so," he said. "But, hell, I've been wrong before."

"Haven't we all," Cam replied, standing up and retrieving his pack. The dogs got up immediately and bounded off the porch. "I still feel like I should try to talk you out of this."

Marlor shook his head. "I want to go find my wife and daughter," he said. "Have to make the big crossing to do that. If it works, good. If it doesn't, what's it matter? Keep this wind to your left as you head back."

"Any critters I should watch out for?" Cam asked.

Marlor shook his head. "Bears and snakes are all denned up by now. Around here, anything else will be more scared of you than you are of them."

Cam smiled in the gloom. "Funny how they know, isn't it," he said. And then he summoned his dogs and headed for the woods behind the cabin. The first snowflakes began drifting down as he reached the tree line. He looked back, but the cabin was already disappearing in a white curtain, along with James Marlor.

Halfway down the mountain, he heard the boom of a .45. He stopped for a moment. Nightfall had come early to the cabin.

33

IT WAS 4:30 IN the morning when Cam got back to his house. What had been snow in the foothills had been freezing rain down in Triboro, and he'd been lucky to get home, given the mess out on the highways. He turned the dogs loose to run around the backyard and then went into the house. The alarm system was still on, and there were no signs of intrusion that he could see. He checked the Mercedes in the garage, but the small markers he'd left to detect intrusion were all in place. They'd told him to get out of town, so he had. Now that he was back, he wondered how long it would take for someone to know that. He retrieved the dogs and put them in the mudroom to dry off. Then he went into the kitchen and checked the phone. The dial tone was stuttering.

Think, he told himself. If, as a cop, you wanted to know whether or not a subject was at home, you'd have three choices: to go there and see, to maintain constant surveillance, or to tap his home phone. An actual phone tap took a court order, but if all they wanted to know was whether or not the phone was being used, the phone company might be willing to tell them that without the paper work. So don't use the phone. He used his personal cell phone to retrieve the message. It was from Jaspreet, asking him to call her. He deleted the message, and then he had an idea. He accessed the menu for the mailbox and changed his greeting to indicate that he'd be away for the next month. Callers were invited to leave a message, which he could retrieve from the road.

What else might they check? The mail. He went back out front, holding a newspaper over his head, as the sleet had started up again. The mailbox was fairly full, although in the usual American proportions of one-quarter real mail to three-quarters advertising. He sorted through it, returned most of the junk mail to the box, and hurried back into the house. His brain was getting fuzzy with fatigue and he decided to quit for the night. The dogs would tell him if anyone came around the house, and maybe daylight would suggest his next moves. At the very least, he had to tell the sheriff about Marlor. Then he realized he probably shouldn't do that. Cam didn't think the sheriff would understand his quasi-complicity in Marlor's suicide.

At eleven o'clock the next morning, Cam pulled his new truck into the underground parking entrance of Jaspreet Kaur Bawa's ten-story condominium building near downtown Charlotte. He entered the code she'd given him onto the keypad and the device buzzed, spat out a ticket, and raised the gates. The ticket told him he could park in any space that didn't have a name and number. He parked, went into the building, found the elevators, and pressed the button for the ninth floor.

The fast elevator popped his ears. When the door opened, he found himself in an ultramodern glass and stainless-steel lobby. The gold lettering on a pair of double glass doors directly in front of him read TIGEREYE ANALYTICS, and a receptionist buzzed him through the glass doors. The doors to the office suites behind her were not glass, and each of them had large keypads in place of door handles, and a glowing red-lighted box at eye level on the doorjamb. The receptionist confirmed his identification and then asked him to take a seat next to her desk. She then asked him to put the five fingers of his right hand into a small glove-shaped plastic box. The box beeped and she told him to remove his hand. Then she gave him what looked like a pair of opera glasses that had a wire attached. She asked him to look into them and open his eyes wide. He saw a green pattern materializing in front of his vision, which turned to bright red and then to a comforting golden color. He heard another beep as the retinal scan was recorded. Then she made some entries on her keyboard.

"You going to want some DNA, too?" he asked.

She smiled. "Not today, Lieutenant. Jay-Kay is expecting

you upstairs in her living quarters. The stairs are right over there."

Cam thanked her and headed for the stairs, which were wide and beautifully carpeted. He'd been joking about the DNA. The receptionist had not. At the landing halfway up the stairs, instruments were waiting to sample his fingerprints and retina, and then more doors clicked open. He turned and went up the rest of the way. Jaspreet was waiting for him at the top of the stairs. He was conscious of tiny video cameras tracking his every move as he approached.

Jay-Kay, in a silvery two-piece silk suit whose style was something between Indian and Italian, looked as dazzling as her surroundings. "Good morning, Just Cam," she said in her delightful singsong voice. "You found it okay?"

"Piece of cake," he said. He whistled when he took in the view of the city from her living room. It looked like her apartment covered the entire floor. "You own the building?"

"A consortium owns it," she said. "I lease it. I never own the place where I live. That way, I can walk away at a moment's notice if it suits me. But I am the only one who works and lives here."

She took him into the expansive living room and offered coffee. He found the light a bit strong and was thinking about putting his sunglasses back on, when she picked up a remote and changed the tint of the floor-to-ceiling windows.

"How many folks work for you?" he asked, savoring the strong coffee.

"The number varies. I don't have regular employees except for Sharon, the woman downstairs. I form teams when I need to, because each job requires specific expertise. Most of my employees are computers."

"And where are the tigers?" he asked.

"Downstairs in the lab. I have a terminal up here, of course. The sheriff was a bit vague as to what he wanted me to do."

"Are you still working with the Bureau?" he asked.

"I have no active contracts going right now," she said. "If they call, of course I go."

"And did the ATF take over the bombing investigation?"

"All these questions, Just Cam. What is it we're doing here, please?"

He got up from the low leather couch, which had begun to make his back ache. "I'm not entirely sure, Jay-Kay," he said, going over to one of the windows. The traffic down in the city streets was not audible. "I'm officially on a leave of absence, which means no badge, no police powers whatsoever. The sheriff wants me to find out if there's a vigilante squad in the Manceford County Sheriff's Office." He turned to face her. "I told him I'd need computer support of the covert variety—a way into old case files and the county law enforcement's E-mail system."

"Looking for?"

"Again not sure," he admitted. "Evidence, preferably. Indications of past cases that might resemble what happened to the two minimart robbers. E-mail chatter about the bombing. What the cops are saying about the ATF's investigation. The sheriff has come around to the notion that he might have a problem. He wants to look into it before anyone else does."

"What will he do if we uncover evidence of such a thing?"

"Bobby Lee? He'll pull the State Bureau of Investigation in and then hold a press conference."

"He wouldn't cover it up?"

Cam didn't even have to think about his answer. "Negative. Bobby Lee Baggett's so straight that he can't cross his eyes."

She put down her coffee cup and joined him at the window. "It just seems a bit strange to me, having observed the federal agencies, that he would employ a single undercover agent to suss all this out, and not, say, his Internal Affairs, or even the feds themselves."

He was conscious that they were just about the same height. He thought he could detect a hint of perfume in her jet black hair. "I think it's more a case of his wanting to know stuff before anyone else does. He has a way of doing that in his outfit. When he asks an embarrassing question, he usually already knows the answer. Plus, cops investigating cops is a delicate business."

"How so?"

"Well, in a Sheriff's Office, all the veterans came up together. We've protected one another's backs on many an occasion. Sometimes we owe our lives to another cop, and we all have to act that way when we hit a tactical situation. There's an assumption of perfect trust. Hard to investigate someone whom you trust absolutely. And afterward, that trust is forever impaired."

"And why will you be able to do any better job of that?"

He smiled. "Because I have an overriding personal interest in finding out who killed Annie Bellamy."

"But not who killed the two robbers in that horrible chair?"

He turned to face her. "Actually, I know who did that. Ready to keep some secrets?"

When she said yes, he told her she'd been right about Marlor's cell phone. He described the discussion in the mountain cabin and what had happened afterward. He also told her about the warning from the mysterious deputy who had paid him a visit. She went back to the couch and sat down when he was finished. "Does anyone else know this? That James Marlor is dead?"

"I don't think so, unless I was being followed. And I have to admit to making an assumption that he killed himself and didn't, say, fire a shot into the woods to make me think he had. He could still be alive."

"But you don't think so."

"No, I don't. He had nothing left to live for, and he seemed determined."

She was nodding as he said that. "He must have had some help," she said.

"Obviously. Somebody steered him to those two guys. He admitted that. And he sent a reply, telling whoever had contacted him where that chair was."

"Which by now they've done away with?"

"Not necessarily," he said, remembering all those approving comments of the cops who had watched the videos.

"And this is not a double standard here?" she asked. "It's

okay for Marlor, with police help, to have killed the two robbers, but not okay for someone else, possibly police, to have killed the judge?"

"All these questions," Cam said, throwing her own words back at her. "Yes, it's a double standard. Annie Bellamy was a valuable human being. The two mutts were not. Plus, that account is squared: Marlor did what he had to do, and now he's dead, too." He paused for a second. "I seem to remember you talking about heads on stakes in the public square?"

She colored slightly and then nodded. "Yes, I did say that. And I have no problem with what Marlor did. I just wanted to be sure you are firm in your convictions, Just Cam. Because if you uncover the police who are doing this, it will be a war. No time for second thoughts then. Especially if they find out what you're doing before you are finished doing it."

Cam stared down at the floor for a moment. He knew he'd crossed a significant bridge when he'd let Marlor do himself in. "Yeah, I understand that. How about you? You still want to get involved in this? It could be as dangerous for you as for me."

"It sounds like an interesting challenge," she said with a shrug. "Besides, I'm an excitement junkie."

He laughed. "Remember those words," he said. "Now, I'd like to see if you can find my new truck."

She gave him a blank look and he explained how he had purchased a new truck. "Every cop on the force knows my old Merc. Not as many knew my old pickup truck, which I suspect is now speaking Spanish. I want to know if my little deception worked."

She picked up the window remote and darkened the windows. Then she picked up a second remote and pointed it at what looked like a blank wallpapered section of the living room's interior wall. Two panels drew back and exposed a square forty-eight-inch flat-screen display. The faces of two Bengal tigers were drifting around the screen in a screensaver motion. She spoke a single command in a language Cam didn't recognize. The tigers growled in unison, disappeared, and were replaced with an organizational chart of the

North Carolina government. A bright cursor was blinking on the governor's box. She gave more voice commands, which moved the cursor down to the Department of Motor Vehicles, and then the screen was replaced with a single box. She spoke a series of words, which caused numbers to appear in the box, and then the screen blinked and a database page that allowed one to search listings for registered drivers appeared. She spoke individual letters that spelled out Cam's full name, and two vehicles came up, along with his North Carolina driver's license.

"How do you happen to have that password?" Cam asked.

"The Bureau gave me one for the last project. It allows access to all state databases."

"They just hand that out to contractors?"

"No, they hand it out for specific case projects. The password is retired when the contract expires. But: the numbers are generated from a sequential list of numbers allocated to the Charlotte field office. I have that list. My machines simply pick a number that hasn't been issued yet, like the last one I used, plus a few hundred digits down the list. Are those your old vehicles?"

"Yeah, my old pickup truck is still in the system as being registered to me," he said.

"And the new truck?"

"Should be registered to a Cam Bichter, with a *B*."

She made a computer search for that name, but no hits came up. "When did you buy the truck?"

"A few days ago," he said.

"Then the paper hasn't moved through the system," she said. "But none of this will work for very long. The system uses VIN numbers. Eventually, transactions will come up and then there will be a VIN mismatch."

Cam felt his face redden. He should have known it wouldn't work. She piled on a little more.

"The other problem will be insurance. Your new truck is insured, yes?"

"Right. Of course."

"Then your insurance company must report that fact to the

State DMV database. It's the only proof of insurance that the system will recognize these days. Insurance is VIN number–specific. That will blow your cover immediately, assuming someone's actually looking."

"Shit, forgot about that," Cam said.

"Almost every aspect of your life is interlinked these days," she said, causing the screen to fade by issuing another voice command. "Banking, buying or selling anything, medical insurance, life insurance, credit records, and *anything* you do on-line—all are visible to competent eyes."

"So if I wanted to mislead someone . . ."

"You might mail a credit card to some Mexican resort," she said. "One of those solicitations that comes in the mail? Put a five-hundred-dollar limit on it and hope someone steals it and uses it. As soon as he does, you're in Mexico."

"That simple?"

"No, not to law enforcement," she said, brightening the windows again. "Law enforcement would check to see if there was a corroborating airline ticket, hotel reservation, or a rental car—things like that—to support your supposed travel. If you really want to dissemble, it has to be seamless."

"Marlor took out a big wad of cash. He didn't want to confuse; he simply wanted to operate off the grid."

"To the right watchers, taking out the big lump of cash in the absence of, say, a purchase of some kind pretty much signals that that's what you're going to do," she said. "Even you reached that conclusion about Marlor immediately."

Cam nodded. "The sheriff wants me to see if there's an organized death squad operating in the Manceford County Sheriff's Office," he said. "He also wants to know if cops were connected to what happened to Annie. But I don't think I can do anything on the bombing case without bumping up against the federal investigation."

"I would agree," she replied. "They are tracing back on the explosive and trying to solve the question of the timer. They will generate a suspects list and try to connect them to the bomb or its components. And they will pursue the police angle as well, I think. They will look into any disciplinary judgments against police, and then examine the individual police officers for motive."

"Exactly what I would do," Cam said, thinking of Kenny Cox. "And then I'd start interviewing—in depth. Assume they're there, and assume they're organized. Rattle cages."

"Yes," she said. "But if *you* start doing any of that, the Bureau will detect it. That would be a problem."

"How about we work it from a different direction, then," he said. "Let's look at criminals. People like Flash and K-Dog who did crimes but didn't take much of a fall for them. Criminal defendants who went through Bellamy's court, who either walked or waltzed. Who then maybe got dead."

She smiled. "Now you are postulating search criteria," she said. "How far back?"

"Five years? Ten? Hell, I don't know. Pick a window. Maybe start with all the court records on criminal cases in Bellamy's court. Then build a disposition record for each of them. Some will be in jail. Some will be free. Some will be dead. See if there's a pattern to the dead ones."

She sat down and picked up what Cam thought was a magazine, except this one had a screen. She was using a fingernail as a stylus to write on the screen as he talked. "And then," he continued, "see if we can tie in arresting officers, or testifying officers. Find out who did the investigation of each case."

"Are we looking at large numbers of names here?" she asked.

"No," he said. "Each field office has only three, maybe four detectives. Sergeants. The same names will keep coming up. We'll need a way to tie them together."

"That's what my tigers do, Just Cam," she said. "They look for relationships. It's usually a matter of entering enough data."

"Can you do all that remotely? Without having to go the courthouse?"

"If the documents have been stored electronically, yes. The sheriff can get me access. If things are on paper records, it will require a hand search."

"I know all of our daily records have to go on computer," Cam said. "Hopefully, the court has the same requirements. In the meantime . . ."

"Yes, what will you be doing?"

"I'm going to be looking into something called a 'cat dancer.'" He told her what Marlor had told him. He mentioned the name White Eye Mitchell and said that he was going to start out at the Cherokee Indian reservation in the southwestern part of the state. He saw a glimmer of recognition in her eyes.

"I know that area," she said.

"The night rallies?"

She smiled. "Those are just urban legends."

"Sure they are," he said. "Probably like cat dancers, whatever the hell they are."

She stood up. "Call me tonight."

"On my home phone or my cell?"

She smiled patronizingly at him. "You might as well give all that up, Just Cam. Use whatever phone you want to. You simply don't know enough to deceive effectively."

"Swell," he said.

34

AS SOON AS CAM reentered Manceford County, he picked up a tail. From what he could see in the rearview mirror, it was a Sheriff's Office cruiser, not Highway Patrol. He checked his speed, which was about ten miles over the limit, but other vehicles had been passing him until the cruiser showed up. He could see a crowd of cars beginning to bunch up behind the police car. Finally, after about three minutes, as he approached an exit ramp, the cruiser closed in and flashed its headlights. Cam dutifully put on his own turn signal and pulled off on the exit ramp. There was a BP gas station immediately to the right and he pulled the pickup truck into the station and then drove around back. The fact that the deputy had not used his light bar should mean that he just wanted to talk.

The cruiser pulled up alongside, nose-to-tail, and Cam ran the window down. He recognized the deputy as one of the sergeants from the High Point field office. The officer said good morning and passed a pager over to Cam.

"How'd you make the truck?" Cam asked. "I just bought it."

"Yeah, I know. One of our new guys moonlights down at that dealership. Said you'd come in and gotten you a new truck. Red one-fifty with dealer tags. Sheriff's secretary said you'd be coming back from Charlotte right about now and to give you that pager. Have a great day, Lieutenant."

Cam grinned as the cruiser pulled off and headed back to raise hell with interstate traffic. It was still a small town. And Jay-Kay had been entirely correct. He set the pager for vibrate instead of ring and put it in his pocket. Then he followed the cruiser back down onto the interstate. So all of his efforts to pretend he'd left town had been for nothing. And how had the sheriff's secretary known he'd be northbound on 1-85, headed toward Triboro? Because Jay-Kay had probably called the sheriff and requested some access, that's how. But if a lowly probationer knew he was still driving around the county, then whoever was working with that night visitor from another county could also know that. Hell with it, he thought. I'll head home, get some stuff, and then head west to the reservation. Then I won't have to pretend that I've left town.

As he turned onto the westbound ramp of interstate 40, the pager vibrated in his pocket. He pulled it out. The little window read "Tilly's 10." Cam was surprised. Tilly's was a biker bar at the edge of the truck warehouse district on the outskirts of Triboro. It had a rough reputation and had been the scene of many public disturbance calls and even a few knifings and shootings. The only reason the sheriff let it stay open was that it was a great place to pick up parole violators. Bobby Lee's theory was to give the pond scum a place to congregate, and then the cops would know where they were. But Tilly's was no place for a discreet meeting, as the sheriff was known there on sight, and Cam himself would be spotted pretty quickly. On the other hand, it was not a place that cops hung around unless they went in force looking for a specific bad guy. So, Tilly's?

He was tempted to call in and suggest someplace else, but the sheriff had been specific about no phones and no e-mail. Okay, he'd go down there tonight and then try to talk Bobby Lee into going somewhere else. In the meantime, he'd spend the day packing up for his trip to western Carolina.

At 9:45, Cam drove past the biker dive. It was an ugly windowless steel building with a single red neon sign announcing the name of the owner. Tilly Hogg weighed 285 and sported a greasy black ponytail and beard, a massive paunch, and forearms like tattooed hams. He'd adopted the name Tilly because it provoked insults and then fights, and he liked to fight. His real name was Raymond, and he'd fight over that, too. There was a dirt parking lot on three sides of the building and a Dumpster row out back. The lot was treeless and surrounded by ten-foot-high chain-link fencing with angled-out barbed wire on top. The only way in or out was through two chain-link gates manned by a couple of shaved-head mammoths decked out in the obligatory studs, chains, and black leather. There was a herd of Harley hogs parked nose-out around the building, while the rest of the lot contained some muscle cars, pickup trucks, and even two heavily chromed semitractors. White spotlights shone out from the roof over the parking lot, making it almost impossible to see much of anything in the compound from the street. A forceful stream of bar smoke rose out of single ventilator cowl up on the roof, and Cam could hear the thump of a heavy-metal bass as he drove past. The two gate goons didn't even look in his direction. To them, he looked like any other truck driver headed down into the warehouse area to pick up his next over-the-road gig.

When the local cops wanted to sift through the garbage at Tilly's, they'd bring a SWAT team or two, surround the compound, roust the gate guards, and put chains through all the Harleys' wheels. Then one team would loose a pack of K-9 shepherds through the back door, while another would mace whatever came spilling out the front door. Cam had brought Frick along for his meeting tonight, and she sat attentively in the backseat, looking hard at the bar as they drove past. He'd put her spiked collar on, mostly for effect. Frack had gone ballistic when he realized he was getting left behind. Cam had had to crate him up just to get out of the house, but when it came down to it, Frick was the fighter.

Cam was wearing jeans, his steel-tipped SWAT boots, and a sweatshirt under an unzipped windbreaker. The Peacemaker hung down from a left-hand shoulder holster with six in the holes instead of the usual five. He had a double-barreled over and under .38-caliber Derringer in his right sock and a twelve-inch-long shiny black canister of pepper spray canister sitting on the seat by his right thigh. From five feet away, it looked like a Maglite.

The Sheriff normally drove one of those half pickup truck, half SUV hybrids. Cam had tried to spot one of these in the parking lot, but the floodlights effectively blinded him.

He drove down two blocks and then began a surveillance circle of the area, looking for stakeout vehicles or any other indication that other cops might be in the vicinity. He looked at his watch. It was almost ten o'clock. He doused his headlights and drove back up the street until he was half a block from the gate into Tilly's. He pulled over and left his vehicle running, waiting to see who or what might show up. He checked the pager in his pocket to make sure it was on and that he hadn't missed a message, but it was blank.

After ten minutes, a lone Dodge muscle car came rumbling down the street from the opposite direction and nosed up to the gates. One goon lifted the latch and stepped out to talk to the driver, while the other one came out and went around to the other side of the car, his right hand held inside his jacket pocket. Cam could just make out a white face on the driver's side, and then there was a mass of bleach-blond hair sticking out the window as a female lifted her head from the driver's lap. There was much guffawing at the gate and then the first goon waved at the other one to open the gate. The Dodge burned rubber as it leapt forward into the lot. The gate muscle closed the gate again, both of the goons still laughing.

Cam looked at his watch again: 10:00 P.M. There was no way Bobby Lee Baggett could have gotten through that gate by himself, and Cam wasn't willing to try it without substantial backup. "Tilly's 10" had been the message. Tilly's at ten o'clock. Clear as a bell. He decided to wait and watch for another thirty minutes and then get the hell out of there before he attracted some unwanted attention. The patrons of this particular bar would be popping crystal and chasing it with whiskey. They wouldn't think twice about beating a cop to death, putting his body in one of those Dumpsters, and then setting fire to the Dumpster.

Thirty minutes came and went. He'd watched as a brace of obnoxiously loud Harleys had been admitted, each one sporting a pair of protohumans of uncertain gender. But there was no sign of Bobby Lee or any of his troops anywhere on the street. He checked the pager again, but it remained blank. He checked his cell phone to see if there were messages but found none. At that moment, a fight broke through the front door of the bar, with two bruisers beating on each other with what looked like pieces of furniture. The gate guards watched as more bikers spilled out into the parking lot. Cam saw his opportunity and ordered the dog to lie down. Then he started up his truck and swung it out into the street in a lazy U-turn away from Tilly's. He left the lights off until he was pointed away from the commotion behind him, then drove down the block and made a right toward the trucking warehouses. He had to wait at a stop sign at the next corner for three big rigs to cross, which is when he became aware that there was now a vehicle behind him. From the height of the headlights, he thought it might be a semi, but the shape was wrong.

As the last truck cleared the intersection, Cam drove straight across, going deeper into the warehouse complex. The headlights followed without so much as a pretense of halting at the stop sign. He gave Frick another down command, not wanting whoever was behind him to see her distinctive head in the backseat of his truck. He turned left at the next corner and drove down the full length of a warehouse that had two dozen trucks backed up to articulating ramps. He could see forklifts working the freight at one end as he drove by. The vehicle stayed with him, and now he thought he recognized the shape of a Suburban in his mirror when it turned to follow him.

Okay, so who is this? he wondered. No signals were being made, and the pager in his pocket should have been buzzing if Bobby Lee was back there. The Sheriff's Office had some Suburbans, although they tended to favor Ford products. The feds liked Suburbans, he remembered as he made another turn—to the right this time—and sped up to drive down along the back of the warehouse. To his left was a line of trees, and beyond that was the stagnant ditch that had once been Cross Creek. The Suburban stayed with him, going right through the stop sign, just as Cam had done. He knew that the main drag out of this complex would take him back past Tilly's, and that was a direction he didn't want to go. He wondered if there was a way to page the sheriff, but he didn't know any of the numbers. Now that he thought of it, that was odd—the Sheriff had said he wanted the pagers to be a two-way channel. So maybe this page had come from someone else.

He drove down past two more blocks of warehouses and then he had to turn right because the creek and the perimeter road made a dogleg turn to the right. The warehouse parking lots were well lighted and filled with trailers awaiting their trucks. They were also surrounded by high chain-link fences, so he couldn't duck into one of the parking lots. He turned right again, which pointed him back toward Terminal Avenue. The Suburban stayed behind him, neither closing in nor falling back. At the next corner, he saw a semi rig pulling out of the gates beyond a warehouse's loading-dock apron. He turned right and went through the gate as the semi pulled clear, ignoring the angry yell from the elderly gate guard. The Suburban had had to stop to let the semi get through the intersection, but it then turned right and came up to the gate as the guard was trying to slide it closed. Cam drove over to one of the empty loading docks, turned his pickup truck around as if he were going to back up to the dock, and then stopped.

There were trailers on either side of him, but he'd left enough room to drive out if he had to. He left his lights on and the engine running. A forklift driver up on the dock backed out of a nearby trailer with a load, but if he saw Cam he paid no attention. Cam saw the gate guard arguing with someone sitting on the driver's side of the Suburban, and then, to his surprise, a very large man dressed all in black appeared around the back of the Suburban, grabbed the gate guard, and shoved him into the backseat of the Suburban. He then slid the gate fully open and got into the backseat himself, slamming the door shut behind him.

Show time, Cam thought, and there are at least three of them. A driver, someone in the backseat to hold the gate guard, the big guy, and maybe even a fourth in the right front seat. He put his foot on the brake, dropped the truck into drive, and waited as the Suburban came over to where he was parked, stopping about fifteen feet in front of him. All four doors came open at the same time, and as soon as he saw figures in the doors with what looked like baseball bats, he floored it, his truck leaping forward and hitting first the door on the driver's side and then the left rear door, slamming them into them before the men had gotten clear. He swerved left, stomped on the brake, hit reverse, and this time backed up at full speed along the other side of the Suburban, aiming for the doors on the right sides, although by now the men who'd been getting out were diving out of the way of the roaring pickup truck as his rear bumper stripped the doors right off the vehicle. He slammed on the brakes again, put it in park, opened the front passenger door, and sent Frick out the door with a "Get 'em" command. Then he piled out the other door and rolled under the adjacent semi, pulling out the .45 as he went and ending up in the prone position behind the trailer's jack stand.

The shepherd achieved complete surprise, lunging at the nearest of the men on the right side and knocking him down in a frightening display of teeth and growling. From underneath the trailer, Cam couldn't see the top half of the fourth man, but he could see that he had a baseball bat in one hand and a gun in the other and that was enough. These boys weren't here to talk. Aiming at the man's legs, he fired once with the .45 from under the trailer and saw the heavy bullet hit him in the right shin, causing him to scream and windmill backward toward the loading dock, gun and baseball bat flying. He swung the gun around to set up on the man wrestling with Frick, but the guy was already down on the concrete, trying to protect his arms and face from the snarling shepherd. His bat was lying on the concrete.

Cam glanced quickly at the Suburban to see if the other two were getting out, but his position and his own pickup truck blocked the view. Just to make sure, he took careful aim and fired two rounds high, one through each side of the Suburban's windshield. He knew that the trajectory was such that he wouldn't hit anyone in the vehicle, but the big slugs did a satisfying job of showering safety glass all over the interior. He rolled then, in case someone was setting up on him, emerging at the back of the trailer. Frick was still shaking the man down on the pavement like a terrier with a rat. The man Cam had shot was wadded up in a fetal position against the loading dock, holding his broken leg and moaning. Cam sprinted toward his pickup, kicked the gun lying on the concrete under the Suburban, and then opened the door and yelled for Frick, who released the man, bounded over immediately, and jumped into the truck. He could see faces on the loading dock now, and men pointing at the two men down on the concrete. Cam slammed his door and burned rubber as he headed for the gate, which fortunately was still wide open. He hung a two-wheeled turn to the left and bolted out of the warehouse area onto Terminal Avenue, driving back up toward Tilly's. The two gate goons stared at him as he flew by. He was tempted to throw a couple of rounds in their direction just on general principles, but he was past them too quickly. He checked his rearview mirror, but there were no headlights visible behind him.

He slowed as he reached the end of Terminal and turned right onto the access road just as two semis came rumbling by, headed into the warehouse complex. He saw some blood on Frick's muzzle in the glare of their headlights. He'd trained her to run at full speed right at the target, knock the man down, deliver a dozen or so bites to the arms and hands, and then latch onto a coat or a shirt and shake him until he went limp and stopped resisting, all the while making as fierce a racket as she could. Frack didn't have it in him to go on the offensive like that, although he was fully capable of all that and more if somebody came into the house or attacked Cam. At ninety pounds, Frick did just fine, and the sudden appearance of a German shepherd coming at you full tilt, ears flat, about nine yards of ivory showing and a wolf's roar in her throat, was usually enough to paralyze any attacker.

"Good girl," he told her repeatedly as he drove up the access road to the freeway at normal speed, still trying to control the shaking in his arms. "Very good girl." It had begun to rain, and he switched on his wipers. The good news was that he'd gotten away from four assailants, none of whom would be in the mood to do much of anything for a while. The bad news was that four men had sucked him into an ambush by using the supposedly secret communications channel that he and Bobby Lee had set up. If those guys were cops, they'd probably manage to get out of there before the Sheriff's Office showed up in response to the warehouse calls. They'd dump the gate guard somewhere and then ditch the battered Suburban, which was probably a throwaway drug seizure, as quickly as they could in some accommodating auto junkyard. The bullet wound would be harder to explain at an ER, but cops occasionally incurred a few self-inflicted wounds when they'd mess around with their own gun collections. All it would take would be one buddy corroborating the "accidental" circumstances, and then it would turn into a line-of-duty paper drill, along with a lot of ribbing from fellow officers. The dog bites might be a tougher proposition to explain, however.

He tried to recall faces, to remember if he'd ever seen any of those guys before, but the only thing he was pretty sure about was that they were not Manceford County cops, as had been the case with the older deputy who'd come calling at his house. The truth was that he still didn't *know* anything about his attackers. It might easily have been one cop with some buddies, or just a leg-breaking squad for hire. There'd been no badges flashed or anyone yelling "Police officers. Freeze!" at him. So if they were all cops, then this thing was a whole lot bigger than Manceford County.

35

CAM CLEANED FRICK UP and removed the Holly-wood spiked collar, making sure she hadn't been injured in the melee. Then he'd put both dogs out back to patrol the yard. He'd had to use some steel wool to get the Suburban's paint smears off the left front bumper. His cleanup wouldn't withstand examination by a good forensics team, but a casual look would show no damage or marks. The rear bumper showed nothing except a slight deformation in the standoff bar, and he couldn't do anything about that. He'd cleaned the .45 and reloaded it, and he'd washed his hands in paint thinner and then orange sand soap to get powder residues off. Then he carefully vacuumed the pickup truck to get the dog hair out of it. Thinking defense, he slipped a big three-ball trailer hitch, angled high, into the receiver at the back of the truck, and then called the sheriff.

As usual, the sheriff was in uniform when he arrived at Cam's house. Cam handed him a cup of coffee and then they sat down at the kitchen table while Cam told him what had happened earlier. The sheriff nodded at the end of Cam's recitation.

"We had a disturbance call at that warehouse area just after twenty-two-thirty," he said. "By the time the responding units got there, both vehicles involved were gone. The gate guard verified the part about their snatching him up at the gate."

"He wasn't hurt?"

"No. Shook up, scared, but not hurt. They pushed him down in the backseat and told him to close his eyes and be still. That's what he did. Said the two guys on the left side got swatted pretty hard when you hit the doors. He was fixing to climb out over the guy in back when you shot the glass out of the windshield. Thought that was a good time to get back down and stay down. They stopped about a block away from the scene and rolled him out on the street and then took off."

"Minus the doors on the right side."

"Presumably, although they were not found at the scene."

"Anyone see me?"

"Not really. All the truckers could talk about was that dog."

"She evens the odds right out," Cam said.

The sheriff grinned then. He loved dogs, especially police dogs. "I don't understand how they got past the two responding units," he said. "Suburban missing its doors, no windshield. And our people were on-scene within five minutes."

"If they were the two I saw, they were faster than that," Cam said. "But look: I was summoned there via a text pager. How did that happen?"

The sheriff sipped some coffee. "I don't know. I got my pagers from the evidence locker. Throwaways. Got four of them." He looked over at Cam. "I still have all four."

"So someone in evidence control must have run his mouth," Cam said.

"People talk about me and what I'm doing all the time," the sheriff said. "But you're sure these weren't Manceford County people?"

"They weren't Manceford County cops, I know that," Cam said. "But, I don't *know* that they were cops at all."

The sheriff nodded. "There's the rub. You didn't take the first warning, now we get this shit. Guys with baseball bats and guns? People who've obviously operated as a team before?"

"T've got more," Cam said. He then told him about catching up with Marlor, their little talk on the front porch, and what Marlor had said he was going to do. The sheriff listened in silence, an expression of growing disbelief on his face.

"And you just let him do it?"

"He told me he was going to kill himself, but not when or how."

"Why didn't you just arrest him? Bring him in? Get him a shrink or something?"

"Per your instructions, Sheriff, I can't arrest anybody. Besides, I didn't necessarily disagree with his plans."

The sheriff gave him an exasperated look but then nodded slowly. "And he admitted to doing the two shitheads but denied the bombing?"

"And I believed him. If I were on the stand right now, I could say that it was a dying man's testimony. He had no reason to lie."

"And he thought cops were the ones who gave him the lead to those guys?"

"Yes, sir, but he wouldn't reveal where the e-mail came from. Said he didn't know and didn't care." He told the sheriff about Marlor's comment regarding the cat dancers.

"What in the hell is that all about?"

"I have no idea, but I think that's my next step. Get out of Dodge for a while and go see what I can find. You'll have to decide what to do about Marlor."

The sheriff sighed, finished his coffee, and got up to put the cup in the sink. "Man," he said.

"I also told Jay-Kay Bawa, that computer consultant," Cam said. "She may or may not feed back to the feds."

The sheriff came back to the kitchen table and sat down. "They haven't said a word since ATF took over the bombing investigation," the sheriff said. "Not even the random evidentiary question."

"If I go out to the western counties, shouldn't I be back in full status?" Cam asked. "I could end up needing local backup."

"If those guys were cops, and from out of the county, who could you trust out there?" the sheriff asked. "Plus, if I put you back in full status, everyone here would know as soon as the first little old lady in payroll said something."

"Do the paperwork. Put it in your safe. Give me back my creds and my tin. If someone calls in, say the right thing. I've got my own weapons."

The sheriff smiled. "Feeling naked, aren't you?" he said. "Been a cop your whole working life. You let Marlor kill himself because you weren't sure of what you were without the badge and the ID."

"Maybe," Cam said somewhat defensively. "But I also thought that what he said he was going to do made sense. It seemed like . . . justice."

The sheriff shook his head. "Justice is what the system metes out," he said. "Marlor admitted to kidnap and murder. It's not up to us to say how that plays out. It's up to us to bring him in and let him face trial." He frowned. "In a way, your letting him do that is not a whole lot different from the cop—if it was a cop—who told Marlor where those mopes were."

Cam felt his face flushing. "Well then, Sheriff," he said, "if that's how you feel, good luck with your problems—all of them. I think I'll go take that world cruise now."

The sheriff waved his hand. "Don't get your knickers in a knot," he said. "You know that technically, legally, I'm right. Morally, personally, well . . . I don't know what I would have done with that poor bastard under the same circumstances. I know what I'd *preach* about it. But . . ."

Cam waited. The sheriff was well and truly stuck. Normally, he would have been running to the feds or at least to the SBI with this problem. The feds weren't an option, not as long as they were keeping him at arm's length until they were satisfied that the Manceford County Sheriff's Office was squeaky-clean. But in the meantime, he was probably the only asset the sheriff could put in play, especially outside the county.

"All right," the sheriff said. "You hit the road for points west. I'll get Surry County to retrieve Marlor's body. See what you can find out about the dancing cats or whatever it was Marlor was babbling about. Call me at home, tell me where you land, I'll FedEx your stuff. I'll do the paperwork myself tomorrow morning."

Cam nodded. "And I'll use Jay-Kay Bawa as a conduit if I need information from the various LE databases," he said. He hesitated. "I still think you should go see McLain, tell him what you're doing."

"He won't return my calls," the sheriff said.

"Call him again. Say you want a meet—on your turf—or he can watch the evening news and get your message that way. The feds hate that."

The sheriff gave him an appraising look. "Damn, Lieutenant, you're getting slippery in your old age. Tell me this: You still trust Kenny Cox?"

Cam was surprised, but he nodded. "I'm ninety-nine percent sure he isn't part of this. He's too smart to get into vigilante work."

"Ninety-nine?"

Cam thought about it. He couldn't quite define what his reservation was. "Kenny screwed up, got burned by Judge Bellamy, hated her, and made no bones about it. Everybody knows that. Plus, he thought that electric chair was positively wonderful. Plus . . ."

"Yeah?"

"Kenny's one of those cops who live for the edge. He *likes* being a cop and he likes chasing the bad guys. It's his whole life. That's why I don't think he'd jeopardize any of that by doing vigilante stuff."

"Unless he was getting a little jaded, maybe?"

Cam shrugged. "I don't know. We all get bored occasionally. Kenny *could* get that way. I just don't believe he'd act on it. Probably why he spends all his off-duty time chasing women. He can get as much or as little excitement as he wants."

"Okay, because I think I need an inside man as well as an outside man. I want to fold him into what you're doing. I'll also talk to McLain. If he has anything on any of my people, he'll have to show me."

"You want me to go *through* Kenny?"

"No, I want you to come to me, exclusively. But if I need to move assets in your direction, I'll use Kenny. In the meantime, write me up a statement on what happened tonight. Mail it to me at my home address. You taking those dogs with you?"

"Absolutely," Cam said.

"Great idea," the sheriff said. "No question about whose side they're on."

36

FINDING WHITE EYE MITCHELL turned out to be easy. Cam drove out to Pineville, county seat for Carrigan County, and rented a cabin. He used his personal credit card to pay for it, so Jaspreet and her tigers would know where he was. He took one day just to settle in and tried some trout fishing, which gave the sheriff time to send his credentials and badge. The following day, he checked in with the Carrigan County Sheriff's Office and told them he was looking for Mitchell. The man was known locally as one of the backcountry guides who took clients out into the Smokies. One sergeant said that Mitchell was in his late sixties, maybe older, possibly part Indian, part who knew what, but not someone they considered a problem. They'd even used him a couple of times to help search for missing hikers. That said, no one in the Sheriff's Office could tell him how or where to find the man. He supposedly lived up on the edge of the park, but beyond that, no data. They suggested a tour of the roadside gin mills in Carrigan and perhaps Cherokee County and in the towns up on the margins of the Indian reservation. "Just ask around," the sergeant recommended. "Eventually, the word will get to him, and more than likely he'll find you."

Cam piled the shepherds into the truck late that afternoon and dutifully made said rounds, bought more barely touched beers than he had in a long while, and struck out across the board. Only one bartender said he recognized the name, and none of the locals had seen Mitchell for a long time, especially now that fall had arrived and with it the end of the heavy tourist season. Cam told everyone he talked to that he was staying in the Blue Valley cabins off Route 16, that there was no trouble, and that he only wanted to talk to Mitchell.

He got back to the cabin just before 11:00 P.M., brought in some firewood from the front porch for the woodstove, let the dogs run around for ten minutes, brought them back in, and hit the sack. The other cabins appeared to be empty, which was no surprise, given the season and the altitude.

The next morning, he was awakened by a low growl from Frack, who was standing in front of the cabin's single wooden door, hackles up. Frick was trying to see out the front windows, but the outside shutters were still pulled closed. Cam checked the time and saw that it was just after 7:00 A.M. He got out of bed and pulled on jeans, boots, and a shirt over his long johns. Then he found the Peacemaker, checked the loads, and quietly ordered both dogs to sit. He opened the front door and found a swarthy, gray-bearded man sitting in one of the wooden rockers with his back to Cam. He was wearing one of those black mountain-man slouch hats Cam had seen for sale in some of the saloons the previous night, a sheepskin-collared denim jacket, jeans, gloves, and intricately tooled boots with, the tops of which were covered in deerskin. The man looked sideways at Cam, revealing why they called him "White Eye." His pupils were a disturbing silver color, reminding Cam of animated ball bearings.

"You lookin' to talk to me?" the man asked in a gravely voice.

"You Mitchell?" Cam asked.

The man nodded once. "Let me gather up these dogs," Cam said.

"Ain't no need," Mitchell said. "Dogs don't bother me none. And I ain't carryin', so you can put that hog leg away, you want to."

Cam hefted the .45 and then stuffed it into his belt. "Come on in, then. We'll get us some coffee."

The man got up and walked through the door, following Cam. Both dogs stared at him, and he stopped and put out both hands, palms down, in their direction. Frick came over first and sniffed cautiously, then Frack. They seemed very interested in the scent of his jacket. Mitchell sank down into a squat and deliberately bared the back of his neck to Frack, who sniffed again for a good fifteen seconds, established his dominance, and then walked away. Frick came closer and did the same thing, running her nose over the back of his head and hair before she, too, walked away and sat down next to Frack in a corner of the room. Cam could see that they were both watching Mitchell, but there was no longer any tension in their pose. The mountain man had, for the moment anyway, completely disarmed them.

Cam got the makings for coffee going and invited Mitchell to take a seat at the table in the single room, which doubled as a living room and eating area. Mitchell took off his hat and coat and put them on the floor. He was whip-thin and his gray-white hair was shiny with oil and pulled into a tight ponytail. His clothes smelled of wood smoke, but they were clean. Cam got out two mugs and sat down at the table. The gun in his belt pinched his belly, but he ignored it. He rubbed his own growing beard, wondering if it would ever get as expansive as Mitchell's. It was certainly going to be as gray.

"I'm a lieutenant in the Manceford County Sheriff's Office," he said, trying not to stare at those ball bearing–like eyes. Mitchell nodded. His hands were down on the table and bore signs of the outdoors.

"I need to know what a cat dancer is," Cam said.

Mitchell regarded him for a moment. "Why you askin' me?" he said.

"A man told me I should ask you," Cam replied. "A man called James Marlor. You know him?"

Cam saw no flicker of recognition in Mitchell's eyes at the mention of Marlor's name. "Nope," Mitchell said calmly.

"Well, he's dead," Cam said. "Killed himself. Lost his wife and daughter in a holdup that went bad back in Manceford County."

Mitchell blinked, looked away for an instant, but didn't say anything.

"Before he killed himself, he caught up with the two holdup men who had killed his family. Caught up with them, took them prisoner, and then put them in a homemade electric chair and fried them."

Mitchell's eyebrows rose a fraction of an inch. "Sounds right," he said.

"Well, officially, we cops take a dim view of citizens doing that kind of shit."

"Officially," Mitchell said.

"Yeah," Cam agreed.

"What's that all got to do with me?" Mitchell asked.

Cam hesitated. He didn't know this man, or what his relationship had been to James Marlor, if any. Or to rogue cops who were not from Manceford County. The coffee smelled ready. He got up and poured them both a cup. He decided to keep the Bellamy bombing out of it. "I caught up with Marlor. Talked to him before he died."

"You mean before he killed hisself," Mitchell interjected.

"Right. Just before he did that. There are certain aspects of the case we couldn't figure out. He cleared up some of them, but he then suggested I come out here and ask you about cat dancers. He named you specifically. Made no sense to me, but here I am."

"You watch him do it?" Mitchell asked. He was holding his coffee mug close under his chin. When he sipped the coffee, Cam saw that his teeth were in terrible shape, yellow and even black in some places. He looked right at Cam, who couldn't help but stare. Those silvery white eyes were strangely compelling.

Cam hesitated, then told Mitchell what had happened.

"You a cop," Mitchell said. "Ain't you supposed to stop that kind of thing?"

Cam looked away. "I didn't," he said slowly, "because I sympathized with the man. The alternative was for him to go to jail, maybe even end up on death row."

"For doin' what was right," Mitchell said.

"Revenge killing isn't right," Cam said. "That's what the law's for."

Mitchell made a rude noise. "Law's for goddamned lawyers," he said. He pushed back his chair, finished his coffee. He was clearly preparing to get up and leave. "I don't know nothin' about no cat dancin'."

Cam had the feeling that Mitchell knew he'd been holding back. But he couldn't overcome years of police training. When you did an interview, you told the person as little as possible. That way, whatever you were told should not, in theory, be tainted by hints of whatever it was you were investigating.

"All right," Cam said. "I appreciate your coming by. I didn't see a vehicle out there. You need a ride back somewhere?"

"Walked in," Mitchell said, getting his hat and coat off the floor. "Walk back out, I reckon."

"And you've never met James Marlor?"

"Don't b'lieve so. But I take lotsa folks into the back-woods. Could be he was one of them, but I don't recall that name."

"If I need to talk to you again, what's the quickest way I can find you?"

"Carter's store, up to Cherokee," he said, putting on his hat. "But you'n me? Don't b'lieve we got anythin' much to talk about, mister."

"We might," Cam said, for want of anything better to say.

"Real talk's gotta go both ways," Mitchell said. "Strangers come around these here parts, asking a buncha questions? Most folks ain't gonna know nothing a-tall."

"I'll keep that in mind," Cam said nonchalantly. "Appreciate your coming by."

Mitchell nodded at him, went out the front door, and closed it behind him. Neither dog seemed to pay much attention one way or another.

Cam got up and poured himself another mug of coffee. Okay, he thought, that was a waste of time. The man had said he didn't know Marlor or anything about these so-called cat dancers, and Cam had no reason to doubt him. He decided to ask around some more, starting with the local cops.

Half an hour later, he left the cabin with the dogs and walked over to his truck. There had been a heavy frost the night before and all the windows were solid white. He popped the dogs into the backseat and was climbing into the driver's seat when he saw something on the hood. He got back out.

The hood was covered with a substantial layer of white, but right in the middle there was what looked like a paw print. It was a large paw print, complete with identifiable pads and claw marks, eight inches across, maybe a little bigger than that. Cam studied it carefully and then looked around to see if there were any other prints on the ground, but all he could see were his own dogs' prints, which were much smaller than what was on the hood. He examined the big print again. It didn't make sense, just one print. He circled his truck this time, scanning the ground. Nothing except his own footprints and those of the dogs. But that thing was huge, and it definitely looked like a cat's print. He'd seen bear prints before, and this was different.

He walked back over to the cabin and searched the ground around the small building for Mitchell's boot prints, but there were none. Just his own and the scattering of the two dogs' prints from where they'd come out of the cabin and done their usual morning romp, Frack insulting trees and Frick checking out the scents left over from the night. But there was absolutely no sign of where Mitchell had walked in or out, either. He looked up into the surrounding hills, where birches, pines, and a host of bare-branch hardwoods stood frosty sentinel duty on the slopes. A crow lifted off from a distant tree and started raising a racket. How had he managed that, Cam wondered. Walking in and out without leaving a trace?

Then he thought about the paw print. Maybe this was Mitchell's way of telling him something about cat dancers after all. He shivered in the cold mountain air.

37

HE SAW TWO SHERIFF'S cruisers in front of the local Waffle House when he drove into town, so he pulled in. He'd quit going to Waffle House about five years ago, when'd he'd begun to watch his girlish figure, but felt right at home with the sudden aroma of cigarette smoke, hot grease, bacon, and road-grade coffee. Two bulky deputies were having breakfast at the counter, so he took a stool and ordered his usual. He nodded at the nearest deputy, who'd been in the Carrigan County Sheriff's Office headquarters the day before.

"Y'all find White Eye?" the man asked, stubbing out his cigarette and lighting up a replacement. He was fat but muscular, with a round red face and a belly that strained his uniform shirt. His Glock looked like a toy gun in its side holster. His shiny green jacket looked to be a size fifty-two, if not bigger.

"Actually, he found me," Cam said.

Both deputies nodded at that, as if confirming something they already knew.

"Get what you needed?" the second deputy asked. He was younger and thinner than the one right next to Cam, but he had the oversize forearms and biceps of a weight lifter. One of the waitresses came banging by behind the counter and refilled their coffee cups in three quick movements while calling in an order over her shoulder in Waffle House code to the grill man.

"No, I didn't. He was agreeable enough, but said he didn't know anything about what I was asking him."

"And what was that, Lieutenant?" the big deputy said, eyeing Cam through a haze of cigarette smoke.

Cam hesitated but then thought, What the hell. "We've got

us a murder investigation going back in Manceford County. A term has come up that we can't figure out—*cat dancers*. This Mitchell guy supposedly knows what it means."

The two deputies glanced at each other and then resumed work on their breakfast platters. Cam could hear a low mutter of operational traffic coming from their shoulder mikes.

"Y'all ever heard that term?" he asked.

Both of them shook their heads at the same time.

"Manceford County," the big guy said. "That's a ways east of here. Who put you onto White Eye?"

"A suspect," Cam answered. "Someone who's no longer alive."

The deputies absorbed this news with equanimity. There were always risks associated with being a suspect. Cats, Cam thought. He remembered the big paw print. "Are there any big cats up here in the Smokies?" he asked.

"There's lots of stories," the smaller of the two said. "Hikers and rafters come back saying they seen a mountain lion. Some ranchers on the edges of the park claim they've lost stock. But officially, the Park Service says they're all gone in the East."

"We've got bobcat, now," the big cop offered. "Coyotes, some say wolves, even, and lots of bears, too." The smaller one agreed.

"One couldn't easily mistake a bobcat for a mountain lion, though," Cam said.

They both agreed that was right. Cam asked if there were other guides in the area. The deputies told him yes but said most of them closed up their operations and headed south to warmer weather during the winter—not enough business.

"But White Eye stays?" Cam asked.

"White Eye does his own thing," the big deputy said, stubbing his cigarette out on his breakfast plate. "He guides, but he's picky. Likes to do unusual stuff, from what I hear. Take folks out to caves, or secret trout pools. I hear he's kinda expensive, too. Picks and chooses his customers."

"Is he really part Indian?"

"So they say," the man answered. "But there's lots of cons

being run up on the reservation, especially around the casino. A lot of those so-called Indians came down here from New York City. But hey, as long as the tourists don't care, we don't care. If a hustle gets out of hand, we smack somebody down."

The smaller deputy pulled his shoulder mike over to listen to something and then nudged the big guy. "MVA 'with,'" he said. "Rock and roll." They both threw some bills down next to their platters, nodded good-bye to Cam, and headed for their vehicles.

Cat dancers, Cam thought. Something definitely there, the way both of those guys had immediately denied it. No discussion, no asking him to repeat it, no back-and-forth between them, kicking it around. Just plain denied hearing the expression and quickly changed the subject. And White Eye, talking cryptically about conversation having to go two ways. It had to have been White Eye who left that paw print on the hood of his truck. Screwing around with him a little bit?

He was walking back out to his truck when the pager went off in his pocket. He pulled it out and read the number. There was a pay phone back in the Waffle House's anteroom, so he went back in. The sheriff himself answered.

"You having any luck?"

Cam described what he'd seen and heard so far. "I think some people around either know what the term means or have heard it. But everyone's being pretty closedmouthed."

"Find a woman," the sheriff said. "Someone who runs something up there. Isn't there a casino? Find the hookers. They know everything, and women like to talk."

"Hookers? Up here?"

The sheriff chuckled. "Hookers are everywhere, Lieutenant, despite your limited experience."

Cam laughed out loud. "How's it coming with the feds?" he asked.

"Had a brain fart," the sheriff told him. "Asked the SBI to broker a meeting with the Bureau and the ATF. We're calling it a 'comprehensive case review.' We're getting together tomorrow in Raleigh. I used the fact that Marlor was dead to break the logjam."

"So he really did the deed?"

"He did. Surry County found the body. One under the chin. Forty-five, like you said."

Messy, Cam thought. Very messy.

"Kenny and the guys come up with anything more on the bombing or what happened at that warehouse?"

"He's checking statewide to see if there've been any reports of 'accidental' shootings in any of the sheriffs' offices," Bobby Lee said. "Nothing yet. I have to tell you, he still doesn't think cops are involved in what happened to the judge."

"Well, it wasn't Marlor," Cam said.

"We have only his word for that. I need you to pull something out of the hat out there, Lieutenant, and sooner would be better than later."

"All right, I'll go find me some hookers," Cam said, and hung up. He decided it was time to go on up to the casino at Franklin and check it out.

In fact, the casino and attached resort hotel were a total bust in the hooker department. The place was ultramodern, filled with families having a great time, and all the games were digital. He then drove out to some of the smaller strip towns on the approaches to Franklin, cruising streets lined with grease-burger joints, guide shops—most of which were closed for the winter—and motels with names like the Wig-Wam Lodge and the Tee-Pee Campground. He drove around for a while, not quite sure what he was looking for, until he saw Carter's Trading Post, which was a faux log building, complete with a porch lined with rocking chairs. Stone chimneys flanked each end, both of which were serving apparently operational fireplaces. He remembered the name from his little talk with Mitchell, so he pulled into the nearly empty parking lot, let Frack out, put him to heel, and went in. The store was exactly what he expected, filled with racks and shelves containing a few thousand tourist trinkets and featuring a sandwich bar in one corner. One of the plainest females he had ever seen was doing paperwork behind the main counter. There were no other customers in the store.

He wandered around, pretending to look at all the Indian souvenir junk, with Frack keeping station by his left hip. He finally went up to the counter and said good morning to the three-hundred-pound woman tending the register. She smiled at him, which positively transformed her face, returned his greeting, and then said hello to Frack, who just looked at her. She didn't seem to be in the least bit disturbed by the huge black shepherd. He asked if he could get a cup of coffee, and she said, "Sure, honey," and waddled over to start a fresh pot. She was wearing Indian garb of some kind that could have done double duty as an RV cover. The pine floor creaked wherever she went.

"It'll be a couple of minutes," she announced while making up the coffeepot. "Where you guys from?"

"Triboro area," he said. "I'm a lieutenant with the Manceford County Sheriff's Office."

"Yeah, I kinda figured you for a cop," she said pleasantly. "My husband's a sergeant with the reservation police force. Great-looking dog. He police-trained?"

"After a fashion," Cam said. "Frack here's more of a thinker than a fighter. The real deal is out in my truck."

"Two are best," she said. "Most bad actors give it up when they see one German shepherd. I don't know why all cops aren't issued a dog from day one."

"Not enough dogs," he said.

She checked to make sure the pot was going and then came back over to the counter. "So you're up here out of season, which means business. Anything we can help you with?"

He was a little bit surprised at her overt friendliness, but then, her husband was a cop. He decided to play it straight and told her what he was after.

"Cat dancers," she said. "Yeah, I've heard some stories, but they're kinda out there, if you know what I mean."

"I'd appreciate anything you could tell me, because right now I am in the mushroom mode."

She laughed at that. "In the dark and everyone's feeding you shit, right?" she said. "Haven't heard that one since I worked for the state. Well, cat dancers. The way the story goes, there's supposedly this secretive group of men who go up into the Smokies and track mountain lions."

"I thought they were all extinct in up here."

"That's the official line at the Park Service, and they do have a point: No one has taken a picture of one for a long, long time. Lots of bar stories, tales of encounters—but not one instance of proof."

"You'd think with all the electronics people carry around today, someone would have a video or a picture."

"Exactly what the park rangers keep saying: 'Bring us a picture that proves you saw it up here, and we'll change our tune.' Hasn't happened. Anyway, these cat dancer guys supposedly draw lots and then one of them goes out and tracks a mountain lion to its hideout, while the others follow behind to see what happens."

"Track how?"

"The old-fashioned way—on foot, nose to the ground. No dog packs. And then comes the hard part. The tracker has to get close enough to get a picture of the cat's face, and then live to tell the tale."

"A picture?"

"Right. Supposedly, that's the whole point: The guy has to be a good-enough tracker to find a cat, find its hidey-hole, and then get a close-up picture of it without harming the cat and while living through the experience. Call it extreme wildlife photography."

Cam shook his head. "Sounds absolutely nuts to me," he said.

She shrugged. "So are those guys who scale the three-thousand-foot vertical rock faces up in these mountains—without ropes, without a partner up top to catch their asses when something goes wrong. Or the guys who go snow-boarding in the avalanche zone, you know? Nutcases, all of them. Thrill seekers. And most of 'em Yuppies from your part of the state—no offense—bored with making money and having to drive a Beamer."

"Has anyone ever seen one of these pictures?" he asked.

She laughed. "No. Which is why most of us think this is

total BS. Especially because a mountain lion is notorious for sensing when it's being tracked, and turning the game around."

"Damn. Well, how about that, then? Any incidents of people getting torn up by a big cat recently?"

She went over to check the coffee and poured out a cup, even though it wasn't quite finished perking. The smell of charred coffee immediately filled the air from the metal burner. "Well," she said, "not exactly. There have been some disappearances in the Smokies over the past ten years. Sometimes it's a hiker who just doesn't come back from some of the more remote wilderness areas. I've got some flyers over there next to the hat rack. We had two rangers get killed by some meth freaks, and we had that one unsolved rape and murder up on the Appalachian Trail five years ago. College girl, and they never caught anyone. Either way, none of that was tied to a big cat."

"But if there are people doing this stuff with mountain lions, it would figure that somebody would get hurt."

"If they're alone—and that supposedly is the game—they wouldn't just get 'hurt,'" she said with a meaningful smile.

Cam thought about that for a moment and then nodded. Right, he thought. They'd get eaten. It was happening out west with increasing frequency—urban bicyclers, children straying from camp, pets, hikers.

"But then you'd have a disappearance. People coming around asking if anyone had seen Joe."

She shrugged, nodded at the board with the flyers on it, poured herself a cup of coffee, and joined him back at the counter. "We get that, although the Park Service people are who you need to talk to. They handle disappearances in the park. But I'll bet they don't get folks coming up here asking after guys who said they were going to chase a mountain lion."

"If there even are mountain lions up here," he said. "You know a part-Indian guy named Mitchell?"

"White Eye? Sure. I'm not convinced he's really part Indian, at least not Cherokee like me. But he seems harmless enough. Does some guiding. Supposedly a good tracker.

Comes and goes. Doesn't say much. The people who use him seem to know about him in advance."

"What kind of people would that be?"

"White guys, your age. Come into places like this and say they need to get ahold of White Eye. I assume he finds them. But look, you should go over to the Twenty Mile Ranger Station for this part of the Smokies. It's on Route Twenty-eight. You single?"

He was surprised by her question but said yes.

"Great. Ask for Mary Ellen Goode. She's the official naturalist, and she's a also quite a looker."

"Well, that clinches it," he said with a grin. Then he frowned and asked if Mary Ellen Goode had a large boyfriend or, worse, a husband. She shook her head. "Not anymore," she said, a strange look on her face.

38

CAM HAD BEEN SHOWN back to Ranger Goode's office after he checked in with the lobby desk, and Mary Ellen Goode was indeed a looker, as pretty as his previous interlocutor had been anything but. Five six or seven, bouncy short black hair, bright blue eyes, a figure that challenged the official severity of her Park Service uniform, and a room-brightening smile. She was obviously a woman who knew she was good-looking and had long since grown comfortable in her skin. He noticed that she also had a Dr. in front of her name on her Park Service name tag, which he'd discovered while making other observations. Her title was park ecologist. He introduced himself, showed ID, and then asked about mountain lions in the Smokies.

"Officially?" she said. "No gotchee. Panthers are considered to have been extirpated from the ecosystem in the Smokies. No confirmed sightings since 1920."

" 'Extirpated'?" he asked.

"Polite word for hunted out of existence. There was one study done by a researcher named Culbertson in 1977 that suggests there were three to six mountain lions living in the park. They were probably descendants of the original nineteenth-century population. But nowadays we think that what people are seeing, if not a bobcat, might be escaped captive-bred western cats."

"Is captive breeding legal?" Cam asked.

"Not in North Carolina, but it's legal to own western cougars in Tennessee. The cats that have been caught or found along the East Coast states are usually defanged or declawed, which would indicate captive breeding."

"But you do get sightings up here?"

"Sure, every year, a half-dozen or so. But no pictures and no sign whenever we investigate the area of the sightings. And some of the people doing the reporting wouldn't know a mountain lion from a mountain goat."

"How big could one get?"

"A hundred and twenty to two hundred and twenty pounds. Six, seven feet long. A rear pad print ought to be eight to ten inches across, or larger."

He thought about the mark in the frost on the hood of his truck. "Big enough to take down a man."

"Oh, heck yes," she said. "Think about playing with your house cat on the sofa until it gets annoyed and starts working those hind legs. Now scale that up twenty times and visualize a two-hundred-pounder landing on you from a tree, knocking you flat on your back on the ground, hard enough to take your breath away, seizing your whole face in its mouth, clamping its fangs through your cheeks and into your sinuses, its front claws stripping all the meat off your baby back ribs while its hind claws spread your intestines all over the trail. All in about five seconds, with the appropriate sound effects."

"I think I need a bathroom," Cam said.

"Exactly. And they can do all that from the ground or from a run, too, as cyclists are discovering in not-so-remote parts of California. Ever seen the films of a cheetah overtaking a gazelle? A mountain lion can do that, too, just for not quite as long a distance. They mainly feed on deer, which are not slow animals."

"And if this happened to a human, what would the cat do with the, um, remains?"

"Consume all the soft and squishy bits first, then drag the corpse to a hiding place, stash it under a pile of brush or up in a tree, and come back for seconds and thirds until everything was gone. Arms and legs would get carried back to cubs in the den if it was a female. Major bones crunched for marrow. Skulls emptied."

Cam tried to push away the grisly images she was conjuring up. "Would they be easy to track?"

She gave him an appraising look. "Track? I think it's your turn, Lieutenant. What's this all about?"

He told her about the stories of cat dancers, reiterating most of what the large lady at Carter's Trading Post had told him.

She started shaking her head about two-thirds of the way through his summation. "Very, very unlikely," she said. "These are highly secretive nocturnal animals. You'd almost have to know where it was denning up and then work back around its hunting range. And even then . . ."

"Then—what?"

"Well, these cats are interesting. They're first-class hunters and even better ambushers. Highly tuned senses—hearing, smell, night vision, footfall vibrations, and just cat sense. You tried tracking a mountain lion without specially trained dogs? The cat would turn that game around right about sunset and you'd probably end up as dinner."

"How about a really good tracker? Indian-good?"

She shrugged. "It's possible, I guess. But I wouldn't try anything remotely like it. Following a bear would be less dangerous than following a panther. And all this just for a picture? No way."

He'd run out of questions, and as much as he'd have liked to have spent some more time with the beautiful Dr. Goode, he knew he should cut it off. He thanked her very much and asked how he could find some of the better guides in the area.

"Yellow Pages?" she suggested with a smile.

"I knew that," he said.

Cam spent the rest of the day dropping by the various guide and expedition shops in the towns of Lore and Trailwood, learning little. That evening, he went for a short walk to exercise the dogs. It was short because darkness came suddenly and the temperature dropped right along with the light. He fed the dogs, left them in the cabin, stoked the woodstove, and went back into town around seven o'clock to find something to eat. The obvious central attraction was a log cabin lodge affair with wraparound porches. The place advertised mountain cooking, whatever that meant.

Inside, the place was divided into two main rooms, separated by the kitchen area. The smaller room was for dining and the larger contained a well-attended bar. There were two people in the dining room, but more like twenty in the bar, men and women. It was complete with jukebox, tables for two and four, a small dance floor, a place in the corner for a live combo, and a forty-foot-long polished hardwood bar. Cam took a stool at the bar, looked over the surprisingly good scotch selection, and ordered a Maccallan on one rock from one of the very busy bartenders.

He finished his scotch, covered his tab, and headed for the dining room. As he did so, three Park Service rangers in uniform came through the front door, and one of them was the lovely Dr. Goode. She smiled and waved in his direction as they headed for the bar, causing one of the young men with her to give him a suspicious once-over. He waved back and then let the waitress take him to a table.

As he was finishing dinner, the rangers left. A few minutes later, Mary Ellen Goode came back in and headed over. He started to get up, but she waved him down and slipped into a chair.

"Had dinner?" he asked.

She shook her head. "I'll eat later." She looked around for a moment to see if anyone was watching them. "Look, I've been thinking about your inquiry. Is this serious stuff?"

He told her about the chair, and then said only that a suspect had mentioned the term *cat dancers* as being somehow connected to the executions.

"Connected how?" she asked.

"Don't know. Didn't know what the term actually meant until the lady at the store told me. But since there aren't any lions, I guess I'm going to declare defeat and go home."

"Well," she said, staring down at the table for a moment. "That is the official Park Service line. But . . ."

He finished eating, wiped his face, and pushed his plate and silverware aside. "Go on."

"A ranger I used to date two years ago told me the same story once. In fact, he was thinking of opening a file on it, except he thought headquarters would laugh. He thought that it might be real, and that the people doing it were dangerous."

"I saw a ranger packing a belt and a gun last night," he said. "We don't associate our national parks with dangerous people. You know, park rangers are all about warm and fuzzy bunny lectures."

Her face clouded. "We have a lot of sworn officers now," she said. "Two years ago, some bikers from Atlanta came up into our park and set up a crystal-meth lab in a camper. Two of our rangers went to investigate the smell, and the bastards gunned them down when they knocked on the door. One of them was Joel Hatch, my fiancé."

"Oops," Cam said. "Sorry."

"Well, bad things happen to good people, don't they? The good news is that an Atlanta field office special team caught up with them in a bar in Blue Ridge, Georgia. Apparently, there was 'resistance.'"

Cam nodded. "Resistance is good," he said. "Saves everyone a lot of time and effort. But I'm sorry for your loss." He wanted to tell her about Annie, then decided to let it go.

"Thank you," she said automatically. "Anyway, I'd forgotten all about the mountain lion business until you asked today. I'd never heard that term—*cat dancers*—however."

"Know a guide named White Eye Mitchell?"

"Only by reputation. Supposedly, he found a missing hiker five years ago, after everyone else had given up."

"'Supposedly'?"

"Well, we think he'd guided the man in. Rumor was that they'd argued, and Mitchell left him out there to calibrate his thinking. There was no proof of that, of course, and the rescuee wasn't talking, for some reason."

Cam nodded. "Could I ask you to pulse your sources up here, see if you can find out anything more?"

She looked at him. "You're leaving some things out. Am I right?"

"Yes," he said. "But I can assure you that my case is as serious as a heart attack."

"Does our local sheriff know you're here?"

"Yes, he does. I checked in with him first thing. But he doesn't have the whole picture, either, and I was able to convince him that that was a good place to be right now."

"Okay," she said. "I'll ask around. How long will you be up here?"

"Don't know," Cam said. "Until I find something."

"Or something finds you," she said softly.

It was his turn to stare at her. "What's that mean, exactly?" he asked.

"I'm not entirely sure," she said. "But the truly wild parts of this country seem to attract all kinds of edgy critters these days." She shook her head, as if trying to dislodge a bad thought. "Don't mind me," she said with a smile. "Too much time alone, I think."

"I can actually relate to that," he began, but then two men came into the dining room from the bar and called hello to Mary Ellen. She excused herself and went to join them. Cam paid his bill and went outside. It was cold but clear, and he felt like taking a walk. The night sky was so filled with blazing stars that he actually stopped in the parking lot to look up at them.

When he got back to his truck, he found a small note stuck into the driver's side window.

"I get off duty at 2300," it said. "We need to talk." This was followed by a cell phone number, and the signature was "M.E.G."

39

WHEN HE GOT BACK to the cabins, he noticed there'd been a dusting of snow in the area—nothing serious, but enough for the headlights to show that a vehicle had driven down the line of cabins sometime after the snow and then back out. Before he turned into the parking space by his cabin, he got out of his truck to see if the vehicle had stopped, but it didn't look like it. Straight tracks; big tires, like his own. He squatted down and fingered the edges of the tracks, which, had this been the movies, should have told him how old they were. Instead, the bits of snow and mud melted in his hand and told him absolutely nothing. Indian scout you are not, he decided.

The snow leading up to his cabin, on the front steps, and frosting the edges of the porch was undisturbed. He let the dogs out and watched them to see if they focused on anything near the cabin, but Frick just ran around, nose down, tail up, while Frack made the trees afraid. He checked the little back deck, where a rusty barbecue on wheels lived, but there were no signs that anyone had been back there, either—unless, of course, they had come before the snow. Enough of this paranoia, he said to himself, and went inside to see if he could raise Bobby Lee Baggett. As he expected, he got voice mail. He left his name and cell number and then went to retrieve the dogs.

As he started a fire in the woodstove, he remembered that he'd left the gun in the glove compartment. He went back out to the truck to retrieve it and took another look around. His was still the only cabin that appeared to be occupied. The only other light on was up at the office at the top of the lane. The sky was partially overcast now and the air smelled as if there was some more snow on the way. There was no wind to speak of, and the only sounds were coming from the truck's engine as it cooled down in the frosty air. He tried to imagine a mountain lion padding silently around the cabins, green eyes glowing in the darkness. He heard a clump of snow fall out of a pine tree behind him and caught a glimpse of a big gray night bird, bent on murder, gliding soundlessly down into the ravine behind the line of cabins. The surrounding foothills were indistinct dark shapes. The cabin park was too low for him to be able to see the Smokies, which began their humped stretch west to Tennessee only about five miles away. He shivered in the night air, called in the dogs, and went back into the cabin, where the woodstove was already producing an agreeable heat. He broke out his Shelby Foote and settled in to read about Grant's expedition against Fort Donaldson on the Tennessee River.

The sheriff called him back at 10:00 P.M. Cam gave him an abbreviated summary of what he had been doing, and told him he'd found out what the term *cat dancers* meant.

"Hopefully it's not too fanciful."

"Actually," Cam said, and the sheriff groaned. He groaned some more once he heard the story.

"Mountain lions? Guys chasing mountain lions for—what, the thrill of it all?"

"For a picture, actually," Cam said. "That, of course, explains everything. I guess it's extreme wildlife photography. Stand by for the documentary."

"Judas Priest!" the sheriff said. "And the rangers told you that mountain lions are extinct up there?"

"Unfortunately, yes. The occasional sighting is excitedly reported—always with absolutely zero evidence."

"And how exactly does this lunacy connect to our problems here in Manceford County?"

Cam began to make Indian chanting noises, indicating that he had no idea, and the sheriff swore. "Look," he said. "Spend another day or so up there, report back in, and we'll see where to go from there."

Cam said, "Yes, sir," and hung up. He went to the front door and looked out. It was snowing again, and this looked like more than a passing squall. He wondered if he ought to go out and put the snow straps on his tires, but he decided against it. The radio forecast had been for snow squalls only.

Half an hour later, he made the call. To his surprise, a man answered.

"I got a note to call this number," Cam said. "Who am I talking to?"

"You want to know about the cat dancers?"

"That's right," Cam replied.

"Where you staying?"

Cam told him.

"Which cabin?"

"The only occupied one," Cam said. "You'll see my truck. You a park ranger?"

"Half an hour," the man said, and hung up. Cam found his notebook and wrote down the phone number, along with a note to get Jay-Kay to ID the number for him. He checked on the snow again, and it was still coming down.

He considered his situation. He'd just told a stranger where he was, and that he was alone in an empty cabin park. There was only one road in and out of the cabin area. If another wrecking crew showed up, it would be a really bad idea to be trapped in the cabin. His problem was that he hadn't brought extreme-weather clothing with him, he had only one nontactical weapon, and he had no backup. He'd just assumed that the phone number belonged to Mary Ellen Goode, the smiling ranger.

He figured he could try calling the local law. And tell them what? he wondered. Frick got up and came over to see what was bothering him. Well, I do have some backup, he thought as he rubbed her ears. Frack came over to get in line for ear rubbing. The shepherds could read his mood like a book.

He put on a second pair of socks, long johns, and a sweater over his flannel shirt. He got his coat and gloves, and happily found a knit watch cap in his bag. He opened the front door and looked out. The truck's hood was already showing an inch or so of snow. The sky was completely overcast, and the whirling snowfall obiterated things far off. The vehicle tracks in the road were just faint indentations now.

Leaving the lights in his cabin on, he locked the front door.

He got the Peacemaker and his Maglite, took the dogs out the back door, and walked next door to the adjoining cabin. He went around the side that was away from his cabin to minimize visible footprints. He tried its front door. It was locked, but the back door was not. He let himself and the dogs inside and unlocked the front door from the inside. The outside temperature wasn't that cold, maybe low twenties, and it was the same in the empty cabin. The dogs had their winter growth, so they'd be all right. He set up a chair so that he could see the snow-covered lane between the cabins, then sat down to wait. The only lights visible were the one he had left on inside his cabin and the amber security light up at the office. He tried the phone in the empty cabin, but it was dead. He thought about going back and getting his cell phone but decided against it. He had the dogs, he had the Colt, and he wasn't where he'd said he'd be. If hostiles were coming, he should have at least a little warning.

After thirty minutes of waiting, he got up and moved around the empty cabin. The mountain cold had begun to penetrate his layers of clothes and he needed to restore his circulation. The shepherds were curled up by the front door. Frack was dozing; Frick was watching Cam. The snow was still coming down outside, and now the security light up by the road was only an amber glow. The smoke from his cabin's woodstove was barely visible.

The caller may have given up the trip because of the heavy snow, he thought. And if it had been a setup of some kind, the baby blizzard going on outside would make that sort of thing pretty difficult. He decided to give it another half hour and then go back to his heated cabin. He checked out the back windows of the cabin, but the falling snow obscured the ravine and hills behind the cabins. He went back to the front windows—no change: heavy snowfall, everything out front losing definition. And then Frick started growling, a deep belly growl that woke Frack right up. He got up and went to the door and sniffed it, then looked back at Frick, who was still lying on the floor, ears up and growling.

"What's out there, killer?" Cam said, and she got up and went to one of the front windows. Whatever it was, Frack hadn't heard it, and Cam certainly hadn't heard it, but he'd learned not to ignore the dogs when they sensed that something wasn't right. He palmed the Colt and began to go from window to window in the dark cabin, taking care not to silhouette himself. Although there was no moon visible, the snow brightened up the night and he could see pretty well in the immediate area around the cabin. Frick continued to growl quietly, although less frequently now. She lay down by the front door. He thought about letting her out, but if it was just a deer, she might get lost in the ensuing chase. A bear prowling for garbage would be another possibility, except they should be hibernating. He'd heard no vehicle noises, so it probably was wildlife.

He did another circuit of the windows—nothing. He thought about going back to his cabin, getting the cell phone, and dialing that number again, but something told him not to go outside. He watched the dogs. Frick had her head down on the floor, eyes watchful. Frack, as usual, watched her, ready to take his cue from his more aggressive partner. Neither dog seemed very anxious to go outside, which told Cam that they just might be afraid of whatever was out there.

Then Frick went on alert at the front door, getting up and staring at the door but making no sound, her hackles up and her body rigid in that position of readiness from which she would launch an attack. Frack moved behind her, also staring at the crack at the bottom of the front door. Cam moved to the back corner of the room, standing in relative shadow, and watched windows. There wasn't a sound from outside—no wind, no crunch of footsteps in the snow, no engine noises. His breath formed little puffs of vapor in the frigid air. Then he thought he heard something out front, but it was a very subtle sound: a soft pressure on the porch floorboards, a muffled creaking noise. Cam crouched down in the corner of the room, pointed the Colt at the door, and watched the front windows very carefully, looking for shapes or shadows against the snow glare. The dogs suddenly went down on the floor, their eyes still locked on the front door but their bodies no longer poised for an attack. In fact, Frick was assuming what was almost a submissive posture, while Frack lay there, his head cocked sideways, listening to something. Cam thought he, too, sensed something out front, but knew he was just reacting to the dogs.

The three of them remained motionless in the cabin for another minute, and then the dogs slowly relaxed. There were no more sounds out front, which made Cam turn slowly on his haunches and watch the back windows and door. He snapped his fingers quietly and Frick scuttled over, followed by Frack. He sat them down next to him in the corner. They nuzzled his hands, their tails sweeping the floor, their relief palpable. Whatever it had been, it was gone, and since their senses were a whole lot better than his, he stood up and walked to the front windows. The shepherds went with him, plastered to his legs. He studied the front yard and the road but saw nothing but more snow. Then he looked down at the porch floorboards and saw a line of large soup plate–size prints in the shallow snow that had accumulated there.

The prints stretched across the full length of the porch and looked a lot like what he'd seen on the hood of his truck that morning. There was a shiny film of ice already forming in the depressions. His breath started to fog the glass, so he could not make out details, such as which way the animal had gone or whether or not there were claw marks, but now he had a pretty good idea of what had come calling, and why the shepherds had been scared.

He checked all the windows again, but there was nothing moving out front. He gathered up the dogs and went out the back door, gun in hand, in case they'd all guessed wrong. He stood for a moment on the back deck, the snow tickling his face. It was coming down hard enough that he could hear it sleeting through the trees. The dogs stayed right by his side, and they were no longer relaxed. He went back over to his cabin and walked around it to see if there were any tracks, but the snow looked undisturbed until he got to the front porch, where there were shapeless indentations in the snow out in front of the cabin. He tried to trace them out to the street, but the snow was too deep. They did seem to go from the front of his cabin over to the front of the other cabin, so the cat had been able to tell where he'd been hiding. But where had it gone?

He told the dogs to go find it, and they reluctantly moved away from him, sniffing the rapidly disappearing indentations, circling close by, but clearly unwilling to go romping off into the dark woods. It's definitely colder out here in the falling snow, he thought as he scanned the shadows in the trees and listened for any sign of wildlife. The dogs were back, looking at him as if to say, Was that good enough? The security light up at the office was barely visible now, and he looked hard at the road to see if there were any signs of a vehicle. Then there was movement in the tops of the trees and he felt a sudden draft of colder air come down from the slopes above him and blow through the line of cabins. The snow went sideways for a moment and both dogs put their noses up to scan the moving air. Frick made that low, rumbling growl again, and Cam felt the hair rising on the back of his neck. He backed toward the porch of his cabin, the dogs going with him while he kept the gun pointed out into the whirling darkness. The wind made a slow moaning noise, and somewhere off to his right a pine top cracked and then fell to the ground with a thump. He kept backing until he felt the steps against his heels; then he stepped up and reached for the door handle.

It didn't move. It was locked. He thought for a moment, and then he remembered he had locked it before going out the back door.

He moved sideways off the porch, still watching the lane and the surrounding cabins. The shepherds were both staring at something in the direction of the office. Cam reached the corner of the building and looked around it into the darkness. He studied the snow, but there were no indentations. He stepped around the corner and, keeping his back to the wall of the cabin, slid sideways along the rough boards until he reached the back corner. Then he realized he didn't have the dogs with him. He called them as quietly as he could, but they didn't come. He swore and edged his way back to the front of the cabin, feeling very exposed in the weird twilight created by the falling snow. He peered around the corner.

The dogs were gone.

He looked around and thought he saw their tracks headed

up the lane toward the cabin office. The wind groaned again, and the snow wheeled in response. Something else cracked out in the woods. Get inside, a little voice in his mind told him. Get inside *now*.

He did. Not trying to be quiet anymore, he crunched through the snow to the back deck and let himself into the cabin. The sudden warmth from the woodstove was very welcome. He closed the back door and then went to the front windows to see if the dogs were visible, but they weren't. He flipped on the porch light, unlocked and opened the door, and called them. No dogs. He closed the door. If they'd gone after a deer, they could be in real trouble, because a deer could run them to death in these hills. If they'd gone after a goddamned mountain lion, they could be in real trouble, period. The wind outside was blowing steadily, rattling the damper in the woodstove's chimney. He threw another log into the firebox and stirred the coals. He knew there was no point in going out there on foot to look for the shepherds. He could easily get himself lost in all this snow, and he was neither dressed nor equipped for that kind of adventure. Then something banged against the back door and he heard the skittering of anxious claws. He unlocked the door and let them in. They ran around the cabin excitedly, panting hard, as if they'd just had great fun with a good chase. He was tempted to yell at them, but then he realized he was very grateful that they were back.

He checked that all the doors were locked and then got ready for bed. Tomorrow, he'd get a trace on that cell number and see if he could track down the mysterious caller. The wind outside blew harder and sleet rattled against the roof. He turned off all the lights, took another look out all the windows, set the Colt on the nightstand, and climbed into the heavily quilted bed. The dogs dropped down near the woodstove and curled up. As he drifted off to sleep, he thought he heard a distant prolonged shriek above the wind coming down from the ravines, but he assured himself that it was just the snowstorm. Of course it was.

40

MARY ELLEN GOODE WAS still smiling when Cam walked into the ranger station the next morning. The day had dawned bright and clear with about a foot and a half of snow on the ground and the temperature at a sinus-clearing ten degrees. The county roads had been scraped and sanded, so he'd made decent time getting over to the ranger station. He'd put on his old deputy's hat and mirrored sunglasses against all the glare, and Mary Ellen told him with a perfectly straight face that no one would ever make him for a cop.

She offered coffee, which he accepted gratefully. He explained the note and the phone number, and her eyebrows went up.

"That's the number for my Park Service cell phone," she said. "But it's right over—" She started looking around her desk. "Well, it was right here. This is the charger for it."

"Whoever left the note knew who owned the phone, then," he said. He wondered if it was someone in this office. He explained about the initials on the note.

"I don't like the sound of that at all," she said, frowning.

"Let me ask you this: If tracks were made by a large animal in the snow, and then there was more snow, and then a crust of sleet froze over all of that, could someone still excavate those tracks?"

She stared at him for a moment. "I couldn't, but we have a ranger on staff who maybe could."

An hour later, they were back at Cam's cabin. A long, tall, gaunt ranger who looked uncannily like Abraham Lincoln was down on hands and knees on Cam's front porch, scraping gently at the snow with a woodworker's two-handled draw knife. Cam and Mary Ellen, trying to ignore the cold, watched from the doorway.

"Normally," the ranger said, "the prints would simply fill up, but you said you saw an ice film. That's what I'm looking for. How deep would you say the snow was when the prints were made?"

"A dusting of blown snow," Cam said. "Maybe half an inch deep, max." Everyone's breath was making puffs of condensation in the frigid air, and now the ranger shifted to a paintbrush as he continued to mine his way down through the snow along a three-foot-long stretch outside of the area where Cam and the dogs had trampled the snow. Two pairs of German shepherd ears were silhouetted in one of the front windows.

"Well, this may all be for nothing if that layer of ice—wait one. Here we go. Here we go."

The ranger shifted from the big paintbrush to a much smaller and finer brush and began to remove snow across the line of his original shallow trench. As he did so, the outline of a paw print began to emerge.

Mary Ellen looked over his shoulder and whistled quietly. "That's a big bastard," she said.

"Yeah, I'd say so," the ranger replied, clearing away the remaining snow almost grain by grain until he had the entire print revealed. Then he brought out a spray can from his field kit and sprayed the entire depression. "It's a silicone-based compound," he said. "Solidifies on cold contact." The material was barely tinted yellow, but it held enough color that the print was thrown into clear relief. This time, Cam could see the tops of claw marks, and it wasn't a happy sight. The ranger sat back on his haunches. "Now that," he declared, "is a large cat. Panther, from the size of it." He laid down another coat of varnish, waited a moment, and did it again.

"And not declawed," Mary Ellen commented.

"Yeah," the ranger said, getting a camera out of his pack. He fired off several pictures from different angles, then swore, fished out a ruler, laid it down by the track, and did it all again. The print looked to Cam to be about ten inches across.

"Are there more?" the ranger asked.

"There was a line all the way across this porch," Cam said. "The dogs came in here by the door and messed stuff up, which is why I had you start in the middle of the porch. There's more on that porch over there."

The ranger nodded and began to extend his trench in the snow. "I need one, preferably two more to get an estimate of stride length. This'll take awhile."

The dogs were getting antsy inside the cabin, so Cam went back in, and Mary Ellen followed. She greeted both dogs affectionately and they returned her favor.

"Great shepherds," she said. "Let me guess: This one's business and this one's pleasure?"

"Right you are," Cam said. "Although the black one can do business if he has to. Mostly, he just scares people by looking at them."

"Works for me," she said. "How'd they react to that thing being out there on the front porch?"

"Not bravely," he replied.

"Smart dogs," she said, shaking off her coat now she was inside the warm cabin. She had a field belt on under her bulky Park Service coat, complete with what looked like a Glock. She saw him looking. "I don't leave home or the office without it," she said. "Ever since . . ."

"Copy that," he said. He went into the kitchen to crank up the coffeepot.

"So tell me, Lieutenant, what's really brought you out here to our neck of the woods? You show up, telling tall tales about cat dancers, somebody steals my phone, makes an appointment he doesn't keep, and now we have the first real sign of a mountain lion in thirty years."

He pulled over a kitchen chair and sat down to wait for the coffee to percolate. She stayed over by the woodstove, nonchalantly trying to warm her buns and her hands at the same time. They both heard the ranger out front say "Yes!" as he found another track.

Cam stared down at the table for a long moment while he tried to figure out how much to tell her. She didn't bug him.

"Did you guys hear about those executions that showed up on the Web?" he asked her.

"Oh, yes," she said. "That was all over the LE networks. I saw one of the videos."

"That happened in our neck of the woods, and I'm working the whodunit."

"All by yourself?"

He smiled. Smart girl, he thought. "For the moment," he said. "We might have a wee bit of federal help."

"Ah," she said. "So there's one game for your federal friends and another one for the sheriff's edification?"

"Something like that," he said. He wasn't willing to broach the possibility that there were vigilantes involved.

"And didn't you have a judge get herself blown up down there in Triboro recently?" she asked. "Was that related?"

"Maybe," he said. "Truth is, we really don't know, but we're keeping our options open. She was the judge who let the two fryees loose on a technicality."

She gave him a shrewd look from the other side of the room. "Liberal judge lets them go, they get rounded up by a person or persons unknown and end up in an electric chair?" she said.

"They killed the wife and daughter of a Duke Energy scientist in a holdup. They walked because of a police screwup. Then said scientist goes off the grid, followed by the two mopes doing a star turn in the chair. He'd been a Ranger back in the army. So . . ."

"And you guys think he did the judge, too?"

He shrugged uncomfortably. She was getting too close to figuring out what he was really investigating. "Like I said, it's early days, and the feds have their own theories—as usual."

"Lest we forget, Park Service is federal, too," she said. "And that's not an answer. We're not necessarily the enemy, Lieutenant."

He was saved by the percolator, which started making gasping noises. He got up and poured coffee into three cups. He handed one to her and then took one out to the ranger, who had uncovered a second track and was beginning to dust a third. She joined him in the doorway, stirring some sugar into her coffee. "How big, Larry?"

"Two meters plus," the ranger said, sitting back on his haunches and blowing on the hot coffee between sips. "Can't estimate weight on wooden floorboards like this, but at that stride length, it has to be seventy, eighty kilos. Big effing cat. This third impression is not very good, so I'm going to work the dirt just off the porch."

"And what the hell was that thing doing here?" Cam asked.

"You let those dogs run around?" Mary Ellen asked.

Cam nodded.

"Then that's probably what it was hunting," she said. "A panther this big would definitely not be afraid of a couple of dogs. Slap, slap, chow time."

Larry had moved off the porch and was excavating the snow at the end of the building. All scrunched up down in the snow, he looked like a grounded stork. Cam went back inside. "So maybe there is something to your cat dancer story," she said. "But what's the tie to what you're investigating?"

He smiled at her. "I'm not sure there is one. Just something some guy mentioned in the course of our asking questions, so here I am. Basic follow-up. It's what we do when we're clueless. There probably is no tie."

She gave him a skeptical look. "My doctorate's in animal science," she said. "My specialty happens to be bears, not big cats. These prints will make for some interesting discussions down at the tavern. But then we're going to have to prove you didn't fake them, of course. You know, Bigfoot Two. Sasquatch comes to the Smokies."

"Knock yourself out," he said. "It's not like I'm looking for a feature story in the *Enquirer*. You've basically answered my questions."

She nodded at him with a faintly triumphant smile. Shit, he thought. She just mouse-trapped me. Dr. Smiley. He grinned at her. "Okay. Nicely done."

"Thank you. And the real story is?"

It was his turn to surprise her. "I can't tell you anything else about this investigation," he said. "It's that sensitive, okay?"

She blinked. He stared at her until she got it. "Oh," she said. "Internal problem."

"I never said that, and that's where we need to leave it," he replied. "No offense intended."

"None taken. How can we help?"

"Cat dancers," he said. "Anything you can tease out of the local woodwork about that term might help. I'll take rumors, hearsay, gossip, all the way to names and addresses. Anything."

"You really are nowhere on this, aren't you," she said. "Okay, I'll get the guys to ask around." She thought for a moment. "At least now we seem to have the requisite cat."

41

CAM WAITED AROUND FOR another hour while the ranger tried to surface more prints, and then, after putting both dogs in the truck, he went back to the headquarters of the Carrigan County Sheriff's Office and met with a Lieutenant Grayson, who headed up their Criminal Investigations department. He directly asked for their help in running down any information they could develop on the cat dancers story and any possible connections to White Eye Mitchell. He described the electric chair executions case, the bombing incident, and the fact that their prime suspect had committed suicide, but he did not allude to suspicions that police might be involved. Grayson, a tall, rangy individual in his fifties, took it all aboard and said they'd look into it, then asked whether Cam would mind if they checked back with Manceford County. Cam, "No problem," and gave the lieutenant the appropriate phone numbers to get in touch with Bobby Lee.

"We heard some talk about a mountain lion this morning," Grayson said.

Cam nodded. He'd forgotten how fast news could travel in a small county. He described the tracks and what the park ranger thought about them. He also mentioned Mary Ellen's comment about the possibility that Cam had faked the tracks.

"Mary Ellen's good people," Grayson said. "They get to listen to a lot of BS at that station. Tourists see the damnedest things: panthers, wolves, king cobras, grizzlies, and I don't know what all."

"She gave me the official Park Service line in the office: Ain't no panthers. Then later, she sort of hinted that that might not be true. Struck me as odd. She seems to be . . . nice.

"She tell you what happened to her fiancé, Joel Hatch?"

"Knocking on the wrong door at the wrong time?"

Grayson tapped a pen on the desk for a moment. "Brother Joel was a bit of a cowboy, especially for the Park Service. *Really* got into the sworn officer bit. TV cop wanna-be, in our opinion."

"Is that what got him shot?"

"What got him shot was that he called in the meth lab, was told to wait for backup from us, and then talked his partner into doing a John Wayne. No surprise to any of us, but we all felt bad for Mary Ellen. And his partner." He gave Cam a significant look. "Mary Ellen's a special lady in this community, if you follow me?" he said.

Caution received, Cam thought as he nodded.

"They get any hairs from those prints?" Grayson asked.

"I believe they did," Cam said. He remembered the ranger going out to the SUV to get some evidence bags.

"Good," Grayson said. "We have some mounted specimens from the early nineteen hundreds here in town, in private hands. They can do a DNA comparison, see if we're talking eastern or western panther. Or rabbit fur stretched over a dinner plate with bear claws glued to it. What's the connection with White Eye in all this?"

Cam hesitated. He was pretty sure that Grayson's sudden shift in topic had been calculated, so he decided to take refuge behind the same line he'd given Mary Ellen Goode.

"There's more to this case than I'm allowed to talk about," he told the lieutenant.

"No shit," Grayson said with an amused look on his face.

Cam smiled sheepishly. "Best thing is probably for your boss to talk to my boss. That way, I'm not going to wander too far off the reservation with what I say or don't say. Personally, I think Mitchell might know something about this cat dancer story, although he says he's never heard of such a thing."

"Nor have I," Grayson said. "Not to mention that that would be a damn fool thing for any man to try with a panther."

"Exactly. This whole thing is probably a dead lead."

"Except for the fact that we have you coming all the way out here from Manceford County, asking around about mountain lions, and suddenly we have what looks like the first confirmed evidence of a panther in many years. Quite a coincidence there, and I assume you feel the same way we all do about coincidences."

"I do," Cam said. "There is one thing, though." He described his casual conversation with the two deputies in the Waffle House, and his suspicion that they actually might know something, too. Grayson made a note, said he knew who they were and that he'd pull that string.

Cam thanked him. "Like I said, we're more than a little bit behind the power curve on this one. And we have feds in our hair just for grins."

"Is there just possibly an IA angle on this deal?" Grayson asked.

Cam looked at him with as innocent a face as he could muster. "Why ever do you ask that, Lieutenant?"

Grayson smiled and said they'd poke around and get back to him. Cam thanked him again and left.

He got back to the cabin park a little after sunset. The skies were filled with ragged white clouds drifting down off the Smokies and the temperature was dropping quickly. As he turned in, he was surprised to see that the security light on the front of the office was out, leaving the line of cabins in even darker shadows than usual. The gloom was relieved by an occasional burst of moonlight on the hard-packed snow. He pulled into the parking notch by his cabin and let the dogs go. After a day of being cooped up in the truck with only occasional tree breaks, they happily took off into the snowy woods. Cam hoped there weren't any hungry *things* out there.

He'd spent the afternoon hitting more of the guide shops and asking around about Mitchell and the wild tale about men tracking mountain lions just for fun. He'd learned exactly nothing. He'd then stopped by the Park Service rangers' office, ostensibly to see what they'd come up with on the prints, but mostly to see Mary Ellen smile again. The prints had been cast into plaster of paris and were going to UNC for evaluation. Mary Ellen was getting ready to go to a one-day conference in Asheville and, while polite and even friendly, she'd made it clear she was busy. Disappointed, Cam had backed out and returned to his cabin.

He could hear the dogs barking at something up on the slopes behind the cabin as he let himself in, but they didn't sound frantic about it. They were just making shepherd noise for the sake of making noise. He closed the door and flipped the light switch up. Nothing happened. So now he knew why the security light wasn't on up front: The power had to be out for the whole complex. The interior of the cabin was almost totally dark, illuminated only by the brief glimpses of moonlight coming through the windows. His breath was visible in the cold air. At least the woodstove ran on wood alone, so while it might be dark, there would be heat. He shucked his coat, hung it up by the front door, and went to reload the woodstove. He was bent over the front of the stove, trying to get a match to stay lit despite a back draft coming from the stove, when he saw something in the corner of the main room that made him become very still. The match began to burn the tips of his fingers, so he dropped it, missing the paper crumpled under the logs completely.

His eyes told him that what he was looking at was a pair of green eyes that were locked onto his own eyes like tracking beams. The eyes disappeared when the clouds covered up the moon, but they reappeared each time the moonlight did. His first thought was, Where are the damned dogs when I need them? They were still outside and still barking, but farther away now. He stared back into the corner, and, sure enough, there was a large feline face surrounding those yellow-green eyes: tawny fur marked with a darker mask and two rounded ears with tufts of white inside. It was a big face, much bigger than he had imagined.

He remained motionless for a long thirty seconds, and then slowly, very slowly, while still down on one knee in front of the woodstove, he fished out another match and struck it up, illuminating the room this time. The flare of light confirmed his worst suspicion: There was a mountain lion in his cabin.

42

SWALLOWING HARD, HE SHOVED the match into the paper, and it caught this time, sending a yellowish cone of light out onto the floor and into Cam's face. He kept watching the cat, which kept watching him. His coat with the .45 was ten feet away, so that was not an option. He'd seen the big cat, and the big cat had definitely seen him. He didn't have to know much about mountain lions to know that at this juncture, after they'd been staring at each other, any sudden move on his part was going to provoke a similar move from the huge cat, with negative consequences likely. His heart had begun to pound and his face was probably a little whiter than it had been a moment ago.

The fire grew as the stove began to draw, and he had to back his face away from the sudden heat. Just that tiny movement, an adjustment more than a movement, summoned a deep, sustained growl from the corner of the room. He could see the cat's face clearly, but not its body. Was it crouching, preparing to pounce? Or just lying there, watching to see what he'd do next?

Okay, he thought, have to do something here. He glanced down into the firebox and saw one thin log that was burning brightly on one end. He'd have to reach through the flames to grab it, but if he grabbed it, threw it at the cat, distracted the damned thing long enough to get to the .45, he might have a chance. The cat growled again, a deep-throated warning rumble, as if it were reading his mind. Those yellow-green eyes never wavered, never blinked. He knew it wouldn't work. He might be subtle about reaching into the firebox, but then his reflexes would take over as soon as his flesh sensed the flames and he'd jerk that hand out of there, and then that big bastard would be on him in one shrieking leap.

Slap, slap, chow time.

He could no longer hear the dogs, and his legs were starting to tremble. He saw the cat's shape change slightly in the deep shadows of the corner, as if it was gathering itself. Hell with it, he thought, and began to edge his hand back toward the door of the firebox.

He never saw it coming. One moment, he was trying to watch the cat while positioning his hand to grab for the burning log. The next instant, he was skidding backward, flat on his back, his head bouncing along the wooden floorboards, with two hundred pounds of wet fur and fangs shrieking into his face. The cat's breath was foul, and two dinner plate–size clawed paws were clamping onto his head on either side. He screamed back, shouting from all the way down in his gut, vaguely aware that he had pissed his pants, his mouth only inches from those long, yellow curved fangs, and then the cat was gone and he was staring up into the rafters, still paralyzed with fear, trying to focus his eyes on something up there. Oh God, not another one. And then he realized he was looking into the grinning face of White Eye Mitchell.

"Ain't she somethin'?" Mitchell said quietly, his eyes appearing to flicker in the firelight from the stove's open door. "You oughta see her brothers."

Cam was speechless after the cat's pounce. White Eye seemed to levitate out of the rafters, dropping noiselessly into a momentary crouch onto the floor. He straightened up and offered Cam a hand up.

"What the *fuck*?!" Cam asked, trying to make his voice work properly.

Mitchell pulled out two chairs, pushed one over for Cam, and then sat down in the other. Cam looked around for the panther and found it sitting like any house cat by the door, but it was still watching him. He sat down gingerly, wondering if he could get to his gun, which was still in his jacket pocket, which, in turn, was hanging about eight inches away from the cat. No way, and besides, White Eye saw him looking.

"You don't need no gun," he said. "You need to be listenin' to me now."

"I say again—what the hell is going on here?" asked Cam.

"You train dogs, right? Well, I train cats. How 'bout them apples, huh?"

Cam just stared at him.

"You wantin' to know about cat dancin', ain't you?"

Cam nodded, still vitally interested in getting his hands on the .45. He'd shoot the cat first, and then Mitchell. That's exactly what he was going to do. And where the hell were the dogs? He could still smell that cat's foul breath on his shirt. He realized he was still shaking. Mitchell got up, went over to the front door, and retrieved Cam's revolver. He came back and sat down, holding the .45 casually in his lap.

"You go in there," he said, indicating the bedroom with his head, "and git yourself dressed for some snow walkin'. Warmest shit you got. Extra everythin'." He glanced down at Cam's trousers. "Dry, too. Night-Night's gonna come along'n watch."

" 'Night-Night'?"

"Go on, now," Mitchell said, waving the gun. "I ain't got all damn night. And leave that door open."

Cam got up unsteadily and headed for the bedroom, where his clothes were stacked on a chair. On some signal from Mitchell that Cam couldn't see, the cat got up and followed him into the room, where it sat down in the doorway and began licking one of its enormous paws, watching him. He heard Mitchell get up and go into the kitchen.

He changed his clothes in the dark and started putting on layers. Night-Night, he thought. He eyed the cat while he dressed. It was a beautiful thing, he had to admit, until it stopped licking and stared at him, one massive paw held motionless right by its mouth. Its eyes glowed as if lit from within, and they were not friendly. It's tame, Cam told himself.

When he was ready, he started for the door, but the cat changed its position in such a way as to stop Cam in his tracks. White Eye made a sound in his throat and the cat turned away out of the door. Cam smelled coffee when he came out of the bedroom. The fire in the woodstove was roaring now, and there was much more light in the cabin.

"Set ye down," Mitchell said. Cam sat, moving awkwardly in all his layers of clothing. Mitchell brought over two mugs of coffee, pushed one across the table toward Cam, and sat down. "I reckon everybody's tellin' you that cat dancin' is bool-shit," he said.

"That's right," Cam replied. There were coffee grounds twirling in his mug. "The rangers said that mountain lions were extinct in these parts."

Mitchell snorted. "Seemed real enough sittin' on your chest, didn't she?"

"They were talking about wild mountain lions, I think," Cam said. "Not tame ones."

"They's wrong about that, too," Mitchell said. "Jist 'cause they ain't seen 'em don't mean they ain't up there. Them rangers like that warm office. Only one of 'em goes deep back country."

"And cat dancing? How about that?"

Mitchell looked him over. "You git around in the mountains any?" he asked.

"Some. But not normally in winter."

"This ain't winter," Mitchell scoffed. "Not yet. I can show you what it is you're askin' about, but you gotta come with me right now."

"Tonight?"

"Right now. It ain't winter yet, but it's fixin' to be."

"Do I have choice?"

"You want to know about this stuff, or what? 'Cause if you do, I'm the man to see. That part you got right."

"I want that gun back."

White Eye shrugged, pulled the .45 out of his coat pocket, opened the cylinder and thumbed the rounds out of it, and then handed the gun back to Cam. He dropped the rounds into his own coat pocket. "Leave it unloaded till you see what I got to show you," he said. "Remember, you the one started this shit."

"What's James Marlor's connection to all this?"

"Don't know," Mitchell said. He got up and kicked the door shut on the wood stove. "Let's go."

"Where are my dogs?" Cam asked.

"They run off when they got a whiff of Night-Night. They's smart dogs. They'll be back. Leave 'em some chow out front. And bring that coffeepot."

43

TWO HOURS LATER, THEY were grinding their way up a narrow mountain road in White Eye's ancient Bronco, and Cam was thinking that *road* was probably not the right word. Track, maybe. Mountain-goat trail. Trace? The vehicle's four-wheel drive worked just fine, but even with that, they were making no more than five miles an hour, if that, and often much less. White Eye had produced the vehicle from behind the cabin park's office, where he'd also restored the electricity. Night-Night loped along behind the Bronco with seemingly endless ease, and Cam was grateful that she was outside and not riding in the backseat, two feet from his neck.

He had no idea of where they were. Mitchell had driven about a hundred feet down the county road toward town, abruptly turned right into what had looked to Cam like an empty meadow, and then pointed the Bronco toward higher ground. The snow wasn't that deep, but it was crusted with ice, which made a crunching sound as they plowed through it, the nose of the Bronco permanently tilted up as they climbed.

About a half hour into the trip, White Eye had taken off his jacket and draped it over the center console as the heater began to kick in. Cam had done the same, piling his outer coat on top of White Eye's. And then surreptitiously, using his left hand, he had picked Mitchell's jacket pocket to retrieve three rounds. He'd quietly slipped these into his pants pocket. He'd have to figure out how to get the rounds back into the .45 once he got his coat back on. He was pretty sure that White Eye meant him no harm.

And yet, he thought. Cam hadn't forgotten the mysterious caller and the feline night visitor that little call had produced. Had that been White Eye's work? How many trained mountain lions were running around out here anyway? He topped off their coffee mugs with the last of the coffee and put the pot into the backseat, which was piled high with gear.

"Where we going?" he asked finally.

"Catlett's Bald," White Eye responded. "Be there directly, long as we don't hit no big drifts and the river ain't full of melt."

"What's a bald?" Cam asked.

"Yonder's some balds," Mitchell replied. Cam looked through the windshield as the Bronco topped a rise, and the sight almost took his breath away. The entire Smoky Mountain range lay before them, wave after wave of moonlit humped granite ascending into the night sky as far as he could see from southwest to northeast. The nearest mountains rose up on either side of the track, thick with bare trees on the lower slopes but thinning out just below the individual summits, to be replaced with snow-covered domes. He knew from his maps that there were some six-thousand-foot-high mountains out here, but they all looked much higher than that from the vantage point of the twisting track.

"Bald refers to the tops, then," Cam said. White Eye shot him a patient sideways look, as if to say, Yeah, dummy, that's why they call them balds. Cam kept looking as they started down the back side of the pass, checking the side mirror to see if that big cat was still out there. He didn't see it for a moment, but then he did. It was trotting along as if it did this every night of the week, and he would have sworn that it was watching him via the side mirror, too.

"So tell me about cat dancers," he said, settling back into his seat as the Bronco nosed down into some bumpy snow. The moonlight outside was bright enough to create glare from all the snow.

"They's seven of 'em," White Eye said. "No more'n that. Don't know who they are. They call themselves Bob, Frank, Jim, and the like, but the way they look when they say them names? Them ain't their real names."

"Young men? Old men?"

"A mix; thirties, fifties, ain't no kids, if that's what you're askin'."

"And what do they do, exactly?"

"First one come to see me fifteen, maybe sixteen years ago now, said he wanted me to find him a mountain lion. Called himself Carl. Early thirties. Big guy, hard, but not pushy about it. Guy you wouldn't mess with in a bar. Had that look about him. That's Carl. Didn't give no last name, and I wasn't askin', seein's he was showin' cash money. Anyways, I told him they wasn't any panthers left. He allowed as to how he knew I had one. That there surprised me some."

"That was a secret?"

"Oh hell yeah. Illegal in C'lina. Legal over in Tennessee, but you gotta pay high for licenses and such. They get 'em from out west somewheres." He looked sideways at Cam again. "I don't b'lieve in payin'—taxes, fees, licenses, any of it—you understand."

"Nice if you can work it," Cam said. "How'd he know you had a cat?"

"Damned if I know, but he surely did. Knew she was tame and that she went with me time to time. Knew her goddamned name even. Said what he really wanted to learn was how to *track* a big cat. Asked him what he'd do if'n he ever caught up with one. You know what he says? Take its picture, he says. Surprised the shit out of me. I told him the notion was crazy and dangerous. He pulls out this envelope with five thousand greenback dollars in it. Asked if I'd reconsider." White Eye chuckled at the memory. "Yeah, that was the word. Reconsider his proposition. Shit. Took me about two seconds."

"So there are wild mountain lions out here?" Cam asked.

White Eye didn't answer for a minute as he maneuvered the Bronco across a frozen creek, shifting down into grandma when the ice crust broke and the vehicle lurched alarmingly. Cam found himself reaching for a handhold.

"Here? Uh-uh. Not here. Out yonder," he said, gesturing with his head at the distant mountains. "*Way* out yonder. Told him that. No vee-hicles. Shank's mare all the way. Twenty, thirty mile in and some more straight up. Expensive damn hike. Said he understood. Said there was more money where that came from. He had time, years if need be. Said he was in shape for it and okay in the mountains, even in winter. I told him that was good, 'cause the best time to track a big cat was in the winter. Summertime, fall? You need kills and scrapes. And even in winter, you playin' with fire."

"Tell me why."

"Big cats got seven lives and six senses. They *know* when someone's fuckin' with them, specially a human, specially on they own ground. 'Bout the time you get a good track goin' on one, they like to have one goin' on you. Trick is to know when that shit's started, 'cause if you don't, cat's gonna take *your* picture, you get my meanin'."

"How the hell do you know where to even start? This park is what, fifty miles square?"

"Not that big; it's more like eight hunnert square miles. Somethin' like that."

"That's still a lot of territory."

"I got me an advantage, comes to scarin' up a panther," White Eye said with a sly grin.

Cam looked at him and then understood. "Night-Night."

White Eye nodded. "Night-Night. Big ole tom up there in them far hills see a human, he's gonna lie down and watch, but he ain't never gonna show his face less'n you piss him off. But a female panther? Tom's gonna sniff that stuff out from *miles* away and he's gonna talk about it."

"Then what?"

"Once I find one, we get the hell out of there. Cat won't usually leave its territory, so when it quits followin', I know where its home ground starts. After that, we'd come back in, Carl'n me, and I show him how to cut sign, track, and stay alive doin' all that, so's he can get his damned picture. Then I get my second surprise. I figger he has hisself one of them telephoto jobs, you know?"

"He doesn't?"

"Uh-uh. Shows me this little damned thing, fit in your coat pocket. One a them throwaway things from Wal-Mart."

"Not much range with one of them," Cam said.

" 'That's the whole point,' he says. 'I have to get close to use this. Real close.' "

"This is the crazy part."

"Damned straight. I tell him, 'You go right the hell ahead.'"

"What did he want you to do?"

"Find him a den. Had to be a female with cubs, 'cause tom's don't den up. Just the momma cats, and then only for a coupla months. After that, they hide the cubs with their kills."

"And he wanted you to take him right to a mountain lion's den?"

"I told him, 'I'll set me up camp a coupla miles away and you get to go creepin' on in there one night and take yer fuckin' picture, you want to. But I hear you scream, I ain't ridin' to no rescue until all the picnic noises stop and it's daylight.'"

"Can you actually get that close?"

"I took that boy into the woods off and on for two full years, every time he could get out here to the Smokies. Summertime, wintertime, everything in between. Taught him how to Injun-walk, how to be hid and stay hid. How to change human smell into animal smell. How to listen. How to look. How to be still in one place—for hours if need be. How to *hunt*. You know what I'm sayin'? And I'll say this—he had the natural-born sense for it. I'd'a swore he done it all before."

"Who are these guys? Do you know?" Cam asked.

The Bronco banged over a downed tree hidden under the snow, rattling Cam's spine and precipitating a dust fall inside the vehicle. White Eye kept it going as if nothing had happened, and then shook his head. "Ain't no tellin'," he said. "Crazy bastards, that's what they are, for damn sure. Deer hunters. Bored with life. *Sportsmen,* they call themselves. Sorta like you."

"Not like me at all," Cam said. "I mean, I'm a cop. We hunt bad guys, but we do it with teams of detectives, technology, and prosecutors. No way in hell would I mess with a mountain lion or any other large wild animal on its own ground. I've never been that bored."

"That's just the word," White Eye said. "That's why they do it, I think. They was bored. Wanted them some real excitement. They was hunters already, but this—this was different.

Real different. Called it a challenge. Got fire in their eyes when they'd come out. Especially Carl. Kept sayin' *extreme* all the time. And I believe it turned into something else once Carl brought out the third one."

"What was that?"

"Took Carl three years to get his first picture, 'long with fifty damn stitches on his back. Goddamned cat came *this* close—he snapped his fingers—"to takin' his fool head off. This was out to the Chop. He'd gone down one a them mountain-climbin' wires to get hisself level with the den, then swung hisself in to shoot that cheap-ass little camera. Cat went right at him, jumped the damn wire. They both fell fifty feet into a creek. Cat screamin', Carl screamin'. Said I wouldn't, but I come a-runnin' anyway, used a rifle to run the cat off, and there was goddamned Carl, flounderin' around in that creek. Deep December it was, blood all over the ice, and all that crazy fucker cared about was findin' his damn camera, his back all tore up—I'm talkin' the whites of his ribs showin'. I mean, *damn*! Hurt me to look at it."

"But he got his picture?"

"Oh yeah, he got his goddamned picture. Coupla months later, Carl brings out a second one. Some common damn name. I forget. Bill, John, you know. Looked a little like Carl. Same money, though, so I wasn't askin' much about names. Trained the new boy just like I trained Carl. Graduation back out to the Chop. Anyways, I think these two turned the whole thing into some kind a test for the third guy. You want to be one of us, first you gotta get your face."

" 'Face'?"

"That's what they called it—didn't count less'n you got a picture of the cat's face from near enough so's anyone seein' it would fuckin' *know* that the guy takin' the picture was no-shit close-up."

Cam shook his head in wonder. A disposable camera was autofocused at eight to ten feet for the best picture.

They broke out of the woods and drove out onto a large meadow at the foot of a massive hill. Cam could just see the summit of the next mountain looming over its top. He glanced at the Bronco's gas gauge, but there was plenty of fuel, even though the vehicle had been grinding through the snow in second gear.

"Yonder's Catlett's Bald," White Eye said, indicating the mountain behind the big hill. He was able to go a little faster now that they were traversing the open meadow, although the snow was deeper. They were running without headlights, and they needed none. White Eye aimed the vehicle at the left side of the hill, where there appeared to be a small pass between it and the edge of the deep woods.

"Fourth one got hisself killed," White Eye said, apropos of nothing.

"Whoa. How?"

"How you think?"

"Cat got him?"

"Oh yeah. Me'n Carl, we was hid out on a ridge 'bout a half-mile crow fly from the den. Whoever this Carl is, he's the boss man. We was out along the back side of Whittier Mountain. They's a canyon back there, where the Bullet River cuts through. This old boy went in after midnight, aimin' to rope down to the den 'bout an hour before daylight. He fucked up crossin' a feeder creek halfway to the cliff, made him some noise. Carl never did hear him, but I did. And so'd the cat. This boy didn't come back, so we went in around noon. Found a foot in the creek, and a hat full of hair."

"And the rest of him?"

Mitchell snorted. "Cub meat."

"You hunt down the cat?"

"Hell no. Cat was just doin' what she was supposed to, protectin' her den. If there's a den, there's cubs. Carl said he tole each one of them sumbitches, 'If the cat wins, the cat wins, and you lose. That's it. Otherwise, this ain't got no point.'"

"Damn," Cam said quietly, but he was beginning to understand. Carl, or whoever he was, had turned this deadly little game into an initiation of some kind. But who were these guys? And initiation into what?

"But doesn't that make the cat a man-eater?" Cam asked. "I mean, what if she gets a taste for it?"

" 'Gets'?" White Eye said. "Mister, they's already got the taste for it, best I can tell. Look at them cats out there in California. They's eatin' folks right and left. And why not? They don't call 'em mountain lion for nothin'. And besides, look at it this way: Most wild animals ain't gonna fuck around with no damn panther. So here comes this two-legged animal, bangin' around on the cat's ground, don't seem to know the fuckin' rules, no respect. Panther's gotta do somethin' about that, 'cause, way he figgers, if it ain't actin' like prey, then it's gotta be a predator, right? Pretty fuckin' logical, I'd say."

"Why do you have one around, then?"

White Eye smiled. "I like 'em. First one I found as a cub up on the Tennessee line twenty-odd years ago. Little fucker, mewin' up a damn tree and starvin'. No claws up front. Got away from some breeder, I figger. Put him in the house, raised him up like a house cat. Used to have me some fun when strangers would come round my place, specially after he growed some. Thievin' white trash comes around at night to steal him one a my chickens? Runs into Night-Night in the barnyard? Come daylight, I'm gonna find me fifty feet a goose shit 'cross my yard."

They entered the narrow pass, straddling a blackwater creek running between the two elevations. They came out into a smaller meadow, with the full expanse of Catlett's Bald rising in a sheer face right in front of them. Cam thought it looked like the pictures he'd seen of El Capitan in Yosemite Park. There was a stand of densely packed tall pines to the left, and the ground rose to the south behind the pines, where there were large bare deciduous trees climbing that slope toward the bald. White Eye stopped the vehicle in the middle of the meadow, but left the engine running. The moonlight was bright enough that the pine trees showed their intense green color.

"Get your gear on," he said. "Time to show you somethin' about cat dancin'."

44

CAM OPENED HIS DOOR and got his coat and over-boots on while White Eye did the same. Cam looked at his watch. It was 3:30 A.M., but Mitchell's grainy coffee brew still had him wide-awake. He put on gloves, a black watch cap, and then an adjustable ball cap on top of the watch cap. He patted the gun to make sure it was in his pocket, then quietly transferred the three bullets to the coat pocket from his trouser pocket when White Eye wasn't looking. He stood down into the snow, as did White Eye.

"You going to leave it running?" Cam asked.

"Yep," White Eye said. "Runs good, but sometimes she don't start so good."

Cam followed in White Eye's tracks as they set off for the stand of pines about two hundred yards away. Mercifully, there was no wind, so the temperature didn't seem that bad. The sound of their boots crunching through the snow filled the night air as they approached the pine stand. White Eye walked right into the pines, which looked a lot like the Ley-land cypress Cam had planted around his house, with dense branches reaching all the way down into the snow. Cam fol-lowed him in, pushing a little to keep up as the other man's figure disappeared into the mass of greenery. They'd pene-trated about sixty feet when Cam broke into a small clearing. White Eye was waiting for him.

"Right here," he said, and Cam looked around, not sure of what was coming next.

"What are we doing?" Cam asked.

"Gonna show you somethin' about trackin' a big animal out here in the real woods," he said. "You wait here. I'm gonna go back, move that vehicle back into that little pass, and then I'm gonna come back through these here pines on foot. Not the same way we come in, okay? I want you to sing out when you hear me comin'."

"That'll be never," Cam pointed out. "This soft snow and everything."

White Eye shook his head, stepping around in the clearing, the crunching sound evident. "Got us ice crust in here," he said. "Even so, I'm gonna come back in here and tap you on the shoulder 'fore you hear a fuckin' thing."

"And why are we doing this?"

"'Cause you don't understand how good I am at this shit," the old man said. "You gotta 'preciate how hard this is 'fore I take you to see a real panther."

Cam looked at him. "That's where we're going? To see a wild mountain lion?"

"You wanted to know what cat dancin's all about, right? It's about lookin' a wild one in the face, so that's what I'm gonna show you, mister. But first, I gotta see if you got any wood sense whatsoever. You stay here in this clearin', and don't go wanderin' off."

White Eye turned on his heel and disappeared back through the pine branches, leaving Cam to watch his own breath condense into tiny ice crystals in front of his face. He waited for a minute, trying to hear the other man's progress through the pines, but now he heard absolutely nothing. Of course, White Eye might have stopped three feet into the dense pines to see what Cam would do, so Cam did nothing for a couple of minutes but move to the center of the clearing. It was twenty feet on every side to the nearest pine tree, so there was no way in hell that guy could come out of the pines and tap him on the shoulder without Cam seeing him first.

Then he heard the Bronco's engine rev up in the distance and the sounds of the vehicle turning around. Based on the sound, which was difficult to locate through all the greenery, the Bronco was indeed going back to the entrance to the meadow, although it seemed to be taking an awfully long time. He fished the .45 out of his pocket and fed the three bullets into it, checking the action to make sure everything was working. The metal was cold, and the cylinder turned sluggishly, but it did turn, and that was all that counted. He put it back into the pocket with a button flap on it and secured it. He listened for the Bronco, thought he could still hear it. It seemed a long way off.

Has that crazy old bastard left me out here? he wondered. He looked up at the sky for any signs of snow, but it was clear as a bell and filled with a million enormous stars. He pushed up the front of the watch cap and listened hard. He thought he could still hear the Bronco, but it could also have been his imagination. But clearly, White Eye had gone beyond the edge of the meadow. He left his ears uncovered, the better to hear the man coming back. And he would hear him, because the air was so still he could hear the fabric of his coat rising and falling with his own breathing. His right hand unconsciously patted the lump in his coat pocket.

Maybe I should move out of the clearing, get myself into the dense pines, instead of sitting out here in the middle, waiting to be tagged, he thought. But then he realized there was no way to do that without leaving a trail of footprints, which would point right at him. Well then, maybe— He stopped thinking and listened. He'd heard something out there.

He cupped his hands behind his ears and slowly turned his head like a radar antenna, trying to focus on that sound. Not footsteps, not the Bronco, something else. Then he heard it again. A low cough, overlaid with something else, something deeper. Coming from—where? There was absolutely no way to tell. And it was a sound he'd heard before. But where? Recently, he knew. And then he knew what it was.

Night-Night.

He'd forgotten all about White Eye's panther, who had spent the last few hours trotting along behind Mitchell's vehicle. Working up an appetite? Son of a *bitch*!

He heard another sound but couldn't make it out. Whatever it was, it sounded closer. He decided not to hang around in the clearing anymore, not if that damned cat was coming.

He thought frantically about which way to go. He and White Eye had come in from the meadow, and their tracks would still be visible. In the other direction, up the slope, were trees—real trees, with big strong branches. He stood no chance against the cat if it could catch him in this tangle of pines. But up a tree, with a .45? Much better odds.

If he could get there.

He put his back to their original tracks and plunged into the dense pines, pushing his way through them for about fifty feet and then stopping. He turned around to see if he'd been going in a straight line, but the pines immediately blocked his view. He was pretty sure he was going straight, but it was very difficult to tell in the woods. He listened for sounds of the cat but heard nothing but his own labored breathing.

Go, he thought. Now.

He turned again in what he thought was the direction of the big trees and started pushing again, ignoring the sharp stings of needles on his face. He knew he was making some noise, but he no longer cared. He had to get out of this maze of green branches. It felt like the damned trees were closing in on him, resisting his efforts to escape, even as his brain told him to stop that shit.

After three minutes of effort, he stopped to listen again, this time for more than just a few seconds. He tried to slow his breathing. He wondered what the altitude was up here, then remembered his ears popping more than once on the way up. He should have come out of the grove by now.

Another cough.

That way. Closer.

Cam looked down at his feet to establish his direction, and he felt his face redden when he saw the two sets of tracks. He was standing in two sets of tracks. He'd gone in a goddamned circle. He felt sweat on his forehead, despite the freezing air. Now what?

Climb a tree. Climb up and see which way was out. But that wouldn't work. The pines would simply bend over the moment he got halfway up.

The stars. Use the stars. Pick a star and keep it in front of you. But *which* goddamned way?

Any damned way. Any straight line, but he had to get out of this jungle. Even if it brought him out in the meadow, he could see again. But so could the cat.

The fucking cat doesn't have to see, he realized. It *knows* where you are.

Then he realized his left foot was higher than his right foot. He was standing on a slope.

Uphill. The oak trees were above the pine grove. Go uphill.

Trying desperately not to panic, he turned in the direction he thought was uphill and began to push through in earnest now, not even trying to be quiet anymore. Just when he was about to give up and try navigating by the stars, he broke out of the pine grove, right in front of the blessed oak trees.

He stopped and looked carefully up and down the line of greenery marking the top edge of the grove. It was a good hundred yards of open snowpack to the nearest tree.

He tried a step. *Deep* open snow.

He listened, but there were no more sounds coming from within the pine grove. Where was that damned thing? Just inside the tree line, waiting for him to move out into the open? His mind formed an image of the great tawny beast loping across the snowpack behind the Bronco with perfect ease, doing it for miles and miles.

He scanned the trees ahead and extracted the .45. Had he put the rounds in the right chambers? If he cocked the hammer, would he get a bullet cycling under it, or an empty chamber?

Gotta move sometime, he thought. He stared at the distant trees, trying to pick one out with branches low enough to get into. He spotted a likely candidate, then turned around so he could walk backward up the hill, keeping the entire pine grove in his sight. He held the .45 close to his belly to keep it warm as he trudged backward up the hill, trying hard not to look over his shoulder to see what might be behind him. It was tough going as the hill steepened, and the snow felt like it was three feet deep, even though he knew it wasn't.

He stopped, breathing hard as he thought he saw something move out on the far right corner of the grove. He stared hard, his eyes watering with the effort, but there was nothing there. He scanned the whole grove again, watching for any signs of movement. Nothing. He looked over his shoulder. His target tree was twenty feet away. It was bigger than he'd thought, with a huge gnarly trunk some seven or eight feet in diameter.

Behind which was—what?

Look at the snow, his brain told him. He did. No tracks near the tree.

He scanned the pine grove again, his eyes moving from left to right, even as he started moving backward again, his mind chanting a simple mantra: There's nothing behind you except that tree. No tracks, no cat. Damned thing can't fly.

He kept watching the pine trees, staring hard into those deep shadows at their bases. Wrong, he told himself; watch the tops. If something's coming through those trees, the tops will stir.

And, oh shit, they were—right in the middle of the grove, right where he'd come out. Tiny little movements in the moonlight, but the tops were definitely moving. Something coming through there. And there were his own tracks, pointing right at him.

Night-Night? Or White Eye? Both?

Then something slammed into his back and he let out a little yelp before he realized he'd backed into his tree. He took one last look around, jammed the gun back into his pocket, and started trying to climb it. The limbs, which had appeared to be close to the ground before, were not so close now that he was right here. He circled the tree, searching for a hand-hold, looking frantically at the next tree, and then one on the other side, then back at the pine grove.

Where the big cat had just come out of the grove and was bounding up the hill, right toward him, eyes flashing in the bright moonlight.

Propelled by a sudden blast of adrenaline, he crouched down into the snow and then leaped straight up, high enough that he could grab a small branch, which broke, dropping him into a heap in the snow. Peering out of the corner of his eye, he could see that the cat was halfway up the hill, coming strong, right for him.

He jumped again and grabbed the stub of the broken branch. This time, it held and he did a one-armed pull-up into the first branch junction. With a second handhold, he was up, off the ground, and scrambling higher.

The cat screamed at him from beneath the tree, causing him to lose his footing and almost fall. He scrabbled around the trunk, looking for more branches, discarding his gloves to get a better hold, while the panther growled at him as it circled the tree, looking up at him—and at the branches.

Oh shit, Cam thought as he pulled himself up into the third tier of branches, some twenty feet above the ground now. Cats can jump. And climb.

He kept circling the trunk now, not trying for any more height but, like a squirrel, attempting to keep the trunk between him and the cat's sight line. The panther circled below, more patiently now, watching him, silent as it concentrated on its prey, its breath making little puffs of vapor.

Fucking thing's working it out, Cam thought. Picking which branch. That bastard's coming up here.

He found as secure a position as he could and put his back to the huge old trunk and his legs out on two separate wide branches. He drew the .45. The walnut grips were cold in his bare hands, and he knew better than to touch the metal.

The cat circled one more time, came around to the side where it had a clear view of Cam, and sat down on its haunches. For an instant Cam thought it had decided to give up. And then it came straight up in one graceful leap to grab onto the trunk with all fours at the same branch intersection Cam had first grabbed. It hung there for no more than a split second, then pulled itself onto the branch stub, never taking its eyes off Cam, not even looking where it was placing its enormous feet, its claws tearing off bits of bark that rained down on the snow.

With another effort, she climbed into the second tier, eyes blazing in triumph as she came up, her breath steaming in the moonlight, total certainty in her eyes. Got you now, human. Chow time. He could smell her wet fur and urgent breath. Got you now.

He braced his back against the tree as she maneuvered underneath him, no more than eight feet away, balancing like it was nothing, with all four feet on a single branch, looking, evaluating. She was huge.

He lined up the gun sight between her eyes and then his training took over. No fancy shooting here, center of mass. The chest. Go for the chest.

The cat gathered herself again, crouching down on the branch, rumbling in her throat as she prepared to make the final leap up to where he was, and he thumbed back the hammer.

All the muscles on her front and shoulders quivered as she got ready. She stared right at him, daring him to move, to run, to even *try* to escape. The words *aim* and *shoot* thundered through his head, and he fired.

The shot boomed out over the meadow and the panther transfixed the mountain air with her death shriek. She tumbled down onto the snow at the base of the tree in a rain of bark. Cam felt the thump of her body hitting the ground. He instinctively cocked the hammer back for another shot, but it wasn't necessary. The huge cat was crumpled in a heap at the base of the tree, its lungs clearly blowing red spray out onto the snow. Cam heard another sound then, yelling and shouting. He turned and saw White Eye reeling through the snow, heading across the open ground between the pine grove and the tree line. He was shouting, "No, no," his arms flailing as he tried to run through the snow like a wild drunk, still yelling. Cam pointed the gun at him as he came up, but the man wasn't even looking at him. He was running to the cat, which was trying to get up but couldn't. There was an awful wet roaring noise rising in its red maw.

White Eye stumbled to a stop, glared up at Cam, and then dropped to his knees next to the cat. Cam expected the cat to try to crawl to its master, but that wasn't what happened. The panther rolled sideways and then back in its death agony, focused its eyes on White Eye, and, in a move too quick for Cam to see, lunged at Mitchell with its front paws, hooking viciously, smashing White Eye's head repeatedly like a boxer working a speed bag before collapsing in the snow with a great groan and a final spray of bright red blood from its gaping mouth.

Cam stared down at the bloody spectacle below him. The cat was now on its back, obviously dead, even though the large muscles in its legs and haunches were still jerking. White Eye was sprawled on his back, his staring eyes wide, the sides of his head not really there anymore, hands clenching and unclenching in the spotted snow.

With shaking legs and with his heart still pounding, Cam began to climb down. It took him longer than expected, and he checked the cat once more to make sure it was finished before making the final drop on all fours onto the ground. He extracted the gun and stayed down for a moment, gathering his wits and making sure that thing didn't get up again. He finally came around the tree trunk and stopped. The cat's body was no longer twitching, but White Eye was. Cam knelt down beside him, trying to ignore the mess the cat had made of the old man's skull, which looked like a broken crock of Jell-O. There's no way he's going to survive this, Cam thought. He looked into Mitchell's eyes, which, after a moment, focused on his. White Eye opened his mouth to speak, but then he choked on fluids rising in his throat. He turned his head sideways for a moment, coughed wetly, and then looked back at Cam.

"God*damn* you," he gasped.

"You killed her, not me," Cam said.

White Eye blinked, as if he didn't understand.

"When you sent her after me," Cam said

"Had your rounds," he gasped. More blood welled out of his shattered head every time he spoke.

"Picked your pocket," Cam said. "Don't talk anymore."

Mitchell tried to reach up and touch his head, but his arm wouldn't work.

"How bad . . ." he whispered.

Cam shook his head. "Will you tell me who the cat dancers are?"

White Eye made another gargling noise in his throat, which was when Cam realized the cat had opened that up, too. Then he was looking back at Cam. One of his strange eyes rolled away for a second before it came back into focus. His right leg had begun to twitch uncontrollably. Brain shutting down, Cam thought.

"Don't know," he said, and Cam had to bend closer to hear him. "They's *all* cops. Same as you. God*damn* your eyes."

Then his eyes lost focus as he choked once and stopped breathing.

Cam sat back on his haunches and swallowed hard. The cat dancers were all cops. Finally, he thought he knew what was going on.

45

HE TRAMPED OVER A mile of hard-packed snow to find the Bronco, which started just fine, he discovered. He drove the vehicle back up to the edge of the oak grove and loaded Mitchell's body. He'd tried to move the cat, but it was simply too heavy, so he found a hatchet in the Bronco, hacked off the cat's head, and put that next to Mitchell's body, covering the whole mess with a tarp as best he could for the trip back. Ordinarily, he'd have left the entire scene alone and called for the authorities, but nothing would be left once the scavengers found it, and there wasn't exactly good cell-phone service up in these mountains. He drove back the way they'd come, getting stuck only once, which cost him a half hour of digging and shoving.

He drove directly to the Carrigan County Sheriff's Office in Pineville, arriving bleary-eyed just after sunrise. The duty officer came out to the Bronco, pulled back the tarp, whistled once, and called the sheriff at home. Cam gave them a brief synopsis of what had happened, then said he needed to get back to the cabin, change, clean up, and get something to eat. He told them that he'd be back at ten o'clock for a detailed statement. That seemed to suit all concerned. After another, much longer interview, he put a call through to Bobby Lee to tell him that something had happened and that the locals wanted him to stay up there for a few more days.

"Something?'" the sheriff had asked.

"Office line," Cam said, reminding Bobby Lee of his own orders. No phones, no e-mails. Cam asked him to call his cell phone from a more secure line.

"How's this tie in with our problem?" Bobby Lee asked five minutes later.

"A small group of cops—revealed to us by a suspect, James Marlor—who are doing this pursuit of wild mountain lions as some sort of an initiation into—what?" Cam said.

"And you think these are our vigilantes?"

"It's certainly possible, Sheriff," Cam said. "Especially if they're from all over the state. Not one sheriff's office, but seven. A loose network of out-there cops who get together periodically to take care of unfinished business. They'd be strangers in Manceford County—like that guy who warned me to get out of town."

"But you said Marlor admitted to doing the two minimart guys."

"With the help of someone in law enforcement who told him where they could be picked up. And the bomb at Annie's house? That wasn't Marlor."

"We only have his word for that."

"There was the shooting incident prior to that—that took two people. Marlor was a lone wolf. I think these guys took advantage of what Marlor was doing to eliminate a judge they despised. Relate the two sets of incidents and we all looked at Marlor."

The sheriff sighed audibly. "You're saying we've got one of these guys in our house."

"Either that or one of them had access to someone in our office who's at least sympathetic to their program," Cam said. "And that might be how this is working. This could be a small cell of doers with a much larger base of sympathizers, cops or admin types who are willing to answer a question without asking too many of their own. Guys who don't want to know what's going to be done with the information, but are willing to pass stuff along for the cause of achieving real justice, like when those two minmart assholes went free."

"You're talking accomplice to kidnap and murder, then," the sheriff said. "Cops would know that."

"I don't know, Sheriff," Cam said. "Yes, they should know that. But I can see some of the cops I know being able to make a distinction between executing somebody and leaking a little information. It's not like they were putting cops or cases in danger; just giving an opinion as to where the likes of K-Dog and Flash hung out."

"But legally—"

"Yes, sir, I know. But these might be new guys, easily influenced by older and more experienced cops."

"So who are the doers?"

"Jaded cops. Senior hard-case guys with ten, fifteen, twenty years of pent-up frustration with the system. Not management types, but street supervisors. Maybe not just cops—maybe some Young Turk prosecutors. Probably they start out as sympathizers and then a select few graduate to actual doers. White Eye told me the group consisted of only seven guys—no more, no less. That's a very small action cell, and you don't get to play with those guys unless you're man enough to do go do something like this cat-dancing shit."

The sheriff went silent, long enough for Cam to wonder if he'd lost the connection.

"You get yourself back here ASAP," Bobby Lee said finally. "I can't move on this at all until I have you here."

Cam said he would be trying to get the sheriff of Garrigan County to contain the incident as much as possible, restrict it to local consumption, but that he'd probably need some backup on that, sheriff to sheriff. Bobby Lee understood and took Sheriff Hanson's office number.

"I have my dogs with me," Cam said. "So I'll need to go home first. Want to meet there? I have the inquest proceedings here tomorrow—that's at two—and then I can be back in Triboro by seven, eight o'clock tomorrow night."

"All right. And make sure you talk to that Bawa woman. She's been calling all damned day."

He got through to Jay-Kay an hour later. She revealed that her tigers had managed to penetrate the statewide records in her search for patterns involving prisoners, defendants, judges, and unsolved perp deaths.

"Penetrate," Cam said. "As in covertly?"

"No, actually, as in freedom of information, with a little

help from some federal resources. But here's the interesting point: We were shut out after only three search sessions. I cannot find out why or by whom."

"Shut out?"

"Access denied, across the board. And it looks like a machine is doing it, as opposed to, say, some sys op at a keyboard."

Cam wasn't sure what a sys op was. "So what do you do next?"

"Now we're doing it my way," she said brightly.

"I don't think I want to hear this," he said with a smile. "New subject: What do the jungle drums tell you about federal interest in me for the bombing?"

"Nothing. Which in itself says something—namely, that there is a stone wall in place. They know I'm working with you, and so no one tells me anything."

"Can you do it your way with regard to that question, too?"

"It's technically possible, but I wouldn't want to. Unlike most state agency computer systems, the federal networks look back at intruders rather forcefully these days. When are you returning?"

"Very soon," he said. "Things got messy up here, but productive in one sense. Tell me, have you had any interaction with Sergeant Cox?"

"Not directly. But shall we perhaps talk about that when you get back?" She replied, all but telling him, Not on an open line, dummy.

Exhausted, Cam went back to the cabin and took an all-afternoon nap. He was awakened at sundown by the sound of someone knocking on the cabin door. The dogs were interested but not alerting him. Nonetheless, Cam still wasn't ready to open the door and find one of Night-Night's relatives wanting to have a word. He asked who was there.

"It's Mary Ellen Goode," a voice called. "I think we need to talk."

Cam was standing behind the door in his long johns, still not quite awake.

"Um," he said.

"I'm sorry. I woke you up, didn't I?" Let's do this: Meet me at the Sky Lodge in an hour." She gave him directions and then drove away.

An hour later, Cam was seated by a window at the Sky Lodge, waiting for Mary Ellen. He'd wondered about the name when he first drove up, as the building was an unpretentious log lodge house from the front. When the hostess took him through the bar and down a flight of steps to the dining room, he saw the reason: A wall-length window looked out over a gorge that dropped at least five hundred feet below to a rushing stream. He ordered coffee and tried to wake up. Mary Ellen came in a few minutes later, and he woke right up. She'd changed out of her Park Service uniform into a dress, put on a little war paint, done something interesting with her hair, and was turning heads as she followed the hostess over to Cam's table. Cam, wearing jeans and a lumberjack shirt, felt underdressed.

"Well, my goodness," he said, getting up. "It's a girl."

She smiled as she sat down. "It's a woman, actually," she replied. "And she's here to apologize for what happened to you up there in the woods."

He sat back down slowly. "Apologize?"

She ordered a glass of wine from the waiter, who dropped two menus on the table.

"I haven't been entirely honest with you about this cat-dancing business. I need to explain some things."

The waiter brought her wine and she put a serious dent in it. "Okay," she said. "Here goes. This concerns my late fiancé, Joel Hatch." She paused. "How do I describe Joel?"

"Lieutenant Grayson said he was a bit of a cowboy," Cam offered. "A TV cop wanna-be, to be precise. Someone who liked the role of cop better than that of park ranger."

She stared down at the table for a moment, not speaking, and Cam wondered if he'd been too blunt. "Did they tell you what happened that day?" he asked.

She nodded. "Not at first," she said, "But then later, I talked to some of the cops involved. In fact, he and I'd had some words about the way he was acting, some of the stuff he was doing. And then, afterward . . ."

"Afterward, you felt guilty because now he was dead."

"A little bit, yes, I did."

"I can relate to that," he said, and told her about the bombing incident and his own complicated relationship with Annie Bellamy. The waiter came back and they ordered.

"I guess I've become a fatalist," she said once the waiter had departed. "I think that when you fail to put a proper value on the people you love, the gods take them away from you."

"I think you take what life has to offer and make the best of it," he responded. "We're not in control. You were going to tell me something about cat dancers?"

She smiled. "Nothing wrong with your focus, is there? Okay, cat dancers. I first heard the term from Joel. He'd heard rumors that White Eye Mitchell was doing some weird stuff up in the backcountry and that it involved feral mountain lions."

"Which do not exist," Cam said.

"Right."

"On the other hand, you never went looking, did you?" he asked.

"No, we have plenty enough to do. The station is undermanned, and the park visitors keep us quite busy. But Joel took off a couple of times in the year before he died, and I think he *was* looking. Then he stopped talking about it."

"But he did use the term *cat dancing*?"

"Once. I remember it. He said it was the coolest thing he'd ever heard of. For Joel, *cool* was a word that usually involved extreme danger. But he didn't say exactly what it was, other than it meant getting very close. Then it was as if he realized he'd been indiscreet, and he wouldn't talk about it anymore."

The waiter arrived with their food, and Cam used the distraction to think about how much he should tell her. He liked her and he trusted her, and she'd already figured out that there was an Internal Affairs angle to what he was doing up here.

"Okay," he said. "Let me ask you one more thing: If you thought Joel was mixed up in something 'weird' involving wild panthers, why didn't you report it?"

"You're a career cop," she said. "You know the answer to that."

He thought for a moment. "Let's see. Everyone knew the two of you were an item, and you were afraid that whatever it was he was doing, it might splatter your own career?"

"Not exactly admirable, is it, but that's the gist of it, yes. You had to know Joel. I rationalized it by telling myself that there simply weren't any more big cats up there in the mountains. Not wild ones, anyway. And even if there were, no one would be fool enough to track one into a face-to-face confrontation."

He nodded. "I would probably have done the same thing," he said. He decided to trust her, made her promise to keep it to herself, and then told her the whole story of why he had come up to the area.

"My God," she said softly when he was finished. "An initiation? And one of them was killed?"

Cam looked around the dining room. It wasn't full, but he still didn't want to be overheard. "That's what White Eye told me. And now that I've seen a supposedly tame one in action, I'm a believer."

She shivered. "They want me to testify tomorrow—at the inquest—about how that could happen. With his own cat, I mean."

"I may need you to testify for me," he said. He stopped when he saw her expression. "*Testify*'s probably the wrong word. What I need is corroboration that I'm not making this up. And, of course, the much bigger issue is that we may have a statewide death squad working."

She sat back in her chair, dinner forgotten, thinking about what he was asking.

"As you can imagine, this thing's being run under a pretty damned tight wrap," he went on. "You can't talk about this. Hell, *I* can't talk about this." Even as he said it, he realized that he just had.

"Because you don't know who's who in the zoo," she said.

"Precisely. I'm meeting tomorrow night with our sheriff and the DA."

"What on earth would I tell my boss?" she asked.

"That you need a few days' leave?"

"I'll think about it," she said. "But damn, Lieutenant!"

"You could call me Cam," he said.

"Sure about that?" she asked sadly.

46

THE DOGS WERE IN semidisgrace on the trip back. He had chided them about not following the Bronco and rescuing his sorry ass from the mountain lion. The looks on their faces said that no self-respecting, intelligent German shepherds would *even* mess with goddamned mountain lions, and besides, full food bowls on the porch had distracted them from doing their duty, no matter how wildly construed. He could see their point, but he still gave them a cold shoulder all the way back to Triboro. That seemed to bother them a lot, at least for the five minutes before they fell asleep in the backseat.

It was just after sundown when Cam got back to his house in Summerland. He turned the dogs loose in the backyard, gathered up his mail, disarmed the alarm system, and went inside. A quick walk-through of the house turned up nothing visibly amiss. He called the sheriff at home and let it ring once, then hung up. He took a shower, got something to eat, and, on a hunch, changed into uniform. Bobby Lee arrived twenty minutes later in his personal cruiser. Five minutes after that, DA Steven Klein showed up. The sheriff was in uniform and Cam was glad he'd changed. He had not shaved his beard, however, and this provoked a fish-eye stare from Bobby Lee even as he handed Cam his official accoutrements. They sat down in Cam's kitchen, and Cam poured out coffee for all hands.

Cam then debriefed them on everything he'd learned up in Carrigan County, along with the details of the final night under Catlett Bald. He mentioned that he had a corroborating witness but said that she hadn't decided whether she wanted to get involved. The sheriff described what Jaspreet Kaur

Bawa had turned up in her database analysis of judges, cases, and walk-away perps who'd subsequently died. Her search went back over a decade, he informed them.

"Seventeen DOA's," he announced somberly, and that brought a muttered oath from Klein. "Two of those may have been prison gang–related, but even discounting those, that still leaves fifteen unsolved cases, including the two recent Internet stars."

"Statewide?" Steven asked.

The sheriff nodded. "Fifteen cases where clearly guilty bastards went free and then were extinguished, leaving us with stone-cold whodunits."

"We need to check on something else," Cam said. "White Eye told me one of the cat dancers got himself eaten. He was kind of vague as to when this happened, and it might be bull-shit, but we should look to see if any cops flat-out disappeared, in the past twelve years, say."

"Why twelve?" Bobby Lee asked.

"Because White Eye said the guy who called himself Carl first came to him about fifteen years ago. He said it took him two years to train Carl to hunt the wild cats. Carl finally got his photo of a cat after three years. A few months later, he brought in the second guy and then the ones after that. Our cluster of unsolved cases involving dead perps seems to go back about ten years, so if it's true, the initiate died some-where between ten and twelve years ago."

"I'll go to SBI with that one," Bobby Lee said.

"Or let Jay-Kay do it," Cam said. "Her computers are al-ready trained to do that kind of search."

"'Trained'?" Steven said.

"Don't ask," Bobby Lee told him, shaking his head. "She tried to explain how that all works and left me right in the damned dust."

"The real question is," Steven said, "How do we smoke these bastards out, assuming they do exist?"

Everyone concentrated on their coffee cups for a moment. A night wind came up outside, stirring the tops of the Ley-land cypresses into a soft sound.

"On the question of whether or not these are related killings, were there any correlative factors in the fifteen incidents?" Cam asked.

"Such as?" the sheriff inquired.

"Manner of death; location of discovery; time of death; wound patterns; probable sequence of events prior to their getting killed, such as abduction, a holding period, then execution, or was it just a drive-by?"

"Don't know," Bobby Lee said. "Something else to check. But how the hell do we smoke 'em out? Turn loose another walk-away perp?"

"I think Mitchell sicced that cat on me deliberately," Cam said. "I think he was an integral part of this group, and they wanted me out of the way."

"You *think,*" Bobby Lee said. "You have a body and a dead mountain lion—a tame one, not a wild one. No one has yet to produce a wild one up there, just like the Park Service people have been saying all along. There's no damned evidence."

"I think we do have some evidence," Cam said. "We have the body of K-Dog Simmonds, found in a diesel-storage tank. That's pretty elaborate for a prison gang hit or the revenge of a drug dealer. Plus the videos of the two executions, out there on the Internet, with corroborative damage to Simmonds's body. We have a guy showing up here in a police cruiser telling me to get out of town. We have the shooting incident at Annie's house, prior to the bombing, which had to have involved at least two people. And we have James Marlor, who somehow knew something about cat dancing."

Cam paused, waiting for comment, but the other two sat there looking down at the table. He then reiterated his arguments for there being cops involved. More silence.

"Okay," he said, "Some of that's circumstantial, I admit. But we've put bad guys away on circumstantial evidence."

"If they're cops," Steven said, "they could just go dormant after what happened up there in Carrigan County, and we'd be left with fifteen unsolved and no frigging idea of who these people are."

"I know one way," Bobby Lee said. They all looked at him.

"Start talking about a show trial. Say we have evidence that there's a vigilante hit squad operating in the state, that we have a star witness, in the person of Lieutenant Richter here, who knows who these people are because the old tracker gave him a deathbed confession."

"Wouldn't that make Lieutenant Richter a tasty target?" Steven asked.

"You said you wanted to smoke 'em out. I believe that would do the trick."

"Lieutenant?" Steven said. "How you feel about being the goat staked out in tiger country?"

Cam let out a long breath. "If that's what it takes," he said. "I don't have any better ideas. I mean, we can chase those corroborative factors, see if we can tie an MO to specific individuals or specific county sheriff's offices, but that might take forever."

"They'll know about Mitchell," Bobby Lee said. "That's been all over the news. They'll know Lieutenant Richter brought him in. They have to be worried already."

"One problem," Cam said. "I don't think White Eye actually knew their names or anything about them, other than that he guessed they were cops. If that's true, and *they* know that, setting up a trap might not work."

"Shit," Steven said. "We're going in circles here."

"Seven guys," Cam said, stirring what was left of his coffee. "Seven guys who are so addicted to danger that they'd track a mountain lion close enough to take a picture of its face; who get together from time to time to hunt down and execute especially noxious perps; and who could organize a bomb at a judge's house, which was under Sheriff's Office protection. All this would take a very different kind of guy."

"Your point being?" Steven asked.

"My point being: Let's ask every sheriff in North Carolina to name one person in his office who might be twisted enough to qualify for membership in a group like this. I think we're looking for senior street operatives—sergeants, probably— who've been through a lot and are hard as nails, pissed off at the system, and capable of getting out there on the edge and going full bore. We've all run across guys like that at one time or another. We usually push 'em into early retirement, too."

Cam saw that the sheriff was giving him a studiously appraising look, as if to say, You've got someone in mind right here in Manceford County, don't you? "You'd have to do that sheriff to sheriff," he said to Bobby Lee.

"And then what?" Steven asked. "Say you get a list?"

"Sweat 'em," Cam said. "Use whatever IA channels we have to find out where they were and what they were doing when Flash was abducted in a hail of blank bullets. Or when Annie Bellamy went into low-earth orbit."

"That's such a shotgun approach," Steven said. "Maybe not even legal."

"Any better ideas?" Cam asked. No one said anything. "Of course, we wouldn't get 'em all, but we might get lucky," he continued. "Nail one, turn him, get the rest. Grind through them. Turn one of the Bureau's interrogation teams loose on them. Tie them physically to Carrigan County. Sweat the wives and girlfriends: Does he go out west a lot? Go hunting a lot? Take a lot of leave?"

The sheriff wasn't convinced. "If they're veteran cops, and they've shared this initiation with mountain lions, you won't get a word out of them. Then what?"

"Invoke the Patriot Act," Cam said. "Send them down to Guantánamo Bay and let some of those retired CIA sweepers go to town. That bombing would be sufficient justification."

"Okay, I agree," Steven said. "If Lieutenant Richter is willing, I think the idea of trolling that deathbed confession within Sheriff's Office circles is the best course of action. If they've hit a judge, they won't balk at taking another cop out."

"Then I'd want some federal help in protecting him," the sheriff said.

"Right," Steven agreed. "We need to work up a plan. They'll need time to organize, make their decision, and then get set up. I need to get with McLain down in Charlotte. Sheriff, let's you and me meet in my office tomorrow morning."

Bobby Lee agreed. Steven said he had to go. Bobby Lee

stayed behind after Klein left. "You okay with this?" he asked as they stood out on Cam's front porch.

Cam shrugged. "As long as we move pretty quick," he said. "I don't know how these guys move around or communicate, but it might not take them all that long to come calling."

"You want some people here tonight?"

"Who you gonna call, Sheriff?" Cam asked. "Hate to have the wrong guy show up as part of my protective detail."

"You think Sergeant Cox is one of them, don't you?" Bobby Lee said.

Cam had to think for a moment before replying. "Who would you offer up," he said finally, "if that question came around about cops who operate on the edge?"

The sheriff nodded slowly. "He's gone over the line more than once. That's why Bellamy hammered him in the first place. Except . . ."

"Except the MCAT was the perfect place for him," said Cam, finishing the sentence for him. "Nobody ran 'em down like Kenny Cox."

"Should I move him out?"

"How?"

"A temporary assignment? A special project, say, with the Bureau down in Charlotte?"

"Wouldn't that be interesting," Cam said. He heard his phone ringing inside but ignored it. "If my theory is correct, they don't let any of the cell members do anything on their own home ground. The out-of-towners come, like that guy who showed up to calibrate me. No, I'd say we find a way to know where he is at all times and then see what happens."

"Hmmh," the sheriff said. "Come in early tomorrow morning. You're awfully isolated out here."

Cam snapped his fingers and both shepherds were at the door in a heartbeat, ears up and looking for a job. "Not entirely," Cam said.

After the sheriff left, he retrieved the phone message. It was from Jay-Kay. "Can you come down here to Charlotte? No phone calls. Just come as soon as possible." Reluctantly he went to make some coffee.

47

IF JAY-KAY WAS SURPRISED to see him at 3:30 in the morning, she gave no sign of it. From her appearance, Cam guessed that she had already been up. He'd known many computer types who worked at night as much as they did by day. He sat in her ultramodern kitchen and filled her in on his trip west. She was dressed in jeans and a sweatshirt and her hair was wrapped in a tight bun. She took a look at his weary face and made coffee, which she did with the same clean, quick efficiency she exhibited in her professional work. The kitchen didn't really look lived in. She winced when he described what had happened to White Eye Mitchell. She wrote down Mary Ellen's name and office number.

"My parents used to tell stories of man-eating tigers taking villagers from their beds at night," she said. "Gave me bad dreams for years."

"I don't think that cat knew what it was doing—or to whom," Cam said. "It was reflexive, and amazingly quick."

She set down a cup of coffee for him and a mug of tea for herself. "You, sir, have a problem," she announced.

"Just one?"

"One is enough," she replied. "I was in the FBI building today, on a nonrelated issue. Two of the agents with whom I worked previously were chatting me up about cars. Naturally, western Carolina came up, and I mentioned that you were out there working on something to do with the Bellamy bombing. One of them revealed that the ATF and the Bureau are split on which way to go with that case."

"Split how?"

"The Bureau has a 'distinctive theory of the case,' as this young man put it. He would not elaborate, but he did say that the ATF thinks you may have had a hand in the bombing because you knew about the great wealth that would come your way if she died."

Cam shook his head. "I'm a cop," he said. "I'd have to have known that I'd be the first guy everyone looked at. And I would also have known that if I were implicated in her death, I'd never see a dime. What's the Bureau's read?"

"Only that they do not agree and are waiting for a line of inquiry to produce some results before they'll go forward."

"I'd forgotten they talk like that. And that's the extent of ATF's theory? I'm the heir and thus guilty of murder?"

"They have ruled out terrorism on the basis of the bomb's physical characteristics, which apparently was extremely crude and entirely too big for the job at hand. Plus the fact that you would have been in perfect position to feed James Marlor locating data on the two chair victims, and that you were the only one who witnessed, as it were, Marlor's demise."

"And now this business in Carrigan County," Cam said. "Marlor points me at this cat dancer club; I come up with the man who trained them to hunt the mountain lions, and he dies in my presence."

She nodded. "The prime suspect in the execution videos was Marlor," she said. "And he died right *after* you interviewed him to find out how much he knew. Then, as you just said the central player in this cat-dancing scheme dies, in your presence. And there's only your word as to what happened in both instances. And you requested the leave of absence after the Bellamy bombing."

"The sheriff suggested that, for Chrissakes!"

"Did he?" she asked. "I thought you requested it."

So I did, Cam thought. Shit.

"The agents focus on paper trails. You applied for it in writing. Why? To take care of loose ends. Which are duly taken care of."

He stared at her and she gave him an impassive look. "You believe all this?" he asked finally.

"No, I don't," she said. "But as they said, it hangs together."

Cam got up to stretch his legs. "You said earlier you'd

found out something about Kenny Cox," he said. "That we'd talk later?"

She stirred her tea for a moment. "Yes, I did. You asked me to run his cell phone calls. I did, both his personal cell as well as his operational phone."

"And?"

"The official cell phone was used only for official calls. There were almost no calls made on his personal phone. Admittedly, he's got a minimal calling plan, the payments autodeducted from his checking account."

"Sounds like mine."

"But you use yours, Just Cam. This one mostly just sits there, and that made me curious. I mean, if all he wanted was a nine-one-one phone, those are dirt cheap. So I went at it in reverse."

"Meaning?"

"Meaning I then did a scan to see what other bills are being autodeducted from that checking account."

"How in the world could you do that?" he asked. "Banks don't hand that information out to just anybody."

She smiled. "I emulate. Or rather, the tigers do. In this case, we emulated an IRS audit contractor's query. It's a routine question during one of their so-called reality audits. Because of budget cuts, the IRS uses contractors to do scut work like account scans. I can't emulate the IRS, but I can emulate some of their contractors. I do it for the Bureau all the time when they don't want to tip their hand in an investigation."

"And a bank just lets you in? Without a warrant?"

"Who tells the IRS to go away? Besides, big banks get dozens of queries every day from credit bureaus, mortgage companies, debt collection agencies, other banks. It's not like they want money, and any IRS query is answered immediately."

"Damn. And what did the IRS find out?"

"That he has another phone account—in a different name. And this is going to interest you a lot, I think. The name is Carl Marlor. Ring any bells?"

"*Marlor!*" Cam said softly. He sat down again. "Holy shit." Then the first name hit him, too. Carl.

The original cat dancer? He thought for a moment, trying to recall White Eye's description of the man who called himself Carl. Big guy. Had a look about him that would keep other men from getting mouthy in a bar. Had he described him? Fair-haired or dark? He couldn't remember.

"And the cell company doesn't check people out to see if they're using a bogus name?"

"Only if the customer wants credit of some kind. The competition in that business is so cutthroat these days, they'd sign up Mickey Mouse. Think of all those eager young men waving cell phones at you in the mall."

"You're saying Kenny has established an identity for this Carl Marlor? He's committing identity fraud?"

"The reverse. He's not stealing someone else's identity for money. He's done precisely what you need to do to have an identity—opened some consumer accounts, paid them through autodeductions so they're always up-to-date. He has an address, which is real. He has no landline phone, only a cell phone—but that's all the rage these days. Plus, the number is real."

"What about a Social Security number?"

"He's using his own. His real one."

"And that doesn't trip up some computer-check program?"

She nodded. "The credit bureaus have Carl Marlor listed, with an interesting notation in the comments section—two names coming up with the same Social Security number. But the explanation appears to be real. He changed his name almost fifteen years ago."

"Legally changed his name?"

"Apparently. There's even a court order on file."

"And that just solves it?"

"There are no fraud implications to paying a consumer bill," she said. "Applying for a loan or credit? That's different, and he'd have to explain it, although a credit check reveals the answer. An IRS audit would catch it immediately, of course, which is exactly what happened when I queried."

"Except he's not stealing or defrauding anyone. It is legal to change your name."

"Yes. And it allows him to create phone records in another name, and thereby make calls with impunity if he *is* doing something illegal. As in many, many calls around the state to numbers that all turned out to be for telephone booths. Especially one in the town of Pineville."

"Recently?"

"Very."

He rubbed his face with both hands. The image of a cop car parked next to a phone booth rose in his mind. He'd seen it all the time. "Tell me," he said. "You said your computers are expert at doing pattern analysis. Could they search the phone records of the phone booths he called and then determine if calls were made from those phone booths to any others on a regular basis?"

"Of course."

He eyed her. "Just like that?"

She smiled. "No, not just like that. But what you're looking for is a geographical area of probability, aren't you?"

He nodded. "My theory is that these seven guys are cops. Either active duty, retired, or even fired cops. I think they're all over the state, and get together to do vigilante business once in awhile. A very secret society, with the price of admission being a picture of a mountain lion taken at eight paces."

"Your cat dancers."

"Not mine, but yes. And I've asked the sheriff to make some inquiries, this time for what we call 'cowboys' in the sheriff's offices throughout the state. If we can get the locale of the phone booths and some names to coincide, we have a shot."

"Is your sheriff on your side in this?" she asked.

"I think so, yes. I've kept him in the loop, and he's a straight arrow. If there's a bad apple in his office, he'll crush it."

"Can you get him to task me for those two pattern analyses? I want some top cover."

"Absolutely," he said. "You think these guys will get onto you when you go poking around?"

She shrugged. "It would depend on where the data is

stored and how much attention they're paying to their on-line accounts. I've got the tigers watching for James Marlor's computer, in case Sergeant Cox has it."

Cam stifled a yawn. "I know there's something else I need to do, but damned if I can surface it right now."

"Look," she said. "You're exhausted. There's a guest suite down that hall. Go get a hot shower and some sleep. Clear your brain. I have work to do in the lab. Go sleep for a few hours."

Cam found himself nodding. She was making perfect sense. Then he remembered the dogs were down in the truck. He explained the problem.

"Take them across the street. There is a ten-acre building site there. Then you can bring them up here."

"They shed," he warned her.

"Don't we all, Just Cam," she said with a sympathetic smile. "Go."

48

HE AWOKE TO THE sound of scratching at his door and looked at his watch. It was 2:30. He blinked. Two-thirty in the afternoon? He got up, found a robe in the bathroom, and opened the door. Both dogs were sitting outside his door, ready to go outside, and their look said, Now would be nice. He groaned and went to find his clothes.

When he got back, he found that Jay-Kay had left him a note in the kitchen. She had fed the dogs. She'd be gone all day, and he was to help himself to whatever he needed. He walked through the living quarters and was struck again by the feeling that no one really lived here. But she had actually gone out and bought a can of dog food, and there was even a water bowl put down. He wondered when she slept, but he felt 100 percent better. He made himself some toast and coffee and then called Bobby Lee.

"You're in Charlotte?" the sheriff asked. Cam thought he heard voices in the background.

"Consulting with our consultant," Cam said, wondering who else might be in the room with the sheriff. "We need to meet. Privately."

The sheriff started to say something, but Cam cut him off, suggesting the bar at the Marriott at 7:30.

He then sat down at the kitchen table with a pad of legal paper and began writing a report, starting with the execution videos. He made it as factual as he could, offering no theories or suppositions. It came to some twenty pages when he was all finished.

Then he wrote another one, this time outlining his theories about what was going on with respect to a vigilante cell in North Carolina. He asserted, in writing this time, that he'd known nothing about Annie's bequest, pointing out that the will had been written back when they were already divorced and no longer living together. He stated that Oliver Strong had been her personal lawyer for many years and that Strong could testify that he had never met Cam before summoning him after she had been killed. He denied as forcefully as he could do in a letter that he had had anything to do with her death.

Then he wrote up a third paper, this one laying out what he would like the sheriff, or, for that matter, the federal authorities, to authorize Jay-Kay to do—pursuant to formal warrants this time—to investigate the personal background of Sgt. Kenny Cox of the Manceford County Sheriff's Office. He suggested that military authorities be contacted to get some sense of Cox's military service and how that had ended. He pointed out that if Kenny and James Marlor were related, then the execution videos probably indicated police collusion in the murder of the two robbers, and that since Marlor had told "them" where the chair was—probably right there in Triboro—there might be further executions. He then wrote out the pattern analysis he and Jay-Kay had discussed during the night, and he recommended that this be pursued as a matter of urgency.

When he was finished, it was almost dark. He went downstairs to the receptionist's area. She was still there, and she helped him to make three copies of what he had written. He addressed one copy to Thomas McLain at the FBI's Charlotte field office. He sent a second copy to Mike Pierce at the SBI. The third one, he packaged up to take to Bobby Lee.

When he finally got near Triboro, he took a shortcut off the interstate, a route leading to the downtown area. Being back in Manceford County, he gunned it, forgetting that he was no longer in a vehicle that would be recognized by local law as being driven by a fellow cop. Five minutes down the road, he saw blue strobes in his mirror. He swore and began braking. The cruiser came right up behind him and the strobes dimmed, which meant that they were grille lights. He looked again in the mirror as he started to pull over, confirming there was no light rack on the vehicle behind him. That made him wonder. The state cops used slickbacks on interstates, but the Sheriff's Office traffic detail did not. And this was not a road the state troopers would be working at rush hour.

He pulled off the concrete and onto the berm. The other vehicle closed it right up tight, which was something else no deputy would do. You always left some space, if for nothing else but to register the license plate on the dash Cam. This guy was *right* behind him. He left his engine running and reached for his ID. The shotgun was still under the seat, but there was no way he could reach for that, not without the cop seeing him bend over. But something wasn't quite right here. There was no one getting out of the cop car behind him. Another car came along and then passed them, briefly illuminating two silhouettes in the car behind him.

Now he definitely knew something wasn't right: Manceford County never ran two officers in a cruiser, and he was in Manceford County. The shepherds, sensing Cam's growing apprehension, were getting antsy and looking for instructions. He gave them both a down command to keep them flat on the backseat, then rolled down both rear windows, as well as his own. He put both his hands high up on the steering wheel and watched his mirrors. Sure enough, both men in the vehicle behind him got out at the same time and started forward. He could see white faces in the glare of their headlights, but not whether they were in uniform. Neither one had put his hat on, which was another thing a deputy always did when he got out to issue a traffic citation. Citizens recognized the hat, even when they couldn't see a full uniform.

These guys were not Manceford County deputies.

The men came forward, and Cam caught a glimpse of drawn weapons, which they were holding in front of them, pointed down in two-handed grips. Wrong, all wrong. He thought about grabbing the shotgun, but there was no time and there were two targets. Rather than turning to look at the one coming up on his side, he kept his head straight ahead and scanned the three mirrors with his eyes. The instant the man on the left drew even with the rear window, Cam barked a command. Both rear windows were suddenly filled with a snarling German shepherd in the twenty-snaps-per-second mode. Frick was working Cam's side of the truck, while Frack was doing the same routine out the other window, causing both men to jump back from the truck. The one on Cam's side actually tripped and sprawled out into the roadway in his frantic attempt to avoid being bitten. Cam slammed the truck into reverse and drove the pickup's protruding bumper hitch ball deep into the other vehicle's radiator, then shifted into drive and peeled out of there, blowing gravel, grille debris, and road trash into their faces before either of them had a chance to use guns. He was doing ninety before he knew it and almost lost it on the next curve, but there were no lights in his rearview mirror just now. He slowed down and checked on his buddies in the back. The dogs were sitting up, their legs splayed due to all the maneuvers. Their claws gripped the seat tightly, but they were wearing their very best "That was fun" expressions. Cam relaxed and rolled up the windows.

The sheriff shook his head when Cam told about being picked up on the road back into Triboro.

"That was on me," he said with an annoyed look on his face. "When I said, 'You're in Charlotte?'"

"Who was in the room?"

"Horace Stackpole. And Kenny."

"Oh no," Cam muttered, startling the pretty young waitress who was putting their drinks on the table. Cam handed over his report package. He described what was in it and said he'd sent one each to McLain and Mike Pierce at the SBI. Before Bobby Lee could protest, Cam related what Jay-Kay had told him about the ATF-FBI split on the bombing case.

"My take is that the Bureau is undecided about us here in Manceford County," Cam said. "The ATF apparently has its own agenda. Something's going on there, and I can't figure it out. Mike Pierce will turn on the right people at the SBI. That's why I put it in writing. It looks a whole lot better coming *from* me than *at* me."

"That'll get you suspended," the sheriff said. "That's the first thing that'll happen."

"Suspension isn't all bad," Cam replied. "Look, these guys have tried for me two times. So far, I've been damned lucky, but the next time it's going to be a long gun, and that'll be all she wrote. This way, we do what we do best: We bring a crowd. Make it official—warrants, court orders. And if you're into suspensions, you'd better move on Sergeant Cox."

"Is she sure she's got that right—that his name used to be Marlor?"

"You can ask her directly, but that lady doesn't mess around with those damned computers."

"And I thought women with guns were frightening," Bobby Lee said.

He sipped his drink. "I hate the fact that there are so damned many people into this hair ball."

"Politically?"

"I can handle that," the sheriff said, waving his hand dismissively. "I'm talking about getting these guys off the street. Did you call in the fake stop out on the connector?"

"Negative."

"Where exactly did it go down?"

Cam told him. "There should be a small lake of antifreeze out there on the side of the road," he said, "even if they did get the vehicle moved."

The sheriff got out his cell phone and made a call. He instructed the Southside district office to get a forensics unit out to the location to see what they could find, then report directly back to him. While they ate, Cam explained his theory on how to correlate the phone booth records with the cowboy list, and Bobby Lee told him he'd already started the ball rolling on developing the list. As they finished, the sheriff's cell phone chirped. He answered, listened, and then said to get every piece of debris bagged up.

"They found it?" Cam asked.

"Yep. They spotted a coyote lapping something up in the vicinity and found the antifreeze, plus a lot of plastic bits and a piece of radiator core. There were some big truck tracks ahead of your scratch marks, so they probably called a wrecker. We'll canvass the tow guys in the area. This isn't going to be that hard."

"That's one dead coyote," Cam said. He knew that farmers used to put out bowls of antifreeze when coyotes and other predators began killing livestock. The animals couldn't resist it, and they died horribly. The biggest problem was that it killed everything in the woods that got within scent of it.

"How are you going to handle Kenny?" Cam asked after the waitress cleared away their plates.

"When will SBI get your package?"

"The Bureau will have it first thing tomorrow, SBI by noon."

"I'll call Mike Pierce first thing in the morning, give him time to read your reports, and then set up an interview with Kenny tomorrow afternoon with the SBI in my office."

"If he's one of them, he'll know about what happened tonight," Cam said.

"Maybe, maybe not. If your theory's correct about them not operating on their home turf, he might not. I think we have a day. By then, we'll have something on that vehicle."

"I guess it could have been undercover state guys," Cam began.

The sheriff shook his head. "They'd have shown ID. Made the usual apprehension noises. And there'd have been runner reports all over the place, somebody got away from troopers like that. I'd have been beeped by now."

Cam nodded. In a way, he'd have preferred that there was another explanation.

"Where will you go tonight?" the sheriff asked.

Cam shrugged. "Back home, I guess." Even as he said it, he realized that that would be a dumb idea.

"Get a motel somewhere," the sheriff said. "Hell, stay right here. This is a hotel."

"I've got the dogs with me."

The sheriff looked around. "That's why God made side entrances and service elevators," he said. "Actually, you can probably get 'em in on that parking garage sky bridge on the second floor. Sounds like they saved your ass tonight."

Cam nodded. He wanted to go home, get a change of clothes, see what, if anything, had happened to his house, but the sheriff was right.

"When would you want me in tomorrow?" he asked.

"Go home in the morning, get cleaned up, and then come in. We'll have us a crowd of helpers going by then."

"I don't look forward to this," Cam said.

The sheriff stared of across the lobby for a moment. Cam thought he'd aged in the past week. "We'll recover," he said finally. "But probably not before we tar some good people."

49

HE ARRIVED BACK AT his house at five o'clock the next morning. The dogs had become restless in the hotel room around 4:00 A.M., and he'd decided that was a good time to get them and himself out of there and home before the morning rush hour started. It was still dark when he pulled into his driveway, and there was a thin mist hovering in the trees. He left the truck in the driveway and put the dogs into the backyard, where he watched to see what they'd do. If there was someone in the house, they'd react just as soon as they cut strange scent crossing the backyard. They didn't do anything but their normal yard patrol, so he let himself in through the front door. The alarm system beeped at him when the door opened, but he hadn't set the intrusion alarm before bailing out the night before last.

He went through to the kitchen and turned on some lights, threw his overnight pack into a chair, and cranked up the coffeemaker. He pulled one of his army mugs out of the cupboard and was just turning to take it to the table, when a voice in the doorway asked him to make it two.

It was Kenny Cox, standing in the entrance to the kitchen. He was dressed in civilian camo hunting clothes, but he had his police utility belt and sidearm. His face and clothes looked like he had spent the night asleep in one of Cam's living room recliners. Cam straightened up and tried not to show his surprise.

"How long you been here?" he asked.

"Since about two-thirty," Kenny replied.

"And the object of the social call is?" he asked.

"Talk. We need to talk to you."

"'We.' So it's true, then."

Kenny came into the kitchen, pulled a chair away from the kitchen table with his foot, and sat down heavily. His .45 thumped against the back of the chair. He was so big that the chair creaked audibly when he put his weight on it.

"Depends on what you mean," Kenny said. "We didn't do the bomb. I want to get that right out on the table. That wasn't us."

Cam just stared at him. He was still absorbing the fact that Kenny Cox really was one of them. That it was all true. Kenny saw the disappointment on Cam's face, shrugged, and rubbed the back of his head with one massive hand. "I know," he said.

"You know what, exactly?" Cam asked, trying to keep the anger out of his voice. He wondered if Kenny was alone in the house. The damned shotgun was still in the truck, the shepherds were outside, and his gun belt was upstairs.

"I know what you're thinking. Relax. There's no one else here, and I'm just here to talk."

Cam crossed his arms over his chest. "So talk."

"We knew it was only a matter of time, once that bomb went off," Kenny said. "We were comfortable that you'd finger Marlor for the minimart creeps, but once the attacks on Bellamy started, we couldn't be sure."

The coffeepot maker quit making its noises and Cam got another mug out of the cupboard. "You helped Marlor find them?"

"Hell yes. Got him the blanks, even ran covert backup for him when he snatched up Flash. Talk about funny."

"Not for Flash," Cam said.

"And not for Marlor's wife and kid," Kenny shot back, showing some teeth. "Those pricks got precisely what they deserved."

Cam poured out coffee for both of them. "We're meeting this morning. This thing is coming together. We've identified fifteen possible victims since you guys got going."

"'Victims'?" Kenny said in a nasty voice. "The real victims came first. Korean shopkeepers murdered for fifteen dollars. The young mother raped in the mall parking lot during a carjacking. The baby thrown out of the car on the interstate during another carjacking. The pizza delivery boy who gets his throat cut—not for the money, but for the fucking *pizza*. The all-star high school basketball athlete who takes a round in the throat from some asshole doing a drive-by, just because he was standing at the wrong bus stop at the wrong time, or because some young dick needed to make his bones to join the Crips. The foreign tourists who get the shit beat out of them and their rent-a-car stolen just because they turned down the wrong street. Those are your victims."

"And how are you guys any different?"

"We're the guys who square the accounts, Cam. The old gods who used to handle retribution are in a nursing home in Florida. Don't you dare call these assholes victims. They were professional slimeballs. All we did was help them run smack into that big sword Madam Justice carries, because the scales don't work so good anymore. And there've been eighteen, not fifteen."

"Kenny," Cam began, but Kenny wasn't done.

"Don't lecture me, man," he said. "You're still part of the problem. I worked out the right and wrong of it a long time ago. We have, and we're comfortable with the equation, okay? Every one of those assholes was a stone-cold doer, and every one of them had been let off by some prissy police work or some weak-assed judge, *and* they'd bragged about it. It's the brag that brings the dancers, Cam."

Cam sat down at the table. "Well, it's over now."

"What, you're gonna tell me you got a list of names?"

"You guys used phone booths to communicate, right? Remember Ms. Jaspreet Kaur Bawa?"

"The princess?" Kenny said. "Absolutely."

"Well, the princess sicced those two mainframes of hers on you personally, Kenny. Bobby Lee's talking to his counterparts in every county in the state, asking for a list of cowboys. He's gonna get a statewide list of candidates, and she's correlating phone booth locations with the call history of your other cell phone. The one in your former name?"

Kenny blinked. He sipped some coffee, eyeing Cam over the rim of the mug.

"They're all cops, right?" Cam said. "Either active or former cops?"

Kenny nodded.

"And James Marlor? Brother? Cousin? What?"

Kenny smiled. "You're doing pretty good so far; you tell me," he said.

"Don't know. But we will."

"Okay," Kenny said. "But you'll never understand it. Not you. Not Mr. Straight Arrow."

"You're right about that, Kenny." Cam heard the shepherds moving around out on the back deck. But of course Kenny's scent wouldn't have put them on the alert. Kenny was a buddy. "And this cat-dancing shit—going face-to-face with a *mountain lion*? What the fuck's with that?"

"You wouldn't understand that, either," Kenny said.

"Try me."

Kenny looked away for a moment. "We needed a certain kind of guy, someone who was emotionally worn-out from playing by the rules. You said you're looking for cowboys, but we're not cowboys. We've been through our cowboy phase. This is another level all together."

"Judges, juries, and executioners?"

"Something like that. We needed serious anger at the system and the capacity to face certain death and laugh at it. To fully and truly not give a shit. And when you face one of the wild ones? That is an acid test, by God. And the biggest rush I've ever experienced."

Cam shook his head in wonderment. "I guess it's a good thing you don't give a shit, because the system is going to grind you up."

"Maybe," Kenny said. "But you're going to need evidence, and evidence is going to be hard to come by. That system you're so hot to defend is going to make it really hard to take us down."

"And that's what your life's all about these days? A bigger rush? Hunting down dumb-ass criminals and executing them? And how many cops have you taken out, Kenny? Guys who got a sniff of what you were doing and maybe asked questions?"

"None," Kenny said. "Never."

"Really? Your bunch tried for me twice. What'd they have in mind, tea and crumpets?"

Kenny frowned. "You were warned. What White Eye was supposed to do was scare you, and I admit that went off the tracks. But that was it. You say twice?"

Cam enumerated the warehouse attack and the roadside stop. Kenny shook his head. "White Eye was acting for us. That other shit? Not us."

"Or your group is coming apart," Cam said. "Someone's scared and acting on his own."

Kenny shook his head again. "Negative," he muttered. "Negative."

It was Cam's turn to look away. Either Kenny was lying or he really didn't know what was going on within his little group of assassins. Cam knew he hadn't imagined these incidents. "And you didn't put the elephant-gun round through Annie's house?" he asked.

"Negative. We didn't plant that bomb, either. In fact—"

"In fact what?"

"Like I said, that's when we knew. I got that same feeling when Jimmie killed himself. We always knew that it couldn't go on forever. And after what happened on Catlett Bald, we agreed to go deep. Everyone agreed."

"All seven of you?"

"Six, after Jimmie. I—we—really didn't expect that. I could understand it, sort of, after the fact. But it still came as a shock."

"Jimmie—He was your brother, then?"

"Yeah. Shit. Jimmie was my older brother. He was the one who started the thing with the big cats. He was up there in the western mountains all the time, working for Duke. You have to understand, now—Jimmie was always a little far-out. That's why I had to leave the army. He and I did some crazy shit and they found out about it."

"But the vigilante bit—that was your idea, wasn't it?" Cam said. "Especially once you realized you had a pretty much foolproof way to prove candidates for your hit squad. If they could face the cat, then they were men enough to whack bad guys and never reveal it."

Kenny nodded. "You called us cowboys. We're not."

"You know what I mean. Guys in law enforcement who ride the edge all the time. The cops who *want* to draw their weapons. Who *live* to draw their weapons. The cops who *hate* the bad guys. Who substitute passion for professionalism."

"You wouldn't understand," Kenny said.

"Got that right. Like I told you, we're meeting this morning. You coming in?"

"I will if there's a warrant, although I don't think you'll get one. You have no evidence."

"I have what we've just been talking about."

"You're tainted. You're the guy who became a millionaire when Bellamy went up. The only thing keeping you from suspension is that the Bureau doesn't believe it."

"I'll take my chances," Cam said. "I know I didn't do the bombing or anything else like that. You, on the other hand, know what you've been doing."

"We didn't do that bombing or the shooting into her house, partner. So who did that? Got any clues for that?"

"My guess is it *was* your cell, if not you personally. We can probably make that stick, too, once we tie you people to the killings."

"Never happen, Cam, because we didn't do that. Just like you didn't do it. So there's a mystery for you: Who did?"

"I give up. Who?"

Kenny stood and zipped up his jacket. "I have a theory, but no incentive to share it with you."

"Where are you going?"

"I'm taking some impromptu leave," Kenny said. "I feel the need to do some dancing. Maybe one last time, especially if you guys do get lucky. You want me in the next two weeks, come on out to the Chop."

"What the hell is the Chop?"

"The park rangers know where it is. Ask that pretty one, Mary something."

"Was her boyfriend one of the club? Joel Hatch?"

"Who told you that?"

"Mary Ellen. She admitted to knowing what cat dancing was."

Kenny scoffed. "Hatch was a fucking jock-sniffer. White Eye blew him off. Bangs on the door of a boiler room at midnight and says, 'Open up in the name of the law!' Shit. No wonder they offed him. Adios, partner."

Cam thought about trying to stop him, but he realized that was pointless and probably not even possible. Even if he pointed a gun at Kenny and told him he was under arrest, Kenny would laugh at him. They both knew neither one of them could ever pull that trigger.

Dawn was beginning to break outside. Cam finished his coffee and went upstairs to get ready for the day's coming festivities. He thought about what Kenny had said. What if the vigilante cell had not done the bombing? If not them, then who the hell had done that? And why?

50

THREE DAYS LATER, CAM was back in Carrigan County, headed for a 5:00 P.M. meeting with the park rangers. His letters had formally initiated the opening of a case-action file by the SBI, which had set up shop in Manceford County to lead the investigation with the full cooperation of the Sheriff's Office and the concurrence of the FBI. Bobby Lee had made his calls to the sheriffs of all the counties in North Carolina, achieving mixed results, as he had expected. Some of the sheriffs had said go away, others had said they didn't have any cowboys, and still others had surfaced a total of nine names. These had been turned over to Jaspreet for her pattern analysis of phone records, phone booths, dead criminals, and the locations and service histories of the nine named officers.

Cam had briefed the sheriff privately on his discussion with Kenny Cox, which, as far as he was concerned, confirmed the existence of the cell, even though they had no substantive evidence yet. Kenny had dropped leave papers down in the personnel office the night before he'd come to see Cam, with the leave address blank. Neither Cam nor the sheriff informed the SBI that Kenny had as much as confessed, deciding instead to wait and see if Jay-Kay's pattern analysis would fold Kenny into the mix. They did make sure that his name was on the analysis target list.

By the end of the second day, Jaspreet was ready to report. She had identified a statistically significant pattern of phone calls that tied two of the target names, as well as that of Sergeant Cox, to the phone booths in the locations where some of the criminals had been killed. She had then gone back and sifted through James Marlor's phone records and found more ties to the same general network of phone booths. One of the two names was that of an active-duty officer, and a search of the relevant Sheriff's Office records found congruent absences over the past five years. The second name was that of senior sergeant who'd been forced into retirement after a suspicious shooting incident. It would have been interesting to be able to tie in White Eye Mitchell's records to the pattern analysis, but, as the sheriff in Carrigan County reported, they'd found no records or even bank accounts. Apparently, White Eye had not believed in paperwork, and his mattress had been his bank. Interestingly, Indian guide White Eye Mitchell had been a police officer in Detroit —his real name was Junious Mitchell Smith—before becoming an "Indian" guide in the Great Smokies. Smith's contract had not been renewed, due to what was termed "temperamental unsuitability." They'd searched his property but had found no evidence of big cats.

The SBI had sent for Kenny Cox's army records, but it was going to take at least two weeks to retrieve them from the federal depository in St. Louis. They would need those records to help them determine why he'd changed his name from Marlor to Cox. None of the MCAT guys, including Cam, could shed any light on Kenny's back story. When they did kick it around, it became clear that none of them knew very much at all about where Kenny went on his free time, and they concluded that perhaps all the stories about him being the Manceford County Sheriff's Office premier assbandit may have been cover and deception. Bobby Lee had decided the final strategy: Cam was dispatched to go find Kenny Cox and convince him to come in. If they could break Kenny, then they'd go after the two other known names and try to break up the entire cell. If Kenny wouldn't come in, or they couldn't find him, they'd let the Bureau handle it.

Two of Twenty Mile's three rangers were waiting for Cam when he arrived at the station. It was fully dark outside and the station had been shut down for the day. One of them was Mary Ellen, and the other, who appeared to be older than she was, introduced himself as Ranger Marshall. He said he was the station chief. After getting some coffee, they repaired to the conference room, where Cam explained why he was there.

"We need to find one of our deputies," he began. "He's become the subject of an Internal Affairs investigation ongoing in Manceford County."

"What kind of investigation, exactly?" Marshall asked.

Cam danced around the true nature of the problem, which provoked another question: Did this have something to do with White Eye Mitchell's demise during Cam's previous visit. Cam said it did. They waited. Mary Ellen pretended total ignorance.

"So what do you want from us?" Marshall asked bluntly.

"I have reason to believe that Sergeant Cox is in an area called the Chop? Does that name ring a bell?"

They nodded. "The Chop is a geological formation in the northwestern part of the park," Mary Ellen said. "It's partly in North Carolina and partly in Tennessee."

"What's the name mean?"

"Think of God picking up a hatchet and making one spectacular ten- to twelve-mile-long chop through the backbone of the mountains. It's a place where a large mountain split down the middle a million years ago. A fast river goes through it, and it's about as remote as you can get in the park."

"How would I get to it this time of year?"

"Helo," Marshall said. "But not for very much longer."

"Weather?" Cam asked.

They nodded. "There's a front predicted to arrive in about seventy-two hours, which will make it impossible to get there."

"Even by helicopter?"

"Think twenty-five feet of snow, Lieutenant," Mary Ellen said, keeping it formal. Obviously, she wanted to keep the fact that they had met off-line from her supervisor. "No place to land except near the entrance, where the winds will be fifty to sixty knots, and no way to get down into the Chop, short of a parachute. If you're going out there, we need to call the park dispatch center in Gatlinburg right now. They have the helos and the pilots under contract who are qualified to do this."

"Are you qualified to go out into a real wilderness area?" Marshall asked.

Cam said yes, although he told them he would appreciate any advice on winter trekking.

"What the hell is this guy doing way out there?" Marshall asked.

"Cat dancing, I think."

"Aw, c'mon," he said with disdain. "I heard about that when you came up here the last time. There aren't any wild panthers left out there. Even that hair taken from the print the last time you were here was ID'd as that of a western cat."

Cam shrugged. "The one I shot had been tamed and trained to attack a human," he said. "I learned that the hard way, if you'll remember. My guess is that none of us knows what's living way out there."

Mary Ellen intervened. "Look," she said. "That's true— that we don't know. It's highly unlikely, but Mitchell was obviously doing something that involved the big cats. Did this guy tell you he was going to the Chop?"

"Yes, he did."

"Any idea of how he was going in?"

"It's been almost four days. He's been coming out here for years, so he probably had some form of transport prepositioned. Snowmobile? I don't know. Here's my other question: Can I get some help with this? I'm comfortable in the backcountry, but I don't know this ground, and I sure won't know it if we get twenty-five feet of snow."

There was a moment of silence around the table, and then Mary Ellen leaned forward. "Did he suggest there's a wild mountain lion out there in or around the Chop?"

Cam nodded. "In fact, I asked him what the Chop was, and he said to ask you guys—that you'd been there."

"Yes, I've been there. I've been all over this park. Most of us have. But I didn't go there looking for a mountain lion."

"Is this deputy going to come back in peacefully?" Marshall asked.

Cam hesitated. "The truth is, I don't know. But this will be between him and me. He wouldn't hurt another cop."

"Just how dangerous is this guy? Is he deranged?"

"Do you know what NAFOD means?" Cam asked. He got blank looks.

"Law enforcement these days is all about teamwork. From two-man partners all the way up to full-blown SWAT teams. You rely on the guy who has your back—for your life. The one guy who cannot function in that setting is a guy who has no apparent fear of death. NAFOD is a military aviation term. A guy who's NAFOD can and probably will get someone on his team killed because he's fearless. Kenny's dangerous in that sense."

"Is this personal, you and him?"

"He was my number two in Manceford County. I've known and worked with him for many years. I thought I knew him, but now I've found out he goes face-to-face with wild mountain lions for the thrill of it. I'm going to ask him to come in. I'm going to tell him I've told the right people where he is. If he says no, we'll leave, and turn it over to some people who probably won't just ask."

"Okay," Marshall said. "I'll go along and help you set up a base camp. I'll show you what the Chop looks like, and how to get into it. But I'm not chasing down any whacked-out cop with a death wish, and I'm not going to pat a mountain lion on the ass, either."

Cam winced at the description "whacked-out cop," but then he nodded.

"And we're leaving before the storm arrives, which means, *if* we can get out there by, say, noon tomorrow, you'll have maybe forty-eight hours to surface this guy, and then we're out of there. Agreed?"

Like I have much choice, Cam thought. "Yes, absolutely, agreed. And for the record, I'm definitely not NAFOD."

They talked logistics for a few minutes while Mary Ellen went to contact the dispatch center. When Cam was ready to leave, she had a flight laid on for ten o'clock the next morning, staging out of the ranger station's parking lot. Marshall got one of the local outfitters to open up his store that evening so they could equip their little expedition. Mary Ellen stopped Cam in the hallway as he was leaving.

"Two things," she said.

"Shoot."

"Billy Marshall is an ex–Marine Corps recon guy. He's commissioned as a law-enforcement officer. The only reason he volunteered to go with you is to keep you safe, but he's taking you at your word that you've been in the backcountry before. Have you?"

Cam said yes. "I'll have my dogs with me, and I've brought my own gear. If he wants to back out, I can probably do this on my own."

She smiled. "He doesn't want to back out. He just wants to know how much danger you're going to be putting him in."

"If he stays at the camp, his biggest problem will be boredom. And the second question?"

"I want to come along."

He looked at her, then understood. "And you want to see if there really is a wild one out there, right?"

"Right."

"If there is, will you testify for me when it comes to it?"

"I will."

"Fine," he said. "One last thing: When it comes to my bringing Sergeant Cox in, I need to do that by myself."

"No problem," she said brightly. "I'm not NAFOD, either."

51

THEY LANDED AT NOON the next day in a clatter of rotor blades, which produced a miniblizzard of blowing snow. The helicopter was a modified army Blackhawk bearing the markings of the state Department of Natural Resources. The crewman got out first, still connected to his intercom umbilical. He stomped around on the thin snowpack for a moment and then gestured for them to come out. Marshall passed the gear bags to the crewman and then jumped out, followed by Cam, Mary Ellen, and the two German shepherds. Cam signaled the dogs to come with him, and then they all backed away from the helo. The crewman climbed back into the side hatch, checked the wheels out of habit for chocks, and then the bird rattled off in a big circle to the east as it climbed, leaving behind a profound silence.

They had landed in a clearing on the top of a pine-covered hill, where the snow was only about six inches deep and solidly crusted. The broad hill sloped down to the west across an open meadow leading to a narrow but vigorous river, beyond which there was a massive ridgeline of snow-covered granite rising almost two thousand feet into the sky. The main ridge ran northeast-southwest for several miles in both directions, but right in front of them was the Chop, a wedge-shaped canyon that looked like God had indeed taken an ax to the ridge. The cut was about two hundred yards wide at the base, widening to almost a half mile at the top of the mountain. The river came rushing out of the cut and then made a ninety-degree left turn to the north and disappeared into a pine forest. The sky above the ridge was a deep blue, and instead of a wind, there was a gentle wave of frigid air rolling down their side of the ridge, smelling of pine and ice.

They set up camp down in a hollow just above the river, three one-man tents for sleeping and a fourth one, which was larger, for the mess tent. Knowing they wouldn't be packing the gear any distance, Marshall had opted for maximum comfort, even though it would be for only forty-eight hours. They hung the food bags in a nearby tree and then Marshall took them down to the river to show them the way across. The entrance to the Chop was in shadow as the afternoon sun began to settle behind the enormous ridge. The river came out of the canyon with a black vengeance. It slowed as it hit the turn and the deep bare-walled channel it had worn in the rock, then broke into a wide, shallow shoal.

"You can get across right here, which will put you on the north side of the river inside the canyon. The river hugs the south wall at the entrance."

"How far back does that canyon go?" Cam asked. The shepherds were down at the riverbank, nosing around the rocks.

"About eight miles to the base of that ridge. It widens as it goes back. In the middle, it's almost half a mile wide and forms a V shape. It narrows again on the Tennessee side, and then widens out again about a thousand feet up. You'll be climbing the whole time you're in there, and it's in relative shadow except at midday."

Cam studied the rushing waters. "And how exactly do we cross here?"

"Rock to rock," Marshall said with a grin. Cam had been afraid of that. He knew he could do it, but he didn't think the dogs could. Marshall sensed the problem.

"You cross, trailing one end of a rope over on this side. We'll walk our end upstream, just below the bend, tie a dog into a bowline, and then you call him. Once he goes into the water, you pull, and the current will bring him down to you."

Cam nodded. That ought to work, he thought, although Frack wasn't really fond of water. Frick, on the other hand, would do anything once. An eagle called to its mate a thousand feet up the rock face of the ridge, and they all took a moment to watch it soar.

"This look like mountain lion country to you?" Cam asked Mary Ellen.

She nodded. "Mountain lion country is synonymous with deer country, and there'll be deer in that canyon. It's got water, cover, and browse."

They stood there looking for a few minutes, taking in the shining granite walls of the ridge, the deepening shadows that were swallowing up the big pines in the canyon, and the muscular roar of the river. Cam wondered if he ought to get going. Again, Marshall seemed to sense his thoughts.

"Let's go get set up in camp and study some topo maps," he said. "If your man's in that canyon, I can show you where he's likely to make a camp."

Cam shivered, both from the cold and from the anticipation of going up into that canyon looking for Kenny. He wondered if Kenny was really in there, or maybe up at that other mountain, which was twelve miles north. This could be a total wild-goose chase, and he said as much to Marshall.

"It'll be a short one, then," Marshall said. "You two go in at first light, and you have to be back here by about noon, day after tomorrow. Those DNR guys will wait for you until the snow starts, but then they're outa here. Me, too, for that matter." He turned to Mary Ellen. "You sure you want to go along on this? Hunting fugitives isn't exactly in your job description."

"Kenny's not really a fugitive," Cam said. Yet, he thought.

"I'm looking for evidence of a wild mountain lion," Mary Ellen said. "The lieutenant here has the fugitive problem."

"I hope you can maintain that distinction," Marshall told her. "Okay, let's go get set up. And after that, how 'bout we catch some fresh trout for dinner?"

Cam awoke that night for no apparent reason and touched his watch to see what time it was. It read 1:15. He was completely bundled into his sleeping bag, with one dog on either side of him in the tiny tent. It was definitely a two-dog night. The temperature had dropped like a stone once the sun went down, and he'd been shocked by the cold when they left the mess tent. Fortunately, there was no appreciable wind, but Cam figured it was probably down in the single digits by now. Frick licked the side of his head once when she figured out he was awake. Then her ears popped up. Something was outside.

Cam listened carefully while he groped with his right hand for the .45 he'd put into the sleeping bag with him. There. A soft crunch of snow—very soft. Frack's ears were up now, too, but neither dog seemed to be alarmed. Cam frowned in the dark. If it was a bear or some other wild animal, the dogs would be reacting very differently. Marshall? Up for a midnight head call? Mary Ellen, looking for a cuddle? In your dreams, he thought, grinning to himself.

Another soft crunch. Closer. The dogs listened but did not bark.

Cam studied the side of the tent, which was made of a white material. Moonlight was just visible through the square patch of air vent at the front closure. Then the moonlight was blocked out by something large, which suddenly lowered itself down to half its height. The dogs were watching but still didn't seen upset.

Cam understood. They knew who was out there.

And so did he.

He sat up in the bag, got his arms free, and unzipped the front flaps. Kenny was squatting outside in the moonlight, his face framed in what looked like an Eskimo parka, a grin on his face. He put his finger to his lips and then gestured for Cam to come out. Then he pointed to the dogs, put his palm out, and made the standard "Down and stay" gesture. Cam frowned and shook his head. Kenny did it again. The dogs had to stay behind. Then he stood up to wait for Cam to get suited up.

Ten minutes later, they walked silently into the woods, heading toward the river. Once they were down by the rushing water, they could talk without disturbing the sleeping rangers. Cam had his gun in his parka, but he really wished he had the dogs with him. They had not been happy to be left behind, but they were German shepherds, and discipline trumped, as always.

"Our stealth helo didn't fool you, huh?" Cam said.

Kenny snorted. "Stealth, my ass. I heard that thing coming when you were still over that ridge back there. Who's with you?"

Cam told him.

"And she's dying to see a wild one, isn't she?" Kenny said.

"I don't think she believes it," Cam replied. "They all feel that any wild ones up here are all captive escapees. They don't count."

"They're wrong. But that's not why you're here."

"Nope. I'm here to bring you back in. Let me rephrase: to ask you politely to come back in. They know, Kenny."

"They don't know shit and they can't prove shit, either, Cam," Kenny said. His eyes glittered in the moonlight. An owl flew over their heads, making pulses in the still mountain air, a movement they could feel but not hear. "All we have to do is go radio-silent for a while, and we're safe. Phone calls and statistics don't make a case."

"We'll do what we always do, Kenny," Cam said. "We'll sift and we'll sift, and eventually we'll get a guy in a room. Then we'll convince him that it's over and that the other guys are all singing, and then we'll convince him to make it easy on himself—you know, Club Fed instead of gen pop in the state prison."

"You don't know us," Kenny said. "We'll do what White Eye taught us to do—hunker down, go into statue mode, close our eyes, zone into the woods, make like a tree. We'll become invisible right before your eyes. You think if you can break one, he'll break the rest. Won't happen."

"Why, because you chase mountain lions?"

Kenny took a deep breath and looked away for a moment. "It's not the cat dancing, per se," he said finally. "It's the frame of mind that got them to go out there and get a face in the first place. Hard-case cops who've had it with a corrupted system. Who would happily kill all the lawyers for thirty miles around them if they thought they could. And you know what, Cam? Some of them think that's a doable little mission."

"Your point being?"

"My point being that they won't talk and they won't break. They've all faced something a whole lot scarier than some fucking wimp-ass prosecutor like Steven Klein. You can't break this unless somebody rolls, and nobody's gonna roll."

The river seemed noisier to Cam than it had earlier. He decided to try another tack. "Okay, if that's the case, come back in with me. Sit in the chair and show us your stuff."

Kenny laughed. It was an unpleasant sound. "I just might do that," he said. "But on one condition."

"What's that?"

"You come with me for one last dance. Over there. In the Chop."

"Been there, did that," Cam said. "With White Eye, remember? He wanted to give me a little demo on woodcraft, and the next thing I knew, I was up a fucking tree, with a goddamned cat climbing up after me. No thanks, Kenny."

"This time, you go up the tree first and then watch," Kenny said. "Just watch. That's what we can do here in the Chop. This is where we trained. The river cuts the thing one-third, two-thirds. You go on the wide side; I'll be on the other. I know where the den is. I want you to see this, Cam. I want you to understand why you'll never break us. Then if you still want, I'll come back in with you."

"This is nuts, Kenny," Cam said.

"Yeah, probably. But let me add a sweetener. You come with me. Right now. Leave those civilians back there. And when we're done, I'll tell you who did the bombing."

"You said—"

"I said it wasn't us. And it wasn't. But I know who did. You come with me, I'll tell you. That's the price of admission. After that, it's your call. I go in or I don't. It's what you really came up here for, isn't it? I'm handing it to you."

"How do I know you don't have your posse up in that canyon? Your guys have tried for me twice already."

"No, we haven't, but what good would that do now anyway?" Kenny said. "SBI knows what you know, right? You've briefed Bobby Lee?"

"I have. He sent me here."

"Well, I have the real answer. I'll tell you, but no one else. Don't you really want to know?"

"Let's get something straight, Kenny," Cam said. "We're not friends anymore. We're not colleagues. You were a cop, a very good cop, but you've crossed the line. Maybe we can't prove that, but you and I know it. You've become a man-eater, and you've developed a taste for it."

"You let my brother kill himself and you didn't lift a finger," Kenny shot back. "You knew perfectly well what he was going to do, and you just—what, walked away? Don't lecture me about duty and doing the right thing."

"Okay, I'll admit it," Cam said. "I've changed my mind about some things as I've gotten older. If a guy wants to end it all, then I think that's his call."

"Hold that thought, Lieutenant," Kenny said, a strange look in his eyes. "And come with me."

52

BY HOPPING STONES, THEY crossed the river just below the big bend. The rushing water was black, smooth, and deep between his feet, and Cam kept wondering what the hell he was doing out here. He also didn't like being in the woods without the shepherds, but Kenny had been adamant: The dogs would screw the whole thing up, and they might get killed in the process. Once across, they entered the narrow canyon, staying on the gravel banks of the river. The entrance was only a couple hundred yards wide and the stone walls of the canyon tossed echoes of the river back and forth. A quarter of a mile in, there was a low waterfall, with a line of boulders forming the top rim. Directly across the mouth of the river, the south wall rose straight up out of the water. Kenny pointed at the line of boulders.

"We'll cross those," he said. "We'll stay on the southside bank for about a half mile, and then cut up into the woods."

"You do this shit in the dark?" Cam asked.

"Negative," Kenny said. "First light. But I have to be in position above the den before then. I'll leave you where you can see the den, but across the river from it."

"How do you get to the den?"

"On a wire, from above. The rig is already up there. C'-mon, we have to move."

"Is the cat in the den?"

Kenny looked back at him with a patronizing look. "Cats sleep in the daytime, boss. At night, they hunt. She's out here somewhere, so try to be quiet."

The stone walls of the canyon reflected some moonlight down into the gorge, but not a lot, so they had to go slowly, climbing over large rocks and deadfall deposited by the rushing stream during higher water. It was close to 4:00 A.M. when they bore left away from the riverbank and up onto a pine-covered hillside. There wasn't much snow on the ground. The walls of the canyon on the north side were sheer and went up in ragged terraces nearly a thousand feet. The southside slope was less extreme, even though it rose to the same height.

Kenny took Cam up the slope on a loose diagonal until they reached a promontory of rock that cut back over to form a cliff over the river, some three hundred feet below them. Pine trees came down almost to the edge of the overhang of rock, and then subsided, leaving a small gravelly clearing. Perched over the noisy river below, Cam felt like he was on the bow of a ship under way.

There was marginally better light up here out of the forest. Kenny handed Cam a small pair of binoculars. He pointed to the rock face on the other side, which was only about two hundred yards straight across from them.

"First terrace up, above the rockfall, you'll see a cave," he whispered. "Black hole in the rock. Not very big. There's an overhanging ledge above it, maybe a hundred feet up."

Cam searched but couldn't find it. Then he did. It was much smaller than he had expected. He lifted the binocs but couldn't make out the overhang in the shadows.

"Twilight's in three hours," Kenny said. "I have to get down there, cross, and get back up above the den before then."

"Why won't the cat hear you coming?" Cam asked.

"Because she's not there, boss," he said. "I hope."

"Do you know where she is?"

Kenny shook his head. "The best deer woods are up-canyon, although she could be anywhere. Including on my route to that terrace." He grinned. "That's part of the challenge. You still carrying that antique?"

Cam said yes.

"Keep it handy."

Cam looked over the cliff and down toward the river, which was still very audible even up where they were perched. "How do you get across?" he asked.

"I rigged a second wire, right down there. I'll go hand over hand, and then there's the rockfall up to the first terrace, and from there I have to do some rock climbing to the second terrace. The wire's set up on a ledge there. The river masks the sound of my going up the rockfall. After that I have to be really quiet, in case I'm wrong about her being in the den. You stay right here. You'll see the whole thing."

"You have a gun?" Cam asked.

Kenny said, "No, just the camera." He pulled it out of his pocket. He'd applied shrink-wrapping of some kind to the body of the camera to protect it from the elements. "That's the deal. I have a short-range can of pepper spray in case things get really out of hand, but this is what it's all about. We have a rule: We don't hurt the cats."

"And the cats?"

"They have no rules."

It was actually a little warmer now that they were in the canyon, but not much. Cam shivered as he remembered being up in that tree, with Night-Night coming up after him. "Kenny, look," he said. "I'm convinced, okay? Let's call it a win and get the hell back to town. I don't need to see this."

"Yeah, you do, boss," Kenny said. "Seeing truly is believing in this little game. But for right now, get back into the trees until first light. These cats can see pretty good in the dark. Here, take this." Kenny passed him a folded-up plastic winter survival suit. "Climb into this thing and back yourself into a pine tree. And try to stay awake." Then he was gone.

Cam surveyed the stone wall across the gorge with the binoculars for a few minutes, taking in the rockfall and the gray terraces rising above the lower slopes in the moonlight. He tried again to see the cave, but now he couldn't. He wondered how many millions of years this river had been carving its way through the granite. The top part of the mountain opposite was covered in snow, but most of the southern face was clear, except where iced-over streams painted silver ribbons down the rock.

He walked back to the first trees, about fifty feet back from the edge of the cliff, and quietly pulled the suit out of its pouch. It was made of some space-age material and was the thickness of kitchen foil. Shaped like a snowsuit, complete with hood, it would contain almost all of his body heat, thus protecting from hypothermia even under extreme conditions. He climbed gingerly into the suit and then made himself a place to sit by shoving aside the lower branches of some pines. He sat down with his back to a tree, patted the comforting bulk of the .45 in his coat pocket, and promptly dozed off.

He was awakened by the sound of sleet pattering on his hood. He opened his eyes to a curtain of blowing snow and frozen ice particles. What the hell? he thought. It was clear a minute ago. He turned sideways and illuminated his watch. It was 6:30. And then the cloud of blowing snow lifted as suddenly as it had begun, to be followed a minute later by another one. When it subsided, he looked over at the cliffs and saw what was happening. A solid wind had sprung up on the top of the mountain, and it was blowing a graceful cape of snow and ice off the top of the ridge and down into the deep canyon. With the approach of dawn, the sky above was no longer black, but gray. He ducked as another wave of frozen precipitation came blowing down, and then he shucked the survival suit and crept down to the edge of the cliff with the binoculars.

Perversely, the approaching dawn had put the opposite face into even darker shadow, so at first he could see nothing over there except the great gray expanse of rock. Second terrace, Kenny had said. He scanned the cliff face again, starting at the rockfall and going up until he thought he could see the ledge that was the second terrace. Then he searched left and right. He had to duck as another wave of ice crystals blew down across the river, and when he looked back up, he saw a flash of light to the right of where he'd been looking. He focused the binocs in that area and finally saw Kenny. The summit wind penetrated down into the canyon for a moment and his eyes watered in the sudden blast of icy air. Should have kept that suit on, he thought.

Kenny flashed his penlight at him one more time and then

swung out on the invisible wire. Cam pointed the binocs down the rock face and finally saw the cave. In fact, everything was becoming more visible as sunrise approached. He looked up and saw that the wind up top had changed direction and was blowing the icy plume southwest, back into the canyon.

He found Kenny again and watched as he slipped down the wire, one arm outstretched to keep from spinning. The terrace apparently overhung the cave ledge, because Kenny was dangling in free space, some twenty feet off the rock face and nearly two hundred feet above the river. Down he went in little jerks until he was about level with the cave entrance, and then he went lower still, five to six more feet. Then he stopped. He spun slowly on the wire and looked over in Cam's direction. Cam, keeping the binocs to his eyes, dropped a glove and waved his bare hand. Kenny waved back, and Cam could see that he had something in his hand, probably the camera. Then he swung around on the wire and began to pump his legs, initiating a swinging motion in toward the rock face. Cam stared into the cave and saw nothing but a black hole.

Kenny swung out and back in, getting closer to the rock face with each swing, using both arms to steady himself now that he was no longer sliding down the wire. Each swing in brought him closer to the rock, until it looked to Cam as if he would hit it with his feet at the top of his arc. He swung out one last time, way out, it seemed, and then back in. At that instant, a shriek erupted from inside the cave, amplified by the cavity in the rock, and the cat appeared just as Kenny swung all the way in and flashed the camera. The cat shrieked again at the flash and Kenny swung back out, twirling now that he longer had to control his aspect to the cave.

But he failed to stop his swing.

As the wire arced back in one more time, Cam watched Kenny's triumphant grin turn to horror as the furious cat gathered itself. He saw Kenny try to stop the swing, pumping hard with his legs, although not succeeding. At the closest reach of the swing, the cat bounded forward from the cave and sprang out across the narrow open space between her and the dangling man. Cam thought he saw another flash, and then the cat was enveloping Kenny in a shrieking, shredding embrace. As the wire went back out, man and beast convulsed for a bloody second and then dropped like separate stones into the rushing black river nearly one hundred feet below, passing out of Cam's line of sight before they hit.

53

CAM POCKETED THE BINOCS and scrambled right down to the edge of the cliff, windmilling his own arms to stop himself as he felt loose gravel slide out from under his boots. He got down on his hands and knees and looked over the edge, but he could see nothing but the river as it crashed along its rocky course in the canyon. He felt suddenly exposed on this jutting, narrow ledge. Still down on his hands and knees, he backed away from the edge before standing up. His heart was pounding and he realized he'd been holding his breath. He had to get down there.

Down where? He hadn't even seen where they went in. *If* they went in, and weren't both smashed on those huge boulders lining the river's tumbling course. He picked up the binocs and went back to the edge to sweep the opposite riverbank, looking for any signs of Kenny's red parka or the tawny body of the cat.

Nothing. Not a sign of anything but that solid black current, grinding away at its evolutionary task.

He rocked back on his haunches, trying to decide what to do. He had to go down there. *Had* to look. Directly below the cave, and then downstream. The river wasn't deep, except where it poured into geologic holes, and there were plenty of big rocks midstream for things to hang up on.

Daylight was coming on, and the cat was probably dead or so badly injured that it presented no danger, nine lives not withstanding. A hundred feet could smash the life and breath out of any animal hitting water. He had no illusions about finding Kenny alive. What the cat hadn't done to him, the fall probably had.

"Hold that thought," Kenny had said. What the hell was it

with these guys? Did being a cat dancer mean you really did want to die? It was almost like one of those guys who, when surrounded by cops with guns drawn and pointed, went for his. "Suicide by cop," they called it. NAFOD: no apparent fear of death.

He made his way down the slope, following what he thought was the same trail they'd come up the night before. Or this morning, actually, he thought. His heart was heavy. Kenny Cox had to be dead. He wondered what signs he'd missed all these years, how many times he'd ignored Kenny's furious rants about how the bad guys were winning and how the lawyers and the judges were killing America in their cancerous pursuit of fees and power.

He paid no attention to his surroundings as he went down, half walking, half stumbling across the slope, starting small avalanches of loose rock and coming close to spraining an ankle several times. By the time he reached the river, he was sweating under all the layers of clothing. The sun wasn't visible in the canyon, but the sunlight was, painting the rocks and trees with vivid color in the pristine mountain air. He stepped out onto a large boulder, wondering if it had come down from the mountaintop and how long ago, and surveyed the river.

Still no sign of Kenny or the cat. All he could do was head downstream, taking periodic looks from any rock high enough to give him a vantage point. He kept getting stuck among the boulders, climbing around some and over some and then finding that he couldn't go forward at all. He was half-tempted to jump into the river and let that powerful current take him downstream to the mouth of the canyon. And freeze to death halfway there, he thought. Then he saw something red about a hundred yards downstream.

Cam yelled Kenny's name and tried to hurry, but he only got himself stuck again. He had to backtrack, splash through pools of icy water, climb a rock to see how to get farther downstream, and then get down and do it all again. Twenty minutes later, he was close enough to use the binocs. He couldn't be sure, but it looked like Kenny was still in his parka, crumpled up against the face of a huge boulder in a tiny backwash of the river's main channel. He yelled again that he was coming, then set out again to navigate the maze of tumbled granite.

When he finally reached Kenny, he had to slide down the side of a boulder to reach the little sandy beach. Kenny lay in a sodden heap on the wet sand. The river was much louder down at its edge, a constant reminder of its unrelenting power. He realized that there was no way back up except to climb the wet rock. He knelt down to examine Kenny.

The cat had done tremendous damage. Kenny's face was clawed, as was the material of his parka. And his hands— Cam had to close his eyes for a moment. Kenny had his knees drawn up tight into his stomach, and the bottom of the parka was redder than the top. His face was a pasty gray, almost white, and his mouth was open slightly. Cam was sure he was dead, until Kenny's chest jerked with a shallow cough.

"I'm right here, man. I'm right here," Cam said, loudly enough to be heard above the rushing water. He wanted to lift Kenny's head off the wet rock, but was afraid to move him. Kenny opened his eyes, blinked, and then tried to focus.

"I'm right here, Kenny," Cam said again, feeling helpless. Right here, and there isn't a goddamn thing I can do for you, he thought.

Kenny's eyes rolled out of focus for a moment and then came back to look at Cam.

"Hoo-ah," he croaked, and tried to grin, not quite pulling it off. "Pocket."

Cam didn't quite hear him. "Pocket," Kenny said again. "Camera."

Good God, Cam thought. All this, and he wants to know if he got his fucking picture—his "face." He looked down at the parka and saw a small lump in the right-hand slant pocket. He reached into the pocket gingerly, got his fingers on the camera, and felt some squishy things under the material— things he didn't want to feel. The camera was attached to the inside of the pocket with a nylon lanyard. Kenny groaned in pain as Cam unclipped and withdrew the camera. It was one of those little throwaways and it was soaking wet.

"I got it, Kenny," he said. "It's right here." He held it up so Kenny could see it. Kenny focused on the camera and then back on Cam's face. He was trying to say something, but no words were coming out.

"Don't try to talk, man," Cam said. "Just hold still. I'll get us some help."

"No. Fucking. Way," Kenny gasped. "I'm done. All done." He grinned again, and for a moment Cam saw the Kenny of old. "One face too many." His chest heaved in a wet cough and he blanched white with the pain.

Cam sat back on his haunches and tried to think of what to do. Little wavelets swept into the pocket from the main river and then went back out tinged with pink. Kenny's lips were working again.

"Bomb," Kenny said. Cam bent closer.

"What, Kenny? Bomb? What about a bomb?"

"Bomb," Kenny said again, visibly weaker. "Not us."

"I know, man," Cam said, putting his hand on Kenny's broken head. "You told me that, and I believe you." He wanted to ask who, if not them, but he was too choked up to care right now. Kenny Cox was leaving the building, and there was nothing he could do about it, not out here, and probably not even back in the world.

Kenny said something, but Cam missed it. He bent down to hear. "Not us. Them. Tell McLain. Look in the mirror."

Cam blinked. Had he heard it right? *Look in the mirror?* Kenny's left hand came up and grabbed Cam's right hand. He squeezed tightly, surprising Cam with the strength of it, and then his head flopped back and he was gone.

Cam pried Kenny's lifeless hand off and stood up. Kenny seemed to shrink before his very eyes, and then Cam noticed that the water seemed to have risen in the little pocket. The sodden hood of Kenny's parka was being tugged by a current that hadn't been there before. Cam looked around. He was surrounded by fifteen-foot-high boulders, but the sunlight in the canyon was much brighter. Was it his imagination, or did the river sound different? And what could change that quickly out there to make it rise?

He looked around again. It was definitely rising. Water was swirling around his boots and coming close to floating Kenny's body. He wanted to get Kenny out of here, up onto the dry rock above, but there was no way he could get himself and two hundred–plus pounds of dead body out of this little pocket. He zipped the tiny camera into his own pocket and began to wedge his way up the slippery rock. When he got to the top, he discovered that the rock he was on was now an island, separated from the shore by a six-foot-wide ribbon of swiftly flowing black water. The river was definitely wider now, casting other streams parallel to the main current throughout the rock-strewn canyon. He didn't wait. He slid down the other side of the rock he was on and dropped into the water, which fortunately turned out to be only knee-deep. He struck out for the next rock, trying to ignore the vise of cold gripping his lower limbs. He got to the next rock and then the next, finally scrambling up onto a wide sandbar covered in baseball-size gravel.

He sloshed across the gravel bar and five feet up onto what looked like the real riverbank, which was littered with shattered dead trees and muddy tufts of flattened grass. The main current was now invisible behind the bigger boulders, but it was definitely making more noise, and he could hear the sound of smaller rocks being cracked against bigger ones as the current reclaimed more and more of its channel. He felt a cold wind rise as he sat down and pulled off his soaked boots and socks. He looked west and saw the edge of a black cloud building up over the high ridge about six miles away. He thought he saw a curtain of rain sweep out of it, but it was probably sleet. Somewhere upstream, it was probably raining. Not good.

He wrung out his wet socks as best he could and then put them back on, fighting with his boots to get them laced. He had to get back down the canyon and across that line of boulders at the elbow before they, too, became submerged and trapped him in the canyon. He had no illusions about what could happen: There were clear signs fifty feet above him of how high the river could run, and it would be even higher in the narrow defile below. He got up and started downstream as fast he could go, trying not to look at that dark horizon forming above and behind him as he threaded his way through the boulder field and the snags.

54

THIRTY MINUTES LATER, HE sensed that the gorge
was narrowing, which meant he should be getting closer to
the entrance. He was sweating despite the cold air as he
worked across a slope that was densely padded in pine needles. He had nothing like the clear view of the formation that
he had seen back at the base camp, but the north face of the
canyon was no longer terraced, and he remembered threading
his way through this dense stand of pines on the way in. After
this, the canyon walls would converge at the entrance. He
wondered if the stepping-stone rocks were still above water,
and what he would do if they weren't.

He stepped into a hole and went down with a grunt of
pain, barely catching himself on the limbs of a tree. He
pulled his wet foot out of the hole and massaged his throbbing ankle. A gust of wind came down the canyon and bent
the tops of the pines with a high whistling sound. He was
startled by a brace of quail that flashed out of the trees some
fifty feet behind him in a hard flutter of wings.

And then he heard the cough.

He froze as the hair on the back of his neck rose. Something had flushed the quail. And he'd heard that guttural
cough before.

The wind rose again, bending the pines this way and that,
lifting some of the needles up off the ground in little dust
devils. The sunlight seemed to be changing color, turning
from yellow to silver.

He couldn't just sit there. He had to get down the canyon,
closer to where the others were. They'd have discovered he
was gone by now, probably at sunrise. They'd know where

he'd gone. They'd be coming in, or at least Mary Ellen would. He hoped so at least.

He got up and tested his ankle. Passable. He hauled the .45 out and checked the action. Stiff with cold, but serviceable and mostly dry. He took his bearings and began to walk east, down the slope, keeping the high stone walls on either side of his line of advance. He walked while turning in slow circles, fully aware that the cat had all the advantages in here. It should be injured after that fall, but maybe not—house cats survived falls from trees. He decided not to stop and listen—the cat wouldn't make noise, and he couldn't hear much over the sound of the river and the wind anyway.

Keep moving, he told himself. Keep going down. Away from its den and territory. He had a fleeting vision of Kenny's body washing out of the little cove and being tumbled down the river gorge. He wondered if he ought to fire a shot to alert them. They had to be wondering where the hell he was, and maybe the shot would scare off the cat. Right.

He lifted the .45 high and fired once. The noise was incredible in the confines of the canyon, the shot echoing back and forth off the rocks walls. If one was good, two was better. He fired again, this time into the pines behind him, in the general direction of that menacing cough. And then once more, make it three, the standard signal for distress in the woods.

C'mon, rangers.

He didn't stop moving, though, continuing his ungainly pirouette through the pines, watching every shadow, where he was putting his feet, ignoring the shooting pains from his ankle, and still sweating. From exertion, he told himself. Sure. Would these damned trees never end? He realized he'd started moving slightly uphill, so he adjusted his course back down toward the now-muffled sound of the river, brushing pine branches out of his face, imagining that huge cat slinking along his trail, nose down, tail switching, unimpressed by the gunfire. He strained to hear any answering signals, but there was nothing but the sound of his own breath and the constant swish of pine branches as he pushed through the grove, the trees seeming denser now as he batted at branches with the gun barrel, always turning, watching for any signs of the tawny beast. Had it fled? Did it even know what gunfire was? How the hell had it survived that fall?

The sound of the river suddenly grew louder. He plunged out of the stand of pines into a small clearing, where at last he could see where he was. The river was a hundred yards down and to his left, hidden behind a boulder field. It sounded much stronger now. The canyon's entrance was no more than a quarter of a mile in front of him, marked by a sharp prow of granite to his right, which curved north like a big stone paw.

Then he realized something: The river came out of the canyon and turned north. He was on the *south* side of the canyon. He didn't have to cross the river. He could just keep going, right? Now that he thought of it, why in the hell had Kenny brought him that way, crossing the river not once but twice? He tried to shake the sleep out of his eyes. He sensed he was forgetting something. He was very tempted to find a warm rock and rest for a few minutes. But then he glanced back at the distant tops of the big ridge and saw that the dark cloud bank now extended in both directions for as far as he could see. Something was pumping up the river, and it had to be coming from that approaching front.

The pines ahead of him were larger, but there was lots more space between them. There'd be no getting through that boulder field until he got down to the actual canyon entrance, so he elected to keep going on the southside bank. He listened carefully for any signs that there was something following him in the dense grove at his back, but he could hear only the river. Where were the rangers? Had they heard his three shots?

He set out for the canyon entrance, keeping an eye on his back trail as he moved in among the large pines. He was conscious after awhile that the ground was rising to his right, the carpet of pine needles changing to a fine granite gravel. He passed through a blowing mist of falling water coming from a weep high up on the rock walls above him.

He kept watch for the cat. He had two rounds remaining in the .45, since for safety reasons he never carried a round under the hammer. One round had done in the previous cat, so all he'd have to do would be to hit it. Assuming he saw it coming, that is.

He stopped in midstride as he realized he could see a small slice of the river to his left and below him. Why was he climbing? He was tempted to climb one of the trees to see where the hell he was in relation to the actual entrance to the Chop. Why not? he thought. I should be able to see the base camp if I get high enough.

But then there came the sound of something behind him. He backed up to a big tree and froze, gun held in both hands. He could just barely see his footprints in the gravelly ground, and he stared through the trees from left to right, trying to see what had made that noise. Colder air began to settle through the tops of the pines. He looked up and realized that the soaring stone walls of the canyon were closer now. They should be opening, not closing on me, he thought.

He hesitated. He was beginning to get the sense that he was walking into a trap. He was definitely forgetting something important. It had to do with why Kenny had brought him across the river twice. He closed his eyes and tried to visualize what he'd seen when they landed yesterday, but he couldn't raise the image of the Chop's entrance. Dark and too many trees. Plus, he was very tired.

Climb a tree, he thought. See where you are. Orient yourself. Then proceed. He looked up and sighed. What with the altitude and his own fatigue, he wasn't sure he could climb a tree right now. And the last time he'd climbed a tree, that damned cat had come up after him.

Okay, climbing a tree was out.

He pressed on, no longer bothering to watch his back in order to make better time. He was intent on getting out of this canyon. The rangers had given him forty-eight hours, but the weather front was obviously not going to wait that long. He didn't want to be in this canyon if the river really rose up, and he sure as hell didn't want to get back to the meadow and find only one tent standing.

He came to another line of dense-pack pines, stubbier than what he'd been going through. The river had changed its tone, sounding more like a flood than a rapid. He plunged through the pines, sure that the way out was just on the other side, and finally burst out onto a wide gravel beach. A blaze of sunlight revealed that he'd made it to the canyon entrance. The river swung north to his left in a wide silvery arc, although it looked to be twice the size of what it had been before. The meadow up above a stand of pines on the other side was visible, and the little cluster of tents was still there. That was the good news.

The bad news, however, stopped him cold. He now understood why Kenny had brought him across on the other side, because where the river made its turn, the current had scoured the south bank away to nothing. The gravel beach narrowed down into a spit that lay submerged about a hundred feet in front of him, after which there was only a sheer rock cliff rising out of the flowing water a couple hundred feet up the south wall of the canyon. The river swept through its turn with barely a ripple along that southern edge, indicating deep water. The distance to the other shore from the gravel spit was a good two hundred yards. The benevolent sunshine seemed to mock him as he stood there, trapped on the wrong side of a rising river.

As he surveyed his predicament, the mountain lion stepped casually out of the pines about thirty feet away and looked his way.

55

CAM FROZE WHEN HE saw the cat between him and the riverbank. He tried to think what to do. Step back into the stand of pines? Pull out the .45 and start blasting away—with both remaining rounds? Do the fifty-meter dash straight ahead and then jump into the river?

He stared at the big cat. It did not appear to be injured or even marked. He then wondered if it was the same cat that had mauled Kenny, or was it a different one? A mate? The cat looked right back at him, its black mask clearly etched in the bright sunlight. Its tail began to twitch. Cam quietly extracted the Colt and held it down at his side.

There was no point in going back into the trees. If the cat wanted him, it would have the advantage in there, and Cam would probably never see or hear it coming. The trees were too insubstantial to climb, and it was probably a couple hundred feet back to the nearest big pine.

The cat made that guttural coughing sound again and lay down on the gravel, its entire body pointed right at Cam. He'd seen house cats do the same thing when they had a mousie out in the middle of the living room carpet. For a crazy moment, Cam was tempted to walk over there, right at it, and see if he could shoot it like he'd shot the other one, right through the long axis of its body. But then he saw the muscles in the cat's shoulders coiling. It lifted its lips at him, baring yellow fangs.

He looked longingly at the water, but there was no way he could outrun that thing if it charged. *When* it charged. He slowly knelt down on one knee, took a two-handed shooting stance, braced himself as best he could, pointed the .45 at the cat, and cocked the revolver. The cat growled when he moved, but it still didn't charge. Its tail was whipping back and forth now, its agitation clearly growing. Cam focused on its face along the blade sight picture and then dropped the point of aim slightly. If he fired now, he could probably hit it in the chest, but the shot would be slightly downhill and just far enough away that the drop of the round might result in a clean miss.

He commanded his lungs to expand and tried to keep his eyes from watering as he waited, the big Colt getting heavier in his hands by the minute. The cat began to inch forward on its belly, taking his measure the whole time, its eyes glaring in anger. Cam refined his aim point as the cat made its approach, still belly-down on the gravel, its breathing becoming audible as it made its move. Cam remembered reading somewhere that this was the time to make himself as big and tall as possible, to make the cat pause, but he didn't want to disturb his shooting stance. He had only two rounds, and he'd probably only get off one shot before the damned thing was all over him. He remembered what the mortally wounded beast had done to White Eye, that speed bag hammering with those three-inch-long claws. And Kenny with his shirtful of innards.

The cat stopped, twenty feet away now, and began to quiver all over. Its head was down, giving Cam less, rather than more, of a target.

Then he remembered the camera.

Holding the gun in his right hand, he unzipped his left parka pocket and brought out the little disposable, slick in its plastic shrink-wrap covering. Being careful not to make any sudden jerking moves, he brought the camera up, pointed it at the cat, armed the flash, and fumbled for the shoot button. An instant later, there was a bright flash and the cat shrieked at him. He did it again, and a third time, and each time the cat yelled at him. But its eyes were blinking now and the flash had clearly upset its attack pattern.

He fired it again and again, and each time the cat reacted. After the sixth time, he put it back in his pocket and reset his shooting position. The cat was no closer, but it was still blinking furiously. Its tail was, if anything, whipping back and forth more vigorously, but the cool, careful "Here I come" expression on its face was gone.

At that instant, two shapes burst out of the trees between the cat and the riverbank.

The cat sensed and reacted to the new danger before Cam even knew what was happening. It whirled around on the loose gravel, still down in its crouch, and, flat-eared, fangs bared, roared at the two shepherds. They stopped in their tracks, spewing gravel out in front of them, and then spread out, one on either side of the cat, each one keeping about fifteen feet away, their fur and hackles up and showing more teeth than Cam had thought possible. Frick was to Cam's right on the downstream side, while Frack held position nearest the stand of pines.

They'd left the cat one avenue of escape, which was to dive straight into the pines, but the lion wasn't having it. It roared again and feinted at Frack, who answered with a pretty impressive roar of his own and even more ivory. He stood his ground, much to Cam's surprise, while Frick kept moving, down on her belly now like the cat, growling and showing teeth, making the cat turn to keep her in view even as Frack started to slide toward his right. Cam was still so surprised to see the dogs that he hadn't done anything, but now he did. He scooped up a handful of gravel and threw it at the cat's back.

The lion whipped around and shrieked at him, giving the dogs another chance to adjust their positions. They clearly knew they were no match for an aroused mountain lion, so they weren't getting closer, but they weren't leaving, either. The cat now had three threats to deal with, and it was getting even more agitated. Cam realized he had a body shot now, but, to his own amazement, he found himself reluctant to take it. We started this, not the cat, he thought.

Run, goddamn it, Cam thought. Get out of here. He threw another handful of gravel. The cat spun around again, and this time both dogs feinted at it.

That did it. The cat shrieked one final time and then, in a

blur of fur, leaped into the pines, easily clearing twenty feet without touching the ground, and was gone. The dogs ran up to the edge of the pines but wisely stopped, barking their fool heads off. Cam felt a wave of something like cold nausea sweep through his own plumbing and suddenly had to sit down. Frick came over and licked his face and neck, while Frack paced back and forth in front of the dense trees, nose down, as if he was trying to pick up the cat's scent. Cam could still see that final leap, from a standstill, the same distance the cat had been from him, he realized. Even with the gun pointed right at it, he'd probably never have gotten even one shot off.

He had a sudden urge to answer a call of nature, so he got up and walked over to the riverbank, where the rushing water was visibly moving smaller stones along in the marginal current. Frick followed him, and then so did Frack.

He praised them while he took care of business, then lowered the hammer on the Colt and put it back in his pocket. He zipped the camera back into his parka. If that thing was working, Mary Ellen would finally have her proof.

"So where are the rangers, guys?" he asked. He saw that the dogs were both pretty wet, so they'd managed to get across somehow. He looked across the river at the north bank, but he didn't see anyone over there. The big rocks he'd crossed with Kenny were now small mounds of turbulence out in the sweeping current. He knew what they were going to have to do: They were going to have to go into the river right about here and let the icy current take them through the entire turn and then strike out for the far bank.

He still had Kenny's binocs around his neck, so he used these to survey the other side.

It was doable, *if* he could survive the cold water, and *if* he didn't get slammed up against one of those now-invisible rocks by the current. As if confirming the urgency of the situation, he realized that the tips of his boots were now underwater. He looked back up into the high ridges above the canyon and saw that the dark cloud to the west was now taking lumpy definition along the entire mountain range. He could clearly see curtains of rain sweeping out of the cloud, which meant the river was by no means finished rising.

He wondered if the dogs would follow him into the river, or if he should tie them to him somehow so that they would all stay together. But with what?

They sat down before him, as if to say, That was fun. What's the next game, Pop? He knelt down to rub their heads, which is when the mountain lion erupted out the pines in a dead run and came right at them, eyes blazing, covering the gravel in twenty-foot bounds.

56

IT SHRIEKED AGAIN AND pounced at the now-clustered targets, mouth agape, front paws and claws spread wide, blotting out the sky. Cam barely managed to throw himself backward out of the way even as the dogs instinctively flattened, and the cat landed in the water, instead of on top of them. In an instant, it was swept away by the hungry current, even as it tried to turn back, legs thrashing, still determined to get at them. Cam, sitting on his backside, his elbows in the water, watched in shock as the mountain lion disappeared into the rumbling black river. He thought he saw its head pop up again quite a way downstream, but then he lost it again. Then the gravel under him shifted down into the current, and it was his turn to go for a ride.

He yelled for the dogs, but they just stood there as he was taken out into the middle of the incredible current, his lower body constricting with the sudden cold and his lungs refusing to work due to the shock of it.

Swim, his brain yelled at him, but nothing was working, and then his right knee whacked something underwater. It spun him around in a whirling pirouette, which completely disoriented him. He yelled again for the dogs to come, but he couldn't see them and now had to concentrate on getting to the right side of the river and out of the powerful center current. He couldn't swim, only thrash around while his brain tried to cope with the fact that he was hurtling downstream, totally out of control, the bank to his right a blur of trees and small rocks. He realized his body was shutting down, recalling all the blood from his extremities to his brain in response to the freezing water. The waterlogged parka was dragging him down.

"Gotta go, gotta go, gotta go," he started chanting through chattering teeth, and he kicked out to get across the current, but the river kept turning him, so that every time he thought he was going toward the bank, he wasn't. Then he heard someone shouting, and he caught a glimpse of Mary Ellen on the far bank, trotting downstream, yelling at him.

He hit another rock, and this one pinned him for a moment, causing a small tidal wave of water to rise up over his face. For just an instant, he thought, This is too hard. Just quit, just stop this fighting. He really couldn't breathe, but launched out again, using the rock as a fulcrum, and actually made headway toward the bank. He hit another rock, this time with his stomach, and folded around it, helpless to straighten out and swim again. He kept his head above water and laughed hysterically at his predicament. The current was strong enough to pin him to the rock, and there was absolutely nothing he could do about it. His hands felt like two frozen bricks.

He looked up and saw that he wasn't that far from the bank now, if he could only get off the damned rock. At that moment, he saw two black ears coming downstream at him. Frack swept by, a look of total terror on his face. Cam grabbed out for the dog and snagged his collar. The weight of the dog pulled Cam off the rock, and a moment later they were both rolled into the shallows by a standing wave in the current. Mary Ellen waded out into the water with a long branch in her hands. Cam grabbed at it with one hand and, holding on to Frack's collar, she pulled the both of them to the shallows.

"Where's Frick?" Cam gasped, not letting go of the black shepherd's collar.

"Don't know," she shouted above the roar of the river. "Gotta get you dry, right now. You're blue in the face. Let go of the dog."

Cam pried his fingers off Frack's collar and tried to sit up. All those soaking layers felt like a shroud, and he realized he'd been lucky they hadn't drowned him. Then Frack barked and jumped through the shallows, stopping short of the real current. Cam looked. There went Frick, sailing by like a furry cork, ears and snout up like little sable periscopes, but much too far out in the center current. Cam yelled to get her attention, but she went on downriver and disappeared around a bend.

Cam got up and started to trudge down the bank. Mary Ellen caught up with him as he began to stumble badly, his leg muscles too cold to function adequately. Then the roaring in his head got louder than the river and he passed out.

He awoke to the sound and feel of a fire and saw Mary Ellen Goode coming back toward him with an armload of driftwood. He'd been dragged to a sitting position and placed against a large rock, and she'd built a fire in the gravel on the riverbank. The sunlight was no longer bright, and there was a cold gray haze. His parka lay in a heap next to him, his boots were upside down on sticks, and Frack sat on the other side of the fire, watching him intently. His knee hurt and he felt like he'd been punched repeatedly in the stomach, but all his extremities were responding to commands. The front of his clothes felt damp and stiff, but his back was still soaking wet. He shivered and coughed up some water.

"Welcome back," she said, dropping the driftwood near the fire. "We thought we were gonna have to leave you out here." She pointed with her chin at the massive dark cloud bank building up behind the high ridge.

"Any signs of my other dog?" Cam asked.

"Not yet, but she was swimming strong," she said. "That cat probably made it out, too."

"You saw it?"

"For about a second," she said. "I had binocs on you when you came out on the point over there. I was trying to figure out how to get your attention, but I didn't bring a gun. That was pretty close."

"We'd met before," Cam said. "Where's Marshall?"

"Up at camp on the sat phone, hopefully getting a helo in. The weather jumped the gun on us. Where's your deputy?"

Cam just shook his head. He didn't want to deal with that right now.

"Did you find him?"

"He found me. That's where I went last night."

She nodded. "We kinda figured that out when we saw two sets of tracks. Marshall just thought you'd decided to go in on your own. I was disappointed. I wanted to go up there with you. See if this stuff was true."

Cam thought about the camera in his parka, but he decided he'd keep that factor off the table right now. He rather doubted the film had survived immersion, even with the shrink-wrap. It was, after all, just a cheap disposable.

Mary Ellen hunkered down by the fire and pushed coals together. "We heard the shots," she said. "But the river had come up by then. We had no way to get across."

"Don't worry about it," Cam said. "You got me and Frack out of the river. Thank you." Then he began to shiver uncontrollably.

She came around the fire, sat beside him, and folded her arms around him. He sank into the warmth of her gratefully, and she held him until he stopped shivering. Then, hearing distant shouting, they drew apart.

Marshall came down across the open meadow and joined them by the fire. "Three hours," he said. He eyed Cam and the waterlogged shepherd. "Been swimming, I take it. Where's your deputy?"

Cam looked out at the rushing current and said only that Sergeant Cox was dead. Both rangers just stared at him in surprise.

"You mean he's in the river?" Marshall asked, glancing sideways at the rumbling water.

"Yes," Cam replied.

A sudden gust of cold wind made them look over at the ridge, where the approaching front looked like a black wave building up on the distant back range. Cam thought he saw a flicker of lightning off to the right. The rock on the eastern face was changing colors in the intermittent sunlight.

"How high's that ridge?" he asked.

"Almost five thousand feet," Marshall said. Another cold gust blew down from the meadow in the direction of the approaching system, flattening the dying grass. "Three hours is going to be close. They asked if we could ride out the frontal passage. I told them no."

"Good answer," Mary Ellen said. She studied the cloud bank again. "We could, I suppose, if they have to abort. But that mess could be wild when it comes down this side." She turned to Cam. "Can you walk?" she asked. He said he could.

"Good. We need to get back to the camp, get it ready for load-out."

Cam lurched to his feet, grunting when he put weight on the knee, and then helped Marshall douse the fire. It wasn't hard, as the river had risen to within five feet of where he'd been sitting. Cam took a last look downstream to see if Frick was coming, but there was no sign of her. He dreaded the thought of leaving her out here.

"Can you guys do the camp?" he asked. "I'd like to go look for my dog."

Marshall looked at Mary Ellen, who nodded. "Okay," he said, "but be back in two hours—max. And if you see that thing start down the slope, *run* back to camp. The tops of that ridge are about twelve miles away, believe it or not, but that storm may come down like an avalanche."

Cam gathered up his wet parka and put on his boots, then went to look for Frick.

Two hours later, he trudged back up the hill toward the waiting rangers, Frack alongside, but no Frick. He'd scoured the riverbank, tramping downstream for an hour, then reluctantly turned around. The sky above was getting dark gray now as the approaching front began to descend over the mountain. The temperature had actually risen a bit and the air smelled of moisture. He'd put the parka back on; it was almost dry now. His head felt like it did when he had a bad cold coming on. The rangers had most of the camp taken apart and bagged up, but they'd left the larger tent up in case the weather did manage to beat out the helicopter. Mary Ellen handed Cam a cup of hot soup from the Primus stove.

"No luck," he said as he wrapped both hands around the hot metal cup. She handed him a bologna sandwich as he finished the soup. He ate half of it and then pitched the other half to Frack, who was waiting outside the tent's front flap. "I didn't find any bodies, either," he said. "Except for one deer."

"Mary Ellen says she saw the mountain lion," Marshall said. "So I guess it's official."

Cam nodded, still not wanting to talk about what had happened to Kenny. Marshall cleared his throat.

"We're going to have to file a report," he prompted.

"I know," Cam said. "And I'll give you a debrief at the appropriate time. Do you guys have a secure phone at the station?"

Marshall laughed. "We're the Park Service, remember?"

"The Sheriff's Office will have one," Mary Ellen said.

Cam nodded. "I'm going to make a report when we get back in. How about I let you guys listen in to that? Save me from having to do it twice?"

"That'd be fine," Marshall said. "I mean, I know we're not—"

Cam cut him off. "Yes, you are. You need to know this. My deputy was killed by that cat."

Marshall blinked. "Oh" was all he could manage.

"But it wasn't the cat's fault," Cam said. "Kenny was cat dancing."

"Oh my God," Marshall said. "That's real?"

They all heard the sound of an approaching helicopter at the same time, which ended their conversation. They came out of the tent and started taking it apart. The wind was rising, and there was more of the cloud bank on their side of the ridge now, although it didn't appear to be roaring down at them yet.

The helicopter came in from the east, circled the landing zone once, lined up with the wind sweeping across the meadow, and then put down just below where the camp had been. It was the same crew who'd brought them in.

They began throwing bags into the hatch as soon as the crewman got it open, crouching to keep below the rotor blades. Cam definitely saw lightning flash across the big ridge and down into the Chop, which by now was ominously dark. When all the gear was loaded, they put Frack aboard and climbed into the aircraft. The crewman took one last look around the landing area, spoke into his intercom, and then hopped aboard. He slid the hatch closed and checked that they had fastened their seat belts.

The helo rose smoothly and immediately banked down toward the river. Cam looked out across the snow-covered meadow and saw the unmistakable shape of a German shepherd bounding across the frozen snow in pursuit of the helo. He yelled to get the crewman's attention and then pointed below them. The crewman looked out, said something on the intercom. Frack, in the meantime, had spotted his partner out the window and started barking. The crewman listened and then shook his head.

"No go," he shouted. "Pilot says we're outta here."

"Bullshit," Cam yelled back. "You can't leave her here to starve."

The crewman tried again as the helo gained altitude. Below, and now behind them, Frick valiantly tried to keep up, as if she knew they were in the aircraft.

The crewman made a disappointed face and shook his head again. This time, Cam unbuckled, got up, signaled for Frack to follow him, stepped past the strapped-in crewman, and opened the hatch between the crew compartment and the cockpit. He signaled Frack again and the big dog went through the door and began doing the monster mash on the two pilots: furious barking, lots of snapping teeth, saliva spraying the sides of their helmets. Cam had to steady himself as the helo swerved violently a couple of times, and then the pilot, clearly getting the message, turned the bird around and prepared to put it back down on the ground. Cam called Frack back into the cabin, ignoring the amazed look on the crewman's face. He thought he saw Mary Ellen grinning from behind her oversize sunglasses.

They landed again and the crewman slid open the door. Cam jumped out and called to Frick, who was a good hundred yards away but still gamely coming on. She put on a few extra knots and managed to jump right into the hatch once she got there, claws scrabbling on the metal deck. Cam got back aboard and buckled in after some serious reunion greetings from both dogs. The helo lifted back off with an angry lurch. There was some lengthy conversation on the intercom between the pilots and the crewman, who kept eyeing Cam and the two shepherds. Cam hauled his .45 out of the parka pocket and began popping empty shells out of the cylinder. The crewman stopped talking when he saw the gun, and for the rest of the flight back to Pineville, he sat as far from his passengers as he could, his sun visor pulled completely down. Behind them, the winter storm finally spilled over the ridge and buried the Chop under the first winter storm of the season. Cam hunched into his still-damp clothes, remembering the feel of Mary Ellen's arms around him. It had been a long time.

57

CAM AWOKE IN HIS motel room with a violent chill and had to collect his wits for a moment to remember where he was. He'd reported back to Bobby Lee from the Carrigan County Sheriff's Office, and, as promised, he'd let the two rangers listen in to his report of what had happened to Kenny up on the mountain. The sheriff took it all in and told Cam to return to Triboro the following day. They'd found him a motel room, where he'd proceeded to crash after telling Mary Ellen he'd meet her at the local pub that evening.

Now his head hurt, his knees were really sore, and he was pretty sure he was running a temperature. He tried to get a look at his watch but he was having trouble getting the little dial light to come on. He decided to take a hot bath to see if he could shake off the chills. Afterward, he staggered back to bed and got under all the covers. Then the room became unbearably hot, so he got up and turned on the air conditioner full blast. He lay there wishing he had some aspirin, then began talking to himself about how he might manage to find a store. Then he heard voices outside. There was a knock on the door, followed by another. Finally, the door was opened from the outside, revealing a worried-looking motel desk clerk and Mary Ellen Goode.

"Knock, knock," she called as she came into the room. Cam smiled weakly, and tried to say something, but he only managed to chatter his teeth at her. She shivered in the icy room and turned off the air conditioner. She thanked the clerk and closed the door behind him. "Look at you," she said, shaking her head. "You stood me up, you know."

"Wha—what time is it?" he asked between feverish chills.

"Eleven-thirty," she said. She found his room key card and

said she'd be right back. Twenty minutes later, she fed him some Tylenol and made him drink a bottle of water with it.

"Thanks for checking on me," he said. "I've never crashed like this before."

"It's called 'post-incident letdown,'" she told him. "We see it all the time after a rescue. People survive by running on adrenaline; then the body exacts its price." She hesitated. "I'm sorry about your deputy."

Cam nodded, even though it hurt his throbbing head. "He was a good guy and a good cop," he said. "I still can't quite believe it."

"That he was one of them?"

Cam said yes. The Tylenol was beginning to work. There were sounds from the room next door: a muffled male voice, followed by girlish giggling.

"Kenny told me that it was all real. That they helped James Marlor fry those two guys. They were proud of what they'd been doing."

"And the judge?"

"No," he said. "He said they didn't do that. Then, at the very end, he said something that didn't make any sense at all. Something about looking in the mirror. I think it was just final delirium."

"And you feel like shit because you had to leave him there."

He nodded. "Yeah. I know there was nothing I could have done, but you just don't leave your wounded out there."

"Was he still alive when you climbed out?"

"Well, no, but still . . ."

The noises from next door became more amorous and less frivolous.

"They're doing better than we are," Cam said with a weak grin.

Her smile brightened the room. "You guys, you never quit, do you? There's the bottle of Tylenol, and you need to drink another water. Want to try for breakfast?"

He thought about breakfast and his stomach generated a wave of nausea, which she apparently detected. She moved the wastebasket nearer the bed. "Sorry I brought that up, so to speak," she said. "Why don't you call me when you're operational. I'll go back with you after the inquest, if you really think I can help."

He nodded, not trusting his stomach just now. He closed his eyes. There was something else he needed to tell her, but he couldn't think of what it was. Then the lights went out and he heard the door close. Things reached a climax of sorts in the adjacent room. Some guys have all the luck, he thought.

58

"LOOK IN A MIRROR'?" Jay-Kay said. "If I look in a mirror, I see myself."

They were sitting in the living room of her Charlotte apartment. Cam and Mary Ellen had convoyed back to Triboro and met with Bobby Lee and Steven Klein. The sheriff had been as interested in what she had to say as in what Cam had told him. Then the three of them, minus the DA, had all gone down to Charlotte at the request of Special Agent McLain of the FBI's Charlotte field office. Cam had briefed McLain on events up in Carrigan County. McLain took notes without comment, as did two other special agents who sat in. Cam was a little uneasy at the fact that the feds weren't saying anything, but Bobby Lee did not seem too worried about it. They'd broken for coffee, and McLain had disappeared for a few minutes. He'd come back and suggested quietly that Cam, Mary Ellen, and the sheriff meet him at Jay-Kay's apartment in an hour.

Cam was still sore from his encounters with various river rocks and had to get up and walk around while he talked, but the fever, thankfully, had gone in the night.

"It was practically the last thing he said," he told them. "He was pretty much delirious by then. That damned thing gutted him."

The sheriff was visibly upset about losing Kenny and even more upset that Cam had had to leave his body up there in the mountains. He'd asked Mary Ellen if there was any chance of doing a body recovery, and she'd said not until late spring. And by then, of course . . .

"Did he positively admit to you that he'd helped to execute those two robbers?" McLain asked.

Cam nodded. "His brother built the chair and did the deed, but Kenny steered him to those two guys. I suspect he may have helped more than he said, but we'll never know now. He was adamant about the bombing being someone else's work, though."

McLain frowned as he considered what Cam was telling him, making Cam wonder how high his own name was on McLain's suspect list. "And the chair?" McLain asked. "Where is that?"

"Out there somewhere. Marlor said he'd told the people who helped him where it was."

"Okay," the sheriff said. "We have two possibles, based on Ms. Bawa's research. Neither of those men has been injured lately, by the way."

"The cell was supposedly limited to seven members," Cam said. "We have two possibles, plus Kenny and Marlor. That leaves three unaccounted for. One of them could be the injured party. Jay-Kay, did your search go after that data, too? Line-of-duty injuries, medical leaves?"

"It did and it didn't," she replied. "Medical information is in a more privileged category than time, leave, and attendance records, but I believe the state office in charge or medical insurance is going to help me with that."

"Do they know that?" the sheriff asked.

Jay-Kay just smiled. The sheriff didn't pursue the matter.

"Back to this mirror business," Cam said. "Let's assume Kenny was telling the truth."

"Why start now?" the sheriff asked grumpily.

"Deathbed confession?" Cam suggested. "He had nothing to gain from lying. He swore they didn't do the bombing at Annie's house. And then he said, 'Tell McLain: Look in the mirror.'" He turned to McLain, who was staring absently at the floor. "What do you think he meant, Special Agent?" he asked.

McLain looked up at him suddenly. "What did you just say?"

"I said, 'What do you—'"

"No—the sergeant's words."

"Tell McLain—"

"Yes," he said. "That makes more sense. Earlier you said tell 'them.' Damn, damn, *damn*!"

Bobby Lee leaned forward. "There's a second cell?"

"And?" McLain said, a sick look in his face.

"And this one's federal," Bobby Lee replied. McLain nodded slowly.

"This isn't news, is it?" asked Cam from his position near the window. "You already suspected this, didn't you?"

McLain hesitated and then nodded again.

"Which is why you went radio-silent on us all of a sudden."

"I had the same problem the sheriff here did," McLain said. "I didn't know whom I could trust. Those agents at the meeting today? They're here from Washington on temporary duty. After you told me about the bombing, I got our Professional Standards people into it."

"When I was doing a Web scan for James Marlor connections for your office," Jay-Kay said to McLain, "they told me not to bother with federal connections, that he wasn't in any of the various nationwide criminal databases or even AFIS. Said they'd already looked. I never did verify that."

McLain groaned. "He'd have to be in AFIS," he said. "He'd been in the service. Everyone in the military gets fingerprinted."

"In your searches, Jay-Kay, did you stay exclusively in the state system?" Cam asked.

She nodded.

"Will someone please tell me what's going on here?" Mary Ellen said.

McLain ignored her. Cam thought the special agent looked as if he were facing bureaucratic execution, and maybe he was. Vigilantes in a sheriffs office was one thing, but in the Bureau? "This thing is worse than I thought," McLain said. "Here's what I suggest: Jay-Kay, can you let Ranger Goode stay here with you? I don't think she should go back to Triboro right now."

"Why would she be any safer here in Charlotte?" Cam asked.

"Because you lost Sergeant Cox," McLain said. "People are going to be pissed. And they saw her come in with you."

"Why would I be in any danger at all?" Mary Ellen asked.

"You probably aren't, Miss Goode," McLain said. "But until the sheriff and I get a better fix on who's involved in this mess, I'd prefer to have you nearby. Sheriff Baggett, are we agreed on that?"

"Absolutely," Bobby Lee replied. "You obviously think the two cells knew about each other?"

"Yes," McLain said. "And that would be a lethal combination, wouldn't it. What I really wonder about is whether or not any of our people did this cat-dancing thing. I'm visualizing the people in our office, and I can't think of anyone."

"It might not involve your people," Cam pointed out. "It could be ATF, DEA, CIA, you know, any of them."

The meeting broke up, with Mary Ellen agreeing to stay there at Jay-Kay's apartment while Cam and the sheriff went back to Triboro. McLain promised to be in touch the following morning with a proposed plan of action.

59

THE NEXT DAY WAS taken up with meetings and more meetings as Cam attended to the administrative consequences of a deputy's death under extraordinary circumstances. McLain did not call with his plan of action, and the sheriff said that DA Klein had told him to wait for the feds to take the lead. Cam talked to Mary Ellen once at midday to make sure she was okay, and he found out that she had been spending some time with Jay-Kay as that wizard pried the lids off of several supposedly secure state data systems.

At the end of the day, Cam stationed himself outside Bobby Lee's office and waited. The sheriff finally called him in at 6:30.

"Where are we?" Cam asked without ceremony.

"Have you had a nice day, Lieutenant?" Bobby Lee asked. "Because I've just had a wonderful day. Want to hear about my wonderful day?"

Cam sat down. "Show you mine if you'll show me yours," he said.

The sheriff actually cracked a smile. "JFC," he said, which was about as close to real swearing as Bobby Lee ever came. "It's been alphabet soup, by the hour: FBI, SBI, ATF, ADA, ME, IA, and so on. By my count, the only one missing was the CIA. How'd you do?"

"About the same," Cam told him. "Spent a lot of time on rumor control. McLain never did call?"

"He did not. Some anally oriented individuals from the Hoover Building in Washington did call, however. I think I'm ready to start my own vigilante cell." He paused and then became more serious. "How're people taking all this?"

"Inquiring minds want to know WTF," Cam said. "And

I'm getting some cold shoulders. As in 'You were there at the end. Where's our guy?' "

The sheriff got up and went to the single window in his office. The lights out in the parking lot were on, and yet there were still many personal vehicles parked there.

"I can tell you that you did the right thing," he said. "But that'll be small comfort the next time you go into Frank's Place. Kenny Cox drew some serious water around here. Despite what he'd been doing."

"Maybe *because* of what he was doing," Cam said. "I really may not be able to stay on after this."

Bobby Lee gave him a strange look. "You may be right about that, Lieutenant. You came back. Kenny Cox didn't. People're gonna remember that."

They were interrupted by a call. The sheriff picked up the phone and identified himself. He listened for a long minute, wrote something down, said, "Okay," and then hung up.

"That was the ops center," he announced. "Apparently nine-one-one got a call advising me to check my E-mail. Said if we liked the fry-baby videos, we'd love this one."

Cam felt a chill as the sheriff went over to his computer, opened his E-mail, looked at it for a moment, and then initiated a download. Cam came around behind him to watch. It was a video, and the sequence was the same as before: a black screen, followed by the chair materializing out of the darkness.

"Oh shit," Cam said softly.

The figure in the chair wore a hood, as before. The humming sound came rumbling over the computer's speakers, making one of them buzz. Then came the electronically distorted voice.

"All rise," it began, repeating the mocking introduction to a court session. The humming got louder, then diminished slightly. "Tell the lieutenant he has something of ours, and we want it back."

"What the hell?" Bobby Lee said. "Is he talking about you?"

Sure sounded like it, Cam thought. And the voice was saying "We" now, instead of "I," he noticed.

"The lieutenant has a face that belongs to us. He didn't earn it. We want it back. We'll trade. This face for our face."

With that, a robed and gloved hand descended over the back of the chair and lifted the hood from the face of a clearly terrified Mary Ellen Goode.

Cam felt his gut tighten. This was definitely not supposed to have happened. "This face for our face. And Richter's the designated mule. We'll tell him where and when. Play ball, or she fries and dies."

The screen faded out to black and both of them stood there in shock.

Cam somberly explained to Bobby Lee what the term *face* meant to the cat dancers. And then he remembered something: He had brought back Kenny's camera. He had no idea if the film was still good after repeated dunkings, but the camera was physically intact and it was upstairs in his office. He told Bobby Lee.

The sheriff stared at him. He cleared his throat carefully, as if trying to get his voice back, and sent Cam to retrieve the camera so their forensics people could try to salvage any pictures. Cam did that, gave the camera to a tech, and went back to the sheriff's office.

Bobby Lee called McLain's office. He put it on the speakerphone. Special Agent McLain was not available.

"Make him goddamn available," Bobby Lee demanded, to Cam's surprise. "That's not a request. And now would be really nice."

They went on hold for five minutes, during which time Cam called Jay-Kay. No answer. Then McLain finally came on the line. Bobby Lee told him what had happened. McLain swore and said he'd dispatch some people to Jay-Kay's building.

"You know what this is really about, don't you?" the sheriff asked.

"They want Lieutenant Richter, not the pictures," McLain said.

"Got that shit right. And we're not going to play that game."

Cam, thinking of Mary Ellen's white face, started to say something, but Bobby Lee waved him off.

"I think I need to bring a team to Triboro," McLain said.

"We don't deal with hostage takers here in Manceford County, Special Agent," Bobby Lee said. "We talk to them—once—let them know how things stand, and if they don't play ball, we kill them. All of them."

"We need to come up there, Sheriff," McLain said again.

"I think you need to find your consultant. These bastards have the ranger, but where's your wizard?"

"On it," McLain said. "But I still think we need to come up there."

"Come quick, then," Bobby Lee said. Then he hung up and called the operations people back and told them to round up a SWAT team. Cam decided this would be a good time to go out into the parking lot and get some fresh air. As he was standing out there, the lab tech came across the parking lot from the Walker Forensics Building with an envelope. He saw Cam and veered over to give the envelope to him.

"The pictures survived," he said. "Those disposables are water-resistant, to start with. That thing was shrink-wrapped, and the film cartridge was sealed against light." He looked around hesitantly. "Had to be a brave scooter taking those pix," he added.

"You have no idea," Cam told him.

"Is this what happened to Sergeant Cox?"

"No comment," Cam replied, although he was nodding.

"Damn," the tech said with a shudder.

Cam thanked him and opened the envelope. He was surprised that there were about two dozen eight-by-ten pictures in the stack.

Some of them were panoramic scenes in the Smokies, then some close-ups of paw prints in sand and river mud, more shots looking up into rocky ravines, and several of the rock face in the Chop, showing the cave entrance. Then the dramatic ones: the cat coming out onto the ledge, bathed in the flash, already gathering itself as Kenny swung in; a coveted face shot, which had to have been taken when Kenny was no more than eight feet away; a second shot, this one very blurred, as Kenny swung back out; and then one where the cat filled the entire frame as it made the leap out toward

Kenny. After those came the ones showing Cam's efforts to blind the cat, which were mostly out of focus, except for one beauty where the furious animal was in perfect focus. He could just see part of a shepherd in the background. There were some badly overexposed panels, and then a final picture of a campfire scene.

Cam studied this one carefully. The light wasn't very good, and the people around the campfire were all wearing balaclavas over their faces, except for one individual: White Eye Mitchell.

The cat dancers?

He looked hard at the eyes, trying to recognize any identifiable features. He thought one might be Kenny, but then he remembered that Kenny had probably taken the picture. Still, those eyes were familiar. They were all dressed in cold-weather field gear, so he couldn't tell much about sizes and shapes. He studied the bulky coats and hats, looking for anything familiar, such as standard-issue police gear or an insignia. In addition to White Eye, there were four people around the fire. The picture taker would make five, so two had been missing from the party. He couldn't tell when the pictures had been taken.

He hurried back inside the building, where he showed the pictures to the sheriff.

"The Bureau will be desperate to contain this," the sheriff said. "At least until they catch their bastards. Which probably explains why McLain wants us to do nothing until they get up here."

"I need to go check my messages," Cam said, "see if they've started the game."

"You do understand what I was saying earlier, don't you?" the sheriff asked. "They don't want the pictures. They want you. They take you out, there's no one else who can attest to the fact that either cell ever existed. And if they succeed in doing that, your ranger friend becomes entirely expendable."

"The feds might not be disappointed in that outcome," Cam said.

The sheriff shook his head. "No, I can't believe that. They'll want to control this, but not cover it up."

"These guys have made contact. We need to move, not wait for any more meetings. Mary Ellen is in deep shit. I can't sit still for that."

"Wrong pronoun, Lieutenant, but I don't disagree. The professional thing for me to do right now is sideline you and get someone else to run this—precisely because of who the hostage is."

Cam nodded, then thought of something. "Okay, suspend me. Tell me to go home and stay there. Then I might just disobey an order or two. If it all goes south, you can say I was suspended but went out of control."

"Listen to you," Bobby Lee said with a wry grin. "Look, this is the Manceford County Sheriff's Office. We've got us a problem. We're gonna take care of it, as always. Go check your messages, gather up your team, then get your ass back down here."

"We're not waiting for the feds?"

"What's that Manceford County Sheriff's Office motto— the one I'm not supposed to know anything about?"

"Mess with the Best and Die Like the Rest?"

"That's the one."

Cam asked the sheriff to forward the E-mail with the embedded video to him, then went upstairs and checked his voice mail. Nothing. To his surprise, he found the entire team waiting up in the MCAT offices. Word had somehow gotten out that something big was shaking, and his guys' antennas were apparently as sharp as ever. Cam flipped on his computer and then went to sit at the head of the conference table.

"Okay," he said. "Kenny Cox." Everyone waited. He took them through the whole story, finishing with a detailed description of what had happened up in the mountains. At the end, he passed around the photographs of Kenny's final encounter with a mountain lion. Rolling a chair over to his computer, he opened the most recent video and let them all watch it.

"They'll give her back in return for these?" Tony asked, pointing at the pictures. "I mean, they have to know we'll keep copies."

"Only if *I* deliver them," Cam said, and everyone understood immediately.

The phone rang. "Building security says a messenger just brought in what looks like a letter bomb for you, Lieutenant," the duty officer announced brightly.

"Say again?"

"Well, it's a FedEx letterpack-size package, all wrapped in brown mailing tape. Address is hand-lettered; return address has the name I. M. Jones, and we recognized the street address—it's the Triboro city jail."

"All right, do the drill," Cam told him.

An hour later, after the obligatory, if officially confined, commotion, the chief of the explosives-disposal unit appeared in Cam's office and handed him a clear plastic evidence pouch containing a plain white envelope. "Your bomb, sir," he said with a grin.

"Better safe than sorry," Cam replied, taking the pouch.

"You bet," the lieutenant said, and left.

A picture and a hand-printed note were inside the envelope. The picture was of Mary Ellen Goode, without the hood this time, sitting in the electric chair. Her hands, arms, and legs were immobilized. There was a cell phone sitting in her lap, from which a white wire trailed beyond the frame. The note said "Your place. Tonight. Late. Face for a face. We see backup, the cell phone starts the fun."

"If we moved right now," Tony said, "we could get guys in position before it gets too late."

"This is a cell, Tony," Cam said. "More than one guy. They have to be watching. That's why they made this thing look like a letter bomb. As soon as they saw the bomb-squad robot carry the letter out of the building, they'd knew I'd get their message."

"You can't go out there alone, boss," said Horace.

"How about a Trojan horse?" Pardee said. "You go home alone in a big ole Suburban. 'Cept there're three guys hidden under some stuff in the back of the truck. Pull it into the garage, shut the garage door, get out, and go inside. Three SWAT shooters already in the house—better odds."

"Or," said Billy Mays, "we leak some shit to the media wipes, get 'em out front, bring you out in cuffs for a highly visible perp walk, then haul you off in a cruiser. Get it on the TV for the eleven o'clock follies. Then send out a three-pack and pretend to toss your house. Except we send in a dozen guys, bring out nine. Then the next day, we turn you loose, restart the game."

"Nice try, guys," Cam said, smiling. "But we're forgetting something: These are cops, and probably federal agents. Think of what they can do in terms of listening to our comms, knowing when we're BSing. Hell, for all we know, one of those three SWAT shooters you want in my house could be in the cell."

"You can't go out there alone, boss," Horace said again.

Cam sighed. "This time, I think I have to. I got that woman into this. I need to get her out. I've already lost Kenny."

He searched their faces, watched them sort it out. They understood exactly what he was talking about.

60

CAM DECIDED TO GO home to wait for the call. The team, all of whom were SWAT-qualified, went to find out where they were going to assemble.

Mary Ellen Goode had trusted him. She knew nothing that was terribly important, and it was all secondhand at that. And now she was dead meat unless everything worked out perfectly. How likely was that? This is all my damned fault, Cam told himself. He swore as he went out the door, startling some people coming in.

He fed the shepherds when he got home and then checked his voice mail and E-mail. Nothing. He made coffee. The sheriff called. The SWAT team was set up at the law-enforcement center downtown. McLain had called back and said he'd asked for the FBI's hostage-rescue team but was told that would take twenty-fours to set up. He'd canceled it and said he'd have a tactical team up in Triboro by 11:00 P.M. He'd also offered the services of their latest night-surveillance aircraft, *Owl*.

"Okay, I give up. What's *Owl*?" Cam asked the sheriff.

"A glider with a small jet engine. It can operate at night, carries a pilot and one agent with some pretty sophisticated night-vision gear. They can get on top of a situation, stay there as long as there's wind aloft, and they are soundless. Unlike our helos."

"First they have to call," Cam said.

"Don't sit in front of any windows," Bobby Lee told him.

"I've got my mutts," Cam said, looking at the two shepherds, who were sitting on either side of him, fully aware that something was up.

He went around and turned off all unnecessary lights in

his house, then activated the roof spots. The dogs followed him from room to room. He cleaned his Sig .45 and laid out his tactical gear. He had some more coffee. It was only ten o'clock when the phone rang.

But instead of bad guys, the call was from Jay-Kay.

"I'm on Fifty-two from Charlotte," she said. "What's the best way to get to your house?"

"What the fuck, Jay-Kay?" Cam said.

"It's worse than you think," she said. "Give me directions, please."

Forty-five minutes later, she was sitting in his living room. He'd showered and changed into his tactical gear. She was wearing a pantsuit. He offered her coffee, but she declined.

"How did it happen?" he asked her.

"I don't know. I went out for some take-away right after my secretary left for the day; her son had a soccer game, so she left early. I left Ranger Goode in the apartment, and when I got back, she was gone."

"And your security systems?"

"No signs of intrusion."

"Which meant they were feds, doesn't it?" he said. "Agents, or at least other FBI people who were already in your system?"

"I don't know," she said evenly.

"You said it was worse than I thought. They have Mary Ellen Goode. What's worse than that?"

"McLain and the Bureau are playing you and your sheriff."

"Playing how?"

"I'll show you in a minute, but first tell me where your home PC is." He pointed to the study. She pulled out a package of CDs from her briefcase and went to the machine.

"I'm going to execute a wipe disc on your machine," she said. "First, we save all your data."

"Uh, okay, I guess. May I ask why?"

"Because I discovered something while I was showing Ranger Goode some of the Bureau's case files on this vigilante matter." She brought up a file-management program. "I found out that the next time you go on-line, there's a federal computer waiting to suck every piece of data right off your hard drive," she said, her fingers flying over the keyboard. "I've made some other discoveries, Just Cam, and they're not good ones. I think I've been used, as well."

She backed up all his data files onto the CDs and then put one of her own into the machine. Within ten seconds, the monitor went black.

"There," she said. "I killed everything but your on-line service and the underlying OS. It'll go on-line in a minute, and when they trap it, there's a truly nasty little program that's going to be swept up along with not very much from your computer. Then, wipe disc."

Cam wasn't too sure what "wipe disc" meant, but it sounded dramatic.

"Now," Jay-Kay, said, getting up from his computer chair. "That coffee?"

They sat down in Cam's kitchen and Jay-Kay explained that she'd detected an attempted intrusion into her mainframes when she went to AFIS to see if Marlor's fingerprints were on file. "I have the fire wall from hell," she said. "My machines are set up to detect an intrusion and swallow it whole, making the intruder think he's in, when in fact my tigers are going into his machine and wiping out the hard-wired machine-language programming. You know, the firmware stuff that starts the boot sequence. They order up a restart on the way out, and the intruding computer goes dark."

Cam nodded, pretending to understand what she was talking about. "And what happened this time?"

"This time, in the process of blocking the intrusion, the tigers were thrown out. Two IBM mainframes in parallel operation can usually overwhelm most other computers, so this had to be a big federal machine, probably running some NSA code."

"So what's the deal?" he asked.

She sighed. "I'm a federal consultant. I have clearance and access. And yet someone within federal LE ordered up an intrusion. I checked with the sys op at the Charlotte field office. I happen to know her and I've helped her with some security issues. I made a joke of it: 'What, you guys bored? Nothing to do on the graveyard shift? You want to mess with my tigers?' "

"And?"

"Well, she told me that Thomas McLain wanted to find a pattern analysis–report file in my machines and see if they could steal it. To test my security, he said. And they got it."

"Wow."

"Yes, because that means they went in looking for a specific file—by its file name. I delivered that file to the Manceford County system, which is probably how they got the file name." She sipped some of her coffee and then smiled. "Luckily, it's encrypted."

"Can't they break it?"

She shook her head. "This one's based on an optical code with a physical onetime pad. They need to get their hands on the other half of a specific piece of heat-tempered plastic to break it."

Cam got up and started to pace around his kitchen. "McLain's been on the fence the whole time with this mess," he said. "Let's assume there is a second vigilante cell, made up of federal people, operating here in North Carolina. Or that there are feds involved with the cat dancers. Let's assume McLain thinks this is true. What would the Bureau do?"

"The Professional Standards directorate would be all over it," she said. "There would be Washington types in Charlotte as we speak."

"McLain said those two agents at the meeting we went to were from that directorate."

"I don't think so. I don't know who they were, but everyone in the field office would know it if Pro Standards people were in the building. They'd talk about nothing else."

The phone rang again. It was the sheriff.

"I've got Ms. Bawa here with me," Cam said. "She thinks there's something hinky at the Charlotte field office." He recapped what Jay-Kay had just told him.

"Well, they haven't shown up here, yet, either. And Horace just called down. Said he had some news. This new video? Our Computer Crimes people think that the picture is faked—some kind of digital construct. The eyes are wrong. Apparently, a human retina reflects a certain wavelength of light in a video, while a photograph doesn't."

"How sure are we?" Cam asked.

"Well, your ass is not out of the woods," he said. "Because our lab rats aren't willing to bet *their* asses that the video's a fake. So to answer your question, we're *not* sure."

"Terrific."

"We may have one break, though. The lighting was different in this video. In the execution videos, there was nothing visible in the background. In this one, there's a tiny bit of the floor visible. One of our lab guys used to be an over-the-road truck driver. He makes it for the deck in a tractor-trailer— something to do with pallet skid marks. And when you think about it—"

"Yeah, that would be perfect," Cam said, as Jay-Kay came back into the kitchen. "So I guess I still wait for a message?"

"I think we have to assume she's alive and is being held hostage and then see what happens, Lieutenant," the sheriff said. "I've got the SWAT team on hostage alert, and a helicopter set up with the state guys in case that *Owl* thing was bullshit."

"And how about the G-men?" Cam said.

"We'll play that by ear. See what develops. Let's get off this phone, and whatever happens, leave the lady at home."

"Roger that," Cam said, and hung up.

"Your computer is officially wiped," she said. "I left the CDs, but you might want to hide them."

"Did your little bomb go out?"

"Don't know, but if I'm right about the origin of that probe, sometime tomorrow I should get a call to come in and see why a certain network self-destructed. What have your people decided to do?"

Cam told her. She asked how she could help.

"Actually," Cam said, "the sheriff told me to make sure you do not get involved in whatever goes down tonight."

She frowned. "I did not mean going along for the ride," she said. "I meant, how can I help by doing what I do best?"

"I have no idea," he replied.

The night wind had begun to stir outside, so he turned on the gas fireplace in the living room and poured them both some coffee. They sat down in the living room. Frick and Frack took up stations on either side of the fireplace and fell asleep. Jay-Kay reached into her briefcase and pulled out her cell phone to check for messages.

"Now I guess we wait," he said. "I'm pretty sure the Sheriff's Office has my phone up so they can try a trace."

"Might not someone come here to retrieve the pictures?"

"The general sense of it is that they're after me, not the pictures. I'm the guy who can provide direct testimony."

"Surely you've been deposed by now?"

"Yes and no," he said. "The sheriff knows everything I know, and I debriefed my guys on the MCAT. That's good enough for the Kenny Cox problem, but not for the federal problem."

"If there is one."

"Has to be," Cam said. "Why else would those guys have been trying to take me out? Or take Mary Ellen hostage?"

"I think this kidnapping is about getting you neutralized, not dead. Until the bomb, this was a case of James Marlor getting revenge, with some help from inside the Sheriff's Office. The bomb changed everything. I think it was a mistake."

"A mistake? A C-four bomb in a car? That had to be deliberate."

"I think the bomb was supposed to go off and scare the judge into quitting the bench. What they didn't count on was that she would decide to get in the car. That's why they sent the first, fake bomb—to make sure she understood she was in real danger and to make her stay in the house. Once she was killed, they realized they had exposed themselves, unnecessarily. Then you came along telling everyone this had to be someone else, not James Marlor."

"You've been giving this a lot of thought," Cam said.

She was looking at him with that coolly superior expression he'd seen before when she was talking to lesser mortals. Without even looking at the keyboard, she was entering a phone number on her cell phone.

Her cell phone.

A sudden cold thought hit him. There wasn't going to be any phone call. "They" were sitting right in front of him.

She smiled when she saw the comprehension dawn in his eyes.

61

"YOU'RE HERE FOR THE pictures, aren't you?" he asked.

She smiled again. "Full marks, Lieutenant." He started to get up, but she raised the cell phone and told him to sit back down. He remembered the video, the cell phone in Mary Ellen's lap. He sat back down. She extracted a silenced semi-automatic from her briefcase.

"What's that for?" he asked.

"This is just to keep our meeting polite—you know, more for my protection than to harm you."

Cam looked over at the dogs, wondering if he could spin them into action. But she had a gun and could shoot both of them before he could get something productive going. He looked back at her.

"You've been part of this little gang all along?"

"For some time," she said. "I'm their eyes and ears."

"How? And why, for crying out loud?"

"How? I danced with a big cat, just like the others, of course. That's the only way in. I even have a face."

He remembered the eyes he'd thought he'd recognized. Hers. "And the 'why'?"

"One, because the people they kill richly deserve it. You heard the real me in the hallway that day. Heads on stakes and all that. And because it's a dangerous, fast, and incredibly exciting game, Lieutenant. I think I told you that once—excitement is what I live for."

"Oh right, you're the thrill junkie. But you people have to know we have copies of those pictures, and the Sheriff's Office definitely does not consider this shit a game. We've already lost one cop, and if we lose another one, all you guys are going to get dead."

"First, you'd have to find us."

"We already know—"

She leaned forward. "What you *know* is nothing, except what I've revealed to you. Do you suppose I just might have pointed you at the wrong people? Besides, we didn't cause Sergeant Cox's death. *He* did that. He already had *two* faces. That's more than anyone else. He got greedy, and the cat finally won. That happens."

"He did that because your little game was starting to come apart," Cam said. "You could do that shit with impunity as long as no one suspected cops were making hits. Now that we know, 'your game,' as you call it, is over. And we will find each one of you. You taught us how, remember?"

"In your dreams, Lieutenant. Remember, what I did was pattern analysis of real data, which may or may not exist anymore. Wherever I can intrude, I can alter, remember? All we have to do now is nothing."

"*You* were the one who lit this vigilante fuse—back at the hotel when we had dinner. Why'd you do that?"

"The challenge, of course. Plus, if you let me into your investigation, I could control it."

"And it was you who gave me Kenny Cox? Why? He was one of you."

"Because you were already onto him, weren't you? Our theory was that if I gave you Cox, we might still hide the other laycr."

"But now we know."

She smiled. "That's just a new game, Lieutenant. My tigers and I are ready if you are. And we don't have to be in Charlotte, North Carolina, to play. Those aren't my only assets. In the meantime, listen to me. Do you want Mary Ellen Goode back alive?"

"Of course."

"Then you need to suffer some important memory lapses. It's as simple as that. We don't want you dead. We don't kill police. First, you must promise to forget everything you know, and then we will tell you where to find her."

He stared at her. Was Mary Ellen already dead? Were the Computer Crimes guys right? And besides, did this woman really believe that he'd promise to do that, get Mary Ellen back, and then hold to the promise? She'd been working around law enforcement long enough to know that cops would say anything to get a hostage out. He shrugged. "Okay, deal," he said. "So where is she?"

She laughed. "Not so fast. Do you know that the Bureau has requested a warrant for your arrest?"

He shook his head. "Based on what?"

"Based on a chain of circumstantial evidence, Lieutenant, evidence that stains both the Manceford County Sheriffs Office and you. It was one of your people who botched the arrest that precipitated this whole thing. And then you personally become a black hole."

"What's that mean?"

"James Marlor died after you visited him. White Eye Mitchell died while you watched. Sergeant Cox died while you watched. All three explanations of how they died have come from you, essentially uncorroborated. *You* visited the grounds and house of Judge Bellamy when she was under police protection. *You* were there when someone fired a big-bore rifle into her house. *You* are the sole beneficiary of her estate, which is more than substantial. Everywhere they turn, there *you* are, sucking their interest in."

"And I can explain each of those—" Cam began, but she cut him off.

"You can try, Lieutenant, but the Bureau has built a case based on everything I've already mentioned, plus the 'clincher,' as they term it."

"What's that?"

"Some very interesting and directly incriminating data from your own phone records."

"Not possible."

"The pay phones. You've been calling them, too."

"But that's bullshit—never have."

"Telephone company records say that you have. At least now they do. Would you like to verify that?"

She put the cell phone down and shifted the gun to her other hand. "Look," she said. "The government is convinced that there really is a death squad of sheriff's officers in this state. Right now, they think that you're part of it. After all, you are perfectly positioned to help such an effort."

He just stared at her.

"I'm sorry to tell you that I have helped them form that impression and, *and*, I can enrich that impression. Plus, I can do that from *wherever* I want to."

He didn't know what to say. What had she said before? If she could intrude, she could alter? And she'd just erased his own computer, with his acquiescence. Or had she—could she have put something in there, too?

"And what about the federal death squad?"

"What incentive does the government have to pursue that theory?" she scoffed. "None."

"But Kenny said—"

"That's what *you* said Sergeant Cox said, Lieutenant. And even that was ambiguous and spoken in a dying delirium. You said so yourself."

He sat back in his chair. The room suddenly seemed uncommonly warm.

"So you sent Annie the E-mail?"

"From inside *your* office, yes. From your computer, actually."

"And you planted that bomb?"

"No. The man with me planted the bomb; while I was inside with your judge, gaining access to her home computer, and from that, the judicial network."

"Fuck that—*you* killed Annie Bellamy."

"She killed herself, Lieutenant. And didn't I overhear you tell her to come over once everyone left? Maybe *you* killed her, Lieutenant."

He felt a wave of cold rage sweep through him. He could take her. Scream at her like that big cat and leap across the room, bat that pea-shooter out of her hands and then take her lying little head right off. If he attacked her the shepherds would join in. One of them would get her. She read the sudden murderous blaze in his eyes and raised the cell phone.

"If I press send, she dies," she said calmly. He sank down in his chair. "Back to your part of the deal, Lieutenant. Here it is in a nutshell: You must not testify. That's the long and the short of it. When we're convinced that you are honoring your agreement, we will release your pretty little park ranger."

"How long will that take?"

She didn't answer him. He recalled what Computer Crimes had said about the video images. "I think you're lying," he said. "I think she's already dead."

"Shall I hit the 'send' button, then?" she asked. "Although it's not as if there will be a big boom heard halfway across town."

He hesitated. She lowered the phone. "For our part, the executions will stop. We will even leave the feral cats alone. You simply refuse to testify."

"McLain won't buy that," he said. "The Bureau will pursue this forever."

"We'll take our chances with McLain," she said. "We might know him and what he will do with this better than you do, if their E-mail is any indication. They've been arguing with the ATF ever since the bombing as to the true nature of what's been going on, but even they can't ignore the fact that everything continues to point back to you. But if you go silent, and we go silent, they have every incentive to quit looking, don't they, not to mention that's what Washington wants, too."

Cam thought she was wrong about that, but this wasn't the time to argue. "So the real deal is, I take a dive, Mary Ellen goes free, and you guys get away with it?"

"What we did was mete out justice, Lieutenant—justice as propagated by the old gods, not the politically correct ones. And besides, it won't be that obvious, this 'dive' of yours. Remember, you are the evidence. If you don't talk, everyone's case goes dim."

"What about what I've already told them?"

"If necessary, you recant. You're no longer sure. Those were stressful situations—you may have been mistaken."

He wasn't sure of what to say. He'd sat right here in this house and debriefed Bobby Lee and the DA, so in a sense, he'd already testified. But she might not know that. Or did she? Had they gone back to their offices and put it all into a computer report? Which she could have read? On the other hand, what was to stop the sheriff from reopening the whole thing once they got Mary Ellen back? They had some candidates. He decided that he needed to play along right now.

"Even if they didn't come after me," he said, "I'll still have to get out. Retire."

"Yes, you probably will, but that's better than being shot with a hunting rifle through your kitchen window one night, isn't it? You were a military sniper scout? You know how easy that would be to do, yes?"

He remembered the case of the abortion clinic doctor and tried to blank out that unpleasant image.

"Think of it this way, Lieutenant: For now, you will have succeeded—You will have put us all out of business." She looked at her watch. "I have a plane to catch." She put the cell phone on the coffee table. "This phone has a speed-dial feature. Selection zero one activates the chair. Zero two disables the chair. Don't get them confused."

She looked at her watch again. "In two hours, not before, and using this phone, select zero three. You will then get voice mail. Say yes and hang up. Wait five minutes; then select zero two."

"Why not speed-dial zero two right now?"

"Because you hold half the key, Lieutenant. Until the other half is called in, *all* keys turn the chair on. So, do it our way, please."

Still in shock at what she'd laid out for him, he nodded slowly. She went through it one more time.

"When do we get her back?"

She again ignored his question. "I'm going to leave now," she said. "What I have done to you can be undone. Or made even more interesting, should we feel the need for it. I can do it to the sheriff, too. I can build an incriminating coil of ones and zeros around anyone who has a connection to the computer world, which in America, of course, is anyone of consequence. We are *inside* the law-enforcement system, Lieutenant, and in case you missed it, that's a system that is getting stronger by the day. Never forget that."

He stared straight ahead while she walked out of the room. The dogs watched her go and then looked over at Cam.

"I think I'm fucked, guys," he said.

62

AN HOUR AND A half later, he was back downtown in the sheriff's executive office. The precious cell phone lay on the sheriff's desk. Cam's watch lay next to it, its timer counting down the minutes.

The only outsider there when Cam got in was Mike Pierce of the SBI. Cam had described his little tryst with Jay-Kay. The sheriff wanted to get a line on her immediately, but Cam talked him out of it. "Let's do the drill, get the ranger back, and then we can chase the bad guys," he said. Mike Pierce had the scan report Jay-Kay had given them. He highlighted the numbers for the pay phones and went to get some help to access Cam's phone records to see if it was true that Jay-Kay had implicated him.

Cam stared down at the cell phone after Mike left. "I have one big problem with all this cell phone shit," he said.

"What's that?"

"She said all three speed buttons would turn the chair on until I make that other call." He looked over at the sheriff. "What if that's still true after I make that call? Or *when* I make the 'yes' call? What if this is all bullshit and I end up sending the signal that kills Mary Ellen?"

The sheriff frowned, and Cam realized that he looked older and grayer than when this mess had begun. "I'll do it, if you'd like," the sheriff said. "You'll have to say the words, but I'll punch the buttons. I've got the SWAT team standing by, and the ops center is ready to trace the numbers that come up in the window."

Cam sighed and slumped in his chair. "She's got me boxed, Sheriff," he said. "With your support, I can probably avoid a federal prosecution, but if I don't testify, I'm finished in law enforcement."

The sheriff didn't say anything. He did check the watch, which was ticking away on his desk.

"Where's McLain and his tactical team?" Cam asked.

"Don't know," the sheriff said.

Mike Pierce came back into the room, clutching the report. He closed the door and sat down. "Please confirm your home phone number, Lieutenant," he said. Cam gave it to him. Mike scanned the report and nodded.

"You guys didn't go through all the data, right? You read her executive summary and conclusions?"

They nodded.

"Well, she wasn't kidding. She already had your phone number in here as one of the recurring contact numbers in the pay-phone network. She just didn't call it out in the conclusions paragraph."

"Son of a bitch," Cam said. "There it is. How the hell did she *do* that?"

"I asked the tech control people at the phone company that question," Pierce said. "And they said that the call logs are tied to the billing system. They don't keep records on their customers on the off chance the cops might call, but they do keep records for bill generation. You know when you call into customer service and bitch about a bill?"

They nodded again.

"Well, you know how sometimes they make nice and remove a specific charge? The way they do that is by expunging the record of the call. The billing system then does the math. My point is, it's not a secure system. Even a customer service rep in Bombay can do that."

"And she's coming at them with a couple of mainframes," Cam said. "Shit!"

"How much time do we have?" Pierce asked.

The sheriff looked at the watch. "Twenty-seven minutes," he said, and then explained Cam's concern with the speed dial business. Pierce shook his head in frustration. "What choice do we have?" he asked. "They fry her, you're still on the hook, especially with this shit."

"But she faked all that," Cam protested.

"And we have whose word for that?" Pierce asked gently. Cam wanted to hit someone.

"There's more," Pierce said. "We called that woman's number in Charlotte, got an answering service. The woman who returned the call said she was Ms. Bawa's executive assistant. She doesn't know where Ms. Bawa is, but that's apparently not unusual. Just for the hell of it, I asked if you had been to that office. The officer with the dogs? she asked."

"I can explain that," Cam said wearily. "I did—"

Pierce had his hand up, indicating that Cam should stop talking. "I've been going to law school at night," he said. "I think that right now you should follow the lady's advice and say absolutely nothing. The sheriff here vouches for you, and that's good enough for me. But the best option for the feds to solve their vigilante problem is to hang you out to dry, declare a public, if partial, victory, and then take their own manhunt underground. Image is everything to those guys."

"You do understand that this whole damned thing is a setup, right?" Cam said. He realized he was almost shouting.

"You should have taken along some backup," Pierce replied, unperturbed.

"Who?" Cam said angrily. "Sergeant Cox?"

"Enough," Bobby Lee ordered. "Let's focus on getting the ranger back alive, shall we?"

The designated lieutenant for the SWAT team called, asking for an update, and the sheriff told him they'd be making the calls in about twenty minutes. "Hopefully, someone will call into the ops center with the location of the hostage after we do our phone drill."

They all looked at the cell phone and waited as the minutes ticked by. The more Cam thought about it, though, the less he believed there would be any calls, at least not immediately. He wanted to run out of the building and scream at the moon. All of this because some asshole had failed to read two scumbags their Miranda rights? He thought about Mary

Ellen, strapped up in that horrific chair, waiting for someone to do something. How long had she been there? Was she still alive? Had that video been done the night she was taken hostage? Or were all those images fakes, the product of some other mad digital wizard. He visualized the oil-soaked corpse of the one robber lying out on the ground next to that diesel tank. Was that where Mary Ellen was now? "We'd never harm another cop," Kenny had said, but now Kenny was a pile of picked-over frozen bones somewhere up in the western Carolina mountains.

"Okay, we're two minutes away," the sheriff said. "This thing has a signal. You going to do it, or shall I?"

"I'll do it," Cam said, getting up and going over to the sheriff's big desk.

They waited as the watch clicked down, and then jumped when the tiny little beep went off. Cam picked up the phone and hit zero three. He flinched when someone slammed the front door to the executive offices. Zero two killed the chair. Right?

His hands were sweating as the phone rang and rang. C'-mon, he thought. C'mon.

Then it was answered by voice mail. To his astonishment, Cam heard his own voice mail greeting playing. He snatched the phone away from his ear and looked at the number he'd speed-dialed. It was his own home phone.

"Well?" the sheriff said. "Aren't you supposed to say something?"

To my own fucking phone? Cam thought, but then he said the magic word and hung up.

He reset the watch timer for five minutes and they waited some more. Then he took a deep breath and hit zero two. The phone rang once, twice, and then what sounded like a fax machine picked up and stopped. Silence followed and Cam hung up again.

"You're not going to believe this shit," he announced. "The first number I called was mine."

"Figures," said Mike Pierce. "She's got that, too."

63

THEY WAITED FOR ANOTHER hour, but there were no calls. Cam finally called his own voice mail at home. One message, and not the one he had left. He listened carefully, played it again, and then saved it. "Sounded like a tape," he reported. "A trucking terminal on the south side of I-Forty, off the airport road. We're apparently looking for a trailer. They said for me to go alone, or they'd fire the chair."

"No," Bobby Lee said. "No way."

"I got her into this mess, Sheriff," Cam protested. "Least I can do is get her out."

"What you'd do is get yourself killed. No, I'm sorry, but there's a hostage. I'm always sorry there's a hostage. But we go in force."

"How about that *Owl* thing?" Pierce asked. "Send it overhead with some thermal-imaging gear, see if they can find a trailer that's different from all the others?"

"How long will that take?" the sheriff asked. Pierce didn't know, but he went to find out.

Thirty minutes later, they had a plan. The *Owl* would make its sweep and report any targets of interest. The SWAT team would deploy in the rail yards behind the trucking terminal. Cam would drive through the terminal in a lone cruiser, wearing full combat gear, and pretend to scan the trailers with a handheld thermal-imaging device. He'd drive around long enough to allow the SWAT team to get in position behind the trailer, and then they'd pounce. If the *Owl* didn't find anything, they'd regroup and try something else.

It took another hour to get the aircraft in position above the terminal. Cam rode out with his MCAT guys in a Suburban to a location three blocks away from the terminal. Then he shifted over to a cruiser while the guys went to join the SWAT team at the command post. The sheriff and Mike Pierce went directly to the command post in the sheriff's personal cruiser.

Cam reached the terminal in five minutes and drove in past the security gates. The place was a medium-size terminal by Triboro standards—ten warehouses equipped with mechanized truck-loading docks. Some of the warehouses were inactive, but half had trucks and trailers backed up and forklifts operating in lighted doorways. The sergeant at the command and control vehicle announced over the secure tactical frequency that the aircraft was overhead, scanning the empty trailers parked at the back of the terminal. He said there were sixty or seventy trailers out there.

Cam drove around with his window open. The dock workers didn't seem to pay any attention to the lone cruiser prowling the area. Cam could communicate with the war wagon but not with the SWAT team. The aircraft reported that the roofs of the warehouses appeared to be clean, no lurking shooters. Ten minutes later, it reported one trailer had a different thermal signature from the trailers around it. They pinpointed its location along the back fence of the terminal, and the SWAT team went into motion.

Cam continued his prowl, occasionally sticking the thermal-imager gun out the window as he waited for word that the team was in position behind the target. Finally, he was told to drive to the very back and begin a slow sweep of the trailers parked against the back fence. He started using his spotlight now, shining it under the parked trailers, which was the one place the *Owl* could not see.

He drove the full length of the line, hoping like hell that there were no long-gun shooters in the trees, then switched off the spot and turned around. He started back along the line, imaging each trailer carefully as the tactical controller counted down the time on top. He pretended to be interested in one trailer until the war wagon announced that the team was in position in a line of trees behind the trailer park area and that the fence had been cut.

Cam kept driving until he arrived at the trailer designated

by the aircraft. He pointed the imager at it, but nothing came up in the viewfinder. The aircraft confirmed he was pointing at the right trailer. Now it was time to get out of the car. He wanted to do another spotlight sweep under the trailer, but that might illuminate the SWAT people on the other side. The trailer, like all the others, was parked with its foot stand facing the road and the cargo doors facing the fence at the back.

He used his own headlights instead, parking at an oblique angle in order to throw some light under the trailer. He wished he had his shepherds with him—they'd have been able to find anything and anybody lurking out there.

"In position," he announced quietly to his shoulder mike.

"Exit the vehicle and go around to the back of the trailer," the voice in his earphone said. "*Owl* reports no sign of ambush."

Cam swallowed, put the cruiser in park, and got out. The terminal lights did a fair job of illuminating the line back here, but there were lots of shadows. He just hoped that aircraft could see everything for a good five hundred yards around, because any competent sniper could take him out from that distance, body armor or no body armor. He walked carefully around the back of the trailer, shining his flashlight everwhere but back at the fence. He listened for any sounds of the *Owl*, but he heard only a soft wind in the tree line. He could see that the trailer was a refrigeration model, with a squat generator up top and heavy insulated sides. There was maybe twenty feet of space between the fence and the back of the trailer.

The doors on the trailer were locked when he reached the back, so he made another circuit of the trailer while trying to suppress the creeping tingle he felt on his back. Were they here? Had they tumbled to the SWAT team? Was the guy in the *Owl* one of them?

He came back around again to the rear doors. Nothing happened. "Clear," he said to his shoulder mike.

"Team go," announced the controller, and then the whole area lit up as the SWAT guys, looking like storm troopers from a *Star Wars* movie, came swarming through the fence, followed by some portable spots, which soon had the entire area ablaze in blue-white light. More vehicles poured through the front gates of the terminal area and set up a perimeter. The sheriff drove up in his cruiser, followed by the command and control van.

They walked back to the rear of the trailer. "I'm scared to death of what we're going to find here," Cam said.

The sheriff didn't say anything. Cam figured Bobby Lee had already framed Mary Ellen in his mind as being dead, which realistically was the way most cops visualized hostages. That way, when they got them back alive, it was a pleasant surprise. Mike Pierce didn't say anything, either.

The access crew brought over a large bolt cutter to open the doors of the trailer. Cam and the sheriff peered in as the noise suddenly subsided. Two portable spots were rolled up to the fence and their generators started up. The doors were swung open.

Front and center was the electric chair from the Web videos. There was a flat table in front of that, and behind it a one-man tent had been erected in one corner. A brand-new welding machine was set up to one side of the chair, and heavy wires led to the back of the trailer and up the inside front wall toward the refrigeration unit's generator at the top of the trailer. There were empty water jugs, a portable camp toilet, and a pile of army MRE ration containers piled in a trash heap. The generator switched on once the doors were opened.

There was no Mary Ellen Goode.

Cam swore silently.

Two members of the team went in, being careful not to disturb any of the items lying around the floor. They checked the tent, where they found a mummy-style sleeping bag, an old duffel bag, and several scraps of duct tape. After a quick initial exploration, they backed out to wait for the CSI people. Cam could only shake his head in total frustration. Where the hell was Mary Ellen?

"From all appearances," the team leader said, "there was someone being held hostage in this thing. But not now."

"Any signs of violence?" the sheriff asked.

"No visible bloodstains," the lieutenant replied. "CSI will have to confirm that. That chair doesn't smell so good, though."

"Did you see a cell phone in there?" Cam asked. The lieutenant was about to answer when a chirping noise started up inside the tent.

On the third ring, they all heard the trailer's generator ramp up. Red and green lights blinked on across the control panel of the welding machine. Cam and the sheriff exchanged glances and then the sheriff yelled for everyone to back out. The SWAT guys jumped down out of the trailer and joined the general exodus. The generator suddenly went to very high rpm as they swarmed back through the big hole in the chain-link fence. Cam and the sheriff were the last to get through the hole, and as they turned to watch, the chair turned into one massive arc as current flowed through wires attached to the the welding machine. With no one in the chair, its metal arms and legs dissolved in a blazing ball of direct-current lightning, blinding all the cops as they stared in fascination. Then there was a deep red glare at the deep end of the trailer and then it blew up in one enormous fireball, blasting bits of metal, tires, and decking all over the parking lot. The two trailers on either side caught fire from the blast, and half the SWAT cops found themselves sitting on the ground, their ears ringing despite their helmets. Cam had turned away from the searing light and was thus standing partially behind the sheriff when the trailer went up. When he regained his balance and turned back around, the sheriff was sitting on the grass, looking curiously at a foot-long wooden shard that was sticking into his upper chest.

"Medic!" Cam shouted as he knelt down beside the sheriff. His ears were ringing from the blast and he couldn't be sure he'd made himself heard. The sheriff was bleeding, although not very much. He had been wearing his protective vest, but the piece of wood had gone right through him. The part of it sticking out of his back was blackly slick in the harsh light of the portable spots. Bobby Lee coughed weakly and Cam had to hold him upright as he swayed dangerously.

The team's medic came on the run, saw the shard, and

called for an ALS ambulance. Cam backed away as a second medic knelt down and helped keep the sheriff upright. Cam could see that there were other SWAT team members down, but they were all in full body armor and none of them looked to be seriously injured. Most were being tended by other members of the team. The ambulance came through the perimeter, its lights flashing. A heavy pall of bomb smoke lay over the parking lot, and Cam was pulled back to the sights and sounds of Annie Bellamy's yard. It even smelled the same. C-4 again, he thought. So these bastards never hurt other cops, huh?

Mike Pierce came over and watched with Cam as the medics loaded Bobby Lee onto a gurney and then pulled it through the fence to the meat wagon. While some of the cops were spraying the burning tires of the nearby trailers with fire extinguishers, other SWAT team members were standing around the back of the ambulance, saying encouraging things to the sheriff, which meant that he was still conscious.

"That looked bad," Pierce said.

"It was high up," Cam said. "Maybe clipped a lung, but there wasn't much bleeding."

"Not outside anyway," Pierce said, confirming what Cam had been thinking.

"This changes the equation," Cam said.

"We sure that ranger wasn't in there?"

Cam nodded. "It was empty, but somehow they knew the trailer had been opened up. Either they had someone here or it was electronic."

"They told you to come alone. This wasn't aimed at the SWAT guys."

"They had to have known we'd bring a crowd eventually," Cam said. "They might have expected I'd open the trailer, but they must have figured there'd be backup."

"Sheriff's Office bad guys would know," Pierce said. "Federal bad guys might not."

"And where's Mary Ellen Goode?"

Several of the SWAT guys were looking up at something. Cam did the same and saw a small airplane with an oversized

Perspex bubble cockpit and ridiculously long wings swoop low overhead.

"*Owl* says something blew up," the controller announced in a dry tone.

"Go, *Owl*," Cam said glumly.

64

CAM DROVE DOWN HIS street at 2:30 A.M. He slowed as he drove under the lone streetlight in the cul-de-sac. He was bone-tired, still sore from his adventures in the river, and hugely disappointed at not finding Mary Ellen Goode. He'd been on the phone with Ranger Marshall after getting back to Sheriff's Office headquarters, and it had not been a pleasant conversation. Apparently everyone up in Carrigan County would be calling for his head.

Me, too, he thought as he pulled up into his driveway. His ears were still ringing. The house was dark, and the Leyland cypress trees were swaying gently in the wind. The word from the hospital in Triboro was "satisfactory." The sheriff had been the only serious casualty. The shard hadn't severed any major arteries but it had not been a clean wound, and infection was a major concern now. He scanned the front of the house but saw nothing out of the ordinary. He hit the remote for the garage door, but nothing happened. He hit it again. Nothing.

He parked in the driveway and turned off the engine. The streetlight was on, so there should be power in the house. And where were the dogs? They would ordinarily have heard the car, come through the dog door, and run around to the fence in the side yard. No dogs. He was tempted to blow the horn to see what would happen. He hit the remote again, but the door continued to ignore its signals. He checked the little red LED to see if it came on when he pressed the button. It did, so the remote was working.

He unholstered the Sig .45 and got out. Then he got back in and called the ops center to request that a cruiser be dispatched to his house. "Ten minutes," the operator said. Decision time: He could take a quick look in and around the house, or wait for the cruiser. No-brainer. Wait for the deputies.

Two units showed up in six minutes, and the two deputies and Cam went into the house together. The lights worked normally inside, but the dogs were nowhere to be found. The deputies accompanied Cam into every room and the garage. They looked for signs of explosive or incendiary devices, and they checked the windows and doors for evidence of tampering, but everything appeared to be normal. They made a sweep of the backyard, going all the way down to the creek, and then made a quick, if somewhat creepy, walk through the cypress groves on either side of the house.

Embarrassed, Cam sent them away forty minutes later. He knew he'd done the right thing, but still, the expressions on their faces had told a story. The only thing still very much out of order was the fact that the dogs were gone. They never roamed. The wind was steady now and the moonlight was dimming as the sky filled with low-hanging gray-white clouds. It was unseasonably warm. So where were they? He got one of his big flashlights and went back down to the creek line again, checking for signs that they'd gone under the old fence. And then he found the gate open.

He shone his light across the creek, which at this point was no more than two feet wide, and saw some flattened grass on the other side and what looked like a trail going up the hill. The gate was normally locked with a double-end snap, which was now gone. So someone had let them out. Or had sneaked into his yard, discovered two big dogs, and let himself out in a big hurry. Pursued by the dogs? There was a faint chemical smell hovering down in the grass, despite the wind. Something in the creek? He sniffed hard, but he couldn't place it. He called for them, but only the wind answered.

He went back to the house, aware that he was clearly silhouetted by the backyard spots as he walked up the lawn. Had the dogs gone on up into the Holcomb property? And if so, why? Looking for him maybe? Frick might do that, but

Frack would stay behind and watch. And they would certainly come when called.

He yawned. He was exhausted. And yet, if his dogs were nearby and in trouble, he knew he'd never sleep. He went back into the house, got his gear, turned out the spots on the back deck, and went down to the creek. One pass, he promised himself. I'll go up the hill, look around the buildings, then come back. Tomorrow is another day—or rather, today is. I've got bigger problems than two missing dogs.

Get some backup, he told himself as he went through the gate, but then he remembered the looks the two deputies had exchanged. Not again, and if they weren't dog people, they wouldn't be too happy at traipsing through the underbrush in search of his two runaways. The Holcomb place would be spooky by moonlight, but he and the mutts had been up there a hundred times before. He yawned again, then started out up the hill. He kept going, pretty much in a straight line. The farmhouse loomed up to his right, the barns and a topless silo to his left.

He checked the barns first, sliding a large wooden door to one side and scaring off an owl and some other unidentified nocturnal creatures. The place smelled of musty old hay, ancient grease, and decaying wood. Ghostly mantles of cobwebs swayed in the draft from the open door, but there were no other signs of life in the building. A piece of tin on the roof flapped gently in the wind. But no dogs. He looked into the empty concrete garage briefly, saw signs of a teenage love nest with all the appropriate graffiti, and then turned to the house itself.

There was plywood on the doors and first-floor windows, but it had been put up a long time ago and the local demon spawn had evidently been going inside the house, too, as some of the panels, warped and grayed by weather, were stuffed rather than nailed into the window embrasures. Cam had poked his nose in once several years ago, and said nose had advised him in no uncertain terms that he didn't want to pursue his explorations. He didn't really intend to go inside now, other than to call for the dogs. Even as he pulled one of the plywood panels aside, he knew that if the dogs were inside, they'd have been whining at the windows.

Once inside, his search was anticlimactic. An abandoned old house on a windy night should have been at least a little creepy, but with the smell of empty beer cans, rotting Sheetrock, human excrement, fast-food cartons, and mouse droppings, the place was mostly just annoying, even in the dark. He gave up and went home.

65

A WEEK LATER, CAM found himself sitting in his office, realizing that his career as a police officer was all over
but the shouting. His formal announcement that he wouldn't
testify had put the expected crimp in the vigilante investigation. The day after his dogs disappeared, he'd been called
into a meeting with DA Klein and the grand jury foreperson.
He'd told them then that in order to save a hostage from certain death, he'd made a deal with his own voice mail that he
wouldn't testify.

"So what?" Steven said. "She wasn't there, so they didn't
keep their part of the deal. Why should you?"

"Because we still don't have her back," Cam replied, sup-
pressing a desire to add a "duh" to that. He pointed out that
Jay-Kay never had answered his question as to when they'd
get Mary Ellen back, and logically, that wouldn't happen until they knew he wasn't going to testify.

"Are you trying to tell me that the Sheriff's Office is just
going to quit on this one? And even if you all are, you don't
really suppose the feds will just close the book, do you?"

"I can't speak for the feds, counselor," Cam said. "But we
got our vigilante, didn't we?"

"You mean Sergeant Cox?"

"Yes, Steven," Cam said with a sigh. "I meant Sergeant
Cox. And as for the feds, they now know that their fancy consultant was on the wrong side of this problem. And now she's
out of the picture." Until their computers blow up, he thought,
although he didn't say it.

"We have that list. I'll remind you that my office didn't
make any deals."

"You go right ahead, Steven," Cam said evenly. "But if we

get Mary Ellen back in a body bag, that will be on your head, not mine. Plus, Jay-Kay was pretty clear that at least some of the so-called evidence she gave you was not everything it seemed."

Klein, furious, had thrown him out of the office. Cam was sympathetic but not too worried. Much of the cell's effectiveness had been that no one suspected they even existed. And the Sheriff's Office had that list, too. Bobby Lee would work it one day, back-channel if he had to. But first they had to vet the whole thing, because the source of the list was, of course, Jay-Kay. MCAT's efforts to track her down had come to nothing. She had disappeared, leaving behind her office and apartment complex in Charlotte, along with two IBM mainframes running diagnostics on each other with nothing else left in their vast memory banks but some transient electrons. A check of airlines and passport controls revealed no one by that name leaving the country. Her fancy car was gone, and the Sheriff's Office dutifully had a warrant out for the car and its owner. The Bureau reported similar results, although they were a little vague as to precisely which strings they had been pulling to find her. But Cam well knew that if anyone wanted to go off the grid, that woman was more than qualified. She could as likely be in Indiana as back in India.

The sheriff was recovering but slowly. The doctors had beaten one infection but were now confronting another one, and the range of antibiotics was narrowing. Cam had been able to see him twice, and, if anything, he looked sicker the second time. With the sheriff out of action, Cam had become increasingly isolated within the Sheriff's Office, especially after Steven had started running his mouth. He had a similar meeting with the federal authorities from Charlotte. They had most of the secondhand story, of course, but short of imprisoning Cam until he talked to them, the only physical evidence anyone had amounted to one dead minimart robber and bits of the homemade electric chair that had killed him, one dead wilderness guide and the head of the mountain lion that had killed him, one missing Sergeant Cox, the remains of one smashed-up vehicle grille, and bits and pieces of two bombs, one from Annie's house and a second from the trucking terminal.

Cam's bigger dilemma was how to reestablish his good reputation within the Sheriff's Office in general. It didn't take a genius to tell that a slow freeze-out was beginning, and this was reflected in the way other officers in the Sheriff's Office were treating him. There'd been polite hellos, but increasingly the others evaded him: "Sorry, don't have time to shoot the shit right now. Lots going on. You know how it is." The members of the MCAT team had been individually detailed to various training and recertification courses, and there were rumors that the team was going to be broken up, due, somehow, to "budget constraints." Rumors were spreading everywhere, and he desperately wanted to sit down with his contemporaries and tell them why he had recanted.

From his hospital bed, the sheriff advised against that, saying the feds could come back and subpoena any or all of them, forcing them to reveal what Cam had said. He'd talked to Mike Pierce about his status as a potential suspect in the federal books. Pierce told Cam that as long as he kept quiet, nobody should be able to put any hooks into him. Pierce was also the first one to come right out and suggest that Cam take early retirement.

"Hang around for ninety days," he suggested. "Tell Bobby Lee you're going to put your papers in, give him time to either restructure MCAT or appoint a new boss. Then fold your tents and steal away into the desert night."

"Should I go out the front door or the back?" Cam asked bitterly.

"Are you part of some vigilante group?" Pierce asked.

"Hell no."

"Like I said before, if that's good enough for Bobby Lee Baggett, that's good enough for me, too. Which means it should be good enough for your friends, as well. Your enemies can go screw themselves, right?"

The report from the army had finally come in on the incident that had ended Kenny's military career. He had been on a temporary assignment to Fort Huachuca in Arizona. He had failed to return on time from a seventy-two-hour leave. Subsequent investigation revealed that he and his brother, one James Marlor, had been engaged in an illegal hunting expedition on the federal reservation. James Marlor had been injured, and Kenny had taken him to a civilian medical facility for treatment. The ER people had reported to the local police that the injuries suggested a mountain lion attack. Because Kenny was army, the report made it back to Fort Huachuca.

The brothers had indeed been hunting mountain lion, which was forbidden within the installation's vast boundaries. James Marlor had shot a cat. He'd approached the body, thinking the cat was dead, but it wasn't, and it had mauled him. Kenny had killed it, then lied to protect his civilian brother. He was subsequently court-martialed, not for hunting mountain lion but for moral turpitude—that is, for lying to his superiors. He'd been dismissed from the service with a general discharge and had subsequently changed his name to Cox.

Cam wanted to pull Kenny's Sheriff's Office service records to see how he had accounted for those years in the army, but the personnel office had closed out the records upon notice of Kenny's death. At this juncture, Cam wasn't willing to pursue it. There had been a Sheriff's Office memorial service for Kenny, where the sheriff spoke about the sacrifices police officers made in defense of the American way of life, among other platitudes. Department heads were told that Sergeant Cox had died in a hunting accident in the Smokies and that it was pure happenstance that Lieutenant Richter had been sent to look for him at the time of the incident.

Cam's phone lit up for the first time in a week, snapping him out of his reverie. He picked up. It was Oliver Strong, Annie's lawyer.

"Lieutenant, I've heard through the grapevine that you might be taking early retirement. Any truth to that?"

Cam laughed. "Which grapevine was that, counselor?"

"Courthouse mail room, to be exact," he said. "And they're never wrong, as we all know. I don't mean to pry, of course, but if you are going to make a career move, I have some good news and some bad news."

"Bad news first, Mr. Strong. That's been my diet recently."

"Okay, the bad news is that the IRS has sent me a letter saying that we'll need to suspend liquidation of Judge Bellamy's estate because the prospective beneficiary is, and I'm quoting here, 'a person of interest' in an ongoing federal investigation. They cite the law about a bad guy not being permitted to benefit from the fruits of his criminal acts."

The feds reminding me of who has the real power, Cam thought. "'Person of interest'?" he said.

"That's what they call somebody when they want to hang him but don't have enough evidence to take the poor bastard to a federal indictment."

"Okay, I think I understand that. And the good news?"

"Remember that provision about past-due alimony? Where she said that when you retired from police work, she would augment your pension?"

"Vaguely," Cam said. "Although truly, I'm a whole lot more worried about finding a certain park ranger right now than I am about money, pension or otherwise."

"I understand, Lieutenant, but you just might care. Because the way this works, as soon as you put your papers in, you will begin to get the earnings from her estate. Not the principal, of course, but whatever earnings some nine million dollars' worth of investments produces will come to you in quarterly payments. Even at five percent, that will not be chopped liver, as the expression goes."

"Are you shitting me?" Cam said.

"Not a pound, Lieutenant," the lawyer said. "In fact, it's worded so that even if you're fired from the Sheriff's Office, it still works. The relevant clause speaks to your leaving law enforcement permanently."

Cam laughed. "I guess she knew that my getting shit-canned was always a possibility," he said.

"Well, retire, resign, or piss somebody off, but if you leave law enforcement, you let me know, okay?"

Cam said he would, then hung up. He had meant what he'd said: He'd have preferred to have found Mary Ellen wrapped in duct tape in that trailer to all the money in China.

He'd never had big bucks before, and he recognized that suddenly having money might present its own problems, especially if he left under what looked like an increasingly dark cloud. Damned if I do, damned if I don't, he thought.

The phone rang again. He picked up and identified himself.

"You have mail," said a clone of the chipper voice from AOL.

He laughed and hung up, thinking it was a joke, but then, curious, he went to his computer. He did have mail, and it was from JKB@tigereye.com. Well now, he thought. He opened the E-mail.

A color picture began to unfold on his screen. He couldn't fathom it until it was just about done, and then he saw that it was of the interior of a dimly lit cavern that looked fairly large. In the foreground was what appeared to be an enclosure area with three large cages that had straw on the floor and watering troughs toward the back. Each cage was about twenty feet long and ten feet wide, and each had a heavy wooden door at the back.

The cages were empty. The reinforced wire doors at the front of each cage were standing open. All three of the wooden doors at the back were shut and barred by heavy metal strap handles. Superimposed at the top of the picture was a string of numbers, which Cam recognized as GPS coordinates. At the bottom there was a line of text, which read. "The lady or the tiger? Come at noon. Come alone or don't bother."

66

AT NOON THE NEXT day, he stood by his truck and looked across a creek at a very old house trailer and some sheds that were nestled in a fold at the base of a heavily wooded hill. He would have driven into the yard except that he didn't think the rickety wooden bridge in front of him would hold up under his truck. He'd spent an hour finding the place once he'd left the paved road. The final mile had been little more than two ruts through the woods that paralleled the creek. The ruts kept going past this trailer, but the GPS unit on his dash said he was there.

He had come in patrol uniform, even though he had no Sheriff's Office authority in this county. He was alone but not entirely on his own. He'd gone down to the hospital to see Bobby Lee after getting the E-mail, and he'd told the sheriff what he proposed to do. The sheriff looked somewhat better and was lobbying hard to go home. He immediately vetoed the whole idea of Cam going out there alone.

"If these were plain old kidnappers, I'd agree with that," Cam said. "But these are cops. There's no way I can arrange backup out there without them knowing it."

"Then your hostage is a goner," the sheriff said. "You go alone, they can kill you, and then her, and then they're done with it."

"If the hostage were a cop, I'd agree," Cam said. "But she's not. She doesn't even know that much. I got her into this."

The sheriff had heaved himself up from the bed and stared hard at Cam. "Why in the world would you trust these people?" he asked. "Just because they're cops or agents? Just because Sergeant Cox said they'd never do another cop? Want to see the hole in my chest?"

Cam had no ready answer for that. "They made a deal" was all he could muster. The sheriff responded with a rude noise.

"Look," Cam said. "She said if I took a dive, they'd hand Mary Ellen Goode over. Without my cooperation, the whole investigation is stymied. If I get her back alive and then go forward to the grand jury, I'll be looking over my shoulder for the rest of my life, and so will she. If I don't testify, then we're in a permanent Mexican standoff. They stop their shit. She's alive. That's a better outcome."

"You're being a fool about this, not to mention entirely unprofessional. I know she's pretty, but is she really that special to you?"

"I . . . like her," Cam said. "And she saved my ass out in that river. I owe her at least the effort."

"Well, I can't permit it," Bobby Lee said. "In fact, if you proceed with this, I'd have to fire you. So what's it gonna be?"

"I guess you're going to fire me," Cam replied.

"Okay, you're fired. Now, you want me to call the sheriff of Carrigan County, tell him what's going on, and ask him to go out there—wherever it is—with some deputies if you don't call in after, say, two hours?"

"I'd appreciate that," Cam said. "As long as they give me those couple of hours. I'll tell them when I'm going in." He'd paused for a moment. "I really do appreciate the shot."

"And shot is probably what you're going to get, Lieutenant. Now get out of here. I'm a sick man."

Cam sized up the trailer and the yard now. It took up about a third of an acre and wasn't trashed, unlike many of the places he'd seen along the way. There was a chicken coop, an outhouse, two closed sheds, a snowmobile up on blocks, and two canoes upside down on racks under a lean-to. A vegetable garden was rapidly going to seed at the side of the trailer. It was a bright sunny morning, and the place was obviously empty. No dogs, cats, chickens, or any other signs of life, other than a single lightbulb burning next to the trailer's rusty screen door. There was no mailbox or any other indication of whose place this was. The electric utility poles ended with this trailer.

He locked the truck, hitched up his utility belt, and walked across the bridge, which bounced even under his weight. He went up to the trailer and knocked forcefully on the metal wall. Then he saw the white decal taped across the door handle behind the screen door: KEEP OUT PER CARRIGAN COUNTY SHERIFF'S OFFICE EVIDENTIARY EXCLUSION ORDER.

An eviction situation? Cam wondered. Then he bent down and saw the name listed on the label under owner: J. M. Smith, aka W. E. Mitchell.

He stood back up. This was White Eye's trailer? Well, shit, of course it would be. He tried the door, but it was locked, and if he forced it open, he would break the decal seal. He knocked again just to make sure, then went around to the back and tried the back door. Same seal arrangement, and it was also locked. There were shades pulled down over the windows, so he couldn't see anything inside.

The picture in the E-mail had been taken in a cave of some kind, not in a trailer. He looked at his watch. He had less than two hours before he had to make contact with the Carrigan County Sheriff's Office. He decided to forget about the trailer and concentrate on those sheds across the yard. He resisted the temptation to look up into the hills to see who or what might be watching him. If they just wanted to shoot him, they'd have done it by now.

Neither shed was locked. The first shed contained a great deal of camping and trekking equipment, some of it commercial, like the climbing ropes, and some of it obviously homemade, like the makeshift travois. This shed was freestanding; the other one backed up to the hill itself. That's where the entrance to a cave would be, he thought, assuming this was the right spot. The second shed contained boxes of camping supplies, a stack of firewood, and enough canned food to get through a winter. He banged on the back wall but found no secret doors or cave entrances. He tried the floorboards, but they were all solid.

He went back out and looked around. The only sounds

came from the creek and from birds in the nearby woods. If other people lived along this track, they were all staying home. The only other outbuilding besides the tilting outhouse was the chicken coop, which was fifty feet behind the trailer but not near the face of the hill. It was about twelve feet square, built up on a low platform. Its wire and wood sides could be taken down for cleaning, and there was a slanted ramp from the ground up to the entrance hole. There was a fence around the coop, but the gate was open and the chickens were apparently long gone. He went through the gate and poked around, finding only some old feathers and evidence of a lot of scratching. He kicked the four-by-four holding up one corner, and a dog barked. Then two dogs barked.

Cam recognized those barks, but he couldn't figure out where they were coming from. Then he realized they were coming from under the chicken coop. No, wrong, from underground, under the coop. He stooped down to look. He should have had a clear shot all the way under the platform, but there was a square cinder-block structure about the size of a well house under there. He stepped back and lifted one of the walls of the coop and found that he could latch it upright. More barking from underground. He called to them, and they got even more excited. He climbed into the chicken coop, sneezing because of all the feathers, dust, and straw on the ledges, and pulled up a wooden frame on the cloth-covered floor, creating a flurry of chicken feathers. Under that was a hinged wooden hatch with two big handles.

He lifted the heavy hatch and found a ladder going down ten feet into the ground. An orange plug from an extension cord hung on one side of the ladder, and a garden hose was coiled at the bottom of the ladder. There was a crudely wired receptacle and a hose bib just under the hatch coaming. He plugged the cord in and a lone lightbulb came on down below. Suddenly, he saw Frick and Frack circling at the foot of the ladder, whimpering with joy at being found. He pushed the hatch all the way over so that it rested back on its hinges and went down the ladder, his first thoughts on how he would be able to get the dogs up that ladder. Once he reached the bottom, he realized he was in a small cave. The dogs were all over him, and he bent to pet their heads and reassure them. They were thin but apparently unharmed.

He looked around the cave, but there was nothing in there other than the ladder. A second orange extension cord was plugged into the light fixture and was taped along a wall leading down into a narrow passage. The air was cold but not wet, and there was a strange smell, which grew stronger as he stepped into the passage. It looked like it went down slightly and to the left. There were no lights overhead, but there was a dim glow in the distance, so, bending his head, he stepped down onto the smooth rock and followed the passage's twisting course. The dogs followed him, although reluctantly.

The closer he got to the light, the stronger the smell, which he recognized now as spoiled meat, overlaid with a an odor of dung and straw, similar to smells he'd encountered in a zoo. The dogs were plastered to his knees now, obviously frightened. Cam was pretty sure he knew what this place had been used for, and then he rounded a sharp-angled turn and saw the cavern from the E-mail picture opening in front of him. The three cages were directly in front of him. There was a large open area right in front of the cages. The stone floor in front of him was covered in soiled straw, and a single bare lightbulb illuminated the entire cavern. The animal stench was strong as he unholstered his .45 and checked the action. The dogs lay flat on the floor when he stopped. They were both staring intently at the three cages.

Cam made sure there weren't any creatures lurking in the deep muck, then stood still just to listen. The only sounds were a low hum from the lightbulb and the drip of water in one of the passageways leading out the back of the cavern.

"The lady or the tiger," Jay-Kay's E-mail had said. He remembered the story, only here there were three doors instead of two. Her meaning was clear: This was White Eye's very private little zoo. Open the wrong door and you'd get the American version of the tiger. By implication, he should find Mary Ellen behind one of the doors. He called her name, quietly at first, then louder. To his surprise, his voice didn't echo at all, and for a moment he imagined the roof of the cavern pressing down on him. He took the dogs into the first cage on the left and brought them right up to the heavy wooden door, hoping they could tell which door was safe. The door had four iron T-hinges and the boards were rough-cut oak, reinforced with steel straps. One long steel strap was hinged on one side of the door and wedged into a hasp on the other. The dogs would not approach the door, and they scampered back out of the cage as soon as he let go of their collars.

He banged on the door and called again. No response. He tried the same thing with the other two doors and got the same reaction. The dogs were useless. The animal smell in the cages was probably overwhelming to their sensitive noses, so he decided to get them out of there. They'd be equally useless if a mountain lion did appear, especially in a confined space. Slap, slap, chow time. He called them back to the ladder and then hauled them one by one up the ladder and released them outside the chicken coop. He checked his surroundings for watchers and took them to the truck. Then he went back down into the main cavern.

He squatted down on his heels and considered the wooden doors. Lady or the tiger? he thought. Decision time. But unfortunately, here there was no princess in the stands, twitching her hand to tell him which door to open. This place was probably where White Eye had kept and raised Night-Night, although, he told himself reluctantly, that shouldn't have required three cages. But as best he could tell, none of the mess down here was fresh, and with White Eye in the ground, any other cats would have decamped a long time ago, assuming there were tunnels or passageways behind those doors that led outside somehow. The cages themselves were made of hog panels. They didn't seem strong enough to contain a determined mountain lion, even though there were sides and tops to all three. But then if the cats had been tame, it might not have mattered. There were three bolts on each door, though—top, middle, and bottom—so maybe *tame* was a relative term.

He decided on the right-hand door, since that's where he had ended up. He walked in and levered the big strap out of its hasp and swung it up and over behind the hinges. Then, his .45 ready, he pulled the door open. It was very heavy, but it moved silently on well-greased iron hinges. The door was at least eight inches thick, which would certainly have muffled any response to his calls. Inside, there was another passageway, but this one was narrower and much lower than the one he'd walked down to get here. He might fit through there on hands and knees, but he wouldn't want to try it. The air in the passage smelled infinitely better than in the cage room, and it blew toward him in a gentle breeze. The dangling lightbulb swayed imperceptibly on the ceiling, throwing some shadows around the walls. He decided to leave this door open while he checked the other doors, if only to improve the air.

Which one next? He looked down at the floor of the cages to see if he could determine whether the muck was any fresher in one or than in the other. The straw was such a mess, he couldn't tell. The left one, then. He opened it and found yet another passageway, this one a little higher but just as narrow. This time, he bent down and looked at the mud on the other side of the doorjamb. Were those prints? Yes, they were. Fresh? Who the hell knows, he thought. My tracking skills haven't improved since the last time I saw some of these. No fresh air moved out of this passageway, however, so he pushed the door shut, not bothering to reset the locking bar. He wondered how far back those tunnels went, and he wished the dogs had been braver. On the other hand, everyone always said they were smart dogs.

Okay, Jay-Kay, wherever you are, this time it'd better be the lady, he thought. You promised. With a grunt, he opened the center door and saw a shallow rock cavity about six feet deep. It was stacked with cardboard boxes. Hunched in the middle of the stacks was Mary Ellen Goode. She was strapped into what looked like a stripped-down clone of the steel chair in the trailer. Adhesive tape covered her mouth, and a damned cell phone lay in her lap. He started to say something but then saw that she was staring at him with a look of pure terror on her face. Actually, he realized, she was looking behind him.

67

THERE WERE *TWO* MOUNTAIN lions standing in the area in front of the cages, glaring at him. When he turned fully around, they both reacted by lifting their lips and exposing far too many teeth. The larger of the two lowered its head and issued a loud growling hiss, while the other one started to slink off to one side, never taking its eyes off the two humans in the storage room. The door he'd left unlocked in the left-hand cage was now ajar.

Cam took out the .45 and moved as carefully as he could toward the door of the cage. He could see that both cats were in poor shape—thin, almost emaciated, with crud in their eyes and an unhealthy color to their fur. He realized they were starving, which probably didn't help his and Mary Ellen's situation any. He kept the .45 in his right hand pointed in their direction, although he didn't really want to fire that thing down here in a stone cavern. With his left hand, he carefully reached out to the edge of the door and began to swing it shut. This time, the other cat growled at him, although neither one of them made a lunge for the door as he managed to get it shut. He felt for a latch, then remembered he was inside the cage. Both cats began to prowl back and forth in front of the three cages, although they were keeping their distance. Maybe they're tame, he told himself. He wondered if starving canceled out tame.

Reaching through the pencil-thick wire squares, he felt for and finally found the middle of the three latches and pulled the bolt across until it seated in the frame of the door. Then he felt secure enough to go back and get Mary Ellen out of that horrible chair. He let her take off the adhesive tape while he kept one eye on those two cats. If they charged the door, the heavy oak frame ought to keep them out.

"Don't shoot them" was the first thing Mary Ellen said once she got the tape off.

Ever the animal sympathizer, Cam thought. "Won't if I can help it," he said. "You okay?"

"Thirsty," she said. "How did you find me down here?"

"I got mail," he said. "Jay-Kay sent me GPS coordinates. Are we alone, you think?"

As if in answer to his question, there came a loud thump from the direction of the entry tunnel and a squeeze of air pressure in the cavern. Both cats reacted with low squalls. Cam swore. That was the big trapdoor in the chicken coop. He had laid it all the way on its back when he first opened it. There was no way that it could have fallen back shut. Someone had just closed it. Should have left the damned dogs loose, he realized. Mary Ellen understood at once.

"Now what?" she asked.

"Not the end of the world," he said. "In a couple of hours, there'll be people out here looking. I came alone but checked in with Carrigan County along the way."

The cats were prowling closer to the wire doors now, as if trying to figure out how to get in.

"What's in the boxes?" he asked.

Mary Ellen, rubbing her wrists, went to check while Cam watched the cats. She grunted in surprise. "Would you believe dog food?"

"A mountain lion eats *dog* food?" Cam asked.

"Those two would eat each other at this juncture," she said. "I see deer bones in the straw, so this stuff was probably emergency rations."

"Maybe if we fed them, they'd lose interest in us," he said.

"Worth a try," she replied, and went to work with a rusty can opener that was hanging by the door. The cats stopped pacing when she started opening cans and sat down.

"Nice kitty-kitty," Cam intoned hopefully. They both hissed at him this time, but they were watching Mary Ellen.

She found a steel feed bowl under the straw and filled it with six cans of dog food. "Now what?" she said again, echoing Cam's own thoughts. How could they get the bowl through the door without losing an arm?

Mary Ellen solved the problem. She carried the bowl to the cage door. Holding the bowl in one hand and working the bolt with the other, she backed out the bolt and then yelled at the two cats, which promptly slunk back away from the door. She opened it, slid the bowl in, and then rebolted the door.

What happened next wasn't pretty. The larger cat ran to the bowl, as did the smaller one. The larger one whirled on its haunches and attacked the smaller one with a thumping whirlwind of slashing paws. The smaller one shrieked once and then rolled away from the bowl. It lay down on the stone floor and licked its wounds, never taking its eyes off the rapidly disappearing dog chow.

Mary Ellen opened another can at both ends and threw it through the wire to a far corner of the room. The wounded cat pounced on it and began grinding the can in its jaws. It hurt Cam's teeth just to watch it, but Mary Ellen simply opened up another three cans and threw them in the same general direction.

"Really starving," Cam said.

"And tamed males," she said. "And that's the crime of taming a wild animal. Ultimately, somebody forgets, and they starve, which hurts." She opened up one more can of dog food and threw it to the front of the cave, where it splashed.

Cam blinked. Splashed?

He stared through the dim light and saw water at the front of the cavern. There was a steady stream of water coming down the passageway. Mary Ellen saw it, too. She didn't have to say "now what" again, either. The smaller cat was ignoring the water as it savaged the individual cans of dog food. The big guy had licked the bowl clean and was now headed over to the corner where the last can of dog food was being flattened. There was more growling and hissing, but they had evidently reduced the edge of their hunger to the extent that there was no more fighting. The big one started lapping water from what was rapidly becoming a small lake, and the smaller cat joined in. Some of the larger clumps of straw out in front of the cages were beginning to float.

"Does whoever's coming know about this cave?" she asked.

"I doubt it. There are seals on the trailer door, but I didn't see any signs of this little zoo being discovered. But there was no lock on the hatch, so if we can get by the cats, we should be able to get out."

"Get by the cats."

"Yeah, well, they've been fed. Sort of. And I have the forty-five."

She gave him a look.

"I'm not going to drown down here," he said. "I didn't domesticate two mountain lions. I'm sorry about this whole weird business, but—"

"Where'd they come from?"

He started to answer but then stopped to think. Where had they come from? The narrow passageway, the one with no airflow. On the other hand, the other passageway had an airflow, which usually meant access to the outside. No, it had been the left door he'd pushed closed but not locked.

"That one," he said, pointing to the left cage.

"Let's throw meat in there; if we can get them in there, we can lock the cage."

"Damn. I hate women who can think," he said. "I'll throw the meat, and you lock them in."

She rolled her eyes at him and he pointed out that it was her idea.

It worked. The cats darted into the cage after the cans of meat and she slammed and locked the cage door right behind them. They started squabbling over cans and didn't appear to notice they'd been caught.

Cam trotted up the entry passageway to shut off that water. Mary Ellen found him standing under the bare lightbulb, looking up. The ladder was gone and the hatch was shut. There was water pouring around all the edges of the hatch, and a good bit of it was dripping down the wire and onto that bare lightbulb.

"It's gonna get dark pretty soon, he said. "Either we get up to that hatch or we find another way out."

"There're all those boxes," she said. "Pile them up. You're probably tall enough to reach the hatch if you stand on them."

That also worked, but the hatch didn't move. Cam did manage to pull the extension cord down far enough to form a loop, which got the water away from the bulb. But then the water-soaked cardboard boxes began to collapse, so he had to jump down. The floor was wet, but the water wasn't accumulating in this room. It was all flowing downhill to the cage room.

"That right-hand cage had a tunnel behind it," he said. "There was fresh air blowing in. The other one was stagnant. I think we have to try it."

"With no light?" she asked. Her voice betrayed a fear of enclosed spaces.

"I have this," Cam said, hauling a tiny Maglite out of his utility belt. "In a cave, it'll look like a searchlight. Caves are really dark."

"Don't I know it," she replied. "Well, at least we know where the cats are."

But when they got back to the main chamber, the back door to the left-hand cage was wide open and the cats were gone.

68

THEY HAD TO CRAWL on their hands and knees for about fifty feet before the passage allowed them to stand up. The left-hand passage had been a more attractive proposition, except for that one not-so-minor detail. Ankle-deep water rising in the main chamber had pretty much forced the decision: Stay there and drown, or give the other passage a shot.

They made better progress once they could stand up, but Cam was pretty sure they were going down, not up. The passage was only about two feet wide, so they had to step sideways most of the time. Cam led, shining the light alternately ahead and down so that they didn't walk off a subterranean cliff in the dark. The air smelled of old rock and damp, and the walls seemed to press in on them constantly. He could hear Mary Ellen's labored breathing behind him, and he was pretty sure it was not due to physical exertion. He tried to make a joke about her looking to see if her cell phone had a signal, but she didn't laugh.

They finally stepped down into a small cavern. Cam shone the light around and saw that there were three other passages leading out of it. He had no idea which way to go.

He shone the light back into the passage they'd come through. A silvery ribbon of water was pushing toward them through the dust on the floor.

"Look," she said. "If the water's coming down here, it can't flood that cage area, can it? You said people are coming. Let's go back up there. At least that's close to the surface."

Her eyes were huge in the tiny white glow of the flashlight. He thought about it. "They'd never hear us underground. Not unless they'd come over to the chicken coop, like I did."

"They won't search?"

"I was prepared to pull that trailer off its foundations because I knew you were here. They'll see my truck, see my dogs, and think I'm out in the woods somewhere. The trailer's still sealed. They didn't find the tunnels the first time."

"So which way do we go?" she asked, her voice rising. "How do we even decide?"

Her voice was loud enough to create a small echo in the surrounding passages. It was answered by a distant guttural cough. Cam put his hand over her mouth before she could say anything more and pushed her roughly back into the passage from which they'd just come. He swung the light beam across the mouths of the other three tunnels and then turned it off. He bent down and whispered in her ear that a cat was coming. He felt her tense up. He signaled with his body that she needed to back up some more, then got the .45 out, made himself as comfortable as he could, and waited.

Nothing happened for about two minutes, and then there was another cough, louder this time. He felt in the dark for her head and bent backward so he could whisper into her ear again. "The cats probably know the way out. There was air flowing through here when the main hatch was open. We'll follow it."

He felt her nod slightly and then he straightened back up.

They waited. The darkness was absolute. He could feel his eyes trying to adapt for night vision, but there was no ambient light. So listen, he told himself. And be very fucking quiet. He tried to detect Mary Ellen's breathing, but she'd already figured it out.

Those cats could supposedly see in the dark, but not in this kind of dark. But they could smell and they could sense another animal presence. He and Mary Ellen had walked down into the junction cavern, so their scent would be in the dust on the ground, if not in the air.

So turn on the light, he told himself. The cat has all the advantages right now. He had a bad thought: Could the cat be behind them?

No, that cage door had been locked, and there'd been no side passages in the tunnel they'd come through. No, it had to be in front of them.

He pointed the flashlight into the cavern and switched it on.

The cat was three feet away, staring at them, its amber eyes blinking in the sudden shaft of light. Mary Ellen gave an involuntary little squeak, and Cam swallowed hard. He didn't move, and then, almost without realizing he was doing it, he let go the best and loudest imitation of a cat's hiss that he could muster. The cat replied in kind but then bolted across the cavern and disappeared into one of the passages—the one directly across from them.

Cam stepped down into the cavern with shaky knees and helped Mary Ellen get to her feet. They listened for a moment but didn't hear anything.

"I'm guessing there's a way out, and that he went for the tunnel that would let him escape."

"And if there isn't?"

"Let's try it. If it looks like a dead end or we run into more intersections, we'll go back and do it your way."

"What if he's in there, setting up an ambush? That's what they like to do, you know."

"Maybe, but he's the one who ran." He didn't bring up the fact that two cats had gone into the tunnels, but an ambush in these narrow passageways would be just about impossible. On the other hand, so would escape.

He took her hand and they went into the passage the cat had disappeared into. To their vast relief, this one started to ascend. He checked for tracks in the dust and thought he could see some every four feet or so. Then the passageway turned hard right and went up at almost a sixty-degree angle. The slope was wider than the tunnel, perhaps fifty feet up, and littered with loose rock and dirt. He shone the light up to the top of the slope and thought he caught a momentary flash of amber-green eyes. A moment later, some small stones rattled down the slope.

"That what I think it was?" she said.

"Yeah, but it's still running," he replied, sweeping the light across the top of the slope. It was a yellow light now, no longer quite so bright. They'd have to resolve this pretty soon, or go back before the flashlight died entirely.

He went up first, got halfway up, and then slid clumsily all the way back down in an avalanche of dirt and rocks. Mary Ellen tried it, got ten feet higher than he had, and slid back to the floor in the same manner.

"The cat did it," Cam said. He searched the sides of the incline and pointed out some scratches on the cavern's walls. The dirt seemed firmer here, so he tried again, making it to the top this time. Mary Ellen did one more avalanche drill and then finally got up to the top. Cam swept the light around and exhaled in relief. There was only one passage in front of them, and it continued to ascend. He thought the air was fresher up here, although he knew this could just be wishful thinking.

They dusted themselves off, stepped into the passageway, and continued to climb, going slowly in case that big cat was waiting up around the next corner. The incline wasn't dramatic, but the footing was slippery, which indicated water, so Cam switched the light out to see if there was daylight ahead. There wasn't. Just lots more of that stygian darkness. He rested for a moment, listening. He was about to start moving again, when they both heard the sounds of something scrabbling up that rocky slope behind them. Cat number two.

They hurried as best they could, bumping their heads occasionally as the space above dwindled to five feet or less. Cam swung the light behind them about once a minute to see if eyes flashed, but the tunnel twisted and turned so much, nothing could be seen. He thought the air was definitely getting fresher, which was good, but his flashlight was dimming fast. He wanted to switch it off again but didn't dare as long as that other cat was ahead of them. They've been fed, he kept telling himself, and they're more scared of us than we are of them. Right.

When the cat screamed ahead of them, he very nearly tripped over his own feet in his attempt to halt. Mary Ellen bumped into him and gripped his arm. The cat screamed again, a hate-filled noise that ended in a prolonged rumbling growl. Its noises echoed in front of them, as if it were making its stand in another large cavern. Then from behind came an answering noise, this one sounding a lot more lionlike than the one ahead of them. We have you where we want you, it said. Your move.

Cam was tempted to let fly with the .45, but he knew full well the danger of ricochet, not to mention causing a cave-in from the explosive noise.

"Let's go," he said. "Time to face these bastards."

Mary Ellen seemed frozen in place, so he pulled gently on her arm and then she followed. They rounded a corner and encountered a cavern that was not so much large as it was high, a beehive-shaped rocky cylinder that rose nearly sixty feet to a tiny point of visible sky over to one side. There was a deep water-carved fissure running down one side of the wall, which looked like the way up to the opening at the top. The cavern was about a hundred feet across at the bottom, and there was a pool of black water in the center. The bones of numerous animals lay around the pool, and the panther was on the other side, its tail switching angrily. It screamed at them again as they stepped into the cavern. Cam switched off the flashlight, and they could actually see. They edged around to their right so they could watch the passage behind them for the other cat.

"I'll watch the cat," he said. "You study that big crack over there, figure out the best way up."

The cat on the far side began to slink around to its right, watching them every step of the way. Cam and Mary Ellen moved to keep the cat diametrically opposite them across the pool.

"It'll take some climbing, but that looks like the only way up," she said. "Everything else slopes in at the top."

"Right," he said. "Good thing these damned cats can't climb."

The second panther appeared out of the passageway then and growled in what sounded like triumph. The first cat reversed course, and now the two cats closed in on them from

separate directions. The cat on the right was between them
and the fissure. Mary Ellen tugged his sleeve and pointed at a
rough ramp of rock right in front of them, leading up to a
ledge.

By now, Cam had the .45 out. He wanted to accommodate
Mary Ellen's wishes as a naturalist and not harm the cats, but
not at the price of becoming dinner. He pointed it into the
water, aiming in the direction of the second cat, and fired one
round. The noise was terrific, as was the waterspout created
by the heavy bullet. The cat stopped and screamed at them,
shaking water off its face. The first cat, now no more than a
dozen feet away on their right, wasn't impressed and kept
coming. Cam fired again, this time trying to hit in front of the
approaching panther. This produced another scream and a
slashing ricochet that whacked around the inside of the cavern, making them both duck. Mary Ellen jumped onto the
ramp and scampered up onto the first of the ledges. Cam followed, watching the cats, who were stopped now and treating
them to a lively display of teeth and noise. One was still between them and the climbing fissure, but below them.

The cat that had been splashed reversed course and
headed all the way around, apparently aiming to get behind
his partner, who was gathering himself for a spring up to
their ledge. Cam squatted down and aimed carefully at that
one as Mary Ellen struggled to stay up on the narrow and
slippery rock ledge.

Starvation trumped tame as the cat jumped right up at
them. Time slowed down. The cat's huge face filled Cam's
entire vision. It was so strong that it could hang right on the
edge of the narrow ribbon of rock with its hind claws, gather
its immense shoulders, and roar at him. He could smell its
rancid breath and feel the heat of its predatory fury.

He shot it full in the face as at least one fully clawed paw
swiped the air right in front of him. The cat screamed and
tumbled back down the rock, sliding into the pool and disappearing. Cam barely had time to switch his aim before the
other cat was bounding up at them. He fired once and then
again, missing both times, but that was enough to make the

cat overshoot, lose its balance, and fall off the ledge amid the sound of ricocheting rounds. It dropped like the other one into the pool. Mary Ellen lost her grip and slid off the ledge. Cam reached to grab her and joined her in the debacle. They hit the water together and gasped at the icy temperature.

Cam held on to the gun and spun around, looking for that one operational cat. It was right there, swimming powerfully in their direction, making a hideous screeching sound. Cam tipped the big pistol down to drain any water out of the barrel and shot the beast right down the throat. The recoil lifted his arm just as the cat tried to slash him, and then, spewing blood, it sank out of sight.

Mary Ellen had managed to get to the side of the pool, but she couldn't get herself out of the water because of the slippery surface. Cam tried to swim over to her but found his left arm wasn't working. He looked down and saw a mass of blood and other things where his left bicep had been. He hadn't felt a thing, but now he did. Gritting his teeth, he backpedaled over to where she was struggling and told her to wait a minute and catch her breath. His own boots could gain no traction on what seemed like the glass-smooth sides of the pool, but first he wanted to make damn sure the cats were out of the picture. A roil of bubbles broke the surface out in the middle of the pool and then all was still—until the first cat surfaced right next to Mary Ellen, causing her to scream and lunge back out into the pool. One of the cat's eyes was completely gone, the other one showed only white, and the back of the cat's skull was missing. Somehow, it found the edge of the pool and used its long claws to pull itself up onto the dry ground. It rested unsteadily there for a few seconds, flanks heaving, and then hoisted its body all the way out of the water. It tried to stand up but couldn't. It collapsed, convulsed once, coughed, and then died on the rock floor, its front claws still embedded two inches into the dirt.

They treaded water for a long minute, really feeling the cold now but wanting to make sure it was over. Mary Ellen's teeth were chattering, but Cam was silently blessing the cold water as it numbed his ruined left arm. Then he paddled over to where the cat's body lay, hesitated for a second, then grabbed its tail and hauled himself one-armed out of the water. He lay right alongside the panther for a moment. The cat was still warm and it was longer than he was tall. He gestured to Mary Ellen, but she wouldn't come near the panther. He crawled down to where she was treading water and pulled her out ten feet away from the cat's inert body. Then they both sprawled on the floor of the cavern. She hadn't seen his arm yet. He didn't want to look at it.

At that moment, an authoritative voice called down from the hole up top and asked what in the hell was going on down there.

"Better late than never," Mary Ellen gasped.

"County cops. What can I say?" Cam replied, putting his hand on her forehead.

"Sorry about the cats," he said. "Sorry about this whole damned mess."

Feeling a familiar roar in his ears, he clamped his good hand over the wound on his arm. "You better get them down here," he whispered.

She sat up, saw the arm.

Then things got a little fuzzy.

69

A MONTH LATER, CAM sat out on the deck behind his house with a Scotch in one hand and Frick's fuzzy head in the other. Frack lay on the deck, watching as usual. Bobby Lee Baggett sat across from him, also enjoying a sunset libation.

"So I'm still fired," Cam said.

"Well, actually, you've been early-retired. Sounds like fired, but different."

Cam thought the Sheriff was still a little gray around the gills and that he'd lost pounds he couldn't afford to lose. From time to time Bobby Lee would unconsciously put his left hand on his chest over the wound site. Cam knew the feeling.

"Don't remember signing the papers," Cam said, massaging his own bandaged arm.

"Memory is the second thing to go, especially when you get retired."

"What's the first?"

"I forget," Bobby Lee said. It was such a lame old joke they both chuckled.

"What are the feds up to these days?" Cam asked.

"They have identified some 'persons of interest,'" Bobby Lee said.

"That mean what it usually does?"

"Yep. They know who the bad guys are, but can't prove shit. Yet. There's an interesting wrinkle, though, if you can believe it."

"Try me."

"They want to offer that Indian computer wizard immunity if she'll help them tag the federal members of that cat dancer thing."

"She had to have been the one who set that bomb at Annie Bellamy's house," Cam pointed out. "Immunity from a murder charge?"

"I think they're going to pretend they don't know that," Bobby Lee said. "Offer her immunity for being a part of the death squad. Get what they can, then open the murder charge."

"Get her in custody and give me five minutes with her," Cam said.

"Now, now, those aren't the words of a retiree."

"Have they found her?"

"That's the problem. They seem to think you might be able to help them out with that."

"Me?"

"She was the one who sent you the GPS points, right?"

"That was an entirely one-way channel, boss," Cam said. "My chances of finding *her* on the Internet are precisely two."

"One of their computer wienies is going to be in touch. You can at least make helpful noises."

Cam reflected on that and sipped some scotch. His doctors had told him not to drink while on the final course of antibiotics. He had invoked his constitutional rights against cruel and unusual punishment, although he kept it well within bounds. Pretty much.

"I'm going to the County Sheriffs' annual convention in Raleigh next week," the sheriff said. "Gonna have me some 'offline conversations on matters of mutual collective interest.'"

"Share some technical parameters?" Cam asked.

"Those too. What do you hear from your ranger friend?"

Cam tried to flex his left arm. It didn't flex worth a damn. There was too much meat gone from vital places. Mostly he walked around like Napoleon, with his left hand shoved inside his shirt. "Unfortunately, not much," he said.

"Why—'cause you shot those cats?"

"No, because I dragged her into something that turned nasty and dangerous. She was just supposed to testify, and instead . . . well, you know. And then when I declined to testify, I think she began to wonder about me and all my works."

The sheriff nodded.

Cam looked over at him. "I have to hold to that," he said. "Until you and the feds can tell me they have them all in custody, Mary Ellen won't be safe."

"Did you ever explain that to her?"

Cam shook his head. "I wanted to go up there again," he said. "Have a talk. But every cop and park ranger in Carrigan County told me never to come back up there. They think pretty highly of that lady, and I was the guy damn near got her killed."

"Mmm-mm."

Cam looked over at him. "What's that mean?"

"It means that it was those cat dancers, whoever the hell they are, *they* damn near got her killed." He paused for a moment. "Now that you're retired, you're just going to sit back and forget this whole mess, right?"

Cam had to think about how to answer that. "I think I really would like that five minutes alone with Jay-Kay Bawa," he said.

"Feds would hate that."

"I have money now, Sheriff," Cam said. "And more coming. Lots more, apparently. I think that can buy me a certain degree of insurance, of the political variety. Besides, what better thing to do with all that money than to nail the bitch who killed Annie?"

"And what exactly would you do if you found her?"

"That is the question, isn't it," Cam said, thoughtfully. "Maybe knock together another electric chair?" Frick got up and moved away. Frack moseyed over for some head rubbing.

"Sounds good to me," the sheriff said, "as long as we both understand you're just running your mouth." He stretched his legs and rubbed his chest one more time before he got up. "Oh, by the way, there was a letter for you, came in care of the office. I called the sender, told her you had left the force. She asked why, and I . . . well, I kind of filled her in on some things. She asked me to return the letter." He unfolded an envelope from his pocket and handed it to Cam. "Here's the one she sent in its place. I'll leave you to it. Remember who your friends are, and what's important in life."

Cam took the letter but didn't look at it. "You're not disappointed in me, then?"

"Absolutely not," the sheriff said emphatically. "But you need to move on. We'll get 'em. Ain't like we don't know a thing or two."

"'Mess with the best'?"

The sheriff grinned, his teeth white in the night, not unlike a big cat's. "That's it," he said.

Cam took the letter into the kitchen once the sheriff had gone. He sat down at the kitchen table, massaged his arm, and read what Mary Ellen had written. Then he smiled. Jay-Kay and the cat dancers might have to wait awhile after all.

But not forever.

ACKNOWLEDGMENTS

I WANT TO THANK the Sheriff of Guilford County, North Carolina, for his insights on the inner workings of a modern and highly successful urban Sheriff's Office. That said, I've taken extensive liberties in conjuring up characters, methods, and even localities for this story. I also want to thank the United States Park Service for their technical help on the Great Smoky Mountains National Park, although there, too, I've made up a lot of the material on locations within the park and, most important, the existence of feral mountain lions. There is simply no concrete evidence of big cats roaming the Smokies. If on the other hand, you are a proponent of the rule that says the absence of evidence isn't the same as evidence of absence, then you might want to watch where, and when, you walk in the backcountry. Almost needless to say, no one would be foolhardy enough to try cat dancing with a mountain lion, not even the real (and very brave) Kenny Cox, who so graciously allowed the use of his name in this book in connection with an American (Carriage) Driving Society fund-raiser. This is a work of fiction, and any resemblance in this book to actual persons, places, or events is absolutely coincidental.

Read on for an excerpt from
P. T. Deutermann's next book

SPIDER MOUNTAIN

Coming soon in hardcover
from St. Martin's Press

THE ROCK RIGHT BEHIND my head exploded into a spray of razor-sharp granite shards, followed by the echo of a booming rifle up on the high ridge. The back of my neck felt like it was on fire as I rolled to one side and deeper into the rock pile. The shepherds came running, but I yelled them down as another round slashed down the hill, spanging off a rock and out into the hollow below. I made like a snake, wriggling between the bigger rocks, conscious of wetness on the back of my shirt. Another round came into the rockpile. This one ricocheted off about five rocks before passing over my head like a supersonic hornet. The shooter knew I was in there and was hoping for a lucky hit. I was looking for that fabled direct route to China through the center of the earth.

Finally it stopped. My neck still hurt like hell, but it was now dark enough on the hillside that the guy probably couldn't see us anymore. The distant boom of the rifle was still echoing in my ears, and I remained down on the ground for another thirty minutes until it was almost fully dark. Then I crept towards the edge of the rockpile nearest Laurie May's place. The dogs were whining above me, but I told them to stay down until I got clear of the rockpile. Five minutes later, I was able to get into some trees and call them down. Crouching low, I trotted down the hill towards my not-so-secret-anymore cabin.

Somehow they'd found out where I was holed up. Laurie May must have said something or done something to alert one of the visiting cops. I didn't believe she'd intentionally done anything, but either way, I couldn't hang out here anymore.

I waited at the edge of the woods which concealed her

doomed daughter's cabin and watched her house for several minutes to make sure there wasn't a reception committee down there. I finally spotted the old lady through one of the windows in the lantern-light, and decided to go on down. Her front door was open, and I called her name. She came to the door and asked if I had been doing all that shooting. Then she saw my collar and told me to come in right away.

That first round had embedded enough granite dust in the back of my neck to make a good piece of sandpaper, as I discovered when she patiently extracted every speck of it. I was gritting my teeth and wishing for my bottle of Scotch by the time she was through. Then she smeared some foul-smelling poultice on the wounded skin which took a lot of the sting away. I was afraid to ask what was in it.

"How many was they?" she asked.

"I think just one, with a long rifle and a good scope. He had me pinned in a cluster of big rocks." I turned around to look at her. "I can't stay here anymore," I told her. "They'll figure it out if they haven't already."

"I ain't afraid of them no-counts," she said bravely as she put away her tweezers and the cotton roll.

"You tell them when they come that I made you put me up. Tell them I had a great big gun and threatened to shoot your livestock. And we need to burn that bloody cotton—I don't want them to know they hit me."

She threw some sticks in the woodstove, shook the ash grate, pitched in the cotton waste, and then stirred the soup pot. "Where's'at pretty woman?" she asked.

"Over in Marionburg," I said. "She managed to get out of Robbins County, but I don't think she can come back here while Mingo's people are all stirred up. I'm going to hike out." I explained some of what I'd learned in the phone call.

"I'll heat ye some soup," she said. She clanked the firebox door shut. "You know they gonna be out there in them woods. Prob'ly have 'em dogs with'm, too."

"I can't let them take me again," I said. "Especially now that my allies have been backed out."

"Which way you gonna go?" she asked.

"I think the best route will be over the ridges towards Crown Lake. I think the roads will be too dangerous."

She stirred the soup some more. I realized I was really hungry. The back of my neck had settled down to a warm burn, which I hoped was not an infection getting under way.

"If'n it was me," Laurie May said, slowly, "I believe I'd go t'other way. They gonna be lookin' for ye to run for Marionburg town. If'n it was me, I'd go up and over that ridge yonder and hide right in Grinny Creigh's back yard. Ain't none'a them gonna expect you to do that."

Including me, I thought, but she had a point. If that shooter had alerted the rest of Nathan's crew and the sheriff, the woods would soon be alive with the sound of guns being cocked and slavering dogs sniffing out trails. They would, in fact, never even think to look at Grinny's place. She saw me considering it and gave me a toothy grin.

"I'll show ye a shortcut through that backbone ridge, yonder," she said. "Put you into Grinny's place sideways, other side'a them dogs. They's a little cave on the bottom side of her front field. Maybe you can hole up in there, watch and see where she's hidin' them poor young'uns."

And that was the objective, wasn't it? I reminded myself. Carrie had defanged herself when she resigned from the SBI. She had no legal authority to pursue Grinny Creigh. Neither did I, for that matter, but I was here and she wasn't. If I could watch the Creigh place undiscovered for a few days, maybe I could actually put some flesh on the bones of Carrie's theory about Grinny selling children. The transponder was still in place, for now anyway, so in theory, I could call out.

Evidence. We desperately needed evidence.

"Okay, I'll do just that," I said. "The cave big enough for me and the shepherds?"

She nodded and then told me to sit down and eat. I briefly wondered how she knew about a cave over on the other side of the ridge. On the other hand, she was old enough to know damn near everything about these hills.

* * *

An hour later, we turned down the lanterns in her cabin, put them in the front windows, and then slipped quietly out the back door. I had my field belt, the spotting scope, a bedroll, water, and the Sig. 45. Laurie May had fixed up a bag of bread and a couple of hard-boiled eggs. The shepherds seemed to sense our need for stealth; they were sticking close and moving in silence. There was a quarter moon rising above the mountains, so between her knowledge of the path and a borrowed walking stick, I managed to stay upright as we climbed through the rock rubble towards what she had called the backbone ridge. We seemed to be heading right into the side of it as the ground rose, and I wondered if we were going to have to go straight up and over. But then we walked into a dense stand of gnarled pines whose branches were low enough to require constant swatting. Laurie May was moving surprisingly fast for a woman of her age, which hopefully meant she knew right where she was going. After about seventy-five feet of pine needles and bugs going down my shirt, we broke out in front of a crack in the ridge.

"This here broke clean through the 'bone long ways back," she whispered, pointing into a narrow defile which was in total darkness. "They's water runnin' through it, comin' down off'n them sides. Foller it through to t'other side, go down to yer right hand, mebbe twenty rod, to the cave hole."

"Thanks, Laurie May. I'll try to come back out after dark tomorrow. If by any chance Carrie contacts you, tell her where I am. If she comes to your place, try to keep her there until I get back."

She nodded in the darkness, squeezed my hand, and started back into the pines. I approached the passageway through the ridge. Her description of it breaking clean through was accurate. I stepped into the crack and looked up. Sheer rock walls rose on either side of me, no more than six feet between them where I stood but getting wider toward the top, which had to be two or even three hundred feet straight up. The ground underfoot was loose stone and mud, and I could see thin dark streaks of moisture weeping down the sides of the defile. I'm not one to feel claustrophobic, but this passage through the heart of the ridge got me close to it. I tried to imagine what titanic forces could split and then open the whole ridge like this. I had to resist the temptation to keep one hand on the walls to make sure they weren't closing together on me. The shepherds followed nervously, stopping when I did, and picking their footing carefully.

The path through the crack led straight across for about a hundred yards and then slightly downhill, and the water took on some depth as I neared the other end. The air was dank and cold, and the looming rock walls seemed to amplify my every footstep, no matter how careful I tried to be. At the other end, the crack narrowed down to no more than four feet, and it took all my willpower not to bolt the last fifty feet.

Finally I reached the other end and stopped just short of stepping out onto clear ground. The hollow containing Grinny Creigh's place opened in front of me, and I had a good view down the slope and overlooking the buildings and pens around her cabin. My vantage point was a good three hundred feet or more above the cabin in elevation. There was no cover on this side of the ridge except one lonesome pine tree which was tapping the water seeping out of the crack. I hesitated to just step out there; there were dim lights on inside the main cabin, but all the outbuildings were dark. I was facing the south end of the cabin, so I couldn't see anything on the front porch where she'd been enthroned the night I'd been there. And might be tonight.

I stepped just out of the crack and sat down to watch for a while, mostly to get my night vision acclimated to the moonlight. Now that I was out of that sheer-walled split in the mountain I could see much better. The tiny weep spilling out of the crack went straight downhill and disappeared into a brush-covered gully. I used the telescope to scan the compound, looking for any signs of humans or dogs, but there was nothing moving down there. There was a slight breeze blowing across the face of the ridge as cooler air from the upper back ridge poured downhill towards the road and creek way down to my right. Otherwise there wasn't a sound coming from the hollow.

The shepherds lay down on either side of me, and their warm, furry hides were comforting. I settled back against the rock, and my shirt collar reminded me of the rifleman who'd damn near laid me down on the other side. Which further reminded me of the cell phone. I took it out, turned it on, and checked for a signal. One lonely bar, and it wasn't entirely persistent. I switched it back off since I had no way to recharge it.

After a half hour, my back was getting cold so I decided to find the cave. Having no idea of how long a rod was, I elected to simply go sideways down the ridge, moving slowly, and feeling along the rock wall for a cave entrance. I'd gone maybe fifty feet when I heard and then saw the headlights of a pickup truck coming up from the river road towards Grinny's cabin. I was well above their line of sight but decided to freeze in place and sit down again, trying to make myself small. On a full moon night they might have seen me, but I figured I was pretty inconspicuous against the gray rock wall of the backbone ridge.

The truck stopped in front of the cabin and shut down its engine and lights. I halfway expected someone to get out and haul yet another chained body out of the truck's bed. Instead I watched Nathan get out of the passenger side and go into the cabin. Even at this distance he was unmistakable, his stooped figure moving awkwardly up the steps and into the shadow of the porch. I saw a match flare on the driver's side. That was good—the match would destroy the man's night vision should he happen to look up in my direction. I was still pretty exposed and considered moving on down the hill. Then I remembered that motion wasn't the best idea if perchance someone was actively scanning the ridgeline.

Ten minutes later, Nathan appeared out of nowhere at the back of the pickup truck. He had two large dogs with him, which he proceeded to heave up into the bed of the truck. I could hear their claws scrabbling for footing. One of them started barking, and I heard a rough voice yell shut-up at him. Nathan got back in, and the truck started up. The driver turned on his headlights, and now it was my turn to lose all night vision as his brights swept across my position on the hillside. All I could do was hope like hell they weren't looking up here, because there wasn't a stitch of cover anywhere. In the event, the truck kept going and soon was out of sight and sound down the hill. I stayed put until I could see again, and then continued my way down the ridge in search of the cave.

About three hundred feet from the crack, I felt the rock wall give way to a narrow opening. I had a penlight on my field belt, but decided not to take any chances. I sent the two dogs into the cave instead. Hopefully there wasn't a six-foot-long rattlesnake denned up in there for the night, because if there was, we were in for some noise. Both shepherds popped out of the cave a minute later, so I decided it was reasonably safe for me to try it out. The opening was only four feet high and perhaps eighteen inches wide, so I had to duck-walk sideways into the cave. The actual cave curled to the right from the entrance. Once inside, I turned on the penlight and checked the ground for snakes and the ceiling for bats. Nobody home.

The cave wasn't much of a cave—it was just a hole in the rock. It had a sandy floor and went back about ten feet, ending in a crack in the rock that was perhaps a foot wide. The ceiling started out at six feet but rapidly sloped down to no more than four at the back. I shone the light into the crack but couldn't see anything that resembled a passageway, just more gray rock. Fortunately the cave was dry as a bone. I switched off the penlight.

"Okay, mutts," I announced quietly. "We're officially here."

I shucked my bedroll and the field belt and then moved back to the entrance to see what kind of view I had. It wasn't terrific. Because of the way the cave entrance made that initial turn, I couldn't see much of the Creigh place without going back outside. Fine for the nighttime, but dangerous during the day. I went outside and sat down with my back against the rock again. The cave would be okay for holing up, but I needed a watching point that would conceal me and the dogs while giving me a clear view.

There was another problem. Nathan had come back to the cabin to get some dogs. If they were trackers, *and* if he went to Laurie May's, they might track me up to and through the crack. After the shooting earlier, somebody knew I was in the area, and probably where I'd come from. In which case, I didn't want to be holed up in any dead-end cave. They could just stick their shotguns into the entrance and leave the resulting gore to compost.

The cell phone slipped out of my pocket. I picked it up, switched on, and checked for a signal. This time there were two whole bars. I fished around for Carrie's number and called her. She answered on the third ring, and I moved back into the cave's entrance.

"Where are you?" she asked. Her voice sounded a bit off.

I told her, and then asked her the same question.

"At your fancy cabin," she said. "My room at the main lodge was on the government's nickel, which is no longer on offer."

"Good, I'm glad someone's using it. I wish I were there instead of out here in this damned cave."

"You didn't tell me you had all this Scotch here," she said. "I may have overindulged. Just a little."

That accounted for her voice and slightly slurred words. "Good for you," I said. "Having second thoughts about resigning, are we?"

"Yep," she said. "Standing on lofty principle usually means the next step is down. The more lofty, the farther down. I should have eaten something. I've already got a headache."

"Regrets?"

"Well . . ." she said, hesitating. "I've discovered that being in the SBI gave me most of my identity. Now . . ."

"Now you feel naked," I said. "No badge, no creds, no gun, no authority. And guess how I know all this?"

"Yeah, I suppose you do. I'm desperate to pursue this

thing with the Creighs, but I'm no longer a player." I heard a hiccup. "May have fucked up."

"Would they take you back?"

"You know? I'm not so sure. My boss didn't try very hard to talk me out of it, now that I think about it. Of course, he was pissed over what we'd been doing here in the hills."

"Drink lots of water," I said. "Get some sleep. Everything looks better in the daylight."

"I won't," she said. "Daylight means mirrors. What are you going to do?"

"Laurie May suggested I hide out in Grinny Creigh's hollow because that's the last place they'd go looking for me. But Nathan just showed up to get some dogs, so my plan may have to change, and soon. There's no good cover where I am now."

"I should be out there with you," she said. "This is my beef."

"Right now you're more useful to me in Marionburg," I said. Especially with a snoot-ful of Scotch, I thought. "I may yet need extracting if these guys get lucky."

"I suppose," she said. There was a moment of silence, a noise I couldn't identify, and I heard her say *Oh, shit*. Then the connection was broken.

I immediately called back. The phone gave me a canned system message saying it was no longer on the air.

What the hell had just happened? Had the Creighs gone after Carrie? In Carrigan County? I shut the phone off and re-stowed it. I looked at the shepherds, who were lying there alert, awaiting orders. Something told me to get out of that cave and to go into motion. I told the dogs to stay down and stepped out of the cave to reconnoiter. The more I thought about it, the more it seemed that Nathan and his dogs might be on my trail pretty soon, so I couldn't stay up here on the ridge, and it wouldn't be terribly bright to let them catch me in that crack in the rock.

Okay, let's go down to Grinny's—if Nathan and his dogs had tracked me towards the cabin, he'd think his dogs simply wanted to go back to the pen. I hoped.

I roused the shepherds, and we set out down the ridge. There was no cover until I got within a hundred feet of the cabin itself, and then we slipped into a tree line near the cabin. I went downhill along the tree line until we got abeam of the cabin itself. I put the shepherds on a long down and crept to the house-side of the trees, some thirty feet from the porch. This had been where Nathan's black hats had been standing the night they brought me up to socialize with Grinny. The wind was slightly in my face, which hopefully would keep the dog pack behind the cabin from detecting us. Grinny's reputed second sight might present a more dangerous problem. There was some light coming through the curtained windows, but it was yellow and diffused, probably lantern light. I couldn't see anyone inside or on the grounds. I was trying to figure out what to do next when I heard another vehicle coming up the pasture road below the cabin. It sounded like a modern SUV instead of one of the ancient pickup trucks these folks seemed to favor. Whoever it was knew where he was going and drove right up to the front of the cabin. I settled down in the pine thicket to watch as the vehicle, a dark-colored Chevrolet Tahoe, stopped and shut down.

For a long minute, nothing happened, and then the front door of the cabin opened and Grinny Creigh stepped out onto the front porch. A foreign-looking man got out of the SUV and greeted her in the lilting accent of Southwest Asia. He went halfway up the steps and stopped when she told him to wait there, and then she went back into the cabin.

I studied the man as he waited in the dim moonlight. He was perhaps five foot seven or eight and in his late thirties. He had a sharply outlined, close-cropped black beard which joined his moustache, and he had the prominent nose features of Pakistan or perhaps India. He wore khaki trousers and a light windbreaker, under which I could see a cell phone and a pager clipped to his belt. He waited patiently on the front steps, looking around at the mountains and open fields around the cabin as if he'd seen it all before.

The door opened and Grinny Creigh reappeared, carrying

a lantern this time and leading a young girl by the hand. The girl was between eight and ten years old and very thin, with flaxen hair and a pinched, frightened face. Grinny gripped the little girl's wrist as if to make sure she wouldn't bolt as she raised the lantern to fully illuminate the child. The man on the steps examined her carefully, asking her to turn around a couple of times, and then came up on the porch to lay his hands on her. Given what I was expecting, I was surprised to see that he wasn't touching her in a sexual manner, but rather examining her, the way a doctor might. He looked into her eyes and mouth, asked her to cough even though he didn't have a stethoscope, and felt her limbs as if to gauge how well-fed she was.

I experienced a sudden urge to shoot them both and rescue the little girl. But for all I knew, this was a county social services doctor or PA making a house call of some kind, even if it was pretty late. The child was thin and frightened, although she didn't look to be ill. Grinny just stood there looking bored, but not letting go of that slim, bony wrist for one moment. I thought for just a moment that I glimpsed another small, pale face peeking through the curtains at what was going on out front, but then it was gone, like a ghost on the move.

The man thanked Grinny and said that everything was acceptable. Grinny turned the child around and sent her back into the cabin. Then she turned back to the man who had stepped back down to the walkway.

"If'n we had to, how many could you take in one go?" she asked.

The man thought about that for a moment. "No more than one per night," he said, finally. "And that would be difficult. The airport security would notice."

"Ain't sayin' we'll have to, mind," she said. "But there's been some folks snoopin' around, and it ain't been the one's we usually see 'round here, them drug cops, I'm talkin' about."

"Who are they, then?" he asked.

"We don't know. M.C. had one of 'em, but he got away 'fore we could have a little talk with'm."

"Is it about the children?" the man asked.

"Like I keep sayin', we don't know. But if we git cornered up, you could take all of'm, right?"

"The demand far exceeds the supply, always," the man responded. "It's the processing and transport that are tricky. For a sudden oversupply, the costs would be higher, of course."

"Unh-hunh," Grinny said in a sarcastic, suspicions-confirmed tone of voice.

"Let me get something out of the car for you," he said, and turned to go back to the SUV. Grinny stood there for a second, and then reached down behind that oversized rocking chair and pulled a shotgun towards her, which she set down behind her against the door. Her huge bulk completely hid it from view.

The man came back from the SUV with something small and black in his hand and for a second I wondered if he had a gun. Instead he handed it up to Grinny on the porch.

"This is a one-time pager," he said. "Use it once and I will come at the regular hour. Then throw it away. Never use it again because they are able to track such devices now." He pointed up into the sky. "From space, using satellites. Imagine. If you must move them all at once, activate the pager precisely at noon on whichever day you use it. Otherwise, activate it at some other time, it doesn't matter when."

"All right," she said, keeping her right hand buried in her housecoat and close to that shotgun.

"I will be back in a few nights," he said. "I will let your Mr. Mingo know when to meet me."

She nodded curtly at him and went back into the house, shutting the big wooden door and locking it with some kind of metal bar which I could hear thump down into place. The man drove off in his SUV. He'd been just far enough away for me not to be able to get the license plate number.

I sat back on my haunches. Some kind of a transaction had just taken place. The little girl had been approved for sale, confirming our worst suspicions about Grinny Creigh. And there might be more of them, either in the cabin with her or somewhere else, based on her question about having to possibly move more than one in a hurry.

But move them where and to what end? He had said something about airports, so maybe the theories about children being sold out of the hills into global sex slave markets was accurate. I remembered Laurie May's comment about what kind of 'mommas' would do such a thing? What kind indeed.

Two dogs started to bark back in the dog pen. I decided it was time to get out of there. I checked the cell phone, but there was no signal down here at the cabin. The dogs finally shut up after five minutes or so. We moved away from the cabin and went back up the hill, staying in the trees for as long as possible, the shepherds plastered to my side. It was slower going up than it had been coming down, and I was puffing once I made it to the cave. I slipped into the black hole and rested for about twenty minutes, trying to decide what to do next. I kept coming up with the same answer—immediate departure. Then deal with the problem of the children. I tried the cell again. There was a single signal bar showing in the little window, so I told the dogs to stay and stepped back out of the cave to see if I could do better.

My heart sank. I should have heeded my own advice. There was Nathan, standing with two other men in the dim moonlight. All of them had shotguns. A fourth man was wrestling the tracking leads on the two big dogs I'd seen Nathan throw into the back of the pickup truck. I thought about calling out the shepherds, but there were simply too many shotguns.

Nathan swung the barrel of his shotgun towards the distant cabin, and tipped his head in that direction. Clear enough.